THE
MOUNTAIN
STORY

LORI LANSENS

SIMON & SCHUSTER
New York   London   Toronto   Sydney   New Delhi

Simon & Schuster
1230 Avenue of the Americas
New York, NY 10020

First Simon & Schuster hardcover edition June 2015

SIMON & SCHUSTER and colophon are registered trademarks of Simon & Schuster, Inc.

For information about special discounts for bulk purchases, please contact
Simon & Schuster Special Sales at 1-866-506-1949 or business@simonandschuster.com.

The Simon & Schuster Speakers Bureau can bring authors to your live event.
For more information or to book an event contact the Simon & Schuster Speakers Bureau at 1-866-248-3049 or visit our website at www.simonspeakers.com.

Interior design by Davina Mock-Maniscalco

Manufactured in the United States of America

10   9   8   7   6   5   4   3   2   1

Library of Congress Cataloging-in-Publication Data

Lansens, Lori.
  The mountain story / Lori Lansens. – First Simon & Schuster Books hardcover edition.
      pages ; cm
1. Wilderness survival--Fiction. 2. Wilderness areas--California--Fiction. 3. Palm Springs Region (Calif.)--Fiction. I. Title.
  PR9199.4.L36M68 2015
  813'.6--dc23
                              2014034170

ISBN 978-1-4767-8650-6
ISBN 978-1-4767-8662-9 (ebook)

For
Max and Tashi
and
Addam, Andrew, Chloe, and Nathan

Dear Daniel,

A person has to have lived a little to appreciate a survival story. That's what I've always said, and I promised that when you were old enough, I'd tell you mine. It's no tale for a child, but you're not a child anymore. You're older now than I was when I got lost in the mountain wilderness.

Five days in the freezing cold without food or water or shelter. You know that part, and you know that I was with three strangers and that not everyone survived. What happened up there changed my life, Danny. Hearing the story is going to change yours.

It's hard to know when a son's ready for the truth about his old man. The night of your middle school graduation was the first time I *almost* told you; then it was your fourteenth birthday, and fifteenth, and every birthday after. You had a right to be told, but it's never been that simple. To understand about the mountain, you need to know what came before.

Remember last spring when we were visiting colleges? We were on that dark gravel road just outside of Bloomington and I nearly hit the deer. Remember we had to pull off at that truck stop because I couldn't stop shaking? The deer was safe, and you didn't understand why I was so rattled by the close call. Later, when I was calm, driving down the highway toward home, you asked me if I'd ever killed anything—accidentally or on purpose. You'd given me the perfect opening in the perfect setting—we always have our best talks in the car.

You were ready. I wasn't. That night I realized I was never going to be able to tell you the whole story—not face-to-face. If I had to watch you take it in I'd have edited, censored, lied, anything to avoid seeing your pain. But there's no point in telling half a story, is there? Or worse, one that's only half-true.

So I wrote it down. I typed it out as it came to my fingers, because that felt like the most honest thing to do. It's longer than I thought it would be—shorter somehow too. As for the timing of all of this? With you starting Indiana State? When you're older you'll see that there isn't so much a good time or bad time for things, appearances to the contrary. There is just *a* time. Anyway, it'll be good for you to read this while you're away at school. You'll need some time to absorb it, and some distance from me.

The day I got lost with the others—that fateful November day— was the one-year anniversary of Byrd's accident. It was a tough year, and I didn't think it could get worse; then, Frankie, my father, got drunk on Halloween night and killed a young couple with his car. My best friend was gone, my father sent to prison for vehicular manslaughter. I was on my own—no one to keep abreast of my plans. Not that I would have told anyone about my trip to the mountain anyway, because on that cool, gray afternoon, which was also the day of my eighteenth birthday, I had decided to hike to a spot called Angel's Peak to jump to my death.

No one else knows that part of the story. Not even your mother.

My fellow hikers have been with me, in one way or another, since we were lost together all those years ago:, walking alongside me when I'm out with the dogs, quiet when I'm reading in bed, guiding me with whispers when I can't find my way, looking over my shoulder the whole time I was typing out these pages. I'll miss their haunting.

When you were a little boy you'd study me in quiet moments and ask if I was thinking about the mountain. I almost always was. You asked if I ever dreamed about it. I did. Still do—especially now. Sometimes I wake up in a panic. Sometimes I wake longing for old friends.

Your mother? She's always said she didn't need to know all the gory details. Still, we both knew this day would come, and once you're finished with this, she'll have to read it too. I'm afraid I've caged the mountain story for so long it'll die in the wild. Mom wishes it already had.

Here it is, Danny. As you read this remember our family motto—there will be sway.

Love,
Dad

BEFORE

My boyhood home on Old Dewey Road stood among similar clapboard bungalows in the older, grimier section of Mercury, upwind of Michigan's largest rendering plant, with the train tracks near enough that I could distinguish passenger from freight by the way the house shook. A year and a half after my mother's accident—that's what we called it—my father briefly got sober and painted the entire house, inside and out, a dark, flat blue. Drowning Man Blue. Frankie said it was a tribute to Glory. She loved the color blue.

Frankie said I was too young, only four years old when she passed away, to have an honest recollection of my mother, but I do. Glory Elizabeth Truly. In my favorite memory she wears a silky white dress with batwing sleeves—one I've never seen in photographs. She's standing in front of a dressing room mirror, smiling at our reflection, and behind us is another mirror where I discover our infinity. *"Always,"* I say. My beautiful mother laughs and tells me I'm clever before covering my face with soft kisses and spinning me in her embrace. I glimpse us with each turn. Glory looks like an angel in that white dress.

I remember the mornings with my mother the most, watching her get ready for work (kindergarten teacher) while Frankie ("entrepreneur") slept upstairs. We talked in whispers as she made up her pretty face and spritzed her curls with lemon-scented hairspray. Before disappearing out the door, she'd turn to smile and then lay her hand on her heart to say she kept me there, even when she was away.

After she died, Frankie had her name tattooed on his forearm— *Glory*, in a rainbow that arched over the word *Always*. I used to think it would have been truer if the tattoo said *Glory Once* or *Glory Briefly* or, even better, *Sorry, Glory*.

I have never, to my recollection, called Frankie by any name other than his first. My ears were filled with the sound of it, usually shouted, often slurred, by the strangers who came and went from that smoke-choked blue house. Men who slammed doors and broke bottles. Women I didn't know cooking food I wouldn't eat. Children I'd never seen play-ing board games I didn't own. I remember one time Frankie tossed me a package of gum and warned, "Share that with your sisters." I turned around to find two freckled redheads I'd never seen before sitting behind me on the couch.

Glory *Always*? She was only twenty-five (Frankie a full decade older) when she died. I have my mother's smile, I've been told, but otherwise I'm the image of my father. I remember after a second-grade lesson about immigration, I'd asked Frankie the details of my heritage. He told me that Glory's family came from England when she was a baby and that her parents, both older physicians, had died of natural causes before my mother graduated from teachers college. Frankie guessed they wouldn't have liked him. It did occur to me that if Glory's parents had lived longer, I might never have lived at all.

When I asked about his side of the family, Frankie hesitated. He was secretive about his past, like me. "On my father's side we were Trulinos until the nineteen thirties, but then my grandfather decided he wanted a more American-sounding name, so he changed it to Truly and that caused a rift and that's how we ended up in Michigan. On my mother's side we're French Canadian and Cree. My cousins came down to visit us from Quebec one time. They were dark and lean. Badass. I take after my mother's side. That's how come I'm so stealthy. Why I like my feet bare."

There was this rotting cedar porch out front of our blue house from which I'd leap as a boy—towel-cape aflutter behind me—shouting, "I am

Batman," or "I am Superman," but I remember one day I lost my cape, and I'd simply shouted, "I am . . . ME!" Frankie slammed his palm on the kitchen table and hollered through the open window, "That kinda arrogance'll take you to Cleveland, Wolf! Cleveland and *back*!" Whether he meant to encourage, mock, or scold me, I still have no clue. My father has left me, my whole life, in a state of wonder.

One spring day when I was thirteen, Frankie stood up from the kitchen table and announced, "We need to be near family now," like the tragedy of my mother's death was ten *days*, and not nearly ten *years*, old.

"What family?"

"We're moving to California. This summer."

"Okay."

"We'll stay with Kriket till we get on our feet."

I'd never been to California and neither had Frankie. I'd never met his sister Kriket (Katherine) and never knew them to be close.

I figured Frankie had gotten himself into some kind of trouble in Mercury, a debt he couldn't repay, or maybe he'd slept with somebody's wife or girlfriend or sister or mother. You wouldn't think women would go for an unemployed widower in a stained concert T-shirt, but there were plenty of pretty girls around to finger the rainbow on Frankie's *Glory Always* tattoo. "I reek of pheromones," he told me once, flapping his hands around his armpits, encouraging me to take a whiff.

We made a plan to head for Kriket's place in the California desert in late July. Frankie was vague when I asked about the future of the little blue house. (Later he told me he'd lost it in a bet.) He bulldozed Glory's toiletries from their bathroom shelf shrine—the lemon-scented hairspray, prescription ointment for a patch of eczema, an unopened box of decongestant to relieve her springtime allergies—and threw them all into the trash.

"Won't need all this where we're going, Wolf," he said, which made me wonder why we'd needed it where we were.

I spent a lot of time at the Mercury Public Library when I was kid.

Frankie sent me there to borrow books by way of free babysitting. Miss Kittle was the head librarian, a buttoned-up brunette who, along with the rest of the staff, barely tolerated me. I couldn't blame them. I stole doughnuts from the seniors' meetings, made a mess of the shelves, and spent far too much time in the men's room. Still, I loved the library. I loved books. I especially loved plump, berry-scented Miss Kittle.

A few weeks before we left for the desert, Miss Kittle surprised me by calling out my name when I walked through the library doors. "Wolf Truly!"

There was something different about Miss Kittle—her cheeks were pinker and her lips were glossed and her thick dark hair fell in waves over her shoulders. By the look of her face I wasn't in trouble, which confused me.

"I have something for you, Wolf," she said. Miss Kittle had never spoken directly to me before.

"Okay."

"I heard you were moving to Santa Sophia."

Her eyes were even prettier up close. "My aunt Kriket lives there," I said.

"That's where I'm from," Miss Kittle said. "My father still lives there. I visit every summer."

"California's a long way from Michigan." My cheeks were hot.

"I had to move up here to help take care of my grandmother. I miss the desert."

"I'll miss winter."

"Ah!" she said, raising her index finger. Then she reached beneath the counter and drew out a large, heavy book. "You won't have to miss winter."

"I won't?"

"You'll have the mountain," she said, passing me the hefty book. *The Mountain in the Desert.*

The moment I glimpsed the photograph on the cover—a helicopter shot of the pine-rimmed granite peak—I knew that mountain contained my destiny. The details leaped from the pages like some 3-D déjà vu: ten thousand feet at the summit; mother of the transverse mountain ranges; hundreds of miles of pristine wilderness; hunting ground of the Agua Caliente band of Native Americans; habitat of bighorn sheep, mountain lions, rattlesnakes; precipitation ten times higher than what falls in the desert below; torrential rains in spring and fall, blizzards in winter. It was a place I'd never heard of but felt that I'd already been.

"You have to climb to the peak," Miss Kittle said.

"That looks pretty high."

"You take the tram most of the way," she said, turning to the back of the book and pointing to a full-page photograph. "The ride up is almost vertical. Look."

It was.

"This tramcar takes you from the Desert Station—the climate of Mexico—to the Mountain Station—the climate of northern Canada—in less than twenty minutes. Palms to pines."

"Cool," I said.

"You can climb to the peak from there. I only made it once," she confessed. "It was cloudy."

"Too bad."

"Maybe I'll try again when I'm in Palm Springs this summer to visit my father," she said.

"You should."

"Maybe I'll see if you and your dad want to come with me. Frankie—right?" She blushed.

Oh no, I thought. Frankie never came into the library, so I couldn't imagine where the two had met. "Frankie. That's right," I said.

"Do you know where in Santa Sophia your aunt lives?"

"Verdi Village," I said, remembering what Frankie told me.

"Sounds familiar. I think it's gated."

I knew nothing about gates.

"Most of the gated places have golf."

VERDI VILLAGE did not have golf. Or gates. Or shimmering pools. Or tennis courts. Or decorative fountains. Or paved roads for that matter. Santa Sophia was a tidy desert town consisting of mostly guarded, affluent communities. But past the mission-style shopping malls, and beyond the fuchsia bougainvillea and the median beds of white aggregate and flowering cacti, and over the abandoned train tracks, thousands populated the thrice-foreclosed-upon Verdi Village mobile home development that bled out over two square miles of hard-baked, treeless earth.

The original double-wide, pitch-roofed aluminum trailers were run-down, but at least they still had electricity and running water, unlike the second strata of mobile housing grown from the seeds of Airstream and Coachmen and Four Winds. Past that, the vagabonds had erected a haphazard crust of shacks and shanties, shelter for economic refugees, the mentally ill, and bikers. Locals called the place Tin Town.

In those dangerous narrows grew children who knew too much too young but, sadly, always seemed to learn too little too late. It was hot as hell in Tin Town—it set the most records in the state for triple-digit temperatures. I can still smell the unwashed bodies and twice-fried sausage, cigarette smoke and cat shit; and I can hear the discontent like bad radio reception. But mostly I can feel it—the wind, constant through the San Gorgonio Pass, polishing the earth and nourishing the groves of wind turbines along the desert roads.

You can see those ribbons of straight white stalks from eight thousand feet up the mountain. It's a hell of a view.

THE FIRST DAY

The night before I left for Angel's Peak I didn't sleep at all, yet I lingered in my bed until almost noon. Finally I rose, pulled on some clothes, and found the warm wool socks that Byrd had given me two Christmases before. I tied the laces on my hiking boots for the first time in a year and reached for my knapsack hanging on a hook near the front door. I hesitated, and decided to leave the knapsack behind—a moment that would haunt me—because I had no further need of the Swiss Army knife, or food rations, or water, or blankets, and didn't want the things to go to waste.

At the Desert Station, I waited to take what I believed would be my final tram trip up the mountain and, leaning against the wall, took a moment to survey the crowd. The three hikers I became lost with that autumn day were strangers to me, but I'd noticed each, for different reasons, before our fates became entangled. Nola. Vonn. Bridget.

Nola, with her soulful blue eyes and neat silver hair, strode by in her oxblood poncho, and I remember thinking that a person would be able to see that shiny red poncho from space. She was wearing good hiking shoes and shouldering a black knapsack, held a tattered field guide in her slender hands. I took her for one of the park docents who lead the short hikes in the Wide Valley at the foot of the Mountain Station.

She was the first rider to board the tramcar that was about to launch us from the desert scrub to an alpine wilderness, and she took a spot at the window where she'd have a view of the desert. Some people want to watch where they're going, and some like to see where they've been. She turned to catch me staring. I looked away, embarrassed.

Vonn boarded the tramcar behind a group of young people with whom I assumed she was traveling. I'd spotted her earlier, leafing through the Native American history books in the gift shop. She was beautiful, with black hair and dark skin, sharp cheekbones and full lips. She was wearing khaki pants and a blue pea coat, and on her feet, lime-green flip-flops, by which I judged she did not intend to hike.

Frankie used to say there were two kinds of people—the noticers and the noticed. He said that I was the former and he was the latter. Frankie would have described Vonn as exotic, the way people do when they're not sure about a person's ethnicity. I guessed the girl was bira-cial—Caucasian and Latina, or Caucasian and African American, or Latina and African American. She took a place at the window facing the desert and turned away from her companions.

Bridget bounced onto the tramcar seconds before the doors closed and squeezed her way to the center of the gondola, her high, blond pony-tail swinging with each shift of her pretty head. She was dangerously lean, swathed in layers of Lycra, with a warm-looking, fleece-lined Wind-breaker tied around her waist and a pair of costly running shoes on her feet. When she stretched across me to grasp the pole, I felt obliged to move.

She carried a blue mesh sports bag, inside of which I could see a wallet, three bottles of water, and three granola bars in silver foil wrap-pers. I'd taken her for a college senior until she looked up at me to smile, and I saw the ice-blue eyes of a woman in her late thirties. I might have stared a moment too long.

The tram worked on a double jig-back system, with one car heading down the mountain while the second climbed up; hung on twenty-seven miles of interlocking cable strung out between five massive towers bolted into the mountainside. At each of the five towers the tramcar made a transition and rocked like a carnival ride for a minute or two—longer if the winds were high. Riders had strong reactions—especially first-timers. As we approached the first tower I steadied myself. The woman with the ponytail had just opened one of her water bottles. Rookie.

The tram operator, whom thankfully I did not recognize, announced over the microphone, "We're approaching the first tower, ladies and gentlemen. Hold on tight." He paused dramatically. "There will be sway."

"What does that mean?" the blond woman asked.

"Brace yourself," I said, but she didn't hear me, because right at that moment there was a loud thump and a quick drop, and the tramcar began to rock forcefully, and she screamed and spilled her water and lost her balance on the slippery floor.

Taking her elbow to prevent her from falling, I gave the impression I cared.

When the tramcar was steady again, sailing through wispy gray clouds, the woman found my eyes. "You look familiar."

"I ride the tram a lot."

"I've only been on this thing one other time and I took a sedative, so I don't remember."

I looked away, hoping the gesture would discourage conversation.

"You look familiar from someplace else."

"No."

"I can't look down. I have such bad . . . what is it?"

"Vertigo," I said darkly.

"Is it gonna swing like that again?" she asked.

"Four more times."

On the other side of the tramcar a little boy began to cry. He wasn't afraid of heights, or startled by the rocking. He was crying because the clouds had stolen his desert view. I watched the older woman in the ox-blood poncho lean down and pass the crying boy her binoculars. She pointed out a rift in the clouds where he could see the Santa Rosa mountain range in the distance. The little boy smiled. The woman smiled too.

The blonde beside me carried on. "Vertigo. It's not so much I think I'm going to fall but I think I'm going to jump. Isn't that *weird*?"

"Yes," I said.

When she turned to look around the tramcar her ponytail brushed my chin and bathed me in her scent, a bergamot-and-ginger mélange that I found disturbingly pleasant.

"I don't think I'll be doing this sober again," she said.

I lifted my nostrils to the breeze from the open windows, taking in the crisp note of sage as we continued our ascent.

"It's awful to be afraid," the woman said, laughing to hide her nervousness.

She was right.

My attention was caught by the dark-skinned girl in the green flip-flops, who appeared to be staring at me from the other side of the tram. I wasn't sure what to make of her attention or her expression. She looked pissed. I couldn't imagine why.

From years of habit, I turned to ask my friend Byrd. I'd done that a hundred times in the year since his accident. Turned to look for him. Picked up the phone to call. Byrd wasn't just my best friend. He was my only friend. My *brother*. We had everything in common. We even shared a birthday. I whispered in my thoughts, *Happy birthday, Byrd*.

The woman swung her ponytail and opened both eyes and lifted her head to peer out the window. "You can't see anything with the fog. Kind of a blessing."

"Sure," I said.

"Can you buy water on the mountain—?" She interrupted herself to scream again as we hit the next tower.

The air grew colder as we rose. I could smell turpentine from the pines, and chilled zinc in the sediment, marine life, bones and roots and pulverized seeds, ancient odors that spoke volumes of loss. I tried to block out the sound of the nervous chattering woman. Unsuccessfully.

"I broke my training last night," she said. "I'm training for a triathlon and I want to kill myself for having a margarita with dinner. I'm already dehydrated. One bottle won't be enough. Are we almost there?"

Controlling my impulse to correct her, because I could see that she in fact had *three* bottles of water in her mesh sports bag, I said, "You can get water at the gift shop."

"I'm Bridget."

I didn't like the way Bridget was studying me.

"Are you sure we don't know each other? Are you from the area?"

"I'm sure."

"You seem so familiar."

I shrugged.

"I grew up a few miles from here in Cathedral City, but I live in Golden Hills now," Bridget said. "You know it? Near the coast? You know Malibu?"

"No."

"I still come out here to the desert a lot. My mother's got a condo in Rancho Mirage. I thought of moving back, but then I met someone. I'm happy."

Bridget didn't look happy. I wondered if I could start making my way toward the exit.

"He was the Realtor on my hillside Colonial. We're training together. For the triathlon. He's younger. Much younger. Not that it matters. Until the woman gets older. When's the next tower?"

"Soon."

Clutching the pole, she gestured at my baseball cap. "My second husband was from Michigan. Grosse Pointe. He liked the Detroit Tigers too."

"The next tower," I said, pointing ahead.

Bridget screamed again when our tramcar thumped over the transition, and by the time we stopped rocking she was almost in tears.

"The next towers don't rock as much," I said, taking pity.

I noticed that the girl in the flip-flops looked nauseated. I hoped she didn't vomit on the tram. She tightened her grip on the pole, keeping her eyes on the floor as we approached the next tower. The wind kicked up and rocked us violently. Bridget screamed again. She wasn't the only one.

When we finally pulled into the Mountain Station's dock, my head was pounding from Bridget's screaming. I could not get away fast enough when the tram doors opened, and rushed off without a backward glance, even when I heard her shout, "Good-bye!"

Once I'd left the other tourists far behind I slowed my pace, trudging into the woods. I was relieved to see the thick clouds settling low, because I knew it would cut down the foot traffic. Who'd bother with a hard, steep hike without the reward of a spectacular view at the end? The climb speaks to our character, but the view, I think, to our souls.

The sky grew darker as I hiked through the towering conifers, over the rivers of cobbled stone, past the massive white slabs of rock, so artfully arranged by random aspects of nature. I was heading for the rogue trail that would lead me downward through a small meadow and over a hill of rock-hewn steps toward a slender, twenty-foot outcropping, the place Byrd and I called Angel's Peak.

Normally I liked to hike at a brisk pace, but this day I was panting, plodding, pulling my prematurely deadweight, thinking not about the end of me but the sum of me—all the befores and afters that had brought me to that moment.

BEFORE FRANKIE got wasted on premium tequila on Halloween night and lost control of his Gremlin on a dark desert road, he had been a hard-drinking risk taker. *After*, he was a convict and two young people were dead.

Frankie was in the hospital briefly after the Halloween tragedy. He refused to see me there. One of the nurses told me he wouldn't read the notes I left. After a couple of days he was taken away in handcuffs. I took the bus to the prison, but Frankie refused to see me there too. He didn't try to contact me in any way. I was already on the edge after what happened to Byrd. Frankie pushed me over.

I'd decided to end my life on my birthday—some warped tribute, as I saw it—to Byrd, and my mother. The mountain was the most obvious setting, and Angel's Peak the most meaningful place. I started counting down the days from Halloween. A week passed, then two, then I overheard that Lark Diaz was going to be back in Santa Sophia for the weekend to be a bridesmaid in her friend's wedding.

Lark Diaz was never my girlfriend, but she was the girl of my dreams, and the thought of seeing her again made me hopeful. I envisioned our emotionally charged reunion and created a hundred scenarios that ended in a kiss. But on the day she arrived, Lark didn't accept even one of the dozen phone calls I made to her father's house. She wasn't there when I showed up on his doorstep. She eluded me at every turn, until I rode my bike twelve miles to the church on the day of the wedding.

From a distance I saw her perched on the ledge of a gazebo on a small hill of the church lawn, wearing a voluminous floor-length green gown. Her dark hair was pinned up on her head, her neck and shoulders were bare. I lost all sense of caution. "Lark," I called, advancing from the rear.

She didn't turn around, but I knew by the way she stiffened that she'd heard me.

The gazebo was higher than the ground where I stood. There were crates of equipment of some kind piled up behind it. I couldn't get close. "Lark! Did you get my letters?"

She just sat there.

"Did you read them?" My voice sounded strange.

She shook her head.

"It's okay. I just wanted you to know . . . Lark?"

She shook her head again.

"I love you!" I shouted, my heart thumping in my ears. "I love you!"

Lark eased herself off the gazebo ledge and slowly turned to confront me. As she did, she stepped to the left, revealing several dozen wedding guests gathered on the lawn, staring at me pityingly.

"Wolf," she said simply. Her voice bounced against the church wall in the distance. The microphone near where she stood was turned on and had broadcast all that I said.

BYRD'S ACCIDENT. Frankie's imprisonment. The humiliating scene with Lark. I couldn't shake the sense that I was bleeding out, leaving a sticky scarlet trail as I climbed the tumbled stones that would take me through a small grove of limber pines toward the overgrown route to Angel's Peak.

A long branch of spiky chinquapin reached out from nowhere to snag the nylon shell of my parka, and when I stopped to free my sleeve from the yellow bush, I was surprised to spot the girl in the green flip-flops moving slyly through the distant trees. For a split second I flattered myself that she was stalking me, this rare mountain feline. I wondered why she was hiking in such ridiculous footwear and what had become of her friends from the tram.

Byrd and I had rarely seen people hike alone. Sometimes the bird-watchers went out solo, but most didn't stray far from Wide Valley. They'd find a spot off trail, sit on stumps or collapsible canvas stools with binoculars and thermoses of tomato soup, and hope someone might stop to chat on their way to the peak. Byrd and me? We always stopped. We had more in common with elderly birders than people our own age.

I ducked into a shortcut through the trees, climbing over boulders and logs. The forest was still, and the girl had disappeared. I figured she must have been done in by her footwear and gone back to the Mountain Station, or found the group of friends with whom she'd boarded the tram. I couldn't wonder much beyond that because the mountain was distracting me, wafting the butterscotch fragrance of Jeffrey pines up my nostrils, dispatching warblers and chickadees to greet me. I hadn't been up here since Byrd's accident, and I shivered with shame at the purpose of our reunion.

A white-headed woodpecker beat out an introduction as I approached, and I noticed a male goldfinch dancing on the snarled branch of a mountain mahogany. A second finch sang from the sugar pines. I wondered if somehow they'd got wind of my intentions and had come to dissuade me.

Climbing some steps of black-veined quartz, I caught the fragrance of lavender on a stiff breeze from the east. Lavender grows on the mountain, but not at the higher elevations—at least I'd never smelled it before. Curiosity over why I could smell lavender was the reason I lifted my head and looked through the trees, and spied something large and red—the older woman in the oxblood poncho from the tram—moving through the branches an unsafe distance from the main trail.

Taking cover behind some brush, I watched her raise her binoculars. It did briefly occur to me that she might be lost, but I assured myself that she was a seasoned birder and had only stopped to rest. Angel's Peak was waiting for me. Red Poncho was on her own.

Then the branches of an expansive wax currant bush quivered behind the woman and I was surprised to see the blonde with the ponytail emerge. Bridget. So maybe the older woman *was* a trail guide. Bridget drank from one of the water bottles in her blue mesh bag as the older woman drew a banged-up yellow canteen from her knapsack.

The sight of the yellow canteen stole my breath. Byrd had one just like it—a gift from me, purchased at the Tramway Gift Shop. My stomach churned when I heard, even from that distance, the sound of the metal cap twisting over the threads of the spout. Before I knew it I was streaking away through the trees.

Bridget spotted me and called out, "Oh! Hi! Hey, there!"

I hurried on, pretending not to hear, searching the woods for the way to Angel's Peak, which I remembered being left of the granite barge ahead and between two massive wind-worn boulders. I found the boulders quickly enough but was confounded to see that several large sterasote bushes had grown over the trailhead. No way around and no way through. I stood there for a moment, stung by the odors of the wide, volatile bush made pungent by the fog settling around us. Then the wind blew the camphor scent up my nostrils, which caused me to sneeze repeatedly.

Reaching for the knife in my knapsack, I was confident I could hack my way through, but I remembered that I'd left both the knife and the knapsack behind.

The older woman in the red poncho must have heard me sneezing because she started hollering, "Young man? Young man?!"

I looked around for the young man to whom she was referring and realized she meant me. I'd grown tall like Frankie, broad from the weights I lifted alone in my room with Motown blasting on my stereo. I inherited my taste in music from my old man.

I tried to ignore her, but she kept calling, "Young man! Young man!"

"You're off trail!" I shouted back at her as I started toward the pair.

She lowered her voice even though we were alone in the woods. "I'm trying to find a *lake. Secret* Lake."

Secret Lake belonged to me and Byrd. "It's not on the trail map," I said.

"Yes, I know," the older woman said.

"Not many people know about it," I said, coming closer.

"Yes, I know."

Under the red poncho she was wearing a thick outer coat and under that a heavy turtleneck sweater. Up close the lavender smell was strong. She must have noticed me sniffing. "Oh," she said with a laugh. "It's my lavender." She drew a small silk pillow from the pocket of her coat. "I carry it everywhere. Keeps the bugs out when you're in and away when you're out."

I'd never heard any homespun wisdom about lavender repelling insects, but it didn't sound preposterous. "How do you know about Secret Lake?"

Jogging in place on a bed of pine needles nearby, Bridget, her pony-tail bouncing absurdly, took her pulse. "We need to keep moving," she said.

"My husband discovered the lake. There's a rare flower that grows around it. That's why it's off-limits."

"Okay." I didn't tell her I already knew about the endangered mountain phlox.

"You don't want to step on something that's endangered."

"Right."

"I've been there many times," the woman explained. "Just—my husband always led the way. He never got lost."

"Well, you're way off."

"I thought so," Bridget said.

"How could you think so when you've never been there?" the older woman asked politely.

"My sixth sense," Bridget said. "This way didn't *feel* right."

I didn't have time for this. "Head back the way you came, then veer to the north and a little east and catch the trail again. Follow it for a half mile or so, and then up the short escarpment west of the little ranger station and down through the black oak."

"I know the ranger station," the woman said.

"Over the creek and beyond these big boulders to the north a ways, there's this rock formation," I said. I didn't add that my friend Byrd called the giant, phallic rock formation *Circunsisco Gigantesco*. "It looks like a . . . *tower*—you can't miss it. 'Bout half mile from there."

"The *tower*! That's what I was looking for! I thought we should have found it by now."

"Northeast through the little meadow and over the huge boulders straight ahead and around that short ridge. Got it?"

"Yes," she said uncertainly, glancing at her hiking companion.

Neither of the women had taken in my directions. I gestured toward the sulking sky. "Look, Secret Lake's a hard mile and a half from here, and it'll be dark in a few hours. Maybe you should try to find it another day."

A pair of sleek black crows found a branch nearby and I couldn't help but think they were trying to warn us by the way they cawed in our direction. The clouds hung so low and heavy that when the birds flapped away we lost sight of them before they reached the tips of the pines.

"Why don't *you* take us?" Bridget asked. "Could you take us?"

"Yes! Could you?" the older woman asked. "We'll pay you. Of course we'll pay you." She pried open the mouth of her big black knapsack.

I could see that, in addition to the wallet, the knapsack contained a kitschy white wool Christmas sweater and a large plastic peanut butter jar. I wondered if she meant to bait animals for photographs—I'm embarrassed to say Byrd and I did that sometimes—but I didn't see a camera.

She waved a bill. "Twenty dollars? It's all I have. But I could send you a check. Do you have an hourly rate?"

I didn't take the time to explain that I wasn't a mountain guide. I simply shook my head and mumbled, "Sorry," then, without a backward glance, set off through the brush.

But there was that overgrown sterasote bush again, blocking my way to Angel's Peak. With a rapid succession of sneezes I began to rip at the branches with my bare hands, cursing myself for leaving my knapsack on the hook by the door.

The sound of laughter, a familiar baritone chortle, made me pause, and then I heard Byrd call my name—*Wilfred*. This wasn't the first time I'd heard Byrd's voice on the wind, or whispered behind a musical refrain, or crying out to me in the darkness. I looked around for him and instead caught sight of the two women heading off in the wrong direction.

Bridget was leading the woman in the red poncho to the left of where I'd pointed, toward a precipitous drop camouflaged by a shallow wall of manzanita and sage scrub.

I tore back through the trees hollering, "Hello! That's the wrong way! Hello!" But I could not be heard over the wind. "HELLO!"

Mercifully, finally, they heard and stopped. I was breathless by the time I reached them. "Other way. *North*—this is *west*."

"She forgot the compass," Bridget said, rolling her eyes.

I didn't take them through the bushes to show them the deadly drop. Maybe I should have.

The older woman smiled sheepishly. "Can you please just say right or left?"

"You should really head back to the Mountain Station. Why don't you come back tomorrow and get an earlier start?"

"I'll pay you twice your fee," the older woman said quietly.

"I'm not—"

"Three times! I'll pay you three times your fee! You'll have to take my word that I'll mail you a check when I get home tonight."

"I don't want your check. Why can't you just come back tomorrow?"

"It has to be today," Bridget said.

"It's my anniversary. My wedding anniversary. It has to be today."

I guessed by her expression, and his absence, that her husband had recently passed away.

"We came here to celebrate our anniversary every year for forty years."

Bridget sighed. I couldn't tell if she was being sympathetic or impatient.

"If you don't take us we could get lost," the woman said. "You wouldn't want *that* on your conscience, would you?" She was right. I didn't want that on my conscience. A sufficient amount of DNA from my mother had infused my character with character. (My father wasn't exactly the selfless type.) How could I have said no? How could I have shuffled off this mortal coil if my final deed was the refusal of a request for help?

"I'll take you to Secret Lake, but I'm not staying. You have to get yourselves back to the Mountain Station," I said.

"Your mother raised a gentleman," she said with a smile. "I'm Nola Devine."

"Bridget," the woman with the ponytail reminded me.

Too petulant to introduce myself, I brushed past them and pressed on, trying to ignore Bridget performing stag leaps from boulder to boulder in my periphery.

I led the two women back past the bloomless wild flowers and through the flecked gray river of rock between the sugar pines. I remember being slightly curious about Red Poncho's relationship to skinny Bridget, but not enough to inquire. I suppose I didn't want to risk being drawn into more conversation.

Nola sang quietly as we broke through the brush. I don't remember the song—Stevie Wonder, I think. I liked the tremolo in her voice and the way she played fast and loose with the lyrics. She reminded me of Frankie, and how he used to belt out the wrong words to the Motown on the radio in the kitchen. I hummed in my head, until I began to grow anxious that a tender memory of my father might weaken my resolve to get to Angel's Peak.

I raised my fingers to shush her, whispering, "Don't want to disturb the animals."

"Well, aren't we *supposed* to be loud in the forest?" Nola asked. "To scare away the bears?"

"Won't see bears up here, Mrs. Devine," I said. But there were mountain lions, I thought, and bobcats and coyotes.

Byrd leaped into my thoughts once more, and in my mind we were boys again, on the path to Secret Lake.

"ARE THERE bears?" I'd asked Byrd as we boarded the Palm Springs tram together the first time, before I'd even turned fourteen. "Where'd you see the bighorn sheep? Ever see a mountain lion?"

The tramcar launched and my gut contracted as the earth floated away, and Byrd (my friend of only a few days at that point) became a silhouette against the bone-white desert.

I couldn't hide the fact that I was trembling when the tram operator leaned into the crackling microphone to warn about the sway. Watching the tram shadow wash over the steep moraine of scrub oak as we rose, I was all too aware that it was a mere six-inch cable that held us above the jagged granite.

When we hit the first tower I screamed. Byrd laughed so hard he nearly puked, and the rest of the riders on the crowded tram erupted with chortles and guffaws too. Even the driver. Even the bespectacled elderly man standing next to us.

As we approached the next tower, I noticed the elderly man watching me through his bottle-bottom glasses. He appeared to be enjoying the theater of my terror. I gripped the pole and closed my eyes. We hit the tower. I found my balance. I did not scream. Byrd thumped my back in brotherhood. The old man huffed in disappointment.

Through the open window I felt the breeze grow cooler. It smelled like Michigan—conifers and cold earth, wet rock and green grapes. I grasped the pole tighter when we hit the next tower and barely noticed the towers after that. Then I turned toward the rock face because I wanted to see where I was going instead of where I'd been.

Midway up the mountain, before the subalpine zone, I'd caught the sharp odor of camphor, which made me sneeze repeatedly. Byrd smiled when I leaned forward to sniff discreetly at the shoulder of the elderly man.

"That's sterasote you're smelling," he said. "I'll show it to you when we're up there. Smells of nothing when it's dry but like bad medicine when it gets wet."

I sneezed again.

Far below us I noticed a red baseball cap caught on a dead tree branch and tugged my Detroit Tigers hat down on my head. I didn't want to lose it. "Some guy lost his hat," I said.

Byrd looked down at where I was pointing. "Jack's hat," he said, wagging his head. "Been there for years."

"He drop it from the tram?"

"Not exactly." He lowered his voice as he gestured at the precipitous mountainside. "Jack missed the last tram down one day—hiked farther than he should have, later than he realized—and he panicked when he found out he was locked out of the Mountain Station. Jack was a pretty experienced hiker, and he was young, in great shape, so he figured he'd climb down between the tram towers so he wouldn't get lost in the dark. He started down but he miscalculated how steep the mountainside was and he ended up sliding, inch by inch, bracing himself with his heels but basically slipping all the way down this slope here."

"Looks almost vertical."

"Exactly. So by the time he got about here, his pants and his under-wear were gone, burned off by friction, and his ass was this oozing, bloody mess. The soles of his boots were gone, and he'd worn his heels right down to the bone. He slid all night long, six more hours, and finally Jack made it to the bottom and passed out in some dense bush. He just about scraped off his entire ass—he seriously had to get skin grafts for years and they never worked out, and he can't put any weight at all on his left cheek. I'll show him to you—he hangs out at this coffee shop near the museum—sits like this." He demonstrated.

"So the moral of the story is go against your instinct?" I asked.

"It's just a story. What happened happened, and now I'm telling you." Byrd grinned. "I don't like morals."

At the Mountain Station we leaped from the tram, bounding toward the viewing decks, where we stood in the thrall of wide white desert and the blurry seam where it met the blue sky. Palm Springs glistened at our feet. The orchards of wind turbines waved from the distance. Far beyond the city sprawl a lashing of dust outlined the border of Santa Sophia and Tin Town. Byrd gestured to the southeast, squinting. "You see out there—the Salton Sea?"

I did see it, like a mirage, the pale paper lake nearly seventy miles away. The thin air was making me dizzy.

"The Colorado River broke through a hundred years ago and filled the basin there. Poof—there's a lake. This resort grew up around it, but then the lake started to dry out and got salty and people left. It's like a ghost town. Ghost lake. Old trailers half sunk in mud, camping gear, rusted-out cars. You believe in ghosts?"

"No," I lied. "You?"

"Only the ones I've seen for myself," he said.

Byrd called the desire to climb mountains King of the Castle Syndrome. There is powerful symbolism in the act of ascension.

"You should see the view from the peak," he said.

"Let's go!"

"Too late in the day, dude. And you're not in shape."

"I'm in shape."

"Weak isn't a shape."

Having subsisted on snack food and secondhand smoke for some time, I supposed he was right. "Isn't it only three hours? I can do that."

"When you get to the top you're only halfway there," Byrd reminded me. "Plus, you can't climb in those cheap drugstore sneakers. You need boots. Footwear is your number one concern. Have you not learned that yet? Seriously? Storms blow in this time of year and you have to have warm layers and good boots. Rain makes the rocks slippery. Snow. Not in July and August but still—you don't want to know about frostbite. Needs a better name. Something to scare the shit out of you so you never risk it."

"Necrodigititis," I blurted.

"Necrodigititis!" My friend grinned. He liked wordplay. "Come on."

"The peak?" I asked.

"Another place. A secret."

That first time, with Byrd, I made a mental map of the path to Secret Lake as we leaped over a slender stream and waded through the grasses in a round meadow, then climbed up and over the collection of speckled

27

granite boulders, muscling down the other side, past *Circunsisco Gigantesco* and up again to a small mesa, then over the tumbled cairns and the fields of cracking chert. At last we arrived to find a magical oasis alive in the afternoon sun. I would have believed there were elves dancing in the pines, fairies riding the waves of deer grass. The light was different, diffused and dreamy, the lake rippling with life.

"Secret Lake," Byrd said. "It's not on the trail maps."

"Cool," I breathed.

Byrd stopped, planting his feet in the deer grass, closed his eyes, and told me to do the same. "The plates are shifting. Can you feel that?"

"I think so."

"My uncle Harley says that to feel it is a gift."

"I feel something." I didn't want Byrd to think I was ungifted. "Rumbling," I said.

Next Byrd directed me to the cluster of low, spiky white-flowered shrubs on the western end of the small, oval lake. "That's endangered," he said. "That's mountain phlox. That's the reason the lake's not on the map. It's everywhere out here, so watch your step." He couldn't have sounded graver if he'd been warning me about land mines.

"How do you know about it?"

"My uncle taught me everything he knows," Byrd said, and then added, "Uncle Harley knows everything."

After that he led me to a long, smooth slab of granite downwind of the water where we could watch the lake from a slight elevation. But before we settled in, Byrd revealed the perilous drop at the end of it. This would be another good place to watch my step, I knew. Fate isn't kind to the careless.

Sitting there in the cool thin air, watching the rippling waters of that hidden lake, we drank from Byrd's old camouflage canteen, which had a dent in the spout and tasted of tin. I decided to buy him a new canteen—Frankie'd given me fifty dollars from his poker winnings that morning out of guilt for his poor parenting—when we got back down to

the Desert Station. I'd noticed a huge rack of yellow ones at the gift shop. I don't know why I didn't wonder if the gesture was unmanly or worry that the gift would be misunderstood, but I didn't. "We should have binoculars," I said.

"I have some. I'll bring them next time. We need a decent camera too. You can get good money for wildlife shots. I only have an old Polaroid."

We observed a few ground squirrels fighting in the tall grass. I didn't see the golden eagle or the Cooper's hawk or the white-headed woodpecker in the surrounding pines until Byrd pointed them out. I leaned into the wind and caught a scent—coyotes—which my olfactory memory cross-referenced with a disastrous camping trip in Traverse City with my father when I was eight.

Turning toward the scent, I sighted a pair of the wild dogs, mangy and lean, not like the fat pups we'd tossed wieners to at the campground. Byrd saw them too, out past the far end of the sage bushes—the animals were staring us down. One of the coyotes snapped at the air, narrowing his gaze and licking his snout before he and his friend disappeared down the escarpment. "Los Coyotes," Byrd said, grinning. "That's my people."

"Mine too, I guess," I said.

Byrd saw me notice the bump in the sock at his left calf. Grinning, he pulled out a sizable Swiss Army knife.

"Cool," I said. "What's it for?"

"What's it for?"

"What do you do with it?"

"Everything. Make kindling, open cans, skin rabbits."

"You skin rabbits?" I couldn't decide if I was impressed or disgusted.

"I could," he said, proving to me that the blade was razor sharp by using it to scrape a layer from his thumbnail.

"You ever killed anything with it?" I asked.

"I could," Byrd promised.

"If you were starving?"

"If I was starving. Or if an animal was dying. If a bird broke its wing."

"You'd kill a bird that broke its wing?"

"'Course."

"With a knife?"

"With my bare hands if I had to."

"I could never do that."

"You could," he said. "You do what you have to do."

It took us months of shifts at the gas station (where Byrd's guardian, his uncle Harley Diaz, hired me on) to save the money for the camera, tripod, and lens attachments we hoped would bring us fortune and fame as wildlife photographers. Byrd and I took hundreds of photographs in the days we spent at Secret Lake. Sometimes we took turns with the camera, but mostly I was the shooter, Byrd the spotter and keeper of the logbook chronicling our sightings: hundreds of deer, seventeen striped skunks (or the same skunk seventeen times), sixteen gophers, seventy-three kit foxes, a vole (at least we think it was a vole), hundreds of chipmunks and deer mice and wood rats, dozens of great horned owls and golden eagles and hawks and falcons, a hundred woodpeckers and thrashers and jays, those cool yellow tanagers and that pygmy owl and the finches and the blackbirds and on and on.

One time we were hanging out on the slab of rock at Secret Lake when Byrd heard this ticking sound, like a lawn sprinkler, and he pointed to a spot beneath a fountain of mugwort where a huge Southern Pacific rattlesnake was reticulating. I pissed my pants a little when the six-foot-long snake's mouth yawned open and I saw the last twitching inch of a wood rat's tail disappear down its throat. I didn't want Byrd to know I was shaking—he seemed so fearless—and besides, he badly wanted a close-up photograph and so did I.

We climbed down from the rock carefully, quietly.

"We gotta get a shot with its mouth open!" Byrd said calmly.

I crept forward, inch by trembling inch, lifting the camera and finally capturing the snake in my lens. I was about to take the photo when the snake snapped its tail and shook his rattles. I dropped my camera and ran away through the tall grass in the short meadow.

When I stopped screaming long enough to catch my breath, all I could hear was Byrd's laughter bouncing off the rocks. He was *howling* like he'd just seen the funniest show on earth. Then the humor of it struck, and I laughed pretty hard too.

We averaged twenty or more hours a week up there, and in all that time we never once saw another human being at Secret Lake, except, that is, for the memorable night we convinced two college girls to join us there.

It struck me that on this day, a year ago, Byrd and I and those college girls must have just missed Nola and her husband celebrating their last anniversary.

THAT DAY we got lost, there I was leading Nola and Bridget through the pines, my unease mounting with each step. No part of me wanted to see Secret Lake again. It might hold sweet nostalgia for Nola, but for me it was a crime scene.

I was moving at a fast pace, but Bridget and her ponytail easily kept up.

"Is this a high *high* altitude?" she asked.

"Eight thousand feet."

"Do people get sick at this altitude, or does it have to be *Everest* high?"

"Yes."

"At this altitude?" she clarified.

"Even lower."

"Dizziness? Nausea?"

"Yes."

"I don't feel any of that. I think the thin air suits me."

Everything about Bridget was thin, except her hair, and maybe her lips. Of course the air would suit her.

Nola panted some distance behind but never asked me to slow

down. I liked her grit and found reasons to stop so that she could catch her breath. "Not much longer," I said.

"I could go all night," Bridget shouted over the rising wind.

Endorphins. Inhale deeply enough and you're a mountain junkie for life.

Leading the pair down a short hill, I stopped to take in the view. The mountain wilderness stretched out before us—rock and forests and more of the same in graded hues for miles and miles. I was concerned suddenly, about the women getting lost trying to find their way back. "I hope you've both been paying attention."

"I'm good with directions," Bridget said.

Nola paused for a breath, shifting her eyes over the marbled rock and spiny forests. "Beautiful," she sighed.

Bridget lifted her wrist to look at her watch and remembered she was not wearing one. "Already getting kind of dark," she said.

It was. The clouds were moving in, but experience told me the wind could blow them out again just as quickly. Still, sudden storms were common this time of year, and how could I leave the two women at the lake if there was a thunderstorm or, worse, a snow squall?

"He would have been surprised that I came without him," Nola said, unprompted.

"He must have had a compass," Bridget said. "This path isn't marked."

"I think he's watching right now," Nola went on. "Bet he had a good chuckle when we went the wrong way."

"Which way now?" Bridget asked, taking the lead.

"Over that section of boulders," I said.

"Thank God we stopped when we did," Nola said. "We might have missed you."

That was true. As we hiked on toward Secret Lake I kept asking myself what I was doing with these strangers. I slowed down to wait for Nola again.

She reached me, huffing and puffing. "I need to get in better shape," she said.

"I told you that a year ago," Bridget called back.

Nola accepted the bottle of water but declined the granola bar Bridget offered from her blue mesh bag. "I'm still stuffed from lunch," she said.

Bridget noticed I had no water and offered me a bottle. I waved her off and she seemed relieved. "Why don't you have a knapsack?" she asked.

"That doesn't seem like something you'd forget," Nola said.

"We should stay focused," I said, setting off into the patchy fog again.

Bridget, thinking she had something to prove, kept pace with me, chattering until at last we reached the landmark that pointed the direction to Secret Lake.

I stopped to rest, leaning against a tree. "Here's the *tower*," I said, gesturing at the massive rock formation a few yards away.

Nola and her husband must have had their own name for the phallic rock, judging by the way she blushed.

"It gets easier from here."

"I think I remember now," Nola said.

"Do you remember the way back from here?" I asked.

"Yes," Nola said uncertainly.

"I remember," Bridget promised.

The wind teased us from behind as we crossed a shallow meadow and made our way around a hill of tumbled boulders. There was always a breeze on the mountain, but on this day the wind came up fast and hard. The closer we got to Secret Lake, the more agitated I became. I was peeved at myself for skipping lunch, then remembered that I had not expected to live past dinner.

As we neared the lake I could smell the still water and the lichen-frosted rocks and the endangered mountain phlox and the bitter tangle of wild grapes on the south edge beyond the reeds. The ground beneath us pulsed. Pausing to inhale, I felt a quickening. That sense of drawing near, being on the verge of something mysterious and explosive.

I stopped to wait for Nola to catch up again as Bridget carried on, springing from boulder to rock, head down, watching her feet. Then time stood still for a moment as I glanced ahead of her to notice a dense gathering of bees. Before I could warn her, Bridget leaped into the swarm.

"No!" Nola shouted.

Too late. Converged upon by the anxious bees, Bridget opened her mouth and released a piercing scream. She swatted at the insects, and spun around in circles, and jerked her head back and forth, screaming all the while. I could see that her lustrous ponytail was acting as a net and had trapped several of the bees in its lengths. The more the bees buzzed, the louder Bridget screamed.

This is where it all began.

Bridget started to run. The bees still trapped in her ponytail buzzed aggressively and she thought she was being chased by the whole swarm, so she kept on running, stumbling on rocks and leaping over fallen trees, careening in a southwesterly direction to an area of the mountain I was not remotely familiar with. She tore through a pass between two massive granite crags, and vaulted over a mountain-fed stream and through a dense forest of white fir and juniper, and skidded down an escarpment of crumbling sediment and staggered up again and over the boulders at the top of another hill as I followed, hollering, "Bridget! Bridget! BRIDGET!"

I chased her for what felt like an hour but was more likely five or six minutes before I thought to look behind me, and spotted the red poncho caught on a bush where Nola had stumbled and fallen. I couldn't chase one woman and leave the other. I started back to help Nola, but before I could reach her, she shouted, "Go! She'll get lost!"

Distant movement caught my eye, and I was confused to see the teenaged girl with the green flip-flops storming toward us through the brush. Where the hell had *she* come from?

I took off after Bridget once again, scrambling over the rocks, as her screams were snatched by the matrix in the walls and hurled back into the forest to confuse my sense of direction.

Then the screaming stopped. I called out, "Bridget? BRIDGET?"

Behind me rocks clattered, and I turned to see Nola in the red poncho, trailed by the girl in the green flip-flops. I waited until they caught up to me, all of us gasping for breath. Together we spotted Bridget through the haze ahead, stomping on what, to my horror, appeared to be a blond cat.

"My *fall*!" she wailed.

"What the hell?!" was all I could think to say when I realized it was a clip-on ponytail and not a dead mammal in the dirt at her feet.

Bridget's cheeks were streaked with black mascara, her short blond hair sticking up in all directions. She clutched the back of her neck, shouting, "Stung! I got stung!"

Nola forced the panicked woman to sit down on a rock. "Where?"

She pointed to her neck. "The stinger is still in there!"

Beestings hurt like hell, but the hot pain usually fades pretty fast. "It won't hurt for long," I said.

"I'm *allergic*!" Bridget shouted.

I suddenly understood her terror.

"This is not good," Nola said.

The girl in the green flip-flops found Bridget's blue mesh bag and began to search through it.

"I forgot my EpiPen in my suitcase," Bridget said, shaking.

"Oh dear," Nola said. "I don't see a stinger."

"On my neck," Bridget answered, hyperventilating.

"Breathe," Nola commanded.

That seemed a strange thing to tell a woman whose throat was closing from anaphylactic shock.

"Where on your neck?"

Bridget wheezed, pointing.

Nola searched. "No stinger. No sting mark."

Bridget's face darkened as she struggled for air. "There!" she rasped, pointing again.

"There's no stinger," Nola said. "Breathe. *Breathe*."

Bridget pointed once more to her nape. "Right there!"

The girl in the green flip-flops looked too but did not find a sting mark either. I failed to see why it mattered *where* Bridget was stung. She didn't have her EpiPen. Her throat was going to close up and the Mountain Station was at least a mile away.

"I do not see a thing," Nola said. "Not a *thing*."

Bridget wheezed dramatically. "In the middle!"

"Nothing."

Bridget's irritation seemed to be mitigating her allergic reaction. "Look under my hair!"

Nola took a moment to do so. "I don't think you were stung."

"I was stung," Bridget insisted.

"You're breathing pretty well though," I pointed out.

"You are," Nola agreed.

Bridget rubbed her neck, pouting.

The silent girl found my eyes. I took the briefest moment to wonder about her presence, and her peculiar manner.

"I was *stung*!" Bridget swore.

"We should head back," I said, turning to Nola, "in case she has a delayed reaction."

"That's it," Bridget said. "It's a delayed reaction."

The fog had become a viscous soup through which we could see neither earth nor sky.

"It's thick as stew," Nola said. I would quickly learn that Nola had a talent for stating the obvious.

"Are you sure you know the way?" Bridget asked.

Hubris, meet Wolf Truly. "I'm sure," I said, and started walking.

BRIDGET'S VOICE rose as we inched through the clotted clouds. "I can't see *anything*."

Gnarled tree roots slithered back and forth between the slippery rocks, stubbing our toes and catching our heels. The teenager lagged in her green flip-flops but was remarkably surefooted, considering. I caught her scent—red licorice and Dove soap.

"We appear to be in quite the pickle here," Nola said, laughing to hide her worry.

"What's your name again?" Bridget called to me through the haze. "Have I forgotten or did you not say?"

"Wolf," I said.

"Beg pardon?"

"Wolf."

"Wolf? I would have remembered that. *Wolf*."

"Wolf?" Nola repeated. "Did you say your name is *Wolf*?"

"It's short for *Wilfred*. Wilfred Truly."

"Wouldn't it be *Wilf* if it was short for Wilfred?"

"It's just Wolf," I said. "That's what my mother called me. That's the way everyone says it. Wolf."

The girl in the green flip-flops did not tell us her name nor attempt to communicate in any way. It occurred to me that she was mute.

"We need to find our way back," Nola said, adding gratuitously, "before dark."

When we came to a juncture of sorts, I sniffed the air, hoping to catch a scent of the trail home, but all I could distinguish was Nola's lavender sachet, the ginger sweat of Bridget, and the soapy teenaged girl.

"Which way now?" Bridget asked.

"This way," I said, pointing.

We walked silently, for nearly an hour, over the rocks, through the granite passes and the village of thick white firs. We carried on past the cluster of live oak. No acorns, just leftover shells from the rats and squirrels. I was sweating in spite of the dropping temperatures. At some point I realized we'd begun making a gentle *descent*. I knew that the way back to Secret Lake should be a gradual *ascent*. I remember telling myself that it was just a different way, a shortcut that would eventually take us back up. And so I *led* them. That must be said.

Nola's cheeks were pink from the cold. Bridget had zipped her hooded jacket all the way up over her tousled blond hair and pulled her second coat on too. The mute girl was shivering in spite of her pea coat, and I found myself twitching with empathetic pain when I lowered my eyes to her scarlet toes in the green flip-flops.

I found a rock and, leaning against it, yanked off my boots, tore the sub-zero hiking socks—Byrd's gift to me one Christmas—from my feet, and passed them to the girl, stupidly mouthing, *Take them*. She pressed the woolen socks back into my hands, shaking her head.

"We'll be back before it gets too cold anyway," Nola announced with conviction. "But that was a very nice gesture, *Wolf*. Does anyone call you Wilfred?"

I thought of my aunt Kriket. I thought of my father. I thought of Byrd. "No."

The wind danced in the trees, scolding the heckling jays as we trudged on. "Come on, everyone," I said, "this way."

Time on the mountain could be deceitful and disappointing, like the girl I once thought I loved. Time shifted and shrank, bounced and echoed, slept with college professors and rejected true love. We walked on in silence for what seemed like a very long time before we stopped to catch our breath and consider the course.

"I think we came around here," Bridget said. "Remember you pointed out that *tower*? Shouldn't it be right over there?"

We moved forward, unexpectedly knocked off-balance by a patch of small loose rocks when we started down a short slope. We slid only a few feet though, and none of us were toppled.

"That could have been *much* worse," Nola said.

By accident the mute girl and I locked eyes. She blanched, and gagged, and then turned to vomit in the bushes. I tried not to take it personally.

Together with Nola and Bridget, I watched the heaving arch of the girl's spine. Nola moved toward her, but Bridget held Nola back by grabbing the red poncho. I didn't pretend then, or now, to understand the ways of women. I reckoned they knew best when one of their kind wanted to be left alone.

"Are you all right?" Nola called.

The girl wiped her mouth with her coat sleeve and nodded in response—so, not deaf. She rose to her feet and stepped up to join me in the lead.

Bridget shared a look with Nola, and we walked on, until we came to another fork in the overgrowth.

"I wonder what time it is," Bridget mused, crossing her arms over her chest. I judged it to be somewhat later than four in the afternoon. In an hour or so the mountain would be dipped in night, and Nola and I were the only ones properly dressed for the cold. I hadn't bothered to check the mountain weather forecast back at the tram station but I knew, at this time of year, we'd be lucky if there was no rain—or snow. "Let's keep moving," I said.

We plodded on a little farther, up the striated granite and frozen flecked quartz, serenaded by Bridget's chorus of complaints. "I'm so cold. Can we hurry up? The rocks are so loose."

It was clear to me that the silent girl in the green flip-flops was moving as quickly as she could, and Nola faster than I'd have expected, given her age. We continued on over the rocks for another ten or fifteen minutes, which should have brought us to Secret Lake but nothing looked familiar anymore, or rather everything did—the same spiny pines peering out at us from the fog in all directions. The same ragged rocks.

"Hear it?" Bridget said. "Sounds like a waterfall."

We could all hear the sound of a roaring falls, an auditory illusion that the mountain is famous for. "The wind," I said. "It's the wind."

"Sounds like it's this way," Bridget said, pointing left.

"It's the wind," I repeated.

"It does sound like a waterfall," Nola said.

"It does."

"Isn't that where the tourists would be?" Bridget asked. "At the waterfall? Shouldn't we try to find it?"

"The only waterfall is Corazon Falls," I said. "That's six miles away from here—down in the canyon. There's no trail to Corazon Falls. Come on. We need to get back to the Mountain Station."

AN OWL began to hoot in the trees overhead, stopping us in our tracks. It was later than I thought. When we paused in a small clearing to catch our breath I tried to remain calm but I knew we were lost. I'd never been lost before. At least not in a mountain wilderness.

The owl hooted once more. I was sure it was a sign—from Byrd? God?—a warning. "We can't go on," I said. "It's suicide to walk in the dark. We need to find a spot to settle in."

"You're not serious." Bridget stiffened. "Are you saying we're stuck here for the night?"

"We'll be good. We'll be fine."

"Oh my God. Oh my God."

Nola reached out to squeeze her arm. "One night. You can make it through one night."

The girl in the green flip-flops said nothing, but I could see she was afraid. Bridget sniffled, but I couldn't find words to comfort her. Mostly I was irritated that she'd gone running off from the bees in the first place.

We looked around, sifting through the fog for a suitable shelter. Finding no overhangs or caves, we quickly agreed that the site of a large fallen log seemed as good a place as any to wait out the cold night.

Leaning down to clear a spot before she sat, Bridget was startled by a skittering cadre of black beetles moving in and out of a tunnel in the dirt and let out a blood-curdling scream. Backing away from the clattering insects, she caused a cluster of rocks to loosen at her feet and roll down the nearby incline, which was deeper and steeper than I'd first imagined.

None of us wanted to sleep with the beetles, so we decided to roll the log away from their burrow. Nola suggested a flat spot up the hill near some manzanita, which would help block the wind. Agreed, we four leaned down to roll the log away from the offending insects, but we were pushing against gravity and the rocks were unstable beneath our feet. With much grunting and huffing we managed to move the big log only a few yards up the incline. Bridget complained that the beetles were still too close, so we bore down once more.

It all happened so fast. (How many times has a sorry man said those words?)

We were moving that damn log up the hill—and then we were falling, lost in the kaleidoscope of rocks and ocher dust and manzanita and sage, conveyed by round, rushing boulders and silt and brush, hitting the ground with a thud.

It all happened so fast.

Battered and stunned, we rose and, gathering our wits, tried to find one another amid the rocks and soil and the bare-rooted scraps of the bushes that had concealed the cliff's edge.

Nola, having been delivered the farthest afield, coughed and shouted, "Everyone okay?"

I called back in the affirmative and so did Bridget. The girl said nothing, but I could see that she'd landed on the far side of a snowberry bush and didn't appear to be seriously injured.

Bridget cried from some place unseen, "Oh my God. Oh my God," but she didn't scream, which I took to be a good sign.

"What about you, Nola? You all right?" I shouted.

"Fine!" she called out. "I just hurt my wrist!"

I stared up into the gloaming at the height from which we'd tumbled. It was a miracle that one of us hadn't been killed. A miracle.

I turned to find the girl shuffling toward me around a large boulder and was shocked to see that she hadn't lost her green flip-flops. She had a small cut on her cheek and a new tear in her old pea coat but seemed otherwise fine. "Okay?"

She nodded as Bridget emerged from between two large rocks. Her Lycra was torn on her knees, and she had some scrapes on her hands and her cheek. "I lost my sports bag," she said. "It had the granola bars and water."

"We'll find it in the morning," I promised. I raised my hand to adjust my ball cap and discovered it was gone. My Detroit Tigers cap. I hoped I could find that too.

"I have my knapsack!" Nola said triumphantly when she appeared, finally, through some thick brush. "I lost my binoculars. They were around my neck."

"We'll find everything in the morning," I said.

Then Nola raised her hand, stunned as any of us to see a shard of white bone protruding from her wrist.

"Nola," I said cautiously, afraid she might faint.

"Oh, for heaven sakes." She just rolled her eyes like she'd spilled coffee on her blouse and was annoyed with herself for being clumsy. When she moved, blood made a fountain of the sharp bone.

Bridget screamed and turned away.

The girl in the green flip-flops leaped into action. "We need to wrap it up. Does anyone have a scarf?"

So, not mute. I felt the inside of my pockets and found a crumpled black bandana. I gave it to the girl, watching her adjust the bones in Nola's fractured wrist before tying the bandana over the wound. Nola bit her lip to stop from crying out. Must have hurt like hell.

The girl kept pressure on the wound, but Nola was bleeding badly and the bandana soon was soaked through. My heart was racing because I knew how quickly a life could end.

"This is not ideal," Nola said.

"We need more bandages," the girl said. "And a splint."

"What's in your knapsack?" Bridget asked without turning around.

"My Christmas sweater, but I don't think it would work," she said. "Should I try to take off my turtleneck?"

"No," we all said.

Quickly I began to undress, feeling the women's eyes boring holes into me as I removed my coat, hoodie, long-sleeve shirt, and stripped down to the old Bob Seger T-shirt of Frankie's that I'd reached for that morning when preparing my corpse for burial. I realized that I was about to reveal my tattoo to three strangers and turned my back on them before I pulled off the T-shirt. I dressed again, then took some pleasure in ripping Frankie's shirt to shreds, handing the strips to the girl.

Bridget looked around at the darkening wilderness, then she opened her mouth and screamed at the top of her lungs, "*HELP!*"

The sound bounced and echoed against the rock and was swept up again and carried off by the wind.

"Save your breath," I told her. "No one can hear us over that wind. We have to wait till it dies down."

While the girl wound the fabric strips around Nola's wrist, I made a brief search of the rocky vicinity and found a square-shaped, shallow recess where we'd have some protection from the wind. "Here!" I called. "A cave!"

Once we'd settled inside the cave, which was more like a cove, the girl continued to wrap the makeshift bandages around Nola's injury, fashioning a splint with a couple of small branches she'd found. We were all lucky Nola hadn't broken an ankle or, worse, her hip.

"I think you stopped the bleeding," I said.

After Nola's wound was taken care of, we attempted to get comfortable in the tight space. Nola sat beside the girl, the girl across from me, Bridget beside me, but we all touched in some way or other. A blanket of cold fell fast and hard.

"Do you feel that?" Nola whispered as if she didn't want the air to hear. "It just dropped double digits in a split second."

From my pocket I drew the thick gray socks and leaned across to find the girl's hands. She squeezed my fingers in thanks, taking the socks and pulling them over her stiff, bare feet.

"We're going to freeze to death," Bridget said.

"It's only November. It won't get that cold," I lied.

Nola reached for her knapsack with her good hand, fumbling for the extra sweater she'd brought along. "Put this on," she said, pressing the scratchy wool bundle into the girl's arms.

"Those are good socks, but your toes are still cold," I said, repositioning myself so that she could put her cold feet under my long-sleeve shirt.

The girl hesitated, then allowed me to guide her feet under my shirt to the warmth of my bare chest. Even through the wool socks her frozen toes shocked my nipples. "Cold," I said.

"Thanks," she said.

In the dark, I felt Nola and Bridget share a look.

The wind kicked up, roaring into our shelter, and we huddled closer for body heat. I removed my down coat and put it over Bridget's shoulders, saying, "We'll share the coat."

"I'm already freezing to death," Bridget said.

"No one is freezing to death," I said.

"Wolf," Nola said to change the subject. "I've never met a *Wolf*. I met a *Cat* once. And a *Bear*—well—his name was Barry, so they called him Bear. I don't know how it was spelled."

"Try to keep your hand elevated," I reminded Nola. "Lean it on your knee. Keep the swelling down."

"You're very calm in a crisis," Nola said.

I was tempted to point out that we would not *be* here were it not for me. If our paths hadn't crossed, the women would've been at the bottom of a crevice, or lost on some other part of the mountain, or maybe they'd have given up trying to find the lake and headed back to the Mountain Station. If our paths hadn't crossed I would *be* no more.

That's when I noticed that my despair, which had weighed me down since Byrd's accident and been deepened by Frankie's imprisonment, was gone, lost in the fall along with Bridget's mesh bag and my Tigers baseball cap. It was like some switch had been flipped off, or rather, on.

Warmed by my heat, the girl wiggled her toes.

"You have a name?" I asked.

"Vonn," she said. *Vonn.*

Vonn's presence among us was confounding, and equally confusing was the scant attention paid to her by the other two women. I squeezed her feet quite forcefully to prove to myself that she wasn't a ghost.

"Can you make a fire, Wolf?" Nola asked.

"Do you have anything in your knapsack that we could make a fire *with*?" I asked. "Matches? Lighter?"

"I'm sorry but I don't smoke," Nola said sincerely.

"First time I wished someone smoked," Bridget said through her chattering teeth. "I mean I really, seriously wished I smoked cigarettes right now."

"Can't you rub twigs together or something?" Nola inquired.

I didn't have the skills to make a fire without a flame in daylight, let alone in darkness. The air was too damp anyway. "No dry kindling," I said.

"I thought you were a mountain guide. First you get us lost. Now you can't make a fire." Bridget's tone was snarky.

"He didn't get us lost," Vonn said.

"Those darn bees!" Nola said.

Vonn sighed, which caused Bridget to turn on her, hissing, "What should I have done? Let them *sting* me? Without my *EpiPen*?"

Vonn opened her mouth, then snapped it shut.

"I just think it's false advertising if you take money as a guide but have actually zero navigational or survival skills."

"Okay."

Bridget would not let it go. "Well, what's your plan, Mountain Man?"

Mountain Man. I thought I heard a snicker coming from behind a slab of rock. When Bridget asked, "Did you hear that?" I thought she'd heard it too.

"Listen." She waited for our silence. "It sounds like that waterfall again."

"You can't trust mountain acoustics. You think you hear things—waterfalls, airplanes, voices. It's just the wind. No matter what you think you hear up here, I promise you it's the wind."

The wind changed direction with a flourish, and we turned toward it, craned to watch the dense clouds lift, astonished as the valley came into view, the twinkling breadth of the city thousands of feet below us, the tiny lights of the wind turbines in the distance.

Nola announced, "That's Palm Springs!"

Bridget pointed toward the distant northeast. "Look out there. God—it looks like a jewel—what is that way out there?"

It was Tin Town. That was the hell of it. We weren't lost.

"We're not lost!" Bridget cried.

Nola laughed. "What a relief! We can just climb down in the morning!"

"Not exactly," I said. "I'm pretty sure this is Devil's Canyon."

"So we'll climb down Devil's Canyon," Nola said. "We'll have quite the story to tell."

"It's not that simple," I said.

"We'll come out right at that breakfast place!" she said, pointing at the city lights.

"I'm afraid we can't get down that way," I said.

"What are you saying?"

"We can't get down from here, Mrs. Devine. You can't get down that way. We're going to have to try to climb back *up* where we fell," I said.

"Don't be silly," Nola said. "That's too steep for me to climb with my broken paw. Besides, we could get lost again! That's crazy when we know exactly where we are right now! Why would we climb *up* to get *down*?"

"We're not trying to get *down* exactly. We're just trying to get *off*," I said. "I know it goes against your instincts."

"I believe in instincts," Nola said.

"So do I," Bridget said for my benefit. "I'm clairvoyant."

The girl gagged a little. I supposed she was still sick from the tram.

"There must be a trail down to Palm Springs," Nola said. "I'm sure we can find it."

"Trust me, Mrs. Devine. It's a maze of deep canyons and steep rock. You might be able to get down, but you can't get back up and you can't get to Palm Springs."

"It looks like you could just walk down," Nola insisted.

I thought of the story Byrd had told me about the hiker. "One day, a long time ago, this guy named Jack missed the last tram down. He panicked up here alone in the dark when he found out he was locked out of the Mountain Station."

"Jack Mazlo?" Nola said. "Are you talking about Jack Mazlo?"

"You know about Jack Mazlo? He's kind of a legend, right?"

"I suppose."

"I don't know Jack Mazlo," Bridget said.

I told the women about his descent down the tramline trail, which wasn't a trail at all.

When I finished, Bridget sighed. "At least they found the poor man. At least he survived."

"But he didn't," Nola said.

"Sure he did," I said.

"I knew Jack Mazlo," Nola countered. "He died that night, Wolf."

"What?"

"He died that night."

"No," I said. "They found him in the brush near the first tram tower. He goes to the coffee shop. Sits like this." I tipped my hip.

"Have you ever seen him?" Nola asked.

"Well, no."

"Who told you that story?"

"A guy who knows everything about the mountain."

"Jack was dead when they found him," Nola said. "He'd lain there with a broken leg for two days straight is what they figure. No one could see him because of the thick brush and no one could hear him over the tram."

"He didn't get rescued?" I was trying to absorb the awful truth.

"He was only twenty-six years old."

"That's so young," Bridget said.

"Jack and Janice Mazlo. They were neighbors of ours in Cathedral City when we first moved down from Ohio. They had a four-year-old— Little Jack. It was the saddest thing. I heard she moved back to Texas with the boy. I wonder what ever became of them."

"That's an awful story," Vonn said.

I was angry with Byrd for the lie.

"I like your version better," Nola said, leaning forward to squeeze my arm in the dark. "I was heartsick about that boy losing his daddy."

She made me think of my mother, and Frankie, and I was disturbed by the sudden longing I felt for my father, such as he was.

Frankie wasn't ever father of the year, but he was once or twice father of the moment. One time he got free fudge bars for the whole block after he chased down the driver of the Sweet'n'Freeze truck to collect on a debt. I was proud as hell to eat mine hoisted high up on his shoulders.

FRANKIE AND I left Mercury, Michigan, for Santa Sophia, California, in the dark, after cramming our few possessions into our newly acquired green Gremlin hatchback one warm night in July.

A block away from home we noticed a terrible smell and suspected a dead mouse was wedged in some crevice of the cooling system since the odor was considerably worse when the air conditioning was on. Frankie hadn't noticed the smell when he took possession of the car because he'd been smoking. It was an ominous departure.

The roads were quiet, and as we passed the library I turned my head to admire the towering conifers that flanked the walkway, and I remember thinking about Miss Kittle's prediction that I would not miss winter. I tried to imagine the mountain in the desert as Frankie squirmed in the torn vinyl seat, blinking rapidly as he tapped on the steering wheel with the wedding band he still wore, humming some melody of regret.

I didn't know if he regretted what he paid for the smelly green Gremlin, or if he regretted his life in general, but I was pretty sure the agitation came from the "aspirins" he'd shaken down his gullet a short time before—amphetamines to keep him awake on the drive, I guessed. Maybe he regretted taking the pills.

We'd pulled out of the driveway on Old Dewey Road, with the windows down, anticipating a week on the road. I proposed we mark our arrival in California with a ritual: take the Aerial Tramway up the mountain and then hike the remaining few thousand feet to the peak on our first day.

"We can't take the *tram*. We gotta *climb* the bitch!" Frankie said, slamming his hand on the dash.

"You probably shouldn't call her the bitch, considering she's named after a saint."

"I'm not superstitious, Wolf," he said, driving the wrong way out of town.

"You mean religious," I corrected.

"I know what I mean," Frankie said, signaling right, then left, but not making either turn. "We're going to climb—like men—all the way to the peak."

"I think that's a long way."

"Supposed to be a hell of a view. A father should see that with his son," Frankie said.

Unlike most adolescent boys, I found the idea of climbing a mountain, or of doing anything at all with my old man, highly appealing. "First day there."

"First day there. We'll go up in the afternoon and watch the sunset," Frankie said.

"The book said the climb takes all day though, Frankie, and that's just from the tram station to the peak. And you should only attempt it if you're in amazing shape."

"I'm a *rock*," he said, falling into a coughing fit.

I had to take the wheel so he could huck some mucus into a rag he'd found on the floor. "Maybe you should stop smoking."

He wiped his nose on his shirtsleeve, trying to focus on the road. "I'm letting things get to me," he said. "I've been letting things get to me, Wolf. This hasn't been an easy time. There's been a lot of pain. A lot of disappointment. Heartache."

It was true.

"I am not getting what I need from this world. You understand?"

I did.

He blew his nose again. "I need to get my shit together."

"You do," I agreed, which irritated him.

"That's what this move is all about. Clean living. That's what I need. Your California sunshine and your orange trees and your lemon trees and your olives and your avocados. That shit'll extend your life thirty years or better."

The thing that got me was you could see on Frankie's face, even as he was saying it, that he wasn't sure he wanted thirty more years.

I offered only a weak protest when he suggested a quick stop at a friend's house, which was, he said, on the way out of town. The fact is that I wanted to be anywhere but trapped in the rank Gremlin with my sniffling, ring-tapping, hyped-up father.

The farmhouse where Frankie was to meet his *associate* Warren was a fifteen-minute drive from the blue house on Old Dewey and still officially inside Mercury city limits.

"You sure about this?" I asked as we scuffed up the porch steps.

The odor of cattle from the neighbor's pasture was earthy and raw. I breathed in the scent and was startled when the porch light flickered on above our heads and a diminutive man with a wiry beard opened the door wearing a woman's turquoise bathrobe and mud-caked cowboy boots. I was three inches taller, but he could smell my fear.

Warren led us down the long hall, squeezing sideways past dusty stacks of newspapers and cardboard that drove me to sneeze uncontrollably. "Tell your kid to quit being an asshole," he said.

"Be respectful," my father warned.

Frankie told me to wait in the kitchen, where tomatoes festered in a basket near an ashtray. I watched my father follow Warren's bathrobe down to the end of the dusty hall, breathing through my mouth.

The wind drove against the trembling pane, as I strained to look out over the plowed fields and the dimly lit pasture beyond. I missed my mother. All at once leaving Michigan felt like leaving her. My misery grew as the cool night slipped in under the kitchen door.

As was my habit, I'd brought a book along. I learned young that when we left the blue house we wouldn't be going to a Tigers game, or a Lions game, or the Metro Beach, or a skating rink, or a splash park, or a park of any kind, or the zoo, or a movie, or even the mall or the grocery store. We would be going to a house, sometimes a small office, an alley, or a parking lot where Frankie would disappear for an hour or longer. Without a book, I was alone, or worse, alone with other people's children, or someone's drunken wife, or sad sister, or bitter secretary, or sometimes just the dark.

I opened my novel, but it was hard to concentrate because of the noise coming from where Frankie and Warren had retired to talk business. I heard Frankie start to rant, then Warren to agitate, and it went on like that for nearly half an hour. The silence, when it came, was deafening.

For a moment I was paralyzed. Finally I got up to venture down the hallway and found my father slumped on the floor of a bedroom near a pile of dirty blankets. The back window was open, and I could see Warren in the moonlight making his way across the rutted field, hugging a pillow to his robe, headed for the dense forest beyond. How far could he get? Why the pillow? Why the forest? What the hell?

I sank to my knees and tried to lift my father's heavy head. His hair felt coarser than I'd remembered and his neck more muscular than I'd imagined. How long since I'd touched him? *Years?*

As a child I sat on his lap, breathing in his scent (Camel Filters and Irish Spring on good days), listening to his heartbeat, tracing the rainbow *Glory Always* tattoo with my dirty fingernail. "What else did she like to do?" I'd ask, and Frankie'd tell me stories about my mother's affection for books and libraries, and rainbows, and secondhand clothing stores, and baking, and how she was always looking for ways to go back in time instead of ways to move forward. No detail was too small: "Glory loved peppermints—always had a tin in her purse." I remembered the peppermint smell. And the little tin.

The window banged against the sash as I steadied his lolling head and searched his neck for a pulse. The scent of urine burned my nostrils, and I almost collapsed with relief when I felt the warm puddle at my knee, but my panic was reborn when I realized that Frankie's urine stream didn't effectively prove he was alive. In fact, I had no knowledge whatsoever of which bodily fluids the dead were capable of releasing.

I settled my father down on the floor and tilted his head back to clear his airways, then leaned over him, like we were shown on the dummy in health class. After covering Frankie's mouth with mine, I exhaled hard for three seconds, then stopped and repeated. I realized I'd forgotten to pinch his nose, then I couldn't remember when to blow and when to pinch. I tried to blow again. What if I was suffocating him? I became aware of his teeth, the taste of his saliva—he'd eaten something with cheese at dinner. I stifled a gag. Again I felt for a pulse.

Funny what you remember—a frying pan filled with cigarette butts on the bedside table; brown splatters on the wall, blood or maybe coffee; dog hairs on the plaid blanket, a dirty white bra on a hook by the door like it was something you should remember to grab on your way out. Nothing illegal if you didn't count the filth. Warren must have taken his contraband with him in the pillow. How far could he get in a lady's bathrobe?

The clock mocked me. Why did a guy like Warren need a clock? I pressed my ear to Frankie's chest, relieved to find there, faint and uneven, a heartbeat. I leaped into action, calling his name, slapping his cheeks. His color was ash.

This, of course, is the part where I call the ambulance. I remembered seeing a phone in the kitchen and ran to it, fumbling for the receiver. I lifted it, then put it back down, then picked it up again, and put it down once more. If I called for an ambulance the police would become involved. Frankie, if he survived, would go to jail or rehab, and I would fall into dreaded *care*.

Returning to my father, I noted the wind driving in through the open window, carrying the stink of manure. I stood over Frankie for a beat and then reared back and kicked his leg hard. He didn't move. I kicked him again. I kicked him once more, harder, and he startled me when he gasped. Like his engine had been ripped, Frankie coughed and sputtered a little and started breathing again. I believe that I saved my father's life that night while attempting to put him out of my misery.

I helped him to sit up, and as Frankie dropped his head to puke on my jeans, I patted his back and was seized by an overwhelming instinct to protect him. Many years later I'd recognize the feeling as paternal love, which is not as strange a thing for a child to feel for a parent as you might imagine. I wiped Frankie's mouth with a crumpled napkin from the floor and for once didn't find his confusion funny. I stroked his stubbled cheek and told him that I was so, so sorry and that everything was going to be fine. It was the truth—at least the first part. He couldn't seem to decide if, by waking, he'd just won a prize or suffered a crushing defeat. I resisted the impulse to say I loved him. I don't know why. "Okay?"

"Warren," he said, after a moment.

At first I took it for a directive. "Warn who?"

"Blue bathrobe." Frankie blinked, recovering a memory.

"He thought you were dead."

"Whoa."

"So did I."

Frankie sat up. "Did you call for an ambulance?"

It was a simple question, but the answer contained the essence of our complicated futures. I shook my head. "No."

Something passed between us then, a mantle of sorts, though Frankie was as reluctant to bestow it as I was to receive. "Good," he said.

It wasn't the move to Santa Sophia that changed things for Frankie and me. That moment came before the desert, the night we started out for California, in the filthy farmhouse on the outskirts of Mercury, Michigan, where we both learned that I was my father's son.

MY FATHER had many, many bad habits, but one of his good habits was to keep a full tank of gas. His motto was: *You never know how fast you might need to leave or how far you might have to go.*

That's what I remember most about the trip from Michigan to California—stopping for gas. Our meals consisted mainly of service-station food—Gatorade, pork rinds, and potato chips, which Frankie saw respectively as a fruit, a protein, and a veg. I developed chronic indigestion and got black circles under my eyes. My lips cracked and bled. I thought I was getting scurvy.

For miles and days the most my father ever said was "Hot."

I was grateful for the distraction of my books. Sometimes the books made me think of the pretty head librarian.

Before we left for Santa Sophia, on a day Frankie and I were supposed to be clearing out the garage, Miss Kittle showed up at our blue door on Old Dewey Road. I already knew she wasn't there to see me when Frankie pounced on her. He must have been right about the pheromones.

Frankie'd found a picture of Miss Kittle, torn from an article in the local paper, beside my bed and thought it was funny as hell that I had a crush on her. I think that's why he decided to date her.

A few days after her first visit I came home to find Miss Kittle on the ripped chaise beside the broken porch, sunning herself in a strapless summer dress. Frankie grabbed the newspaper and suggested I keep *Kitten* (that's what he called her) company for the duration of what he assured us would be a protracted bowel movement.

I took the chair beside Miss Kittle, closing my eyes, pretending to like the sun too, but mostly so I wouldn't be tempted to stare.

"You excited?" she asked.

"Sorry?"

"About moving to the desert? About the mountain?"

"I can't wait to ride in that tramcar."

"And don't forget the peak."

"I'm going to be a mountain climber. Like the guys in the book you gave me. I want to climb Everest like Norgay and Hillary."

"Adventurous men."

"Definitely."

"I like an adventurous man," Miss Kittle said, which honestly made me wonder why she was with Frankie, who had only *mis*adventures. "In some cultures boys are considered men when they turn thirteen."

"Which I already am," I reminded her.

"Which you already are," she agreed.

"And a half," I said, reaching deep inside the front pocket of my jeans. "Thirteen and a half."

"You can do anything a man can do," she said, focused on my hand. "What are you doing now?"

I pulled my short stack of baseball cards from my pocket, grinning. "My best trading cards," I said. "I got Al Kaline today. Did you bring more books?"

"I brought a book about native uses for plants," Miss Kittle said, reaching into her bag. "See, Wolf. Here—redweed. This is important. Take a good long look at it."

She sounded serious, so I did take a good long look at the photograph in the book. "You know this plant by the ruby pods and the white flower. The little seeds from the pods are brewed into a tea or dried and smoked. They were used by Native Americans in a male rite-of-passage ritual. Don't ever get close to it. Don't ever, God forbid, ingest it."

"Like poison ivy?"

"If you drink it or eat it or smoke it, it induces visions."

"Cool."

"And multiple organ failure," Miss Kittle said, wagging her finger. "I knew a boy who died from it in my senior year. His father was the police chief. They went around with tracking dogs and dug up all the bushes. You won't see redweed within fifty miles of Santa Sophia now. But if anyone ever does offer you redweed, you don't accept, right?"

"Okay."

When Miss Kittle shifted in her chair her dress rose up even higher and I was shocked to see her bare right flank. My baseball cards fell from my hands, scattering at her feet. She smiled at me as she swept them into a little pile with her bare toes, accidentally flashing me each time she moved her legs. *How could a grown woman forget to wear underwear?*

"Maybe I'll come see you and Frankie when I go back to visit my father in late August," she said, seemingly unaware of her wardrobe gaffe.

"Cool," I said, looking away when the button on her sundress threatened to burst open at her chest.

"So it's a date," she said, leaning closer.

I was sweating profusely. I looked at my baseball cards in the pile she'd made with her toes. Detroit catcher John Wockenfuss was on top. I distracted myself thinking about Wockenfuss and his unusual batting stance, how he'd turn his back on the pitcher and twist his head all the way over his shoulder. John Wockenfuss.

"Wolf," Miss Kittle said, drawing even closer.

Peering out of the corner of my eye, I saw that not only had Miss Kittle's ill-fitting dress slid up even higher on her thigh, but the button *had* busted open at her chest and one of her pink nipples was exposed too. *Wockenfuss. Wockenfuss. Wockenfuss.*

"Wolf?"

The door opened, and my father appeared. Miss Kittle fixed her dress. I bolted for my room and hid my head beneath my pillow, grateful when some time later I heard the front door slam, which meant Frankie and his *Kitten* had gone out to get drunk instead of staying in to get drunk. Small mercies.

It wasn't until some days later it hit me that Miss Kittle's revealing situation had been an invitation, not a mishap. It took me even longer to realize that Frankie had orchestrated the whole thing. When I confronted him about it later, he said, "Some fathers throw bar mitzvahs for their sons when they're thirteen."

"I asked for a bike."

Soon Miss Kittle stopped coming by. I never heard the details of their breakup. Maybe he cheated on her, maybe he stole from her, or maybe he lied to her. Sadly, she banned us—well, me—from the Mercury library. The bonus was that Frankie had more free time, even if we did spend most it packing up the blue house.

My father said I should keep the library books about Palm Springs and the mountain, and the stack of overdue novels. I did, even though I knew I shouldn't. I still have them.

On the drive to California I looked through the book about the desert hot springs, mildly interested in the thought that millennia earlier prehistoric animals had set foot in the same *agua caliente* that still burbled up from the middle of the earth. I didn't even open the book about the history of golf in the area. I was undereducated in the matter of celebrities current or past, so the books about the Hollywood history of Palm Springs didn't interest me much either. But I pored over the one about rattlesnakes, memorized their detailed markings, and lingered over pornographic close-ups of milky dripping fangs.

The Mountain in the Desert was the book I spent the most time reading though, acquainting myself with the mountain's changing life zones, from desert scrub to alpine forest. The chapters about the Native Americans who lived in the foothills and believed the mountain held the cure for every ailment, physical or spiritual, intrigued me. What if they were right? There were a number of quotations in the book, from naturalists and hikers, who claimed to have seen God on the mountain. When I read the quotes to Frankie he laughed. "Must be the thin air."

The final chapters were about the Swiss-designed tram. I'd never been to a theme park, but I couldn't imagine any roller coaster being more thrilling than that tram ride. To be lifted that high, that fast, catapulted from one climate to another—that sounded like the closest thing you could get to time travel.

I couldn't read once it got dark though. It was hard to imagine cool mountain breezes when I was stuck with Frankie in that crappy Gremlin. I remember looking out the window and not knowing which state we were driving through, Frankie humming along with the radio the whole way, a cigarette burning in the ashtray, day after dismal day.

THAT FIRST night on the mountain with the three women, shivering together in the dark, we were not lost but stranded, with the long night before us. You'd think we would have gone around the circle and told a little bit about ourselves. You'd think we might have taken a minute or two to discuss what just happened and what we should do next. You'd think

that one of us would have cried or freaked out or laid blame. We did none of those things. At least not at first. We were quiet for a long time.

"How's your hand?" I asked, finally, because I could see Nola, in her red poncho, grimacing in the moonlight.

"A little swollen is all." With her good hand she reached into her knapsack for the yellow canteen. "We should drink."

Bridget reached out to take the canteen. "Here, let me do the cap." She opened it and gulped the water, and then passed the canteen back to Nola, who drank modestly before placing it in the hands of Vonn, who took only a very small sip. Our fingers touched when Vonn passed the canteen to me. Hers were surprisingly warm.

The feel of the yellow canteen brought back the memory of the worst night of my life—and that's saying something—one year to the day earlier. I could not bring myself to put my lips on the spout. "I drank a lot at the fountain before," I managed to say. It was somewhat true. I handed the canteen back.

"This really is an adventure, isn't it? I mean it really is," Nola said. "I could never have imagined that today would end like this."

"We don't have much water," Bridget said. "Just the one canteen."

"In the morning we'll find the bag," I said.

"And my binoculars."

"And your binoculars."

"I'm freezing," Bridget said.

"We're all freezing," Vonn said.

There was a long pause. I didn't need to see their collective expressions.

"Maybe some people have a lower tolerance for the cold," Bridget said.

"The cap, Bridget," Nola said.

Bridget reached across and took the yellow canteen back from Nola, saying, "Let me do it, Mother."

Mother? Did she say *Mother*?

In the moonglow I saw what I hadn't noticed before: the shape of the jaws, the slope of the noses. Mother and daughter. Bridget's cosmetic alterations had thrown me off. She'd removed the dent between her brows, which would have deepened in time, like Nola's, and her lips were plump and pouting where Nola's were thinner but shaped prettily. It was clear that, even denatured, Bridget was her mother's daughter.

"How did you get us so lost, Wolf?" Bridget asked plaintively, tipping the yellow canteen for another gulp of water.

"We should ration the water, Bridget," Vonn said.

Bridget pounced. "I thought you weren't speaking to me, *Vonn*? What happened to that? I liked it better when you were doing your silent thing."

Another puzzle piece. Bridget knew Vonn. They were not friends.

"You're so stubborn!" Bridget hissed. "I can't believe you. Even with all this!"

"Studied with the master," Vonn returned.

"Didn't your therapist tell you to *disengage*, Vonn? Can we please just go back to that?"

Nola tsked. "Let her be silent if she needs to be silent, Bridget. Let her talk if she needs to talk."

Sisters? I wondered.

"Retreat into silence," Bridget said mockingly. "Isn't that what you're supposed to do? Retreat into silence?"

"One of us has to be the adult here. I have the most experience," Vonn said.

"You're eighteen, Vonn," Bridget said. "What do you know about being an adult? You think you're grown up because you're running around Tin Town?"

Tin Town?

"Not *now*, Bridget," Nola said.

"Because you've been hanging out with some biker in Tin Town."

"What biker? Who said anything about Tin Town?" Vonn said, turning to Nola for translation.

"I heard you talking about him on the phone," Bridget said.

"You're insane," Vonn said.

Vonn didn't look like a Tin Town type to me. But then she didn't look like a Santa Sophia type either. I wasn't so sure about Bridget.

"You were coming to the desert to help Mim," Bridget said. "Remember? You came to keep her company."

"I did come to help Mim."

"Vonn's been good company," Nola protested.

"Running around Tin Town?"

"Who's running around Tin Town?" Vonn asked. "What is she talking about?"

"I know bikers are trouble," Bridget said.

"What are you all talking about?" Vonn was genuinely bewildered. "Whatever you think you heard—you're wrong."

"Not every person who rides a motorcycle is a criminal, Bridget," Nola said.

Some of my favorite people rode motorcycles. Byrd's uncle Harley ironically had a Honda, and his cool uncle Dantay had a Harley, an entire collection of Harleys, actually. His cousin Juan Carlos had a dirt bike. My cousin Yago rode a Shovelhead, but then again he *was* a criminal.

I didn't understand Vonn's relationship to the other women. "You know each other but it didn't seem like you came together."

"We're the *Devines*!" Nola said it as if I should have known. "Vonn is my granddaughter. Bridget is Vonn's mother."

It hit me then that Vonn hadn't been staring at *me* earlier on the tram. She'd been watching Bridget with her big blond clip-on ponytail, probably wondering what her mother was saying to the tragic boy-man in the Detroit Tigers cap.

"Bridget has a home in Golden Hills. Do you know it?" Nola asked.

"No."

"Oh, it's lovely."

"Near the coast," Bridget said.

"Really just as close to the valley as the ocean," Vonn said.

"Sure."

"Vonn's been staying with me at my condo in Rancho Mirage," Nola said.

"Are you a local?" Bridget asked.

"I'm from Michigan," I said.

"Michigan? But how are you a mountain guide here?" Bridget asked.

I realized I was digging a deep hole with my sins of omission. "I have a friend here. Who I visit. I come here a lot. Hiking."

"That's a long way away."

"It is."

After that came a long stretch of silence, which Nola broke by whispering, "I keep reaching for him. Isn't it funny that I'd still be doing that?"

Bridget and Vonn sighed in sympathy.

"I'm sorry for your loss," I said. I said it because it was the thing people say, but I meant it too. I could feel the vibration from their collective grief.

"It gets cold in Michigan," Nola said. "Ohio too. I grew up in Ohio."

"Even Malibu's too cold for me," Bridget said.

"Once, when I was a kid, it went to twenty below in Macomb County," I said. "Six people died of exposure in one night."

"Why are you telling us that?" Vonn asked.

"I'm saying it won't get that cold here," I said, covering. "I've spent dozens of nights on the mountain. Nights way colder than this. We'll be fine. Just stay close together."

The women seemed relieved, which had been the purpose of my lie. The truth is I'd spent only one night on the mountain. One disastrous night.

Byrd popped into my head. He was never really far from my thoughts—especially on the mountain.

THE GREMLIN'S tank was still more than three-quarters full when we'd passed the WELCOME TO SANTA SOPHIA sign in the dark morning hours.

Frankie was humming softly along with the Beatles while I stared out the window, the mountain looming somewhere in the night. Instead of driving straight to his sister Kriket's house after eight days on the road, Frankie found the Santa Sophia gas station/convenience store.

"Remember, we're going up the mountain tomorrow. Right? We're going to climb to the peak. First day there," I said.

Frankie started coughing. He didn't say anything. He didn't have to.

A rusty cowbell clanged when we entered the store, which appeared to be empty, the cash register unattended. "'lo?" Frankie called.

Figuring the clerk was in the restroom, I took a cold grape pop from the fridge and drank it in three loud gulps, then guzzled two more cans, belching thunderously, while Frankie discovered a surprisingly extensive magazine selection on the rear wall. I tossed the pop cans in the trash.

"I had three pops, Frankie. Don't forget to pay for them."

Frankie nodded. "They carry everything here," he called out. "Look at this selection! Comics. Travel. Hobbies. *Ascent*? *Field and Stream*?" He plucked a comic from the shelf and planted his feet to read.

I'd worked out by now that my aunt Kriket's house was not a place you wanted to race to. My father hadn't once telephoned her while we were on the road, and I wondered if she even knew we were coming.

"Hot as shit," Frankie complained.

It was, I supposed.

Frankie headed toward the bank of refrigerators and took his time selecting a six-pack of his usual brand. "If it's hot like this at night, what must this shithole be like during the day? Who the hell'd go outside?"

"Golfers," a voice responded from the shadows behind the cash register.

A boy, about my age, who had been out of sight, reclining on a lawn chair in the office behind the counter, rose and shuffled toward the register. He was my height, in fact strikingly similar in physique, facial structure, haircut, style. "Old dudes mostly," he added.

We might have been brothers, or at least cousins. The bridge of his nose was slightly broader, his hair darker and thicker, his eyes black, his complexion olive. The differences were defining ones, for I guessed he was Native American straight off and he did not guess so of me.

"Michigan plates," the clerk said, gesturing to the green Gremlin in the parking lot. "I was born in the Detroit area."

"Mercury," I said. "Ways up from Mount Clemens."

"I grew up in Hamtramck," he said. "You know Brodski's Polish Deli?"

"No."

"My grandparents owned it. Best kielbasa. Best pierogi."

"Cool."

"I'm going back there someday. Open the restaurant up again," he said. "You like the Tigers?"

"What d'ya think?" I said, reaching to touch my baseball cap, deeply sorry to find I'd left it in the car. "Left my Tigers cap in the car."

"I believe you," he said.

We nodded in sync, our Michigan connection feeling like more than mere coincidence.

My father joined us, setting his beer and a magazine on the counter, and stared at the boy for a long moment before he said, "Cahoola?"

The clerk jerked his head toward me, expecting I'd interpret, but I was pretty sure Frankie was having a stroke, aphasia being one of the warning signs. It scared the hell out of me when he said it again. "Cahoola?"

The clerk stared.

"I'm part Cree," Frankie said. "That's a northern tribe. I figured if you're from here you must be Cahoola."

Not a stroke. It was worse. "*Ca*hoola." The clerk glanced at me, wearing the merest grin as if to say—*Is this guy for real?*

"I did some reading up on the area, Wolf," Frankie said. (I *hated* my father when he tried to show off.) "Cahoola's the name of the local Native Americans, of which I am one, well, one-eighth. Cree. I'm one-eighth Cree."

I'd done some reading up about the area too, and I knew that the tribe's name, Cahuilla, was pronounced *Kah-wee-ah*. I was careful not to meet the clerk's eyes.

Frankie went on. "The Cahoola Indians have been here for millions of years, Wolf, hunting up on the mountain, fishing down in the desert. The mountain is a sacred place to the Cahoola."

The boy nodded. "Still see some rock paintings up there. Mortars from acorn grinding. Shaman's cave."

"You go up in that tram?" I asked.

"I ride the tram all the time, dude."

"I don't want this." Frankie stopped the clerk from ringing up the magazine. "Just wanted to see what it said to do about snakebites. Their venom makes pudding out of your blood."

If there was a snakebite cure, I wanted to know it. "What *do* you do?"

Frankie's tone mocked the expert advice. "Be still. Remove jewelry. Don't use pressure. Don't use a tourniquet. Don't apply ice. Above all, don't panic!"

"You know better, Frankie?"

"First thing you do with a snakebite? *Piss* on it," Frankie said.

"Piss on it?"

"I read a thing."

"Don't piss on *me*, Frankie," I warned.

Frankie said to the clerk, "You mind if I drink a beer in here?"

After glancing out the store's windows at the quiet, dark parking lot, the clerk tore a can of beer from the foggy six-pack and tossed it to Frankie.

"There's a bush that grows on the mountain," the clerk said slowly. "We make a paste from the leaves. It cured my grandmother's skin cancer. Burned off my uncle's wart. Made my rattler bite look like a flea bite."

"Rattler bite? From a rattlesnake?" I was spellbound.

The boy pulled up his sleeve to reveal a miniscule pimple on his arm. "Everyone I know makes paste from the bush."

Frankie whistled. "There's a cash crop right there."

"We don't exploit nature for profit," the boy said, unblinking.

"No," Frankie agreed. "But if I needed it. For snakebite or cancer? How would I find it?"

"I only know the *Cahoola* name," the boy said, then uttered a collection of guttural syllables that we clearly did not understand. "I'll break it up," he offered. "Repeat after me. Ken eye."

Frankie did, taking great care with the inflection. "Ken *eye*."

"Pretty good," the clerk said. "Ee *it*," he continued, pushing out a long, throaty gurgle.

"Ee *it*," Frankie repeated, imitating the sound perfectly.

The clerk seemed impressed. "You've never spoken a native tongue?"

"Swear to God," Frankie insisted.

"Yo*pu*," the clerk said slowly.

Chuffed by the encouragement, Frankie repeated, "Yo*pu*."

"Say," the clerk finished. "Now say it all together slowly."

"Ken eye ee it yopu say," Frankie said.

My head snapped toward the clerk, whose nod to me was barely perceptible.

"That's *uncanny*," the clerk told Frankie. (Who says *uncanny*?) "Dude, you sound totally *Cahoola*."

"Say it again, Frankie," I said, fearing I'd bust out laughing. I'd never been the guy in on the joke before. I liked it.

"Ken *eye* ee *it yopu* say," Frankie sang loudly.

The clerk nodded sagely, glanced around, and even though we were alone in the store, he lowered his voice to instruct, "There's this nasty old woman who owns the gift shop at the visitor center. She's one hundred and seven years old. She knows everything. She can tell you where that bush grows," the clerk said.

"Right on," Frankie said.

"But you have to say it exactly right. First—this is important—you have to tell her that you're looking for 'the hairy bush.'"

"I'm looking for the hairy bush," Frankie said confidently. "Ken *eye* ee *it yo pu* say?"

I had to turn away.

"There a local paper?" Frankie asked, and nodded his thanks when the clerk sent him back toward the magazine rack.

"Keep practicing," the clerk called.

Frankie took the cue, dancing himself back to the magazine rack, repeating the phrase all the way.

"Your old man's a trip," the boy said when Frankie was out of earshot.

"Is there really a miracle snakebite cure though?" I asked.

He shrugged. "My cousins use sterasote—it's like creosote, but it grows at higher elevations. They use ephedra, ocotillo, cottonwood—all kinds of herbs."

"Which one did you use? That rattlesnake bite *does* look like a flea bite."

"That's because it *is* a flea bite."

We laughed.

"I live in the apartment out back if you need more information about the native flora and fauna."

"You have your own apartment?"

He stared hard at me. "No one's supposed to know. So don't tell anyone. My uncle Harley owns this place. He lets me stay here."

"Cool."

"I have problems fitting in." He said it with a grin, like somehow he knew that I did too. "I'm Byrd."

"Wolf."

"Byron," he offered.

"Wilfred," I matched. So quickly we fell into shorthand. So instantly we understood each other.

Just then the cowbell clanged to herald another arrival, playing out like a scene from those corny old teen movies, in slow motion, with heavy metal rock blasting from the stereo of her car. It was she—*she* of the silken black hair and the deep green eyes and the plush pink lips. She caught me staring openmouthed and sneered in my direction before sliding behind the counter to stretch toward a package of cigarettes in the rack above Byrd's head.

The dramatic makeup she wore—thick mascara and purple eye-liner—made her look fifteen when she was trying to look twenty-one, so I put her somewhere around seventeen. She noticed a beer missing from the six-pack on the counter and thumped Byrd on his forehead.

Byrd pointed down the aisle at Frankie. "They're his."

The fragrance of orange lingered after she walked away from us—not the odor of blossom or juice, but that bitter citrus oil that repels preda-tors. It stung my eyes and made me blink.

"Lark. My cousin," Byrd explained. "She's got demons."

I wondered if Lark's demons were acquainted with Frankie's de-mons, because her body language changed when she saw him. I don't know if Byrd and I exchanged actual words or just gestures with Byrd saying, *Is my hot cousin seriously hitting on your jackass father?* And me re-sponding, *This happens all the time. Check it out.*

We watched a moment longer, Lark's easy smile and swinging hips, Frankie's sideways grin and outthrust pelvis, but when Lark grasped Frankie's upper arm, Byrd called out, "I'm not staying here all night, Lark! You better not be too long! You better hurry up and get back! We're both dead if I get caught behind this counter."

Lark threw a scowl at Byrd and a grimace at me before she sauntered back past us and out the door.

Smiling, Frankie followed, stopping at the counter. "What's your name?"

"Byrd," the boy answered as we all turned to look at Lark's silhouette against the neon light in the parking lot.

"Byrd," I said loudly. "He said his name is *Byrd*."

"Like . . . flapping?" Frankie inquired.

"Like Larry." Byrd grinned.

"Hate the Celtics," Frankie said. "How do you say 'It's good to meet you' in Cahoola?"

"The slang way's simple. Like saying 'What's up?' It's *Yo arra*."

I lowered my face when Frankie repeated, "*Yo arra*."

"The formal version is longer. It's how you'd address an elder, a teacher, or a cop, for example. You add *fah ken ut*. *Yo arra fah ken ut*."

"*Yo arra fah ken ut*," Frankie said slowly.

We repeated that phrase to each other, Byrd and me, a thousand times after that day. It was the bedrock of our friendship. I'd once asked him if we'd exhumed the stupid cliché of the wise red man having one over on the dumbass white man. He thought about it for a moment, because Byrd was a thinker, and then said, "Not cliché, brother. *Classic*."

NOLA WAS restless, wincing in pain.

"We'll get that arm looked at first thing tomorrow," I said.

"Not first thing," Bridget said. "First we have to get back."

At that point, I felt confident that I could find my way to the Mountain Station in the morning. "We'll get back," I said.

"Michigan is a long way away," Nola said.

"Where are your parents? Are they here with you?" Vonn asked.

"They're still in Michigan."

"Are you here on vacation?" Nola asked.

"I came alone."

"Alone?"

"I come a lot. From Michigan. To see my buddy," I faltered.

"All the way from Michigan?" Nola wondered. "How old are you?"

"Eighteen," I said. I did not tell them it was my eighteenth birthday.

"Why didn't your buddy come with you?" Bridget asked.

"Sick," I said. "He was sick, so he couldn't come."

"But he knows you're here?" Bridget asked.

I shook my head. "I didn't want him to feel bad for missing the hike."

"But he's waiting for you."

"No."

"He'll be waiting to hear from you, right?" Bridget said.

"I told him I was on my way back. To Michigan."

"Oh."

I tried to turn the conversation. "Who's waiting for you?"

"Well, if Pip hadn't died a few months ago he'd be waiting for me," Nola said, then amended, "No, he wouldn't. He'd be here with me. He never got lost."

"Someone must be waiting for you?"

"There will be," Nola said, "when they realize we're missing."

"No one knows we're up here, Mim," Bridget said.

"Someone knows."

"No one knows."

"Pip just *hated* getting lost. He would just hate this."

"Don't say *lost*. We can't be more than a few miles from the ranger station. It's not like we're in the wilderness. Palm Springs is right there!"

"No. Of course we're not lost."

"What about all your friends from church and the condo and all the places you volunteer?" Bridget asked.

"I told everyone they wouldn't see me for a few days. I told them all that you were coming out from Golden Hills and we three were going to spend some time together. Do some day trips. That's what we said we were going to do. Never mind. They must count the tram riders in a day and tally it up and know who came and went," Nola said. "I'm sure they do that."

I knew for a fact they did not.

"What about your boyfriend, Bridget?" I asked. "Won't he be worried if he doesn't hear from you?"

Nola turned to Bridget in the dark. "Why didn't you tell me you were seeing someone?"

Bridget was silent.

"The guy you told me about on the tram? The real estate agent?" I prompted. "Won't he worry if he doesn't hear from you?"

"Not that idiot from Camarillo," Nola said.

Bridget dropped her head.

"Does he know you went hiking?" I asked after a pause.

"He's in San Francisco," Bridget said.

"With his wife," Vonn added.

"Oh, Bridget," Nola said.

"And baby," Vonn added.

"Stop," Bridget hissed.

Nola Devine draped her good hand over her eyes. "Girls, please," she said.

"Vonn," I said, letting her name linger on my tongue. "Is anyone expecting *you*?"

"No," she replied.

"What about that guy?" Bridget asked. "The *biker* from Tin Town?"

"I have no idea what you're talking about," Vonn said.

I recalled hearing my aunt Kriket call my cousin Yago's new girlfriend a "mix-race, snot-face Malibu bitch" and also say that the girl had recently moved to the desert. I got it in my head that the girl was Vonn Devine.

Yago was my oldest male cousin, one of the youngest thugs to govern Tin Town. He hated me. I feared him. If Yago was Vonn Devine's boyfriend he would kill me for getting us lost. That seemed like just my luck.

"If you have a boyfriend, we should know," Nola said. "And I'd like to meet him. Even if he's a biker."

"No one is expecting me," Vonn said.

"Are you sure, Vonn?" Nola asked. "It'd be good if your boyfriend reported you lost."

"Don't say *lost*," Bridget said. "We're not *lost*, lost. And, Vonn, why did you even come? You were going to stay at the mountain center, remember? You were going to stay there and get a book to read."

"I was going to, but I thought Mim seemed sad about me not coming along."

"She was sad that you didn't bring sneakers."

"Because we were having the pedicures first. And I forgot."

"So you admit to being forgetful?"

"Even here, even now, one of you is gas and the other is flame," Nola complained.

In the silence, there came the sound of metal clinking against rock. "That was my ring," Nola said. "No one move."

"Didn't I say you've lost weight since Pip died?" Bridget said.

"Have I?"

"You're taking care of Mim, are you, Vonn?" Bridget asked. "You're supposed to make sure she eats."

"She has that part-time job now," Nola said in Vonn's defense.

Bridget found the ring in the dark. "Here it is."

"Thank God. Put it on, Bridge," Nola said. And after a pause, "Happy anniversary, Patrick."

It was moments later—maybe an hour?—when the hooting owl pierced the silence. I thought about the series of shots Byrd and I had gotten of the horned owl in flight and how we'd vowed to have the image of that owl tattooed on our biceps one day. After Byrd's accident I'd gone to this place in Indio with a photograph and told the tattoo artist I wanted the owl on my chest. I didn't want people to see it. I didn't want anyone asking questions.

"You have a car in the lot!" I blurted. "Eventually someone will notice. Eventually someone will check to see if there's an overnight permit registered to that license plate."

"We took a shuttle from the Rancho spa," Bridget said thickly. "*Someone* lost the car keys."

"Someone *gave* someone the car keys," Vonn said.

"Because someone doesn't carry a purse!"

"All of this is my fault, really," Nola said. "I was the one who wanted to go to Secret Lake."

"We took the hotel shuttle so we could get up here before it got too late in the day," Bridget explained to me. "We figured the keys would probably be turned in by the time we got back."

"If the *keys* turn up, and you *don't*, then someone will be looking for you," I pointed out. "What about the shuttle driver?"

Vonn dug her heels into my chest unintentionally as she reached into the compartments of her cargo pants, lifting up to check the rear pockets as if there was still a chance she had the keys. As if it mattered now.

"If the same shuttle driver worked all day, I guess," Vonn said. "If they only have one shuttle. I mean, we weren't guests at the hotel."

"We'll be able to get back in the morning, right?" Bridget asked.

"We're fine," I said. "If there's no fog it'll be easy to get our bearings. We'll climb back up the slope we fell down or find a different way," I said.

Nola asked, "What about you, Wolf? Do you have a car in the lot?"

"I hitched from the tourist center at the main road."

"You shouldn't hitchhike."

I pictured the gentle elderly couple who'd stopped for me in their old white Monte Carlo. They dropped me off and drove away. I've always wondered why they were on that road if not to go to the Desert Station too.

* * *

TIME PASSED. Time flew. Time marched on. I can't remember an over-riding feeling that first night. Rocks continued to tumble from on high to strike the pine trunks beyond the scree. I had to entertain the possibility that an even larger one might follow the small slide we'd caused. I tried not to dwell on negative thoughts though and was mostly anxious for morning light because I wanted to find my Tigers cap and Bridget's bag with the food and water.

The wind drove hard and cold, and I was grateful for the modest shelter of the cave and for the silence of the Devine women, whom I thought must have fallen asleep.

"I have no insulation at all," Bridget said, shattering the stillness. "Twenty-one percent body fat, which is very, very low for a woman."

"Oh my God," croaked Vonn. "Why are we talking about your body fat?"

"I don't want to freeze to death, Vonn," Bridget said. "That's all I'm saying."

"I told you before, no one's going to freeze to death," I said. "I promise."

"You can't promise that. You can't promise anything." Nola piped up from behind her turtleneck. "When it's your time it's your time."

"It's no one's time," I said.

"You don't know, Wolf. Pip looked fine. He turned on the television. I went to brush my teeth, and then came back to bed and he was gone. Without a kiss good-night. Just like that. You just don't know." Nola sighed.

"I'll know," Bridget said. "I think my sixth sense will kick in for that."

"Here we go," Vonn muttered.

"Why do you hate that I'm clairvoyant?"

"You are *not* clairvoyant," Vonn said.

"Don't take things for *granted*," Nola interjected. "That was the point of what I was saying. You don't want to leave with *regrets*. That's all I'm *saying*."

"What do you have to regret, Mim?" Bridget asked. "What could you possibly have to regret? You're the perfect mother. Perfect wife. You volunteer. You give to charity. You go to church. You give free piano lessons to those kids from that place. You pick up other people's litter."

"You sweep spiders onto the porch instead of killing them in the house!" Vonn added.

"There's more to me than you know," Nola said after a pause. "I have regrets."

"I regret I wore flip-flops," Vonn said, and we couldn't help but laugh.

"I don't believe in regrets," Bridget said.

"You believe in horoscopes and numerology," Vonn said. "You believe in ghosts, you think you're *clairvoyant*, but you draw the line at regrets?"

Bridget didn't answer. I found myself wondering about her experiences with ghosts.

"You don't regret that you had to raise me alone?"

"If you're asking me if you were a handful to manage as a single parent, the answer is yes, Vonn," Bridget returned.

"You don't regret that I missed out on having a father?"

"That's in *your* regrets pile. He made his choices."

"You never told him about me," Vonn said.

"Why would I let a man like that ruin your life?" Bridget countered. "I was protecting you. That's what mothers do."

"Do you have regrets, Wolf?" Nola asked, by way of calling for a time-out between her daughter and granddaughter. "Or are you too young for regrets?"

"I do have a regret, Mrs. Devine," I said. "A big one."

"What do you regret?" Nola asked.

"Tell us, Wolf," Bridget said.

"You can tell us," Vonn said.

I wondered then, and have had reason to wonder since, if there are few things so satisfying to a feminine ear as the sound of a man expressing regret.

"I think one Devine is one too many, and I regret the hell out of getting lost with all three of you!"

I'd thought they'd laugh. They didn't.

"Don't say *lost*," Bridget said.

We were all quiet for a time, listening to the wind batter the pines.

"I'm hungry," Bridget said. "I wasn't before, but now I'm starving."

"You're not starving," I said.

"I'm a grazer. I eat small meals every few hours. Especially when I'm in training. How long can you go without food?" Bridget asked.

"I knew this girl in high school who went nine days on apple juice," Vonn said.

"There's this rule of three," I said, picturing Byrd walking ahead of me on the trail, telling me about the rule.

"Bad things happen in threes?" Nola said, frowning. "I think we should stay optimistic."

"Not that rule of three. The survival rule of three. There's room on either side, but generally people say you can survive three weeks without food, three days without water, three minutes without air."

"Three *seconds* without faith," Nola said without pause.

THE TENSION between Vonn and her mother didn't keep us from crowding one another for warmth in the little cave. I accidentally kneed Nola's broken wrist. "Sorry!" she said, before I could.

"Why are you apologizing, Mim?" Bridget said.

"It's just a thing people say, Bridget."

"You apologize for *everything*."

"I do not."

"When the guy bumped you with his cart at the supermarket? When the dry cleaner ruined that jacket? When that woman splashed you with her bike? It's your generation."

"I don't know what you're talking about."

"You wouldn't ask for a spoon for your soup!"

"He felt so bad about the lemonade mix-up," Nola said. "Besides, it was a very thick soup."

"I'm just saying, you don't have to apologize for other people's mistakes. You're overly sorry."

"You're *underly* sorry," Vonn muttered.

"Let it go, Vonn." Bridget sighed.

"How can you say you have no regrets?" Vonn asked. "Every person has regrets."

"I don't."

"In your whole life?"

"None."

"This isn't the time or the place, girls," Nola said wearily.

"You don't regret having the *procedure*?"

"No," Bridget said.

Vonn leaned toward me. "My mother had elective surgery on a body part that will be *retired*, like *crossing-guard retired,* in a few years, using money she borrowed from *me*. Then she couldn't pay it back and I couldn't go on my graduation trip last spring."

"It was a cash-flow thing," Bridget said in her own defense.

"You can honestly say you don't regret that?" Vonn asked.

"That one is in your regrets pile too, Vonn. You could have gone on that trip. You should have."

"*You* didn't pay me back," Vonn protested.

"But *you* lost out. Mim and Pip were happy to loan you the money. You cut off your nose, Vonn."

"We would've been happy to loan you money," Nola said. "It's true. You should have gone."

"You don't get off that easy, Bridget! She doesn't get off that easy!" Vonn shouted.

"But she did," Nola said.

Vonn trembled, and I could feel she was fighting tears. "So you are really going to sit there and say you have not one regret?" Her doggedness would serve us well.

"None."

Nola cleared her throat and said, "Well, I have regrets."

"Mim, please."

"I do. Lots of them."

Bridget and Vonn shared a skeptical look. "Perfect wife. Perfect mother. Perfect grandmother. Name one thing that you seriously regret," Bridget said.

"I dug two graves," Nola said darkly.

"You dug two graves?" I repeated, confused.

"JFK said those who seek vengeance dig two graves," Nola said.

"I don't think JFK said that," Bridget said.

"You're obviously not saying you killed anyone," Vonn said. "Right?"

"I made a very big mistake that changed the lives of a lot of people."

"What did you do?" I asked, eager for the distraction of Nola's confession.

"Mim?" Vonn said.

"I hated Laura Dorrie," Nola said into the darkness. "She was my classmate in senior year, the year we moved from Wisconsin to Toledo."

"Where you fell in love with Pip."

"Laura Dorrie thought she had dibs," Nola said.

"So you hated her?"

"I like to think she hated me first," she said. "But yes. On my first day of senior year at Harding High I fell head over heels for Patrick Devine. He was a two-sport athlete. We said *hunk* back then. He was a *major hunk*. All the girls had a crush on him. He sang with the band, and no one thought that was weird. He was a crooner. Just loved all that Frank Sinatra and Tony Bennett stuff."

Nola was there, walking in slow motion down the halls of high school, starring in her own memory. "He looked just like Warren Beatty in *Splendor in the Grass*. I nearly quit orchestra for cheer that first week just so I could get closer to him. First time I loved anyone more than my violin."

"*Violin*? I didn't know you played violin, Mim," Bridget said. "I thought you played piano."

"I was a prodigy," Nola said matter-of-factly.

"You were a *violin prodigy*? I never once saw you play violin."

"Did Pip make you stop?" Vonn asked. "Did you give up violin for Pip?"

"Don't be silly," Nola said.

"So what about Laura Dorrie?" I asked.

"Laura's father owned Dorries' Steak House downtown, not far from the townhome where we lived. The Dorries were very wealthy."

"So you killed him?" I asked.

Nola ignored me. "Laura had the nicest clothes. Little sweater sets and silk blouses and gorgeous wool skirts."

"You were jealous? That's your regret?"

"Laura played violin too," Nola continued. "Before school even started that fall I auditioned for the senior orchestra leader and was told I was going to replace her as first chair. There was a whole *to-do* about it, and her father was supposed to talk with the school principal but he missed the meeting. Everything was made worse by the fact that Laura Dorrie's father had just hired my father as a line cook at his restaurant."

"You said your father was a piano teacher."

"He was also a line cook. His English wasn't good. He had a thick Hungarian accent."

"And you were a violin prodigy," Bridget said. "Why didn't you tell us any of this before?"

"Why would I want to remember painful things?" Nola said.

"But never to mention that you were a *prodigy*?" Vonn said.

"When I was playing the violin it was the most important thing. When I stopped playing it wasn't. I had Pip. And Bridget. And then you, Vonn."

"Laura Dorrie?" I prompted again.

"Right. That first day of school Laura was assigned as my student guide because we both played violin, and she introduced me to the whole graduating class as the new girl whose Hungarian father washed the dishes at her father's restaurant. When I told Laura that my father was a cook, not a dishwasher, she just said, 'Tomato, tomahto,' then she said that she'd *kill* me if I didn't stay away from Patrick Devine."

"You didn't."

"I didn't. And when it got around that Patrick had asked me on a date, Laura Dorrie showed up at my locker, grabbed my wrist, breaking the clasp on my bracelet—which had belonged to my grandmother in Europe, so it was very special to me—and she told me that I was going to be sorry for what I did."

"She broke your bracelet?" Vonn asked.

"Yes, and she didn't even apologize. She just said, 'I don't like thieves.'"

"So?"

"So I fixed the bracelet, but I couldn't sleep that night. I knew something awful was going to happen."

"Another clairvoyant," Vonn said dryly.

"Laura didn't say boo all week long, but I could see in her eyes she was planning something. When the final school bell rang I was relieved the week was done."

"You had a date with Pip that night?"

"He wasn't Pip then. He was Patrick, and I did have a date with him, but my parents didn't know. They didn't allow dating."

"What happened with Laura?" I asked.

"I was walking home and I could hear my mother shouting from half a block away. Then I heard my father's voice. He was supposed to be at work." Nola took a deep breath. "They were speaking Hungarian, so it took a while for me to piece together that Mr. Dorrie had just fired my father and was going to lay criminal charges against him because two boxes of frozen New York strip loins belonging to the restaurant had been discovered hidden under a coat in his bicycle carriage."

Vonn and Bridget murmured their sympathy.

"My mother didn't think for one moment that my father was stealing strip loins from the restaurant. We hadn't eaten a decent cut of beef in years. It was obvious that my poor gentle father was being framed. He said it was because of his accent. My mother was wailing, 'Who would do such a thing? Why?'"

"Laura Dorrie?" Vonn blurted.

Nola nodded. "Laura Dorrie. My poor father had been wrongly accused and humiliated and fired, all because of me."

"So what'd you do?"

"The laundry was sitting there in the basket on the table with the bottle of bleach, and all I wanted to do was grab the thing and start gulping it down. I was that close to the edge."

I swallowed hard because I knew the feeling.

"But I couldn't stand there one more second listening to my father crying in the other room, so I took the bottle of bleach and ran out of the house without my parents ever knowing I'd come home."

"What were you going to do with the bleach?"

"I didn't know. I walked around the block a few times. I sat in the park for a bit. I'd lost the nerve to drink it. Then I had an idea, and headed for Dorries' Steak House.

"The street was more crowded than usual. I went around the back, but it was busy behind the restaurant too, people going in and out of the back door. So I hid in the alley beside the restaurant, waiting until some cars drove off, then I stepped out onto the sidewalk. The steak house had this fancy red carpet out front."

"You poured bleach on the red carpet? That was your revenge?" Vonn asked.

"*That's* your big confession?" Bridget said. "I knew it."

"I had the cap off the bleach and I was all set to pour when I heard Laura's voice coming from the apartment above the restaurant. I'd heard the girls at school talking about how the Dorries' place was like a palace and how Laura had a closet as big as most girls' bedrooms, so when I saw there was a set of stairs that would take me straight up to the open window where these gorgeous white curtains were blowing, I put the cap back on the bottle of bleach and snuck up to take a peek.

"When I got up there, Laura wasn't in the room. I just stood there at the open window. She had this huge canopy bed and silk curtains, and I could see that the door to her closet was open." Nola took a moment to catch her breath. "You would have thought she was a Hollywood starlet—all the clothes in there. Then I remembered the bleach was still in my hands."

"Ah!" Vonn cried.

Bridget inhaled. "Her *clothes*?"

"I waited a minute, then leaned in through the window to make sure she was really gone. She was, but I noticed that there was a package of cigarettes and a lighter on the windowsill and cigarette butts all over the landing. I figured she must smoke quite a lot and I got worried she was gonna need a nicotine fix any minute, then I heard a noise in the hall, then my bracelet snagged on the window ledge and broke again and fell off."

"Oh no," Vonn said.

"It was dark by then. I couldn't see very well, so I grabbed the lighter from the windowsill. It took me a hundred tries to light it, but finally I did. I held it so that I could see the landing, but I couldn't see the bracelet. Then I got thinking maybe the bracelet was caught on the windowsill." Here Nola stopped for a very long beat. "After that, it all happened so fast."

"What?" I asked.

"I raised the lighter. The curtains. They went up—just . . . *boosh!*" Nola said, gesturing with her good arm.

"I ran down the stairs and grabbed this man walking on the sidewalk and showed him where the fire was shooting out of Laura's bedroom window, and he ran into the restaurant to call the fire department. No one was hurt." Nola paused. "Well, that's not exactly true."

"That's a terrible story, Mim," Bridget said.

"That's why I never told you," Nola said.

We were quiet for some time. "What about Pip?" Vonn asked.

"When I made it to the playground in the park where we said we'd meet, Patrick was already there, worried because of all the sirens. I can't say what possessed me, but I told him what I'd just done."

"What did he say? What did you do?"

"He took me to his church. It was quiet and dark and smelled like candles. We just sat there in the front pew for an hour, could have been longer, holding hands. Didn't say a word. All I knew is that I didn't want to drink bleach anymore and the warm feeling I got in that place made me feel like I'd come home."

"Didn't your family go to church?" I asked.

"My mother'd been married before. She said they weren't welcome."

"Pip never talked about God," Vonn said. "I wouldn't have believed he ever set foot inside a church."

"He turned off church at some point after we got married. Close as we were, he would never tell me why. He didn't want to ruin it for me, I guess. That community has brought me a lot of comfort."

"Pip brought you to the church and then stopped going himself. You don't think that's weird?"

Nola shook her head. "He used to say, 'I'm a *glow*er, not a *show*er.'"

"He did," Bridget remembered.

"And he liked to be on the golf course Sunday mornings. Maybe it was that as much as anything."

"Did you ever confess to anyone else about starting the fire?" Vonn asked.

"After being in the church I decided to go to the police and tell them about the accident with the lighter. Patrick said he would come with me. But when we got to the police station there was *chaos*. The fire had been contained but not before it damaged a big garage out back where Mr. Dorrie was hiding thousands and thousands of dollars in stolen goods. Apparently he was the gate for some operation."

"Fence?"

"Fence. Yes. Anyway, the police weren't interested in my confession. They shoved us out of the way."

"So you never told?"

"I never told."

"But it was an accident," Vonn said. "You were a kid. They wouldn't have prosecuted you. It wouldn't have turned out differently if you told. It's terrible that you've regretted that your whole life."

"I'm not," Nola said. "Regrets serve their purpose. You'll see."

BRIDGET HAD fallen asleep and was snoring loudly.

"Deviated septum," Nola said.

Vonn leaned past me, gently took her mother's head in her hands, and changed the tilt of her jaw. It was the first intimate gesture I'd seen between the two women. The snoring stopped, but the wind roared in again.

"It's like an animal. Or a demon," Nola said.

"Her snoring?"

"The wind. The howling," Nola said.

"How's your wrist?"

"It's throbbing more now," Nola allowed. "It's Bridge I'm worried about."

"She'll be fine, Mim. She's always fine," Vonn said.

"You think she's fine, but she's not."

We listened to the wind a little longer.

"Pip used to say, 'She's going to surprise all of us one day.'"

"She surprises me every day," Vonn said.

"She's only human. Just like you. Just like me."

"Was all that about Laura Dorrie true, Mim? The fire? Or did you just say it to make Bridget feel better?"

Nola checked once more to make sure Bridget was asleep before she said, "There's more to the story than what I told. I didn't get to the worst part."

"It gets worse?" Vonn said.

Bridget's snoring filled the cave once more. Vonn adjusted her mother's head again and the snoring stopped.

"The next morning, crack of dawn, I heard a noise in the yard and I saw my father out there unlocking the toolshed in the alley," Nola said. "I went out to the backyard, and I squinted through the broken slats of the shed to see that he was loading up my old wagon with bins of sugar and flour and some tinned foods and the frosted carrot cakes Mr. Dorrie's restaurant was famous for. Then he opened this old humming freezer and took out a big box of frozen pork loins and four boxes of New York strips. It was true. He was a thief.

"He piled it up in the old wagon and dragged it all the way down the alley to the back of an electronics repair store where a bunch of men were waiting with cash. He sold them everything he brought."

"Wow."

"After that I followed him straight to my violin teacher's apartment."

"Oh."

"So you see."

I did.

"Even if my father had been able to get another job right away, I couldn't keep playing. Look what it cost him. His dignity. His soul. I couldn't imagine going on with my violin. Plus, after what I'd done? The fire? I didn't deserve it."

No one said a word for a very long time. For my part, I was wishing that my own penance was as clear to me as Nola's had been to her.

"If I close my eyes," Nola said, "I can still imagine playing my favorite piece."

We could make out Nola's form in the darkness as she raised her left hand and bent her head toward an imagined chin rest. Straining, she raised her injured right hand, holding a pretend bow, and demonstrated "Spiccato. Legato. Marcato. Pizzicato. Détaché. Martelé."

"Air violin," I said, impressed.

Bridget startled in her sleep. Nola reached over to stroke her daughter's cheek. "Shush now. Poor Bridge. Must be so tired. She's been training for a triathlon."

"She told me," I said. "On the tram."

Nola cradled her injured wrist. "Stupid osteoporosis. Drink your milk, Vonn. Doesn't this all feel like a dream?"

No one answered. I don't know why.

"How long will it take us in the morning, Wolf? If you're right and we can climb back up and find our way to the Mountain Station?" Nola asked.

"How long? An hour and a half, give or take," I answered, underestimating. My stomach was churning. "You two need to get some sleep," I said. "I'll keep watch."

Nola yawned. "I don't know how much this wrist is going to let me sleep anyway."

"I'm wide awake. I won't be sleeping at all. Not a wink," Vonn promised. Four minutes later she was snoring in harmony with Bridget. Nola followed a short time afterward, adding the occasional moan of pain to the chorus.

I could only imagine what those Devine women were dreaming about that first night. Laura Dorrie? Tattooed bikers? Deadly falls? Dead husbands? Rolling fields of mountain phlox?

Me? I played my life in rewind, my mind ablaze with scenes from my past.

THAT FIRST night in Santa Sophia, after we left Byrd at the gas station, I remember feeling sick in the stinking Gremlin, bilious from guzzling those grape pops, focused on the brightest stars I'd ever seen in the inkiest of nights. (*Bilious* was a Byrd word, one of those unfashionable words he was hoping to resurrect. *Egads!* No one else I knew talked like Byrd.)

I have some vague recollection of being hauled out of the car and stumbling up some stairs and passing through a squeaky broken door. Hours later I was awakened by a horrible stench and found myself sweating in a threadbare sleeping bag on a ragged linoleum floor with a two-year-old boy defecating beside me.

A woman's voice rattled down the hall, startling the squatting child, who disappeared, leaving his coil of waste steaming on the floor.

When I sat up I looked around the tiny room, counting two forms in each of the two single beds, adults, or almost adults, like me. There were smaller bodies in sleeping bags on mattresses on the floor, most of them young children. Eight in all. The tiny window was open, heat blasting through it like a radiator. The clock read 5:03.

It was my habit, even then, to be prepared for the worst, but I could see that I'd fallen short in priming myself for life in the three-bedroom trailer with Aunt Kriket and her brood. The home's odor, a vintage blend of cigarettes, stale booze, and bacon, was dismally familiar. I could hear my father hacking up a lung in the kitchen. I used to worry quite a lot that he'd get cancer and I'd be alone.

Frankie'd been so evasive regarding his sister because he didn't know the answers to any of my questions. Kriket moved to California as a single teenaged mother and had been tossed senseless ever since by the tempest of crying babies and gone-away men. When we lived in Mercury, Frankie'd get drunk and call her once in a while. I'd hear him crying in his room. I hated her for that. I never wondered until this moment if she'd been crying too.

My father's parents, as Frankie's story went, argued constantly, mostly about whose genetics were to blame for their children's shortcomings; his mother was convinced that Frankie'd got the "lyin', cheatin', stealin' gene" from the Trulinos, and his father was insistent that Kriket inherited the "puta's scratchy snatch" from the French-Canadian side.

One night, after receiving a frantic call from Kriket at the local bar, Frankie's father raced home to find his wife of twenty-five years sprawled out on the kitchen floor, dead from an apparent heart attack. Frankie claims that his old man quietly swept up the fragments of the serving platter that had shattered when his mother fell, then stretched out on the speckled linoleum beside her and had himself a fatal stroke.

The family debt doomed the siblings, and while Kriket moved thousands of miles away to California with her first child's father, Frankie, four years younger, was taken into Mercury Public Care. "Whatever happens, Wolf," Frankie'd warn me at random moments, "do *not* let them take you into care."

Gagging from the odor of the toddler's mess on the bedroom floor, I got to my feet and went to find my father in the unfamiliar trailer. When I appeared in the entrance to the kitchen area, before I could even make out who she was, my aunt Kriket unleashed her animus upon me, pushing back the frizz of bangs from her mingy eyes, saying, "He looks *exactly* like Dad."

I could say that's why she hated me. But it can't be that simple.

"Don't stare, Wilfred," she said.

I took in her sneering, bloated face and slick, dirty hair. "A baby shit on the floor," I said instead of good morning.

My aunt grabbed a roll of paper towels and chucked it at me, demanding, "Austin?"

"Wolf."

"No, genius, was it Austin who no-no-ed?"

"'No-no-ed'? I don't know."

"Was his front tooth chipped?"

"I didn't see his tooth."

"If his tooth was chipped, it's Austin. Dodge is the chub. Them two are toilet training." She poked me in the chest. "Got it?"

I tried to catch Frankie's eye, my cheeks burning.

"Don't let 'em shit on the floor."

This woman was *blaming* me.

"You smack their butt and slap 'em down on the potty." She pointed to a child's plastic toilet in the corner of the kitchen, which at least one of the toddlers had used successfully.

"I'm not smacking any babies," I stated.

"That's how they learn."

"Don't they have diapers or something?"

"You can't train them in diapers, genius."

"Okay."

"Besides, you want to buy the diapers, moneybags?"

"Not really."

"Didn't think so."

"So they just run around naked?" I asked. That could not be right. "Shitting and pissing on the floor?"

"That's why you gotta smack 'em, Wilfred."

Back in that bedroom I had evil thoughts about my aunt as I dropped to my knees to clean the stinking mess. In the dim light I counted nine bodies, one more than before—the toddler who'd dumped on the floor was now pretending to be asleep on a mattress beside a blond boy with a broken tooth who was groaning like he knew he stood wrongly accused. Austin. Woe is he.

One of the sleeping boys opened his eyes and saw me on my knees with the paper towel full of shit. He threw a pillow at my head, yelling, "You *pig!*"

"Seriously?" I said.

The boy, around seven years old, sat up, demanding, "Who are you?"

"I'm Wolf. Your cousin Wolf. Are you Yago?" Yago's name was the only one I knew.

"You don't know Yago?" The boy was incredulous.

I shook my head, looking at the sleeping bodies. There was a resemblance between me and a number of my cousins, even though they'd been fathered by many and sundry. "My father saw a picture of Yago once. He said I look like him."

"If you were *thirty*," the boy said with a laugh. "And a badass *cholo*."

"What's your name?"

"Jagoff," said the seven-year-old.

LATER I found the bathroom and, after tightening the broken showerhead, climbed into the crusty tub and let the water wash over me. I couldn't find any shampoo, so I scraped the dry splinters from the soap holder and rubbed them into my hair. The rusty water, playing chicken with me, alternated from too hot to too cold, and I had to bob and weave so as not to get shocked or burned.

There was no towel, so I just stood there to air-dry, watching the coppery rivulets soak into the grout, listening to a cartoon blaring on the television in the living room. The bathroom mirror was broken, with the top half missing entirely, and I could see only the fogged reflection of my rigid torso and the coarse dark hairs that I'd cultivated near my belly button in the months before we left Mercury.

I hadn't heard the motorcycle pull up because I'd been in the shower, so when I walked into the otherwise empty kitchen, I was unprepared to see a dark, heavily muscled badass cholo taking off his helmet. It didn't take a genius to guess this guy was Yago.

"Hey, *asshole*," Yago said.

"Hey, *dickhead*," I responded, grateful that, thanks to Frankie, *Foul* was my mother tongue.

Yago laid me out with one swift punch to the head. Didn't see it coming. I woke seconds later, blood on the filthy floor where I'd landed. Mine, I realized. My head throbbed. I'd never been punched that hard before.

"Do you know who I am?" Yago hollered at me.

I looked up from the ground. My tongue felt strange.

"You know who I am?" He grabbed my shirt and twisted it at my throat and pulled me to my feet only to slam me against the wall, rattling my skull off the trailer's frame. He took my chin in his free hand and made me meet his eyes. I did see some familial resemblance.

"Yago," I said thickly, tasting blood.

"You know who I am, and you disrespect me?" he asked, spitting.

"Cousin," I said. It hurt to talk. "Wilfred."

(Why had I said *Wilfred* and not *Wolf*?)

"Wilfred?" Yago grinned, tightening his grip on my shirt, pulling me in face-to-face. "That's your name? *Wilfred*?"

"Wolf," I said. "Wolf." Even as I trembled in fear, I couldn't help but notice that Yago'd eaten garlic recently, and drunken whiskey, and smoked a Camel.

"One thing I hate worse than cousins, Wilfred," Yago said. "Leeches."

I nodded.

"Don't go near my shit," he said.

"I don't want your shit," I spat. My heart was pounding. My mouth was full of blood. Never had I felt so keenly alive.

A young woman entered the kitchen to see about the commotion. "That's Uncle Frankie's kid," she said.

Yago cursed under his breath and let me go.

"You're Wilfred, right?" the woman said, turning to me for corroboration. "Our cousin."

"Wolf," I said.

"We met," Yago said, sneering as he climbed a stepladder nearby. He

reached up to remove a small square panel from the ceiling, drew a brown paper bag from the hiding place, and stuffed the brick-size package into the deep pocket of his baggy jeans.

Before he left he slapped my cheek hard. "Don't touch my shit."

The sound of his motorcycle as he revved it just feet from the door, the screeching, screaming, angry sound it made, was one I'd never forget.

"Ever seen a dust devil?" the woman asked when Yago was gone.

I hadn't yet.

"It's like a little tornado—comes from out of nowhere in the desert and starts spinning and kicking up the dust and sand. Then it's just gone. That's my brother Yago."

"Dust devil."

"I'm Faith," she said, examining my cheek. "It's swelling pretty good, but it didn't split. Open your mouth."

I did.

"You bit your tongue."

I spat some more blood into the dishcloth she'd passed to me.

"We don't have ice."

I nodded my thanks anyway.

"My mom and your dad are off playing the slots. They said they'd be back when they're back."

I guessed that when Frankie told me we were moving because we needed to be closer to *family,* what he really meant was that we needed to be closer to *casinos.*

My aunt's other daughters, Patience and Charity, stumbled into the tiny kitchen followed by two more, Grace and Beauty.

"Frankie's kid," Faith said. "Wolf."

"Don't touch Yago's shit," Grace warned me in a whisper.

"You no-go where Ya-go," Patience said. Sounded like good advice.

Soon all of the toddlers and children were done with their cartoons and running into the kitchen, slapping, screaming, biting, pinching. The adults (and semi-adults—because at least three of them were teenaged

mothers) hit the hitters, bit the biters, and pinched the pinchers in what appeared to be a lesson in Darwinism.

I remember sitting there that morning, finding some tragic beauty in the way the sun came in through the cracked kitchen window and hit the stratus clouds of cigarette smoke, making halos around the small children's heads.

No one seemed to wonder out loud if the screaming malcontents just needed a little breakfast.

The cupboards were bare. There was beer and pop in the fridge but no milk or juice. Faith noticed me rooting and called out over the din that Kriket would bring pizza and chicken wings when she came home. Scooping up one of the diaperless babies, she deftly lit a smoke, blowing the cloud away from the child's face, apologetic when she caught my eye. "It sucks here," she said.

"Does Yago live here too?"

"This place is more of a storage locker for him. Comes to hide out sometimes. Pretends he's visiting his kids. That one is his." She pointed. "So's that one."

"How many has he got?"

"Five altogether. But only two of them here."

Making conversation, I asked her about the Palm Springs Aerial Tramway. Faith told me she had ridden it on one occasion and described it as "fine, if you don't get motion sick, which I do," and the mountain as "fine, if you like rocks and trees, which I don't."

I kept my eye on the doorway to the kitchen as my extended family came and went. I was never sure if I was looking at a new cousin or if someone I'd already met had traded one dirty T-shirt for another. It was Yago who I was worried about. I wanted to be gone if he came back.

I'd spent hours and days in Mercury imagining family life, conjuring a big brother to torment me, a little sister I'd tease and protect. I'd never met a relative before, and now I was in a strange place with more than a dozen of them and all I wanted to do was bolt. "I'm gonna take off," I told Faith.

My plan was to find that gas station from the night before and make arrangements to take the tram with my new friend.

My luggage was still in the Gremlin, which Frankie had driven to the casino, and so I had only my jeans, but they'd be far too warm, and my cutoff plaid pajama pants (subbing in for underwear because I had none clean) and the overlarge Bob Seger T-shirt of Frankie's that I was convinced would mostly hide the plaid pajamas. I'd worn flip-flops in the car, and they'd have to do.

I remembered that Byrd's place was called Santa Sophia Gas Stop and got the directions from Faith.

WALKING THROUGH Tin Town, I hummed a little ditty as I passed the rusted mobile homes, waving to some children splashing brackish water in a cracked wading pool and noting the broken strollers, the maimed baby dolls, rusted bicycles, a toy (?) shotgun leaning against a picnic table, refuse, beer bottles, trash bags, and so many cats I could smell their spray no matter which way I turned my head.

There were no trees in Tin Town, and I found myself ducking from the sun the way people do from rain. I remember thinking that the half-hour walk from my aunt's place to the gas station would be no sweat for a fit teenage boy, but even before I'd found the main road, my foam flip-flops were breaking down from the heat of the blacktop, and the spaces between my toes where the thong rubbed were raw.

I'd been so preoccupied by the shabbiness of my new neighborhood, I'd hardly looked up to search the distance, and when I did my breath was taken by the sight of the mountain before me. Miles high and wide, rising up from the desert floor, *alive*, jagged teeth poised to bite the crisp blue sky, a spiny creature whose very existence seemed to dare the daring. I stopped to take her in. I don't know how long I just stood there staring. *Batholith*. I remembered the word from the library book about geology. A magnificent batholith.

The sun beat on my scalp, and I was annoyed to find bits of bar soap clinging to my hair when I reached up to scratch. I walked on, leaning into the hot wind. Never been so parched. I didn't know then how much worse it could get.

Under the slim shade of a palm tree I caught my breath, found my bearings with the help of a road sign, and felt reassured that I was heading the right way. Faith had said I'd find the gas station at the junction of the main road and freeway, guessing at the half-hour distance and confessing, "I could be wrong. No one walks here."

About fifteen more minutes before I got to the gas station, I figured, but twenty minutes later I was struggling along the dirt shoulder looking for somewhere to beg a drink. (Frankie had neglected to leave me any money.) There was no sign at all of the gas station and no place whatsoever to find water. The sun scorched the tops of my feet while the concrete burned my soles through the foam. I was evaporating with each step.

Shuffling along, I was relieved to find a landscaped path that led into a canopy of flowering bottlebrush trees—I never forgot the distinctive flower. I remember the cactus from that stretch of the walk too, cactus being so strange to me—the spiky cholla and the razor-sharp agave and barrel cactus and the beavertail cactus. Of course, I didn't know their names back then, but I respected the hell out of their thorns.

A distant bench in the shade beckoned, so I pushed myself toward it, grateful to rest my fresh-baked feet. But then I needed to pee.

A few yards from the bench there was a roped-off area of brush, dense with aromatic sage and ringed by a cluster of fat beavertail cactus. I slipped under the rope and through a space beyond the manicured bushes to relieve myself of scant yellow urine.

It's there that I found the tangle of redweed clambering up a fallen oak, recognizing it instantly from the picture in the book out on permanent loan to me from the Mercury Public Library—same red seed pods, willowish branches, and velour stems, same trumpet-shaped white flowers. I recalled Miss Kittle warning me about the hallucinatory powers of the tiny red seeds—people died from ingesting redweed. "Every generation has their cautionary tale," she'd said.

The edges of the pods were prickly, and I was careful not to cut my skin and infect myself with its poison when I tore the velvety sphere from the branch. I brought the thing to my nose, gagging because it smelled strongly of diaper. Then I licked it. I don't know why I did that. I was a kid, and sometimes I did dumb things. The microscopic bit of oil from the red seed pod tasted the way sewage smelled. It didn't give me hallucinations or kill me, obviously, but I will never forget the taste of it on my tongue. Like death.

Miss Kittle had said I was unlikely to see a redweed bush because all the plants had been dug up and burned. But I'd found it. I'd found redweed my first day in Santa Sophia. I looked around, marking the place, and had the strangest sense that I wasn't alone. There were shuffling sounds in the brush. I sniffed but couldn't smell much beyond the sand and sage. I called out "Hello?" as I backed away.

Returning to the path, I felt not exactly proud but something—I felt something. I couldn't wait to tell my new friend, Byrd, about the redweed. Enlivened by my discovery, I quickened my pace, but one of my rubber flip-flops snagged on a branch and the damn thing tore in half. I have not worn a pair of flip-flops since that day. You can't hike in flip-flops, or run from a predator, or climb to the top of a mountain.

Deciding I'd be faster in bare feet anyway, I hurled the rubber soles into the bushes. Native Americans walked barefoot, and sometimes slept on the ground where they could feel and see and smell the earth. According to Frankie, I was one-sixteenth Quebec Cree. I began to navigate over the hot ground with fresh purpose, calling forth my thimbleful of Indian blood.

Emerging from the path, I was startled by the sight of a large modern building. A mall? Water fountains? Food court? I leaped a high fence with surprising ease (adrenaline makes us magical) and, streaking barefoot across the thick green turf, bounded toward the building. A sign at the entrance read SANTA SOPHIA HIGH SCHOOL. The doors to the school were chained and bolted shut.

I caught my reflection in one of the windows and stopped to consider the stranger there; some kind of purple hives had erupted on my face and neck, and on my head the bar-soap residue had mingled with my sweat to create a revolting yellow lather. Desperate for a drink of water, I returned to the road, damning the heat, and my feet, and my father, because what the hell.

The sun rose higher and I walked on, calling to mind graphic images of any number of unwholesome fluids (urine, sewage, tomato juice) and arguing with myself about which ones I'd swallow if they were in front of me at that moment.

I am unclear as to how I eventually found the gas station. Seemed like one moment I couldn't walk another step and the next I raised my eyes to see the SANTA SOPHIA GAS STOP sign. My femurs felt unhinged, and my feet were aflame. I was light-headed, operating on a single failing cylinder, and relieved when I saw Byrd through the window—a flash of dark hair behind the cash register. Then I fell to my knees, vomiting copiously on the red vinyl welcome mat.

I couldn't find the strength to lift my head and worried when Byrd didn't appear right away that he hadn't seen me. The next thing I remember is the sound of her voice, the music that rose from her throat when she said, "*Gross.*"

Lark had been the dark flash behind the register and not Byrd. I was too ill to be embarrassed as she, smaller than me by half, lifted me by my armpits and helped me into the store. The cool air instantly began to help my breathing. When she said, "You're okay, I've got you," I believed her.

That beautiful girl drew me down the aisle and into the small office behind the cash register area, guiding me into a chair in front of an oscillating fan. "You walked?" she asked, tilting a straw so that I could drink from one of the two cans of cola she'd snatched from the fridge. "Barefoot?"

I managed a nod.

"Your dad said you were staying at a hotel downtown. That's a long way."

Even in my diminished state I noted that my father had lied to Lark and obviously said nothing about Tin Town. "My feet broke." I'd meant *my shoes.*

Lark was frowning, focused on a spot at my hairline where the barsoap lather had dried. "Pollen from the trees," I lied. I let the air from the fan hit my blotchy face as I drained the cans.

"You have bumps. Purple . . ." Lark said, gesturing to the hives on my cheeks and neck.

"They'll go away." I wondered if they'd come from the heat or from that microscopic sampling of the redweed.

"Did someone hit you?" she asked, noticing the swelling on my cheek.

"I fell," I lied.

She gathered a pitcher full of ice from the nearby freezer and dumped it into an empty bucket and added a large jug of distilled water, then another pitcher of ice. "You know what they say—you only get heatstroke once."

I wondered if Lark meant a person either dies from heatstroke in the first place or is afterward wiser about risking it. She lifted my scarlet feet and put them in the scalding cold water. I fully expected to be enveloped by steam.

"There you go," she said.

I couldn't connect this girl to the contemptuous vision from the night before. "Thanks," I croaked.

When she stood, her nipples braced against the oscillating fan. She must have noticed my strange expression because she sounded a little panicked, asking, "You gonna throw up again?"

I shook my head without confidence.

Lark set a cold cloth on my forehead and smiled like an angel of mercy. "Your dad said your name's Wilfred?"

It was as though she was speaking another tongue in which neither *dad* nor *Wilfred* were familiar words to me. "Wolf. Everyone calls me Wolf."

She smiled. "So you're Canadian? French Canadian or something?"

French Canadian? Did he use that as a *line*? Did it *work*?

"A hundred years ago we were French Canadian," I said. "We just moved here from Michigan."

"What? Is your father some kind of *outlaw*?"

I didn't like the way she sounded hopeful. "Not exactly."

"Witness protection?"

I liked the sound of that and had every intention of lying about our background. "We left everything behind," I said. "The blue house and my school and my street and Miss Kittle at the library and the shed in the alley and my mother's grave in the old cemetery."

"That's sad," Lark said. "Will you ever go back?"

I shook my head.

"But you'll find a nice place here," she said.

Tears began to roll down my cheeks before I had the chance to turn away.

Then the phone behind the cash register rang, and with a frown of apology Lark ran off to answer, closing the office door behind her. I strained to listen, but she spoke for only a moment, in a whisper, then she hung up and dialed another number. I hoped she was not calling an ambulance, or mental health facility.

She didn't return to me, as I'd hoped. Instead, I heard the sound of splashing and realized, with some horror, that she was cleaning my vomit from the welcome mat. Then came the sound of her silken voice as she helped a customer at the register, then another customer, and another. I envied every eye that saw her when I couldn't, each ear that heard her say, "Twenty-six for the gas and a dollar for the Red Vines." I loved the way she said, "Thangz," at the end of each transaction.

I wondered if she would rush back to me if I coughed or cried out. I didn't want her to think I was too pitiful though, or worry that I was too ill, should the urge to kiss me overtake her. If there was to be a kiss, I badly needed a mint.

Managing the few steps toward the adjoining restroom, I wondered what I could say to impress a girl in front of whom I'd thus far puked and wept. I washed my hair in the sink with dispenser soap and dried it with the industrial hand dryer.

I still had no line, but I *had* thought of a conversation starter—the mountain. I would ask if she had been up in the tram. Of course she'd ridden up in the tram! The tram would open up the general discussion about the mountain, about which I knew many interesting facts.

I held my breath as I opened the office door. Lark was gone, and Byrd was there in her place. "Forget it," he said, grinning at my hand-dryer hair.

"Where'd she go?"

"Forget it," he said, laughing. "Seriously. Are you even a junior?"

"I'll be fourteen in November," I said. It was then that we discovered our birthdays were on the same day—one year apart—with Byrd being a year older. That's a hell of a thing to have in common.

"Your face looks like jam, dude. And your hair's gnarly." Byrd laughed. So I did too.

I spotted Lark through the window pumping gas for an elderly man. She saw me watching but didn't smile like I'd hoped she would.

"She's almost eighteen. She's leaving for boarding school at the end of the summer. New York. She'll never come back."

"Oh."

"She'll have New York friends. A New York life. Plus, she's too old for you."

"She won't always be," I said.

"Are those cutoff pajamas?"

I shook my head. "Underwear. Frankie has the car and all my stuff is in it."

"You walked all the way from your hotel in underwear?"

That's when I told Byrd about my aunt Kriket's trailer in Tin Town and why I'd been in such a hurry to escape.

"Your old man's a case," he said.

"You should meet his sister," I said, telling him about her diaperless babies.

"So they just walk around shitting and pissing on the floor?"

"Right."

Byrd turned serious, watching me watching Lark. "Don't even, Wolf. She's cursed. Her last two boyfriends died under mysterious circumstances."

"Is that true?"

"One was a heart attack."

"Wow."

"He *was* thirty-six."

"Her father lets her date thirty-six-year-old men? Isn't that against the law?"

"Her father didn't know," Byrd said. "He would have killed them both."

"What about the other guy?"

"Kitz?" Byrd spat. "Hated that smarmy podlicker. He died of snake-bite. Young rattler—they have more toxic venom."

"Hate snakes."

"I took a bite on the mountain last summer."

"You said it was a flea bite!"

"Not that. This." Byrd twisted his leg so I could see the puncture marks in his right calf. "Hurt bad. But at least it was dry. No venom."

"How do you know if it's a dry bite?"

"You don't expire," he said, grinning.

"Did this *Kitz* guy get bitten on the mountain too?"

"He was taking his dog for a walk over by the high school. You must have passed it on the way here. There's a big area of brush out back behind the path, and there's always rattlers. No one goes back there. They even warned people in the local paper."

"I was just there!"

"Don't go back there." Byrd was serious.

"Why was Kitz there?"

"Masturbating?" Byrd guessed. "Why were you back there?"

I remembered. "I found redweed."

Byrd looked at me hard. "You know what redweed is?"

"I know."

"You sure it was redweed?"

"The white flower with the red pod."

"Where?"

"Back in the brush behind the high school."

"You know they call it dead weed?"

"I know."

"You know why?"

"I know," I said. "I know."

"The sheriff sent out volunteers on horseback with packs of tracking dogs and they cleared it from here to the Santa Rosa. My uncle Harley has pictures of all these law enforcement dudes with shovels and hoes. He was there."

"Should I go back there and pull it out?"

"To the den of rattlers? No."

"Okay."

"And don't tell *anybody* ever." He said this last part solemnly.

Lark appeared at the doorway, eyeing us warily. "'Don't tell anybody ever'—what?" she asked. Then to me, "What'd you do to your hair?"

"Nothing," I said.

"What were you talking about? Don't ever tell anybody what?" she asked again.

I shrugged. She smiled. "Secrets, huh?"

"No secrets. I just said not to tell anybody I get to ride the tram for free," Byrd said, covering.

"Okay." Lark shrugged and sashayed down the aisle. The cowbell clanged on the door, and she disappeared once more.

"Harley? Because he rides a Harley?" I asked, continuing our earlier conversation.

"Harley because his mother named him Harley. Uncle Harley has a Honda but he doesn't ride much anymore. He's got a warehouse full of classic cars. He donates one to charity every year. Everyone around here knows Harley."

"That's why you get free tram rides?"

"That, plus my uncle Dantay is the head guy at Mountain Rescue. I used to hike with Harley but not much anymore. He's like—fifty." He laughed. "He's cool but he talks too much. Everything is a lesson. This flower is for that. That shrub is for this. He just wants me to know my culture. It's cool, I guess."

"Frankie says we have Cree blood on his mother's side," I said.

"I grew up Polish," Byrd laughed. "Well, I am Polish—half."

"Don't you want to learn all that Native American stuff? I would. I *do*."

"When I was a younger I did and then . . . It's not that I don't want to know." He thought for a moment. "Sometimes a guy wants to feel like he *learned* something without being *taught*."

I had no experience with cool uncles or interested teachers or guiding parents. Miss Kittle was the closest I'd come to having a mentor. "Right," I said.

"I have four uncles, three aunts, twenty-two cousins altogether," Byrd said. "My uncles all try to be my father. Harley, Dantay, Gabriel. They're all cool, I guess. Jorge and Gabriel work at the casino with my uncle Harley. Before he joined Mountain Rescue Dantay was a stuntman in the movies. He's got crazy tattoos."

"People get lost on the mountain a lot?"

"All the time."

"Is it easy to get lost up there?"

"Not if you're with me."

"Dantay lets me ride dirt bikes around on his property. I'll take you over there sometime."

"What about the tram?"

"Day after tomorrow, my day off from here, we'll meet at the base of the station at eight a.m. You got a bike?"

"Yeah," I lied.

"Bring water. Warm coat. Good shoes."

"Coat?" I laughed, considering I'd nearly just died of heatstroke.

"It can get cold up there. Weren't you ever a Boy Scout? *Be prepared.*"

I thought to ask, "Where do you go to school?"

"Correspondence."

"I'm starting the high school in September."

"SSHS, huh? Tell people you know the Diazes."

"I don't know the Diazes."

"I'm a Diaz. So's Lark."

"What about Tin Town? Are there Diazes in Tin Town?"

"Have you looked around? We're not all out on the *rez* anymore, dude. We have management jobs in the casinos. We work in real estate. We own half the Mattress Kings in the Coachella Valley."

"Okay."

"I'm just messing with you," Byrd said, laughing. "There are a few Diazes in Tin Town. But most of my uncles and cousins are rich. The Diazes rule SSHS."

Lark startled us when she leaned in to grab a set of car keys from the rack near the door. The sneering minx from the night before seemed to have returned to possess her. "Come on," she said to me impatiently. "You need a ride home."

I grinned at Byrd, and then followed Lark down the aisle toward the door. Byrd called out to me from behind the register. "Yo!"

I didn't turn around when we said in perfect unison, *"Arra fah ken ut."* I was the happiest I'd ever been in my life.

The air was warm and the sun still high when Lark led me out of the gas station. I was hypnotized by the sway of her heart-shaped behind and soon felt the familiar tug of divergent blood. Not about to show my appreciation while wearing cutoff pajama pants, I pictured the unusual batting stance of John Wockenfuss, as I always did in such moments. We all have our beta-blockers. He is mine. Nothing personal to John Wockenfuss.

Clearly I could not get into Lark's car without having my gratitude noted. What if she screamed? What if she hit me? What if she didn't? *Wockenfuss. Wockenfuss. Wockenfuss.* My stomach churned but had no influence over my predicament. I looked away from Lark's bottom, concentrating on my ravaged feet. Burned flesh. Beautiful Lark. Torn toes. Sublime Lark. *Wockenfuss.*

Lark turned around, glowering, and said, "You're going with him."

I followed her pointing finger to a sleek black car at the far end of the lot. "He's waiting," Lark said, and then disappeared.

Or rather it was I who disappeared. Passed out.

Next thing I knew, I was in the passenger seat of a moving vehicle (not just a moving vehicle but a Cadillac Coupe Deville) with a large male presence beside me at the wheel. "I'm sorry, sir," I offered. "I am not myself." It was the God's honest truth.

"Heatstroke."

"Yes."

"Do you know who I am?" His deep voice rattled the dash.

I took in the huge man in close-up snapshots: aquiline nose—right nostril with no visible nose hair (I'd never before in my life seen a dark-haired man without visible nose hair before). Buffed fingernails on the lacquered steering wheel, squared off with a file instead of bitten to the quick. Massive Adam's apple in his deeply tanned throat, and a humble gold crucifix hanging some inches below. "Are you Byrd's uncle?" I asked.

"I'm Lark's *father*," the man intoned. "You're not going to vomit, are you, son?" He didn't wait for my answer before pulling the Caddy to the side of the road. Unfortunately, I couldn't wait for him to stop the car before bathing his supple upholstery in cola-colored mucus. "Sorry," I choked, pulling my T-shirt off and trying to mop up the mess.

When the huge man came around to open the passenger door, I swung my legs out of the car but couldn't lift my head. I noticed he wore fine shoes—at least I guessed they were fine by the way they were not sneakers or cowboy boots. He had creases ironed into his pants. When he set his hands on his knees to steady his huge frame when he crouched, I saw that he wore a ring on each of his thumbs. No tattoos.

I'd never met such a fine-shoe-wearing, thumb-ringed, bald-nostriled person and was conscious of my own disheveled appearance. I wiped my mouth with the back of my arm. "Are you Uncle Harley?"

He nodded.

I wondered if he wanted to hit me. Maybe he already had. "My head hurts."

"You fell pretty hard," he said. "Does your father have health insurance?"

Frankie didn't have socks. "No, sir."

"Did you eat breakfast this morning?"

"No, sir."

"Thought you'd go for a four-mile hike in the desert without breakfast? Without water?"

"I'm new around here," I said, as if that explained stupidity. "Michigan."

He startled me when he set his giant thumbs on my eyes and lifted my lids to search my pupils. "So SSHS?"

"Sir?"

"You're enrolled at Santa Sophia High School?"

"I know the Diazes," I blurted.

The man grinned. He liked me. I don't know why. "You don't appear concussed."

"Thank you, sir."

I hadn't told Lark's father my address and didn't know it anyway, but he drove directly to Tin Town and through the maze of mobile homes, coming to a stop in front of Kriket's dented mailbox. My aunt peered out from behind her stained bedroom curtains and didn't seem happy to recognize the car.

I could see the green Gremlin parked across the street and was glad that Frankie was back. He'd be a friendly face if he was sober and a familiar one, at least, if he was not. I thanked the big man and was sorry that I had to say yes when he asked if I needed help.

Not a fleet-footed woman, Kriket nonetheless made it to the door before we'd reached the broken front gate. "Harley," she said without warmth.

Harley? Lark's father was *Harley*.

"Your nephew?" Harley asked.

Kriket put her hands on her hips and pursed her lips. "Wilfred."

"Heatstroke," Harley explained. "Rest and fluids."

"Dumbass. What happened to his feet?"

"Flip-flops," Harley said.

"Idiot. What happened to his head?"

"Fainted."

"Moron." Kriket disappeared back inside.

Frankie appeared, an unlit cigarette dangling from his bottom lip, a cloudy glass of whiskey in his hand. "Harley Diaz? I hear you got some job opportunities over at the casino."

Harley didn't hesitate before he shook his head. "Nothing at the moment."

Frankie huffed and disappeared, letting the screen door bang behind him.

I took the trailer steps slowly. Harley stopped me with a firm hand on my shoulder. "Wolf?"

I thought he was going to warn me to stay away from his daughter, now that he knew I came from Tin Town. "Yes."

"You want to be a mountain man? That right?"

"Yes, sir. I do," I answered.

"You want to climb rocks? Plant your flag at the peak?"

"I don't have a flag," I said.

"I'm saying, son, that if you're interested in climbing mountains, you have to remember something."

"Okay."

He stared at me hard. "Most sports require only one ball."

THE SECOND DAY

Just before the sun rose on the morning of that second lost day, I untangled myself from the Devine women's arms and legs and leaned over to check on Nola, disturbed to see how pale she'd become. Her wrist was hidden under the red poncho, but I could guess by the size of the lump it made that it had swollen to frightening proportions. Vonn's face was twisted in pain. Her stomach, I feared. Bridget was snoring soundly.

I stood, shivering, staring down on Nola and Bridget and Vonn Devine. As the sun peered over the purple peaks I was shot with a sudden, intense feeling—one I recognized as love—but it was beyond love, and so powerful it brought tears to my eyes. Then I heard something in the white noise of the wind, not words exactly but a clear message. It was a feeling I'd had once before. I'm aware that people explain such extraordinary experiences away—a rush of endorphins, a surfeit of oxygen, a surplus of carbon dioxide, sleep deprivation, hunger, dehydration. I'm aware that the event may have been self-induced, a product of my own need, but I can only tell you that in that moment I felt God. Make of that what you will.

Outside our cave the ground was uneven, rocky in patches and forested in clumps, with thorny bushes, Jeffrey pines, a few scrub oaks, a dense brood of limber pine, manzanita, wax currant, and a few gnarled mahogany trees. The vegetation was dense, and I couldn't tell how big the area was.

Walking carefully, I maneuvered through the trees perpendicular to the ridge from which we'd fallen, cataloging as I went, looking for any source of food or water, surprising myself with the amount of information I'd stored about Native American plant lore. I remembered an afternoon in the canyon at the foothills when Byrd and I had gagged on raw acorn, attempting to eat a Native American food staple called *wewish*. (Byrd had said, "Know why we call it *wewish*? 'Cause *wewish* it tasted better!") We'd sampled bitter mustard flowers and chewed sweet mesquite beans and nearly turned purple from eating too many mountain berries. If there was food on this outcropping where we'd landed, I was determined that I would find it.

The rising sun steamed the soil, which smelled of worms and minerals. Picking my way through the brush, I scanned the rocks for pools of water and found here and there the shallowest of drinks. The rocks were gritty and the fluid scant, but it was something more than nothing, which was all I'd had since the hissing spout on the drinking fountain at the Mountain Station. My gut was cramping with hunger, my last meal, nearly twenty-four hours ago, a bag of Cheez Doodles from the rack at the gas station. Berries were gone by November though. Ditto the mesquite beans. We weren't at a low enough elevation for mesquite anyway. I thought of the chocolate bars in my knapsack hanging on the hook beside the door.

I remembered thinking, as I drank from that fountain before heading off to Angel's Peak, that it would be the final fulfillment of my boring body's tedious needs. Now it lightened me, *pleased* me to feel such a strong desire for sustenance. All I'd craved, for a long time, was nothing.

Revived by the little bit of fluid I could slurp from the rocks, I walked on, soon with the uncomfortable sense that I was being followed. The granite protrusion on which we'd fallen was about the size and shape of a high school gym, much larger than I'd originally thought.

I caught the whiff of animal—cat—and it did occur to me that a mountain lion mauling would be a fitting finale for a guy named Wolf.

Then I remembered that the big cats didn't spray the same way as the smaller cats. Bobcats wouldn't attack, unless they were rabid. I paused to sniff the air again, but the odor had disappeared and I had to admit to myself that the senses I counted on so heavily were already becoming somewhat unreliable.

From a perch in the sculpture of a dead birch a pair of ravens cawed. The branches shivered and shimmered around me, and the entire woods joined in, groaning with their bows and bends. The wind blew hard in sharp bursts. I felt my spirit soar and moved with swift, strong strides as the symphony reached a crescendo. But then the sky came hurtling through the branches and I found, with heart-stopping suddenness, that I'd reached the end of the earth. It was true, then. We were perched at the mouth of Devil's Canyon.

No view from that huge outcropping inspired optimism. I can see myself—an older boy, or was it a young man?—looking down into the murky depths of the canyons below. Definitely not the way down to Palm Springs. I watched distant Tin Town gag to life in the morning sun and shouted an expletive to the lingering moon.

I was standing there at the cliff's edge when I heard a noise and turned, expecting to find a ground squirrel pawing at the earth. I was startled when a brown hand pushed through the brush to grasp a branch. Byrd, I thought—but it was Vonn.

"It doesn't look good," she said.

"We can't get down," I agreed, gesturing toward the canyon depths.

"We're trapped?"

"No," I lied.

"It's like a huge rock balcony."

"It is."

"Are we stranded?"

"I'm just saying there's no way down from here."

Vonn peered at the drop beyond her wool-socked, flip-flopped feet. "So we have to climb back up where we fell last night?"

"Looks like."

"That was pretty steep."

"Yeah."

"And the rocks were loose."

"They were loose."

"Mim can't climb that. With her wrist . . ." Vonn said. "And I can't. Not in these." She looked down at her flip-flops.

We watched a red-tailed hawk soar past, and again I thought of Byrd.

"Are we in trouble, Wolf?"

"Let's look around some more," I said. Together we scrambled over the rocks and through the trees from the stem to the stern of our boat-shaped outcropping, squeezing past branches, searching all the while for water, food, the blue mesh bag, and, above all, a way off.

At last, red-faced, we emerged at the rocky escarpment we'd fallen down, *the wall* (as we came to call it)—a steep drop about thirty feet wide and forty feet high. "Wow," Vonn said.

We stood before it for a long beat. I wondered if I should confess that I'd never climbed such a steep, unstable rock face, or any rock face for that matter. For all the talking Byrd and I did, we hiked more than we climbed. Even if I remembered the terms from the magazines and books we'd read, I didn't have any rope, or carabiners or technique or experience for that matter.

I tracked the ascent, which ended at the ridge where a cornice projected several feet from the rock wall. Even if I could make it up there, I couldn't see how I'd hoist myself over the cornice. "Easy," I said.

"Could you use that branch to help you get over?" Vonn asked, echoing my thoughts. She was staring up at an ironwood stump with a few long, slim branches that resembled a large hand, where I might be able to pull myself to safety.

"Maybe there's an easier way," I said, leading Vonn through the boulders to the far side of the outcropping. We found another steep drop.

The hawk soaring above us screamed, sounding strikingly like Bridget.

"Maybe we're near her nest or something," Vonn said. "Let's look at the other end."

We moved past the wall again and through a small area of brush to discover another rocky balcony next to ours, attached to a slope that appeared, farther up, to connect to the ridge from where we'd fallen.

"Look!" I said, pointing. "If we could hike up that slope there we can reconnect with the ridge. Get right back to where we were last night."

There was, however, the insuperable problem of a fifteen-foot-wide chasm separating us from the slope, and a deep, dark crevice below. "We could jump it," I said, half joking, staring into the deep, dark void.

Vonn looked down, blood rushing to her cheeks. "Maybe you could," she said. "But I couldn't, Bridget wouldn't, and Mim is *in her sixties,* for God's sake!"

"Devine Divide," I said. "I think I could jump that."

"And if you're wrong?"

"That would not be ideal."

"Mim." Her face fell. "She looks bad."

"Was she awake when you got up?"

She shook her head. "She looked so pale . . ."

We moved closer to the edge to stare down into the depths. The wind came rushing at our backs, and I caught a whiff of camphor and began to sneeze in rapid succession.

"You all right?"

I moved to stand upwind of the sterasote bush in my periphery.

"I can climb back up where we fell," I promised Vonn. "I'll climb the wall and find the way back and get help. Search and Rescue will have ropes and whatever else. Shouldn't take long."

"Even if you can climb up all that loose rock, are you sure you can find your way to the Mountain Station?" Vonn asked.

"Of course." I couldn't fault her for being skeptical.

"Yesterday . . ."

"That fog was dense. And it got dark fast. Look at the sky today. This is excellent visibility. I know how to get to the Mountain Station from here. Come on," I said, "let's see if we can find Bridget's bag."

Vonn burped behind her palm. "Sorry. The tram made me motion sick and it's not going away."

"Maybe it's altitude sickness," I said. "Tell me if you feel dizzy or faint."

"It's my stomach," she said, gingerly touching her abdomen.

It was possible that Vonn had sustained an internal injury in the fall. One more thing to worry about.

As we started back toward the cave, we looked for the bag, but I kept my eye out for edible plants too. "Look for berries," I said. "But don't eat anything unless you show it to me first."

"What else?"

"Acorns. Pinecones. Flowers. Sometimes you find wild apricot bushes. We're pretty far below the Mountain Station. The fruit would be gone probably, but one time this guy said he got lost out this way and found the apricots dried on the branch."

"Mim makes apricot preserves."

"Why do you call her Mim?"

"It's how Bridget said Mama when she was a baby. And my grandfather was Pip. It just stuck."

"Why *Bridget*?"

"Instead of *Mom*? I don't know. I don't know anything according to my mother."

"Did you always call her Bridget?" I didn't tell her I called my father by his first name.

"When I was little I called her Mama." She shrugged. "She knows nothing about me."

"So you don't hang out in Tin Town?" I was hung up on the idea that Vonn knew Yago. He was popular with women. Vonn was his type. The thought of my cousin Yago with Vonn Devine sickened me but I had to know.

"No."

"I didn't think so," I said, trying not to sound relieved.

"Once," she clarified. "One party."

"Oh."

"It was my birthday. Labor Day. We'd lost Pip just a few weeks before. A friend—not a friend, just this girl I barely know—dragged me to this party in Tin Town, then ditched me. The party was outside. People had little fires going everywhere. It was crowded. I drank too much wine. No big deal. Turning eighteen is supposed to be cool, but I don't remember much about that night."

"Yeah."

"How did you spend your eighteenth?"

I didn't tell her that my eighteenth birthday was yesterday and that she and her mother and grandmother had foiled my plans to leap to my death. "Nothing special."

Vonn stopped behind me, pointing up. "Look!" she whispered.

I'd hoped to see Bridget's mesh bag caught on a low-hanging branch. Instead, I saw a falcon—an enormous taupe-and-brown raptor with a creamy speckled breast, the largest I'd ever seen. I was pretty sure that it was a gyrfalcon, although none had ever been sighted on the mountain as far as I knew. I wished like hell that Byrd could see that great, winged beast, gripping the pine bough with such swagger.

"I think that's a gyrfalcon."

"Oh," she breathed.

"You don't see them outside Alaska."

"*Alaska?*"

"He's lost. Wonder how he got here."

"I didn't know birds got lost."

In unison, Vonn and I said, "Wish I had my camera."

The bird flew away. We smiled and walked on, scrambling over boulders, Vonn's borrowed wool socks wedged into the thongs of her green flip-flops, which were, lucky for her, made of sturdy foam.

"Bridget used to be into photography. She has an amazing camera."

"Should have brought it," I said.

"Her new boyfriend borrowed it. I hate him."

"The Realtor/triathlete?"

"She's into body fat and curb appeal now. One of her boyfriends before this managed dog shows. Guess what?"

"She bought a dog?"

"She bought a dog *salon* with the money from her settlement from the plastic surgeon, which she'd planned to put toward nursing school because before that she was obsessed with dating . . ."

"A doctor?"

"A sick rich guy," Vonn said.

"Okay."

"What about you?"

"My father's in jail."

"For?"

"A long time."

"That's not what I meant."

"I know."

"When did he go to jail?"

"Halloween night."

"A few weeks ago?"

"Yeah."

"Sorry. Scary story?"

"The worst."

"Mother?" she asked.

"Died when I was little," I said, wishing I used the word *young* instead.

"You have no one else?"

I shook my head. There were a few employees at the gas station who would notice I was gone, but none would miss me. Besides, I'd left a staff schedule on the door and a note saying I was going on vacation.

Even Harley didn't check on me much anymore, since I'd told him to stay away. "You? Father?"

"*Step*father. Three of them. Second was the cosmetic surgeon who started *that* whole train in motion. Third left her for a *much* younger woman. Bridget just told me about my biological father last year."

"Thought I recognized you," I said. "Don't we have Misery 101 together?"

"Second period with Mister Yurfukt," she said.

The screaming eagle sound we heard next was not the gyrfalcon—it was Bridget, calling, "VONN!"

We charged through the brush to find her, ashen in the granite cave, pointing at Nola's injured arm, which now we could see had swollen grotesquely in the night.

"It's just a nuisance!" Nola said.

Vonn bent to look at it. "Let me loosen the bandages a little."

I barely had the stomach to watch.

Nola was in surprisingly good spirits, even as sweat pilled on her forehead. We gathered around staring at her massive forearm. "I feel like Popeye. *I am what I am.*" No one laughed.

"That looks bad, Mim," Vonn said.

"Not the best," Mim agreed.

"I went with Wolf to look around and where it *seems* like we could walk down into Palm Springs. There's a ridge, and it's not just steep, it drops off, like a thousand miles down."

Bridget clapped her hands, getting our attention. "I have good news. I have to share this with you."

"Here we go," Vonn muttered.

"I had the most vivid dream last night."

"You and your dreams, Bridge."

"I dreamed we were rescued."

"You're absolutely certain we can't climb down?" Nola asked, turning to me, ignoring Bridget.

"Did you hear me, Mim?" Bridget asked. "I had one of my future-dreams."

"Future-dreams?" I had to ask.

"Because she's clairvoyant," Vonn reminded, and then resumed our discussion. "The problem is that where we fell last night—there's this wall of rock; it's steep. You can't climb it," Vonn said to Nola. "And Bridget can't. And I can't. Wolf is going."

"He's leaving us here?" Nola looked worried.

"He'll get help."

"Listen." Bridget raised her hand.

We could all hear the approach of the staccato motor and the distinctive whirring blades. We could hear it clear as day. We leaped to our feet, scanning the horizon, zigging this way and zagging that, jumping on boulders, climbing onto the roof of the cave, straining for a better view.

"Helicopter!" Bridget hollered, jumping up and down and shouting. "Helicopter! HELICOPTER!"

At first it sounded like it was just beyond the neighboring peak. When it didn't come into view right away, Nola shouted, "I think it's coming from that way!"

Bridget waved the red poncho at the blue sky.

"Over there," Nola pointed.

"No! This way!" I shouted, waving my arms along with the women as we waited to spot the rescue helicopter.

All this, in spite of the fact that I *knew* that helicopter searches of this part of the mountain were rarely possible due to the unstable air. Byrd's uncle Dantay had told us sobering stories about a few dramatic mountain rescues from Devil's Canyon, some successful, most not, *never* by helicopter. Dantay had warned us against exploring this part of the mountain.

Minutes passed and the sound grew closer, and we jumped and shouted at the unseen aircraft. "Over here! Please!" The wind became a swirling vortex, and I wondered if we'd be sucked up into it, but then it stopped. The sound of the helicopter disappeared, not gradually—it was just gone. We watched the sky a good while longer, but eventually Bridget dropped the red poncho and Nola sat down to rest on a stump.

"Just the wind," I said.

Bridget clapped her hands to get our attention. "He'll come back!"

"There is no *he*," Vonn said. "It wasn't a helicopter. You heard Wolf. It was the wind."

"I don't care what you and Mim think, Vonn. I know what I know. I dreamed about our rescue. It was the most vivid dream I've ever had. I'm telling you. We are going to be rescued."

"Dreams are just dreams, Bridget."

"Unless you're me."

"Unless you're crazy."

"When I was pregnant with you I dreamed that you were going to be a girl. And you were."

"Fifty-fifty," Vonn said.

"I dreamed that we'd get that house by the water. And we did."

"You and Carl put in the only offer," Vonn pointed out.

"I dreamed Carl was going to leave me. And he did."

"Everyone predicted that one, Bridget."

"I dreamed I'd get that job at the Four Seasons."

"You also dreamed Mim and Pip were going to drown on that cruise."

"We almost didn't go!" Nola said.

"And you dreamed you were going to marry that Norwegian guy from LensCrafters."

"It's true, Bridge," Nola said. "Remember the Norwegian guy?"

"This one is different," Bridget said. "The feeling. It was . . . I'm standing there and there are rescue men with the orange vests and I know without a doubt that we are going to be saved and it feels like nothing I've ever felt before. It's the greatest moment of my life."

"I'm sure it will be the greatest moment of all our lives, Bridget," I said. "But forget about helicopters. Not with this wind."

"We should put my poncho on the top of a bush or hang it from a branch like a flag or something," Nola said. "Just in case there's a plane. Maybe they could see it—even from high up?"

"Good idea." I picked up the poncho, and Vonn and I stretched the red plastic fabric over some cottonwood, though I worried it'd blow away.

"Use the hand grips to secure it. See—they sew grips on the inside so you can hold on to it and it doesn't blow around in the wind," Nola instructed.

I looked at the sky. "I'm going to climb that wall and hike back and we'll have some rescue guys back here with baskets and ropes in no time."

"I do like a man in uniform," Nola joked.

"See, Bridget, we don't need a helicopter rescue," Vonn said.

"Imagine being buckled into one of those baskets," Bridget said.

"Screamer suits," I said. "That's what Mountain Rescue call them."

Bridget took offense. "Because people scream? Do they think that's funny? People scream because they're afraid. Anyway, in my dream there were no screamer suits. And I wasn't afraid. I was the opposite of afraid. There was no screaming. Besides, I wouldn't do it. I would not let them buckle me into one of those. You would not like to see them try."

I glanced up, checking the sun, and guessed the time to be around 7:00 a.m. I was determined, if not confident. "Let's go."

Vonn and Bridget helped Nola to her feet, and together we made our way through the brush to the spot where we'd fallen.

Nola moved slowly, maneuvering around the trees and bushes. The pain in her wrist must have been awful.

We found a collection of large, smooth boulders in the shade of some pines where she could rest her back and keep her injured arm still. "I'm fine," she said. "You don't need to fuss."

"You both should search for Bridget's bag," I urged Vonn and Bridget. "Be careful. The cliffs come up on you fast."

"Maybe you should wait, Wolf. Drink some water and have some granola bar before you climb," Nola said.

I dismissed the idea of waiting for the recovery of Bridget's lost bag. I had no doubt that I would climb the wall on my first attempt and return with help within hours—by lunch, I remember thinking. I figured we'd be on the tram heading down to the desert by noon.

Making my way through the debris, kicking the scree and scrambling up the larger boulders, I finally met *the wall*.

"No problem," I said, and was immediately sorry.

The boulders near the bottom were the least stable, and I made several comic missteps before I found my footing. "All good," I shouted back to the women.

The wall was shot with vertical and horizontal fractures, and bands of white feldspar and rusty manganese, like an abstract painting. I could feel the Devines holding their breath as, with sweat gathering on my upper lip, I prodded with my fingers and toes to test the stability of each boulder. One felt looser than the next, but eventually I began to pull myself, inch by inch, up the steep face toward the ironwood stump near the overhang.

My feet were not clever about how to seek out steps, and my hands were not smart about where to find holds. I kicked to make toe hooks and heel hooks, felt for pockets where I could jam my fingers, and knobs to pinch and slopers to cling to, breathing snoutfuls of dust and sediment, thrutching ever upward.

Taxed by the hot sun and the sheer physical effort of the climb, I paused to catch my breath and looked up to find that I still had three-quarters of the wall to navigate. My hands were torn and bleeding already, so I paused to wipe them, one at a time, but I lost my grip and bounced from front to back over the choss, transferred by the tumbling rubble to the bottom of the wall. I got myself up and shook my limbs to find nothing irreparably damaged or torqued in the fall.

When I turned I saw the three Devines fretting beneath the brooding pines and called, "I'm fine! Bridget! Vonn! Start looking for the sports bag!"

They rose, disappearing together down the path we'd made earlier. I wiped my bloody palms on my parka and prepared to tackle the wall once more, now desperate for a drink from the water bottles in the mesh bag but glad that at least I had a smaller audience to witness my thrashing, graceless ascent.

Shrill birdsong snuck up on me as I climbed again, bouncing off the jadeite in the rock. I clung, turning left to find a dozen little birds perched on the branches of a tall dead cedar. Those small gray birds inspired me. I reached for the next grip, which I could see above my head to the left, then the next, and the next. But the muscles in my forearm were so pumped with lactic acid my fingers wouldn't grip. I cringed as the cramp took hold, grateful that I hadn't climbed higher. I maneuvered, one-handed, back down to the earth.

"All good!" I called out to Nola, waiting for the cramp to subside. I was pretty certain then that we would not be rescued by lunch.

Bridget and Vonn burst through the trees, clapping at the sight of the empty wall, assuming I was on my way for help. Their faces when they saw me there with Nola? Let's just say my sense of failure was already complete and I'd made only two attempts.

"Can't find the bag?" I asked, distributing the guilt.

Vonn shook her head.

"Maybe I took it off," Bridget said. "Because we were moving the log."

"Do you remember taking it off?"

"No."

"Maybe it got stuck in a tree," I said. "You have to keep looking."

I wiped the blood off my palms again and returned to the wall, deciding to attempt the climb from another angle, a vertiginous route where I hoped I could reach a particular ledge, and from there grasp the longest branch of the ironwood stump. I heaved and hoisted and grunted, but when I got there I found the ledge was too shallow for two big feet in hiking boots. The branch of the *hand* I'd planned to grasp was broken—the only broken branch on the ironwood. I made my way back down, cursing all the while.

When I reached the rubble at the bottom I shouted, "Right side looks a little friendlier. I'll try that next."

"You need water!" Nola waved the yellow canteen.

I did need water. I felt faint. But I shook my head and started for the other side of the wall.

My bloody palms made the rocks slippery and my progress slow. Try and try again I did, from one angle, then another, but each time I failed to reach a safe perch from where I could grip that ironwood. At some point I realized that I was drenched in sweat and overheating in the big coat. With some difficulty I managed to find my way to a spot where I could take off the coat, tying the arms around my waist.

The sun beat down as I climbed. No matter which direction I took, I'd invariably hit an obstacle and was forced to climb back down again. It went on like that for hours.

I couldn't escape memories of the past, voices of the dearly, or nearly departed. My mother. Frankie. Byrd. I couldn't help but remember the day Byrd and I first stumbled on Angel's Peak.

WITHIN A short time of moving to Tin Town the mountain became my refuge from Kriket and Yago and that loud, smoky trailer. I attended my freshman high school classes sporadically, preferring to spend my days on the mountain with Byrd. When it was clear I'd grown in strength and stamina, Byrd decided that I was ready to hike to the peak. The mountain had already changed me.

Byrd reminded me that it got cold, sometimes very cold, in early autumn on the mountain, so I'd borrowed an old coat from the musty closet at my aunt Kriket's—one I was certain did not belong to Yago—and put on my Detroit Tigers cap, knowing Byrd would wear his too.

He had procured climbing boots for me—he wouldn't say how or where—and he had a knapsack with the day's gear: binoculars and camera (the old Polaroid of his uncle's, hilariously huge but so cool to see instant photographs in your hands). He'd also packed the yellow canteen I'd bought him, two large bottles of pop, some packaged burritos from the gas station, and a bag of peanuts in the shell.

The trail to the peak was hard and steep, and soon I was sweating and out of breath. After only an hour of hiking uphill I was struggling. I expected my friend to be encouraging, but he mocked my efforts with words I'd never heard before—*scut, varlet, yawt*—spurring me on with his insults, laughing when I almost puked.

It turned out that every rocky step was worth the view even if the day was overcast. We stood there, silent above the dense white sea of cloud. It was the first time I felt that God feeling.

"Air's thin," Byrd said. "Feel it?"

I felt a loving presence all around me and a deep connection to all living things. I didn't want to ask Byrd if he thought it was because of the diminished oxygen. I didn't want to break the spell.

"Feels like another dimension," Byrd said.

"Frankie was going to hike up here with me," I said.

"He should. The mountain could change his life."

"How could the mountain change your life?"

"People say when you're standing in the center of those lines," Byrd said, pointing to a spot beside me where five fractures intersected to make a star shape in the rock, "you get answers to questions you didn't even know you had. Answers that can change your life."

"Cool." I stepped onto the cracked rock star.

"Supposed to hit you like a bolt of lightning—the answer, I mean."

"Like what?"

"Like my uncle was engaged to this one girl, and then he stood on the star and all he could think of was his ex, so he broke off his engagement and got back with his ex. To be fair, that didn't last too long."

"That's it?" I said.

"That was a bad example, but there are stories of dudes getting lottery numbers in their heads and this one guy got this image of his future where he was dressed in a fancy black suit and he quit drinking and went back to college and became a lawyer. Stories abound."

"Stories abound," I repeated, laughing. I was still getting used to the way he talked. "Has it happened to you?"

"I don't believe in that crap," Byrd said, and laughed. "I'm only here to pass it on."

I stood waiting for the thunderbolt, but nothing happened.

It had been an almost perfect day—the first part of it anyway. Alone for nearly an hour at the peak, we used the peanuts to lure a ground squirrel to within an inch of Byrd's head. I have the Polaroids to prove it. They still make me smile. Sitting there, baiting the squirrel, we'd been comfortably quiet, Byrd expressing my sentiments exactly when he said, "Doesn't feel like we just met."

On our way down we'd gone off the path chasing quail but didn't think much about it. Byrd had a hell of a good sense of direction. But we'd gotten turned around in a grove of tall pines and without a guiding sun in the darkening sky, we took one or two, then three and four wrong turns and came upon a deep crevice, much deeper and wider than the one I faced with the Devines.

Overhanging that crevice, protruding from the mountainside, was a long and slender outcropping—it must have been almost forty feet.

"Looks like a harp," Byrd said. "Or a wing."

It did look like a massive wing attached to the side of the mountain.

"We have to name it," he said.

I was having trouble hearing him over the wind, which had kicked up considerably. Pointing at the granite projection, I said, "Eagle's Wing."

"Eagle's Peak?" Byrd shouted.

"Angel's Peak," I called back.

Angel's Peak. Byrd and I exchanged a look. For all Byrd's talk of preparedness and caution and respecting the mountain's boundaries, neither one of us hesitated as we scrambled down toward that winged outcropping and, with about as much caution as we'd show the average sidewalk, skipped out to the end of the perilously slender extension to look down at the deep dark below. I shudder now, to think of it.

It accommodated both of us, but just barely, as we stood at the far end of it looking down. The wind began gusting from all sides. We held our ground and sang out "Detroit Rock City," a KISS anthem we both knew well, our voices sampled by the feldspar and quartzite—rock stars.

Being a year younger I didn't have quite the weight or muscle Byrd had, and when the wind started blowing more fiercely, the force of it moved me. I acted cool when Byrd found a small rock at his feet and dropped it into the depths, counting until it hit bottom. "You know the free-fall equation?" he asked. "That's about two hundred feet."

The wind came at us again. This time it brought tiny pellets of snow. I lost my breath for a moment and that's when it hit us both that we were standing on a tightrope of rock over a canyon with an early winter storm bearing down.

I could see that Byrd was scared too. "Don't move," he said. "These rocks will be slippery as ice in two seconds."

"Okay," I said. I watched the quickly accumulating snow.

"It'll blow over," Byrd said. "It won't stick."

The storm didn't blow over and the snow did stick, and the temperature continued to drop. We shivered as time slipped into the crevice. The relative safety of the mountainside seemed a thousand miles away.

"What if it's like this until dark?" I was freezing, shaken by the wind, starting to feel dizzy. Vertigo.

"Right now we're going to sit," Byrd said. "The sound of your knocking knees is distracting."

Slowly we turned to face the mountain, and then carefully squatting down we sat astride the rock. I didn't like that I was in the lead by default.

"Start heading back."

"On our asses?" I asked.

"That's right."

"Might take a while." I was terrified to move, and when I finally did begin to pull myself forward, my hands slipped on the icy rock and I lost my balance. "I can't," I said. "It's too slippery."

"Go slow," Byrd said.

"I'm freezing."

"No one's freezing. Don't think about the cold."

"I can't think of anything else," I said. "Except how far down that is."

Byrd did not look down. "Tell me a story."

"What's that?"

"Tell me something."

"What?"

"Anything," Byrd said as we inched forward. "Just talk."

"What for again?" I stopped, craning to look at him.

"A distraction. Just tell me something."

"A story?"

"Tell me about your friends in Michigan." We shivered, maneuvering over the snow-glossed rock.

"I don't have friends in Michigan."

"*I don't have friends in Michigan*," Byrd repeated—his mimicry was masterful. "Make something up. What about life with Aunt *Kriket*?"

"Depressing."

"My father died of a heart attack at thirty-one years old. My mother got cancer a few years later. I left my grandparents in Hamtramck and moved here. That's my story. *That* is depressing. That's why I wanted you to go first."

"Are you making that up?"

"I am not."

We continued to shimmy forward as the snow fell around us, both startled by the sound of a rock hitting the wet depths.

"How old were you when you moved to the desert?" I asked.

"Seven. I remember my grandparents saying good-bye at the airport. I was torn up about leaving them."

"Why'd you have to?"

"Their health wasn't good. It was the only option. When my flight escort came we all clung to one another—the woman had to pull me out of their arms. I tried to find them before I turned the corner but they were already walking away, holding each other up. I never saw them again."

"My father lost our house in a bet," I said to lighten the mood.

"Wow."

"He had six girlfriends move into the house after my mother's accident."

"At once?"

I laughed.

"What happened to your mother?"

Another rock fell into the deep crevice. The boney ridge of the wing seemed to be coming loose. I stopped, but Byrd said, "Keep going. All the way to the end."

"Okay."

"Keep talking. How many girlfriends?"

"Six," I shouted over the wind.

The snow was falling faster and harder. "Why'd they have to move in?"

"To cook and clean? They never lasted long."

Behind me Byrd lost his balance and fell against my back. I tilted with his weight but clung hard until he was steady again. As we got closer to safety we could see that one of the big rocks that joined the mountain to the slender outcropping was gone, relocated somewhere far below.

I turned around, pointing out the gap between the outcropping and the mountain to Byrd.

"We have to stand," Byrd said, reading my thoughts. "And step over it."

"Right."

"It's slippery," Byrd cautioned. "Take my hand."

"No," I said. The wind pelted us with heavy snow.

"Take my hand!"

"If I fall I'll take you down too!"

"Are you going to fall?"

"I don't want to!" I shouted over the wind.

"Then don't put that out there!"

I rose slowly, steadying myself on my knees, arms in the air like a surfer. When I was on my feet, I glanced over my shoulder to find Byrd holding out his hand to help. "Step over it," Byrd said.

I refused Byrd's hand, stepping cautiously over the loose rock. "I'm fine," I said, and then I slipped and started to fall.

Byrd risked his life diving to save me that day. He somehow managed to launch us both forward to the mountainside, where we landed on the cold, hard rock.

"Close call," I said, and we laughed absurdly, inanely. We laughed until we ached, then rose and started back through the snowy wilderness to the Mountain Station.

"Snow's pretty as hell," Byrd said.

It was.

A FINE blue sky emerged later that afternoon and I remember seeing it as a victory. Byrd and I had climbed to the top of the mountain, and not only that but we'd also survived a sudden storm at Angel's Peak.

I was feeling very good about my new life in California, until I saw Yago's Shovelhead parked beside Kriket's trailer. I don't know why Yago hated me so much. I nearly didn't go inside. But when I got closer I saw that the Gremlin was there too. If Yago tried to start something, Frankie'd have my back.

I crept inside, hoping to make it to the sleeping bag on the floor in the bedroom without detection. The air was thick with cigarette smoke. I tried to stifle a sneeze but couldn't.

"Get in here, Wilfred!" Yago called from the kitchen.

I stepped inside the small room. He was alone.

"Did you slap my kid?" he asked.

"What? No!"

"Did you slap my kid?"

I turned to find a half dozen children staring up at me blankly. I wasn't sure which of the boys was spawn of Yago.

"I never would," I said.

"Then how are they going to learn?" Yago asked, pointing to a pile of toddler shit under the table.

I shrugged, relieved I'd been accused of neglect, not abuse, and started to turn away.

"Get back here," Yago said.

Kriket and Frankie emerged from the bedroom down the hall. They looked drunk or high or both. "What's going on?" Kriket asked, herding the kids out of the room.

"Wilfred needs to clean his mess," Yago said, pointing to the coil.

"Clean it up, Wilfred," Kriket said, waving the smell away from her nose.

Frankie wasn't really paying attention. He looked up at the clock on the wall and seemed anxious. "That right?"

"Five minutes slow," Kriket said.

"I gotta go."

"Where?" I asked.

Frankie grabbed his car keys from the counter. "Out."

"Should I come?"

"No."

"You got a mess to clean," Yago reminded.

"Frankie?" He knew I needed his help.

Frankie smiled at Kriket and Yago, pulling me aside. "Man up," he said. "You can't expect me to fight your battles anymore, Wolf."

"Yago outweighs me by sixty pounds," I said. "You know he carries a gun?"

"You can't rely on me for everything. I won't always be here."

"I rely on you for nothing," I said. "You're never here."

"Where you going, Frankie?" Kriket was suspicious.

"I'm meeting a guy. Remember, I told you before?"

"A guy?"

"The job interview."

"Thought you were gonna start working for me, Uncle Frankie," Yago said.

"I will," Frankie said. "But there's this casino job . . ."

"Fine. But set your boy straight before you go."

At that moment I noticed that Frankie had a brick-size brown paper bag stuffed into the waistband of his jeans. We both pretended that I hadn't seen it as Frankie zipped up his jacket. Was he stealing from Yago? Probably. On the one hand I applauded the bold move, but what if my cousin found out and blamed me for his lost inventory? I considered ratting out Frankie to save myself a beating. I didn't.

Frankie glared. "Just do it."

"I do the dishes," I said. "I clean the toilets. I take out the trash."

"And you clean up the shit," Yago said.

"Frankie!"

"It's a job interview," he said. "I can't keep the guy waiting." The door slammed behind him.

I swallowed hard as I watched the Gremlin pull away.

Yago threw a dirty dishrag at my head. "Clean it up."

I stood my ground.

"Clean it up, Wilfred," Kriket said.

"Clean it up," Yago repeated calmly.

I remained defiant, even as Yago grasped the back of my neck with his thick fingers and even as he forced me to my knees and even as he slammed the left side of my face into the brown mess.

If there ever was a casino job, Frankie didn't get it.

BACK ON the mountain with the Devines on the second day, it was midafternoon, the sun scalding. I was hanging on for dear life when the boulder I'd used to spring myself to my current position came loose, fell with a thud, and rolled toward a cluster of pines. I checked to make sure that Nola was all right down below, and then realized that the fallen boulder had left me stranded. Nowhere to climb up and no way to climb down. My muscles began to spasm, and I shook, clinging to the rock.

In an attempt to slow down my breathing, I thought of my mother in her billowing white dress. The two of us, twirling in the mirror. Again and again and again. My mother the angel shouted over the wind, "Go to your left, Wolf! Move your foot to your left!"

I moved my foot to my left as my ghost mother'd instructed and found the toehold I hadn't seen before.

Choking on dust, I climbed down the wall and made my way back to Nola, leaning on the rock beneath the pines.

"I didn't know if you could hear me up there over the wind," Nola called on my approach. "I was yelling at you to go to your left. You took the longest time to move."

I was exhausted and irritable and needed to let off a little steam. I took the parka from around my waist and hit the rocks and brush with it, again and again, whipping it until a cloud of feathers exploded from the seam of the sleeve.

Nola ignored my outburst, focusing instead on the place in the rock where I'd broken the brittle branches with my coat. I'd uncovered an unusual pattern of divots. "Those aren't natural," she said.

She was right.

"They look like mortar holes." She pointed out the worn concave bowls dotting the smooth, flat stone next to the one where she was seated. The pain in her wrist was bad, and she nearly fainted when she moved to get a closer look. Even so she sounded like a schoolgirl when she squealed, "They are! Wolf, they *are* mortars. Here! Metates! These are Native American grinding stones! Look here and here!"

Food had been processed on this rock—hundreds, maybe thousands of years ago—yet it didn't make sense. "There's no water source here," I said.

"Maybe there was a spring or waterfall then? Maybe this was a seasonal hunting camp?"

That was plausible, until we remembered that there was no way to get to where we sat—certainly the Indians had not scaled several hundred feet of granite from the lost canyons below. Nor leaped the fifteen-foot crevice. Nor jumped off the ridge where we fell. "There must be something we're missing?" Nola said.

"I don't have time to wonder," I said. "The sun sets early."

Nola examined the sky as I walked back and forth, scanning the wall, squinting.

"You need to drink something," Nola said.

"I'm good."

"Really, Wolf!"

"Where are Vonn and Bridget?" Mostly I wanted to divert Nola's attention.

"Still out looking for that bag," Nola called. "We'll all feel so much better when they find it. And my binoculars!"

"And my hat," I added.

"Was that your lucky hat?"

I looked around, raising my arms to the wilderness in answer.

"Your generation just goes straight to sarcasm."

I started back for the wall.

"You need to rest," Nola called.

"I'm fine," I shouted back.

"You need water."

"I'm fine."

"Wolf, your coat," Nola shouted.

"I'm good!" I barked.

"Wolf! What if you have to spend another night up here? You need your coat! You can't go up without your coat!"

My memory flooded with the smell of my childhood, those gray Michigan winters, sick-making with the car exhaust and cigarette smoke and dusty furnaces blowing all night long. Freezing my skinny ass off all the way to school because I wouldn't wear the winter coat I had to nag Frankie to buy me every year.

"Your coat!" Nola shouted again.

I carried on, pretending not to hear her. I interpreted her caution about the coat as a lack of confidence in my abilities. I was pissed at her—genuinely pissed, steaming—for putting the possibility of failure into my head. Why would I need a coat? I was going to get up there and back to the Mountain Station long before night fell, wasn't I?

I strained toward a skull-shaped knob, snagged by fear. Nola was right, of course. Only a fool doesn't prepare for a worst-case scenario. You can't imagine how much it irritated me to have to climb back down and collect my parka. I didn't look her in the eye as I swept my coat off the rock. I hated her for caring. I hated her encouragement.

"Wolf," she said sharply, and I ignored her.

After tying the sleeves of my coat around my waist I began to climb once again, sneezing from the clouds of sediment that shook loose with each grip. At some point I became distracted by a mass of breccia—a conglomerate of rocks studded with other rocks—that reminded me of the headcheese one of my first-grade classmates used to bring for lunch and made me hungry and nauseated at once. I swallowed hard, reaching for a grip in a fracture just a little beyond my arm span, but found myself stranded once again with no recourse but to climb back down.

The sun was vicious and the wall was mean. I felt a stab of resentment toward Bridget and Vonn, who were sauntering around in the shade of the pines looking for the bag. And toward Nola for being helpless and burdensome. I hated them all just a little, but they'd saved my stupid life.

So there I was, up the wall and down the wall from this way and then from that. With each attempt I looked back to find Nola's smiling face. She'd hardly taken her eyes from me the entire day, sitting there by the ancient grinding stone, elevating her arm like I'd told her. I don't know when I realized that her lips were moving. She'd been praying that whole time.

I continued to find myself between a rock and a rock. Every ounce of energy I expended climbing to a certain height was doubled by the effort of climbing back down. I thought of Byrd, not so much wishing he were there but that I was not. The wind sounded a call to surrender. I didn't realize I'd closed my eyes until I opened them.

I wasn't alone.

"Byrd," I said, curiously aware that I was hallucinating. "I'm hallucinating, Byrd," I told my conjured friend.

"Is it cool?" he asked

"It's a little cool."

"You look like excrement. Come on." He reached beyond a jagged lip to reveal the sturdy grip I'd been unable to see and began to traverse the wall, guiding me toward the steps and grips.

I've had many conversations with myself about Byrd's appearance on the mountain. At that moment I didn't care if the vision of Byrd had originated with me or apart from me. I was only grateful for my surging strength. It wasn't the first time I'd heard my friend, or seen him in the *spirit* realm. (I believed my mother to be in heaven, but I was confused about what had been done with Byrd.) I followed him, straining for holds that I should not have been able to reach. "Thanks, buddy," I remember saying, but he was gone.

"Byrd!" I called out, panicked.

"Crows?" Nola shouted from far below. "They've been there all day!"

I craned awkwardly to look up beyond the ridge to where she was pointing, and in so doing caught my jacket sleeve on a jagged fin of rock. The coat came untied from around my waist and slid down my thighs. I spread my knees to catch the coat but only managed to loosen it further. Unable to let go, I could only watch helplessly as my parka floated to the ground and landed in a cloud of dust. I'm pretty sure I heard God laughing. Maybe it was Byrd.

Climbing back down, I felt every aching cell of my body. My lungs were burning, my eyes were seared, my head, shoulders, and nose torched, not to mention that I was also hot with shame over my failure. I wanted to whip my damnable coat against the damnable grinding stone until there was nothing left but shredded nylon and feathers soon scattered by the wind. Panting, I took a seat on a smooth boulder beside Nola, who passed me the yellow canteen.

"My friend had one exactly like this," I said.

"Pip got it from the gift shop," Nola said. "You see a lot of these around."

It was the wind, of course, but in the moment it sounded like Byrd, shouting into my ear, "Drink it! Drink it, you eejit!"

I brought the spout to my lips, allowing a small quantity of fluid into my mouth. The metal was cool and smelled of Nola, and Bridget, and Vonn Devine. The canteen. That yellow canteen.

"Drink some more," Nola insisted, pushing the yellow canteen back into my hands.

"I'm all right," I said. Grabbing my dusty parka, I tried to stand but couldn't.

"You need to rest," Nola said. "There's plenty of time."

There wasn't plenty of time. Darkness was snickering just behind the peaks. I rose, but my knees buckled again and brought me down to the rock on my bony ass. Nola tried to rise but was beset by dizziness.

"We make quite the pair, don't we?" she said.

Clouds were gathering on the horizon, and I prayed to God for the

mercy of a little cloud cover to cool my burning skin and relieve my stinging eyes. *God,* I thought, *please help me get up that wall. Please help me
take them home.*

I had to blink when a skink, this little blue-tailed lizard, darted out
from the brush near my feet. Was it a sign? There was a sound then, a
ticking sound, and I was reminded of the rattlers and their affection for
the sun. I snapped to attention, scanning the surrounding rocks. I don't
know if I was being paranoid, prescient, or just fooled, like we all were,
by the puckish wind.

When Bridget and Vonn stepped out of the brush again with no good
news about the mesh bag, I took the moment to tell them, "The rattlers
come out when it's warm like this. Watch out around the rocks."

"I am *terrified* of snakes," Bridget said.

So was I. "Don't bother them and they won't bother you."

Vonn stumbled, bracing herself against the trunk of a tree. Fearing
she was going to hurl again, I turned away to afford her some dignity. She
didn't heave though, and when I looked back at her we locked eyes. I saw
something in her expression. I couldn't say what it was. She shrugged,
deflated.

"Keep looking," I said. "We'll all feel better when we have more
water. Just watch your step."

"If there are snakes out I'm not going anywhere," Bridget exclaimed,
sprawling on a bed of boulders.

"They like the rocks," I said again.

Nola raised her voice to her daughter, "Bridget. Please! We need that
water!"

"We've looked everywhere for that stupid bag," Bridget said.

"Keep looking," I said. "We can't give up."

"Why aren't you climbing?"

To me, Nola said, "I've been sitting here wondering why no one calls
you Wilfred. It's a good name." She could see that I was exhausted and
was stalling for me. "A smart person's name."

"Seriously?" Vonn said. "Mim? The names thing again?"

"*Wolf* just sounds so mean. And you're not mean at all!"

"I can be mean," I said.

"I'm named after my great-grandmother on my father's side," Nola explained. "Her name was Lonya, but the nurse got it wrong and when she saw that my little bracelet said Nola my mother was too superstitious to change it."

I was grateful for the rest.

"Bridget's named after Patrick's grandmother. I wanted Bridget to name Vonn after one of the grandmothers or aunts on my mother's side. I just think names should mean something." She sighed. "We used to pass names down with our china and linens and photographs, and now everything is new and made up. I don't know."

"I don't like my name. *Bridget*. It sounds so fidgety. I just wish it were something calmer. Something that suits me better. Autumn. *Season*."

Nola turned to Vonn. "Normally I don't like naming children after cities and states. I do like Georgia for a girl."

"I like the old-fashioned names," Vonn said.

"Millicent? Gwendolyn?" Bridget asked.

"Clara. Virginia. Annabel," Vonn said.

I must have fallen asleep because the next thing I remember is Vonn helping me to my feet.

The blood rushed to my head when I stood, and I had a glimpse of my future. I'd never thought much of my future before that moment, not beyond the wilderness trips and extreme mountain climbing I'd do with Byrd, or the fantasies (which don't count) of driving a Lamborghini with Lark naked in the passenger seat on some deserted road. *Future*. I remember turning that fat word over in my mind, desiring it, like food and sex. I must have been smiling, because when I looked up Bridget was smiling back at me.

"We're going to get rescued. I know it. I have a very strong feeling about that," she said.

* * *

WHEN YOU'RE in the wilderness, minutes pass like hours, and days like years. or in a split second your whole world could be spun on its axis. It was about four hours past noon, judging from the sun, when I felt the brutish wind driving in from the north. I was making my way down the wall after my ninth failed attempt. There were scarcely two hours of daylight left.

Bridget was there when I reached the bottom, shouting, "Do you hear that? Can you hear that?"

The sound was unmistakable, and yet I knew it was a lie. Nola sat up, scanning the sky. I didn't dare waste my limited reserves of strength celebrating another deception. I didn't even turn to look at the sky when Bridget shouted, "The helicopter!"

Her optimism was infuriating. With time leaking through our fingers I'd have only a few more chances to make it up the wall. I didn't feel like wasting my breath telling Bridget not to waste hers. It was the wind. Only the wind.

I found a rock on which to rest. In time Bridget and Vonn stopped waving.

"What if no one even knows we're lost yet?" Vonn asked.

Bridget didn't correct Vonn this time. "It sounded so much like a helicopter."

"Or a waterfall," Vonn said.

Nola agreed. "Waterfall. Yes. Are you sure that waterfall is as far as you said?"

"Corazon Falls? It's miles and miles."

"So it couldn't be what we heard."

"There's no helicopter. There's no waterfall."

"I think the wind sounds like a train," Nola said. "A freight train."

"The tracks rolled right by our house in Michigan. The wind does sound just like a freight train sometimes."

"All I care about is the helicopter," Bridget said, sighing. "I'm so thirsty." We watched her pick up the canteen and sip from it.

"Eventually someone will notice that one of us is missing, and they'll send Mountain Rescue to track us," I said. "They have equipment. A great team of dogs too."

I pictured Byrd's uncle Dantay throwing a long rope ladder down from the top of the ridge. Uplifted by the image, I stood, ready to tackle the wall again.

"Have you been in trouble up here before? Have you been lost up here?" Bridget asked.

I turned to find the Devine women staring at me. "I've never been lost up here," I said. It was the truth. "My friend's uncle heads up Mountain Rescue." Also the truth. "The tracking dogs will pick up our scent."

I started up again, chanting a rhythm as my feet found boulders and my hands found grips. Higher and higher I climbed, calling on happy memories to fuel me; Glory in the dressing room. Glory. Byrd. *Always*.

I was certain this particular maze of steps and grips was the one that would put me in reach of the ironwood, but I was wrong. That's when I heard Byrd's voice again, like he was shouting right into my ear. "What's your plan, *Mountain Man*?" I smiled in spite of myself.

Climbing back down took the scant energy I had left. When I collapsed at the bottom the three women were all there. "You were so close," Nola said, passing the canteen to me.

I drank sparingly. Vonn merely wet her lips before passing it to Nola, who passed it to Bridget, who stopped to watch us watch her. "You think I'm going to guzzle it like he did. I won't. I want to. Not like you all don't want to."

The sound of a roaring waterfall ripped through the silence. We all heard it and turned to watch the trees, like somehow we might witness the deception—catch them in the act. How did the wind in the pines sound like a waterfall? Or a freight train? Or a helicopter? What cruel magic transformed the air as it cut through the towering sugar pines and

140

the fragrant Jeffrey pines and the practical lodgepole pines and the dense white fir?

"We have a little more than a cup of water left. No food," Bridget said. "What if we get stuck here another night?"

I recalled the quick glimpse I'd had inside Nola's black knapsack when they first asked me for directions and blurted at her, "Peanut butter! You have food!"

"I don't have food," Nola said, wide-eyed. "I don't have *peanut butter*!"

"Why would she have peanut butter?" Bridget asked. "She doesn't even eat peanut butter."

"That was Bridget, Wolf," Vonn corrected. "In the sports bag she had peanut granola bars. Remember?"

"Right," I said, eyeing the women one by one. "Right." It hit me that they were in a conspiracy to keep the food for themselves. Chances were they'd already found the blue mesh bag with the water and had eaten the three granola bars and the peanut butter too.

Turning to Vonn and Bridget, I urged, "We need that bag."

I must have sounded desperate, or threatening, because Vonn shared a look with her mother and they went off into the brush again without a word of protest.

"Don't give up, Wolf," Nola said. "There has to be a way up that wall."

"Why are you lying about the food?"

"Excuse me?"

"You have a jar of peanut butter in your knapsack," I said.

"I do not," she insisted.

"You have crackers in there too? Are you holding out on all of us or just me?"

"I would not hold out. I would never hold out." She glanced around to ensure that her daughter and granddaughter were out of sight before she dug into her knapsack with her good hand and took out the plastic jar, passing it to me gingerly.

"Okay." The plastic jar was not filled with peanut butter but something that looked like ashes. "Is this . . . ?"

"Yes."

"The urn they sold me was so heavy," Nola said. "I couldn't lug that thing up here. I bought some disposable bags, but at the last minute I realized they were snack-size. I needed something lighter that had a tight-fitting lid and . . ."

"Why is it a secret?"

"Bridget was against cremation. Since she was a child she's . . . we had to take her to a shrink . . . so many fears and phobias. Superstitions. She thinks she's clairvoyant. Poor thing. I suppose that's my fault for indulging her, but it comforted her as a child to think she could tell the future. Is that so bad?"

"No."

"You don't know if you ruined your kids or if they were born that way." She paused. "Anyway, Bridget wanted to know that Pip's body was at the cemetery where she could visit him."

"So you buried an empty casket?" I asked.

"It's done more often than you think. He's been in the urn in the closet for *months*. Just been driving me crazy. I used to think I'd go nuts from his snoring but this . . . it's like I can hear him yelling to be let out."

"Okay."

"I thought our anniversary would be the right time to sprinkle his ashes on the mountain. I was going to do it when Bridge wasn't looking."

Nola's choice of *sprinkled* instead of *scattered* made Pip's remains sound like cake decoration. "He wanted to be . . . sprinkled . . . at Secret Lake?"

"That was my idea," she admitted. "We never talked about it. We're barely into our sixties. We were still raising Vonn half the time. We talked about grades and allowance and curfew. Sometimes it was golf and cards and what we were going to make for dinner. We didn't ever talk about

dying." She paused again. "We should have though. Your loved ones should know your final wishes."

"Yes."

"I can't leave him in the jar."

"No."

"He hated peanut butter," she said. "We kept it in the cupboard for Vonn."

"Oh."

"I didn't think he'd be in there for long."

"Right."

"Just it was the only clean plastic container I could find."

"Sure."

"I feel terrible you thought I wouldn't share with you if I had food."

"Sorry." I noticed beads of sweat collecting on her forehead and a dark cast beneath her eyes. Her arm appeared even more swollen, if that was possible.

She attempted to find a more comfortable position. "Has anyone you loved ever died, Wolf?"

I nodded.

"Do you feel them sometimes? Their presence?"

I couldn't answer.

"I feel Pip like he's still here. I keep going to tell him something and every time it's like a slap in the face. It happens a hundred times a day."

"It's hard to break the habit of thinking a person's alive."

She stopped. "Who do you think of as still alive, Wolf?"

"My mother," I lied.

"Since Pip died I haven't seen the point of carrying on," Nola said. "Now . . . here . . ." She didn't have to tell me. I knew she'd changed her mind.

* * *

LONG SHADOWS crept over the rock below me as I started up the wall once more. My fingernails were shredded, my palms ravaged, but worst was my sagging spirit. This would be my last attempt before darkness fell.

Midway up I paused to rest and heard, even from this distance, the sound of Nola humming below. I recognized the melody as a classical piece—a violin concerto from the old film version of *Much Ado About Nothing*. It was the only thing that I could remember from my brief time as a freshman at Santa Sophia High School. Most of the other students fell asleep during the film-appreciation class, but I was transported by the music. Korngold was the composer's name.

Nola's humming stoked my adrenaline and drove me on up the wall and soon I was climbing higher and faster than I had all day up a route I'd not considered, accompanied by the weeping violin. And there I was, inches away from the ironwood. I reached, and I strained, and finally I gripped a branch of the dead tree. I tugged and felt its roots deeply anchored in the rock. I paused to consider the best angle to hoist myself over the cornice.

The wind died completely. All was still, and I took a moment to look out over creation. "Thank you," I said out loud.

That's when I realized that Nola wasn't humming anymore, and I peered down to find her splayed awkwardly over the smooth rock metates where she'd been sitting. Even at a distance I could see that there was blood pooling into the mortars where she'd hit her head. I felt quite certain that Nola Devine was dead.

The fickle wind kicked up again, driving in from the north like a train. I shouted for Vonn and Bridget, but they couldn't hear me over the gusts. "Mrs. Devine!" I called, but she lay there motionless. "MIM!" But the wind howled louder and my voice was lost in its refrain. "NOLA!" I shouted anyway. "BRIDGET! VONN!"

I don't remember climbing down, and I don't remember stumbling over the loose boulders to reach her, but I do remember taking Nola's good hand, relieved to find a pulse. Blood was still dripping from the gash in her forehead, but I'd seen more blood than that in one of Frankie's six-pack-pirouettes into the bathroom sink. I had no strength to lift her, yet I did and thanked God.

I carried Nola to the cave, fearful for the first time since we'd become lost that one of us, or all of us, might die here. I covered her with my parka, then used the sleeve of my hoodie to stop the bleeding on her forehead. Bridget and Vonn appeared, looking drained and defeated. Bridget did not scream when she saw her mother's head wound, which made me shiver. Vonn and I shared a look.

Nola woke, confused by how she got there, her injured arm hot to the touch. I could smell her wound festering beneath the cloth bandages. "We should look at it," Vonn said.

Bridget stepped away when her daughter began to peel back the crusty brown fabric strips, which gave way to the freshly bloodied layer of the black bandana. "We have to clean it. We have to redress it. What can we use?" Vonn asked, looking around, swallowing a gag.

"Leaves," Byrd whispered from the trees.

The wind caught the trees and spoke to us all. "Leaves," it said.

"Leaves," Vonn echoed, like she'd heard too. "Don't some leaves have medicinal powers? Like, aren't some antibacterial?"

"You know anything about that, Mountain Man?" Bridget asked.

"Sterasote," I said, aware that had the bush not blocked my path to Angel's Peak, I might not have thought of it when she asked.

"Never heard of it," Bridget said.

"You know it by smell. I smelled it somewhere here. After we fell. Native Americans used it for healing everything. We could make a paste. Mash it or something."

"A poultice," Vonn said.

"Stay with Mim," Bridget instructed Vonn as she took my hand and dragged me into the brush. "Where? Where is it? Come on. It's going to be dark in two minutes."

We searched through the brush, my eyes darting here and there. I couldn't remember where I'd smelled that camphor smell, and I started to panic that I was remembering the one that had blocked my way to Angel's Peak and that indeed there was no sterasote bush here.

When we came to a small clearing where Jeffrey pines framed a scarlet sunset, Bridget stopped. "Is my mother going die?"

A bad infection could kill a person, and our circumstances were, as Nola would say, *not ideal*. I figured Bridget knew it too. "No," I lied.

I carried on, taking Bridget by the hand when she faltered. "Vonn will blame me if something happens to Mim," Bridget said.

"It's not your fault."

"I ran from the bees," Bridget said. "If I hadn't run from the bees we would have gone to the lake and we would be home right now."

"It's not your fault you're allergic to bees."

"Other things *are* my fault," she said. "And it looks like I'm not allergic anyway."

"Maybe you weren't stung."

"I was stung!"

"Okay."

"Imagine if your whole life you thought you were allergic to bees, then found out that you weren't. Just imagine thinking something your whole life, then finding out it isn't true."

"What would you have done differently?" I asked Bridget as we searched for the sterasote bush. "If you thought you weren't allergic."

"Smelled more flowers," Bridget said with a shrug. "Isn't that a funny, stupid cliché? I would have stopped to smell the flowers, which I've never really done because I'm afraid of bees. Especially the roses. I would seriously stop and smell the roses."

The wind chased us in circles. I lifted my nose, praying to catch a whiff of the sterasote bush, but my keenest sense, overwhelmed by frustration, had abandoned me. The cold wind bit my nose and cheeks, and when I looked back to find long shadows over Bridget's slender face, I cursed the coming night.

She moved to take the lead, but we found no sterasote bush through the pines or near the cluster of brittlebush or beyond the spiky chamise or through the common juniper.

Night was closing in, and I was annoyed when Bridget stumbled over a loose boulder and fell to her knees, then frustrated to find that she was weeping. She clearly wasn't injured. All I could think was—*we don't have time for this*.

Bridget looked up at me and asked again, "Is she going to die?"

"No."

"It's a bad infection."

"She'll be all right."

"I can't lose my mother, Wolf."

"Shh." I didn't know how to comfort her.

I kneeled down beside Bridget, taking her heaving shoulders, and drew her body close to mine. The warmth of her gave me such comfort as I'd never known. We found each other's eyes, and at that moment I caught a draft from the west and began to sneeze fiercely. "Sterasote," I managed to say.

I rose, helping Bridget to her feet, and drew her over the rocks and through the trees searching for the sterasote bush, whose odor grew brighter as we got closer. I covered my nose with my jacket. "Be careful. It's over here, close to the edge."

We found the bush and began to yank at the small, stubborn leaves. Quickly we snapped the dry fibrous stems, stuffing our pockets with what we hoped would be a miracle cure for Nola.

Armed with the sterasote leaves and stems, we charged back through the brush, but as we drew near the cave we were frightened to hear the strangled cries of an injured beast—a horrible screech that sounded like no night bird I knew. We scoped the trees as we hurried on.

But it was Nola who was making the terrible sounds, as Vonn, blinking tears, cleaned the festering wound with the edge of a credit card. Her ability to stomach the task impressed me.

Vonn looked up. "What took so long?"

We emptied our pockets of the sterasote into the mortars in the rocks near the wall. Bridget started to pound the stems and leaves into a slimy mush with a round stone she found nearby, squinting against the vapors from the plant's volatile oils. "This stinks," she said.

Together we ground the sterasote into a thick paste, while a few yards away Nola endured the vigorous cleansing of her wound.

When I ventured back to check on Vonn's progress, I wish I hadn't. "How can you do that?" I wondered aloud. "Without hurling?"

"You do what you have to do," Vonn said. "I'm almost ready for the paste."

When I returned to the metates to collect the mashed sterasote with a fresh plastic credit card from Nola's wallet, I remarked on Vonn's ability to handle the rancid wound.

"She gets motion sick on anything that moves but she's fine with everything else," Bridget said. "I have vertigo and she gets motion sick. We wouldn't have come but then Mim confided about the secret anniversary ritual with Pip. We could see she didn't want to go alone."

Bridget stopped mashing the sterasote, her attention caught by something moving on the rock beside me. *Please, God, don't let it be a snake.*

I glanced down and discovered a fat ground squirrel an inch away from my hand. I could have snatched him, then and there. And what? Thumped him dead with a stone? Torn his flesh with my fingers and teeth, sucked his warm blood? I was revolted by the thought, and would not have believed that later I'd have some graphic and disturbing fantasies about doing all of those things. "Git," I said.

Bridget turned to look in the direction of the cave. That very morning she'd been the most optimistic of us, so sure about the helicopter, so certain of our survival. Mountain time being as it was, she'd had a rapid shift in spirit. "What if we don't make it, Wolf?" she asked.

"Well," I said slowly, giving the question full weight. "When I was a kid I spent a lot of time at the library. I've read a lot of adventure books, true stories, and I guess, if I broke it down, I'd say the most successful people in the most impossible situations are the ones who are sure they're gonna get out of it, and they go on thinking that, even if they die trying. So that's what we're gonna do."

We fell silent. Agreed.

BRIDGET AND I approached the cave to find Nola propped up against the rock, pale and stoic. Vonn looked at the sterasote—a mound of green pulp on the credit card in my palm. She leaned over to smell it, cringing, then suggested we apply the pulp directly to the wound. "We need a clean bandage to put over top."

"My brassiere?" Nola offered.

"*Brassiere*," Vonn said, snorting at the word. "Here, use my *brassiere*." In several deft movements she removed her bra and a long tank top undershirt without taking off the Christmas sweater Nola had given her. After scooping the sterasote mulch into one of the bra cups, Vonn bound it with the undershirt while Nola shrank in pain.

Something caught my attention—a scent on the air—and it must have been a strong scent to overpower the sterasote. I found myself sniffing the wind, a grin splitting my lips. The quiet blue fragrance meant *rain*. I felt instantly buoyed. "It's going to rain tonight."

"Are you sure?"

"How do you know, Wolf?"

"I can smell it. We have to figure out a way to collect the rainwater."

Nola peered at me from under half-closed lids. "My poncho," she said. "There's no seam in the hood. The plastic'll hold water."

Vonn went to the poncho, and turning the hood inside out, saw that it made a large leakproof container in which to collect enough rain to fill the canteen.

"Good idea, Mim," Vonn said.

"Make sure those grips on the poncho are wrapped tight around the branches," Nola said, shivering in pain.

As Bridget and Vonn set about securing the poncho, Nola whispered to me, "It's bad, isn't it?"

"It's not *good*, Mrs. Devine. You need a doctor."

When Bridget finished with the poncho she pulled me away from the cave, punching me hard on the arm. "Why would you tell her that?"

"I think she knows."

"*You* know nothing! You said you knew the way when you didn't! You said you could climb the wall and you can't! You said tracking dogs would come and you said we'd find the granola bars. You know nothing!"

I walked away before she could say anything more, taking my place in the cave with Nola and Vonn.

"What was all that about?" Vonn asked.

I shrugged, relieved that Bridget stayed outside to cool off. She was right. I'd made promises only God could keep. When she pressed in beside us a little later, I avoided her eye.

There were scents that rose up to me that night, microscopic particles that brought odors from far away; fry grease from the fast-food joint a few miles down the highway, diesel fuel, dry rot in a wood cabin, dead koi in some distant pond. We watched the lights of Palm Springs grow in the darkness, and Vonn, mooching my thoughts, said, "I hate that it's so close. It's like starving with a tin of food in your hand and no way to open it."

"Dying of thirst on the ocean."

Bridget said, "One of these times, when we think it's a helicopter it won't be the wind."

"They will never fly a helicopter here," I said more harshly than I needed to. "Never."

"My dream."

"The air in this part of the canyon is never stable long enough for a helicopter to search. Even if they're looking for us right now, they're not using helicopters to search Devil's Canyon."

"That so?" She didn't believe me. I could hear it in her voice. Bridget's faith in her dream was absolute.

ONLY NOLA slept. Bridget and Vonn were restless, shifting and sighing. It was cold.

"I can't sleep," Vonn said.

"Me either."

"We need to think of ways to make the time go faster," I said.

The owl flapped invisibly above us as coyotes howled in the distance. Beside us Nola kicked in her sleep. I turned to look at Bridget with her dry lips and wide eyes. Vonn's toes burned against my flesh. Her face had grown subtly longer.

"We need a story," I said, thinking of Byrd. "A distraction."

"No more stories," Bridget begged. "I can't get Laura Dorrie out of my head."

"Games then. Games will make the night go faster."

"Were you in love with my father?" Vonn asked, startling Bridget. I could tell from her voice that Vonn wanted the answer to be *yes*.

"I was *eighteen*, Vonn," Bridget said plaintively.

"Did you love him?"

"I worked at a hotel bar while I was taking some college classes," Bridget began. "I was engaged. I guess I was bored. He used to come in with clients. He'd flirt with me. He flirted with all of the girls. He was older and handsome and sophisticated. I was driving to work on the freeway one night and my engine started smoking. You'll never guess who pulled over. I'd just shaved my legs. Felt fated."

"Was he stalking you?"

"He was heading back to work from one of his son's baseball games. He'd just had a fight with his wife."

"They had four boys. Didn't you tell me that?"

"The whole thing only lasted a couple of months. When I found out

I was pregnant, I called him at work, but before I got to tell him about you, Vonn, he told me that his wife had found out about the affair and it was over and he would call the police if I came anywhere near him or his family. He was a creep."

"But if he'd known about me?" Vonn said. "He would have wanted to meet me."

"His family was everything to him."

"Apparently not," I pointed out.

"Maybe he was a creep but he was my father. I have a right to know him," Vonn said.

Bridget turned to me, explaining, "My first husband was much better father material."

"Except he wasn't my father."

"I hoped he would be forgiving."

"No psychic dream to predict that one?" Vonn began to cough, and then she doubled over and swept her hair back from her face to vomit. I was alarmed to see the release of some dark-colored stomach contents splash on the moonlit rock. I was pretty sure it was blood. A slow bleed. Nothing seemed out of the realm of possible, especially when it came to bad luck. The thought of losing Vonn terrified me.

"You good?" I asked, rising to kick loose gravel and soil over the mess. "Maybe we should change the subject."

"No," Vonn insisted, swallowing hard. "I'm all right. I'm all right. I want to hear this."

"Hear what?"

"The story."

"I've done my best," Bridget said. "There's no story."

"I'm going to meet him. When we get back. When we get home. I'm going to introduce myself."

"Okay," Bridget said. "Do you want me to arrange it?"

"No," Vonn spat.

"Do you want me to come with you?" Bridget asked.

Vonn paused. "Maybe."

The wind blew hard into our little shelter, displacing the warm labors of our breath. My nose flash-froze. "Damn," I said. It hurt. Pressing Vonn's toes into my warm chest beneath my shirt, I wondered what I would look like with my nose blackened from frostbite. I considered the before and after photos, then had a horrifying thought that I might lose my keen sense of smell along with the tip of my nose.

I could still smell rain. Where was the rain? "Favorite movie?" I asked.

"I don't want to play," Vonn said.

"Romantic comedy or drama? You need to make categories," Bridget said.

"If you have a favorite movie you don't need categories. Favorite is favorite," Vonn said.

"You said you weren't playing."

"I'm not playing."

"Food?" I suggested.

"Dessert or main?" Vonn asked.

"You said it was gonna rain," Bridget thought to mention.

I remembered that I'd vowed not to make any more promises I couldn't keep. "I still think it will."

They were fading before my eyes, by the hour, the minute. I knew that if we stayed on the mountain much longer, Nola would perish from her infection. Next to go would be Bridget—with scant fat reserves she'd succumb to hypothermia, dehydration. Vonn would go after that, frostbitten toes joined by frostbitten fingers and then blindness, and then that chill, sleepy farewell.

I found some deep sense of calm in accepting the reality of our situation. Had I not forced the truth on myself, I might have accepted Bridget's prophetic dream about the helicopter rescue, and settled for Nola's limitations, and agreed that Vonn couldn't go anywhere with her flip-flops. Instead, I did the math and listened to my instincts, both telling me that we would all die if we stayed where we were.

I looked toward Nola in the dim light of the cave to find her turned toward me, smiling weakly. "Was I asleep?" she asked.

"For a little while," I said.

"Anything good happen?"

I laughed, and then shook my head. "Nothing good, Mrs. Devine. But nothing bad either." I saw the hint of her smile in the darkness.

"I've just been sitting here thinking that maybe I could use the straps of your knapsack to make some kind of loop. I need something to help me get to that ironwood stump under the cornice," I said.

"That is very resourceful, Wolf."

We were silent for a time, watching the night sky. Vonn lifted her legs on either side of me. Wordlessly I drew her feet beneath my shirt again. Even through the thick wool socks I could feel her toes melt on my skin.

"I wonder if animals are getting at those granola bars. I'd fight a badger for those things," Bridget said.

I pictured crows pecking at the ripped silver foil. "You'd have found the wrapping."

Nola sighed into the darkness before she said, "Bridget, I want them to play my music. You know that piece? The sad one I always played on the console."

"Why?"

"The violins," I said.

"How did you know?" Nola smiled through her confusion.

"The Korngold," I said.

"You know that sad music she's talking about?" Bridget asked.

"From school. Nola was humming it when I was climbing earlier."

"I wasn't humming," Nola said.

Even in the darkness I saw my confusion in her eyes. "You were humming it, Nola. I recognized it from a film-appreciation class. It was the professor's favorite piece. I heard it a thousand times." I hummed a section to remind her.

"That's it!" she said, brightening. "You do know it!"

"Nola, you were humming it. Then you stopped humming and that's what made me look down."

"I never heard any humming," Bridget said.

Vonn shrugged.

I shivered, anxious about my confusion and what it meant.

Nola leaned in to squeeze my arm. "Play it over and over again on a loop at my memorial."

"Oh, Mother," Bridget said, and then bit her tongue.

"Over and over on a loop," Nola repeated. "Five or six times. Then let the folks go. No words. Let the music speak."

"Here, Mim, put the parka on," Bridget said, moving the knapsack at her feet. There was a pause and the air changed in the cave as Bridget's hand found the peanut butter jar in the knapsack. She pulled out the large plastic container, holding it up in the waning light. "What the *hell*?"

Nola was in no shape to protest or explain.

"Give me the jar, Bridget," I said calmly. She handed it over without a fight.

"Is this *food*?" she asked. "Looks like protein powder. Have you all been . . . ?"

I saw myself in her expression—wild-eyed and paranoid. "It's . . . it's Pip," I said.

"Pip?" Bridget stared.

"Oh, Bridget," Nola said. "I should have told you. I should have told you both."

"Ashes?" Vonn said. "But . . . ?"

Bridget paused for a long moment, then tilted her head toward her mother. "I thought you'd pick the eighth hole at the Doral."

"His hole in one! Oh, Bridge, I didn't even think of that!" Nola croaked.

"I didn't know about Secret Lake."

"With our anniversary it seemed the thing to do," Nola said. "So you knew about the ashes all along?"

"When I came up for Vonn's birthday in September I saw the receipt from the crematorium and found the urn in the closet."

"I sewed a plastic pouch full of ashes into all of those little sachets too," Nola said.

"The lavender sachets?"

"That's weird," I said.

"Could that be against the law?" Bridget asked.

"Why didn't you tell me?" Vonn said.

"I didn't know how you'd react."

"I like it," Vonn said. "I think Pip would too."

"Roses for me, please," Bridget said. "I love the smell of roses."

"Is everyone gonna pick their ash sachet scent now? Isn't that weird?" I said.

Vonn giggled, which made me, for a second, deliriously happy.

"Do people really have their loved ones' ashes in sachets all over town and I'm only finding that out now?"

"I've heard of people wearing tiny vials on chains around their necks," Bridget said. "But I think Pip's the only one I know in a sachet."

"When Jack Mazlo died," Nola said, "his mother asked Janice for some of the ashes."

"To make sachets?"

"She put the ashes in a plastic bag and sewed the bag into Little Jack's favorite teddy bear so his father could always be with him."

"Oh."

"She was Maltese, so we thought maybe it was a cultural thing."

"Did Little Jack know about the ashes?"

Nola nodded. "He wouldn't go anywhere without his teddy bear. He called it Daddy Bear."

"I hate sad stories," Vonn said.

"When you get older you think of sadness in a different way," Nola said softly.

"I'll like being sad?"

"It's not that you *like* being sad, but you start to see the value of it. You don't judge sadness so harshly."

I wished I had a sachet containing my mother's remains. Something lemon-scented. Or maybe peppermint.

"Everybody on the block had an opinion about Little Jack and the Daddy Bear. I thought it was terrible at the time. Now I'd love to think that what's left of me could comfort some sweet child. I don't want to be scattered though. I'm more an outdoors *liker* than an outdoors *lover*, and I'm not big on the ocean, so I don't want to be thrown off the back of some squid boat."

"*Squid* boat?" Vonn and I said together.

"And don't bring me back here," Mim said emphatically. We all laughed. "I was thinking a small urn for the mantel or even the kitchen counter if one of you keeps the condo."

"Oh my God, Mim," Vonn said.

"I don't mind being split in half if that's what you decide. I like the weather in Golden Hills."

I did not confess my growing fear that none of us would survive to fulfill Nola's final wishes. "Done," I said.

"Sprinkle a dash around the boxwood near that bench at my church too," Nola added after pausing to think. "That's a comforting place for me."

"Close your eyes now. You need to sleep," I said. I didn't want Nola to see my fear, but she must have sensed it anyway.

"You're doing a good job of keeping us all going, Wolf," she said.

What a crock, I thought.

* * *

THE WIND drove into the cave, lying to us about rescue choppers and waterfalls. The owl hooted overhead, not wise anymore, just irritating.

"Buttered noodles," Bridget said idly.

Vonn laughed. "When you could imagine anything."

"I know. Buttered noodles and that key lime pie that Mim does with the graham cracker crust. I haven't had that in years."

"She made it for you three days ago," Vonn pointed out. "For when you got here."

"I didn't eat it. There's some in the fridge right now." She laughed somewhat maniacally. "Ow!" she cried. "I split my lip."

"We should try to sleep a little," I said.

"I'm afraid to sleep," Bridget said. "I don't want to dream. What if I have a future-dream where the helicopter *doesn't* come? Where we don't get rescued?"

"Seriously, Bridget," Vonn said. "Don't you think you would have had one dream or vision or whatever about getting lost up here in the first place if you were really clairvoyant?"

"It doesn't work like that."

"It doesn't work at all."

"You have no faith."

"You have no track record."

"Maybe I haven't told you about every single dream that came true," Bridget said. "Maybe I kept some of that private."

"Like what?"

"Nothing."

"Like what?"

"I dreamed your father called me a liar when we went to knock on his door. His kids were there."

"But that didn't happen," she said.

"But it could have. It still might."

"We live in completely different worlds, don't we?" Vonn asked in earnest.

"We're not spending another night here," Bridget said confidently. "Mark my words."

"The most important thing," I said, "is that we're going to keep at it. Right? We're going to find that bag, and I am going to get up that wall."

We spent most of the rest of that second night in silence, watching over Nola, ashamed by the relief her warm forehead brought our cold hands, startled by her spastic pain, envious of what appeared to be her periods of deep sleep.

Too cold for conversation, we considered the morphing clouds and listened for helicopters and rescue calls. My hands were stiff, mercifully numb to the stinging scrapes on my palms. My fingers seemed not my own. Sometime in the night, the cave was flooded by the distinctive sound of Bridget's whistling-flute snores. Vonn reached over and adjusted the position of her mother's jaw to make it stop—just as she'd done before. It worked, briefly. When Bridget started to snore again, Vonn gently adjusted her head once more. Then Vonn happened to glance at her grandmother. Her face went slack. "I don't think she's breathing."

We leaned in a little closer, startled when Nola coughed. Then Nola opened her eyes to meet mine in the darkness. She was afraid. I could see it. But instead of being filled with dread I was flooded with determination. I would not let Nola Devine die. I was sure there had to be some way to safety. If there were metates, the Native Americans had to have found some way off this horrible rock-ship, so what the hell was I missing?

"YOU'VE BEEN awake for two days straight," Vonn said.

"How did you know I was awake?"

"You're so dehydrated I can hear you blink."

"It's going to rain," I reminded her.

"So you said," she said, struggling to sit up.

Coyotes howled in the distance as Nola shouted, not asleep but not altogether awake, "Let the dog out, Pip!"

"Does she have a dog?" I asked, panicked that there was some poor animal somewhere with no food or water.

"No," Vonn said. "She's talking about her pug, Brutus. He died a couple of years ago."

Time passed. Five minutes? An hour?

"Do you think anyone is looking for us yet?" Vonn asked.

"Yes," I said, though I had no reason to think so.

"Wolf, do you believe in . . . fate?"

"I don't know."

"It's just that if being here, on the mountain, right now, stopped you from doing something else, would you see that as a sign that you were not meant to do that thing? What I mean is, do you believe the universe—Mim would say God—is trying to tell you something? Maybe even punish you?"

"Trying to tell me what?" I asked, tensing.

She sighed deeply. "Well, if you were going to do something? But you couldn't do it because you got lost, isn't that a sign or whatever that you shouldn't be doing it?"

"Doing what?"

"What you were going to do?"

It's hard to describe my state of mind, because there's no parallel for this in regular life. My senses were duller, my reaction time longer, my grasp of reality a little tenuous, but I was also acutely aware of my decline, which made me question everything in a spiral of paranoia.

We'd been deprived of sleep, water, and food for two days, plus I'd begun the journey less than robust thanks to the pernicious habits of the depressed and suicidal (not sleeping, not eating, negative thinking), all to say—I thought Vonn was baiting me about my plan to jump off Angel's Peak.

"Who told you?"

"What?" She looked confused, hurt by my tone.

"Who told you what I was going to do?"

"Wolf?"

Something was scaring her. I realized it was me.

"What were you going to do?"

My mind was racing for a way to cover my blunder. "I was going to go hike off trail."

"Hike off trail?"

"I was following some bighorn tracks."

"That's it?"

"That's what I was going to do."

"Follow a bighorn. By yourself? Aren't those things scary?"

"They're cool."

"What if it charged?"

"It was a lamb we were chasing," I said. I was aware that I was struggling to keep my thoughts on track.

"*We?*"

"I."

"What were you going to do when you found the lamb?"

"When I found the lamb?" I pressured my abdomen with my fists to stop the muscles from spasming. "I was going to photograph him."

"But you forgot your camera," Vonn guessed.

"Yeah. You? What were you going to do?"

I was having trouble breathing.

"Why don't you have a knapsack?" Vonn asked.

"I didn't bring one."

"I know. I'm asking why?"

"I forgot it at home."

"You must feel so stupid. Do you think about it? Do you obsess about it? How much water had you packed? Food? A tent? Did you have a tent?"

Yes. Yes. Yes. "I don't see this being positive, Vonn."

"Are we going to die here?"

"No," I said. "Maybe." I was thinking about the lamb.

* * *

I'VE NEVER told anyone about the lamb.

In late spring the mountain meadows were painted in purple lupine and coral root, explosions of amber wallflower and scarlet snow plants busting up through winter decay. Byrd and I had stopped on our way to the peak to talk to a middle-aged birding couple about their morning hike. The husband was excited to share with us that they'd spied a peregrine falcon, rarely seen, in the meadow outside of the Mountain Station. He'd gestured at the saddle-peak beyond. "We couldn't follow it off trail though," he said with a shrug.

Byrd and I shared a look. The man was pointing in the direction of Secret Lake. We changed our plans and elected to spend the day searching for the peregrine falcon. With Byrd in the lead, we searched the pines for a sign of the rare bird. Then he stopped and I stopped too, because in front of us stood the most magnificent female bighorn sheep, and behind her, careening comically into her rear because he was so coltish and clumsy, her lamb. Both animals regarded us sideways, all four of us in a quandary about our next step.

We were aware that any quick movement would cause them to bolt and that if they became separated from each other it would be disastrous for the lamb. We were so close I could see a tick moving on the ewe's nose. We stood there with ear-splitting grins watching the pair sniff us on the wind.

The squawking ravens who settled in the pines overhead seemed to rankle the mother bighorn, and she turned an eyeful of accusation on us. Her horns were not as long or curved as the males of her species, but they could hurt pretty bad if they gored a guy in the ribs, or worse. The ewe lowered her head. Byrd and I muttered expletives.

Then the ravens began to heckle more insistently from the pines, spooking the lamb, which jetted off through the brush. The mother turned, sprinting after her baby.

Byrd and I could see that the lamb was heading toward a cleft in the rock that dipped into a short meadow that led to a deep drop. The mother had gone the other way, up into the dense pine forest where she'd lose track of her lamb's scent altogether. We set off after the lamb.

Then it happened. The lamb jumped too close to the edge, scrambled, then fell to a shallow ridge below. It was only an eight-foot drop, but it was enough. Byrd and I climbed down the rocky incline to him. It still hurts to remember the way it was lying there, both front legs broken, bleeding, bleating. I couldn't read Byrd's face. It was strange, he looked so calm.

"Can we save him? Byrd, can we save him?" I already knew the answer. It was unfair that I made him say it out loud.

I could hardly look at the bleating creature, but the damn lamb kept finding my eyes. It was pleading with me. I didn't know if it was for life or death. I watched Byrd reach into his left sock for his Swiss Army knife. He pulled open the blade.

The lamb's cries bounced off the granite. I covered my ears and closed my eyes, unprepared to bear witness.

"Help me!" Byrd shouted, pounding my leg. Reluctantly I bent down to hold the poor animal still.

"Throat," he said.

I held the lamb in a lock and closed my eyes, waiting for the sound of tearing flesh, preparing for the warm gush of fluid, eager for the silence and the stillness that would follow. But there was a strange pinging sound, and when I opened my eyes I was confused to see the knife on the rock beside the terrified lamb and Byrd disappearing through the brush. I picked up the Swiss Army knife, and with one swift cut performed the brutal act of kindness.

Heading down in the tram that night, we noticed some uneasy riders glancing our way. Byrd gestured at my blood-splattered jacket. "Maybe you should take it off."

"Yeah." I did.

"Guess you're stronger than you think," he said, focused on the white desert. To this day I can't decide if Byrd had tested me or failed himself.

* * *

NOLA WAS wheezing in her sleep. Bridget, snoring uncharacteristically softly.

"They sound like cats," Vonn said, echoing my thoughts. "You said before there were mountain lions."

We were not going to see a mountain lion or bear on this outcrop—I was sure of that. "There's hardly a dozen ground squirrels here. Slim pickings for a mountain lion."

"There's us."

"Don't put that out there," I said, half joking. "Don't put that out in the universe."

"You think the universe has ears?"

I shrugged. "My friend always said that."

She hesitated. "You know how people turn to God in their darkest moments?"

"I guess." I thought of the sunrise, how astonished I'd been, moved to tears.

"Isn't that like being a fair-weather sports fan? Do you think—if there's a God—he sees it like that?"

I shrugged.

"Can God see us now, do you think? Does he know we're stranded on this giant ledge?"

I paused for a long moment before I realized I didn't want to speculate. I couldn't bear to think God was aware of our suffering and couldn't reconcile his nature if he wasn't.

"Do you believe?" I asked.

I'd felt God on the mountain that morning when I rose, but he seemed so far away now.

"I'm waiting for a sign," Vonn said.

Bridget shifted in her sleep then, and rolled out a minute-long single-stroke snare-drum fart. Then she started snoring again, loudly, and

Vonn and I nearly shared a seizure from laughing so hard. When we stopped, Vonn fixed her mother's head.

After a pause, she said in a quavering voice, "I might have been the one who lost the keys. I'm not sure I gave them to Bridget."

"It's okay, Vonn," I said. "It was just a mistake."

"If we hadn't gone to the spa for my stupid pedicure that I insisted on, we wouldn't have lost the keys, and we would have gotten up here earlier in the day when it wasn't foggy. Maybe we would have found the lake. We wouldn't have met you. You wouldn't be lost, Wolf. It's my fault. What if God is punishing me?"

"For losing the car keys?" I wanted to assure Vonn that what I felt in the sunrise had no judgment or wrath, but I didn't. Even then I thought people should come to their own conclusions in matters of God. "That wouldn't make sense."

"Or other things," she said.

Interpreting God's motives—even ascribing motives—seemed absurd. "We're here because we're here," I said. "Still, a few prayers couldn't hurt."

"MY TOES are numb again," Vonn said, pressing her heel into my ribs sometime later. "You said to tell you."

I could feel her stiff, frozen feet through the socks and was sickened to think of the deadly pathology at work on us all. I took her left foot in my own cold hands, rubbing vigorously, trying to restore circulation.

"Hurts," she said, squeezing her eyes shut.

"I know," I said. "Burns."

"Burns," she agreed. "Am I getting frostbite?"

Necrodigititis. I managed to coax the warmth back into the ball of Vonn's foot but her toes were hopelessly cold. "If it hurts it means blood is circulating. That's a good thing. Let me keep rubbing them," I said.

"Why is it taking so *long*?" Vonn asked. "Why can't they *find* us?"

I prayed to God they would.

"I'm so thirsty," Vonn said hoarsely.

"It's going to rain," I said again.

Nola was groaning in her sleep, Bridget snoring in concert. Vonn fixed her mother's jaw again and the snoring stopped. "I learned to do that when I was little. I slept with her for years."

I nodded.

"How will the rescue dogs track us if it rains?" Vonn asked. "Doesn't that wash our odor away? What about our footprints?"

"Depends how much and how hard it rains," I said. "We need the fluid. We want the rain."

The mountain made her mournful music: the howling wind, the hooting owl, those granite bass notes playing reverb with the canyon. I felt every cell in my body shriveling, my muscles worn from the day's futile climb. When I shifted I had the sense that my brain was quivering in my skull. All I could smell was sterasote. The lights from Palm Springs mocked us. Tin Town stared back at me like the glowing debris from an explosion.

Did I fall asleep? I'm not sure. I remember that I was startled by the thought that it had been some time since Vonn had complained about her toes. I started up a vigorous massage with my clumsy hands. "Feel that?" I asked.

"Numb," she said.

I pinched the flesh of her big toe as hard as I could.

"It doesn't feel like we just met," Vonn said, oblivious to the pinch. I remembered Byrd saying those same words to me years ago.

I worked my stiff fingers around her toes, my own hands aching from the effort.

"You must regret that you got distracted from tracking the bighorn," Vonn said.

"What?"

"You must regret you saw Bridget and Mim."

I paused. "I don't."

She stared at me in the dark. "No matter what?"

"No matter what," I said. Then I leaned over in the dark, grasping Vonn's arms and pressing my chapped, icy lips to hers. We stayed that way for a long moment, breathing in the other's scent. It was not a kiss, exactly—we were too cold and hungry, our mouths and lips too dry. It was something more, ripe and mature and wise and complex, but I don't think there's a word for it. So many details in that kiss, and something else, something in particular that I wouldn't name, not yet, but knew I had to revisit.

Beside us Nola groaned in pain.

"Is she unconscious or asleep?" Vonn asked. "I'm scared."

"She'll be fine. She's strong as an ox."

"She's old, Wolf. She takes bone pills! You take bone pills when your bones are like sawdust."

"Ox. Bones. Sawdust. Stop talking about food."

She laughed, but just a little. "Days or hours?"

"What?"

"You know what I'm asking—days or hours?"

"You can't talk like that. You can't think like that. I got close to the ridge today. If only I had a rope to help me reach that second branch."

"My coat?"

"We need our coats."

"What about your idea to use straps from the knapsack?" Vonn said.

"Yeah. They won't be quite long enough to make a good rope though."

"Right," Vonn said, trying to stay positive. "We'll use the straps, and the rest of the underwear?"

"Mim's *brassiere*?"

"Mim's brassiere," she said, smiling.

"It's a plan. We make a rope. I climb all the way up. I get help. We'll be home by noon tomorrow."

"It's a plan," Vonn said.

I continued to knead the flesh of her feet, relieved when she started to whimper.

"Hurts," she said.

"That's good. It's good that it hurts."

She watched me for a long while, then said, "You know about those Andes plane-crash survivors from the seventies? The rugby players."

I did.

"Did you read the book?"

"I read the book."

"You remember what they did?"

They famously turned to cannibalism to survive. I didn't want to say it out loud.

"I can't eat Mim." She burst into tears.

"We won't eat Mim." I took her in my arms. "We won't eat Mim."

"Promise?"

I paused. "We'll eat Bridget."

There was a moment of silence before she laughed. "You're sick."

"You too," I said. A compliment.

We watched from our perch in the cave as the owl hooted through the gloom, then disappeared on flapping wings. "Good!" I called. "Go!"

"Think he's been watching us?" Vonn asked.

I did, but didn't want her to think I was flaky.

The silence stretched. When the wind kicked up to interrupt my meditation I was peeved, and turned my face toward it. Vonn nudged me in the ribs again, saying, "My feet, Wolf."

"Do you believe in God?" I asked.

"Well now," she said. "Duh. Haven't we already had this discussion? I'm the fair-weather believer. Remember?"

I'd meant to ask her if she believed in *ghosts*, for a second earlier when I'd turned into the wind I'd seen something move. I was sure it was Byrd again, or maybe my mother, the ghost-angel. I checked Nola to make sure she was still breathing. The woods were quiet save for the distant hooting owl, then the sound of snapping branches.

We scanned around for danger and decided it was just the wind.

"My feet are blocks of ice."

They were. Tucking her right foot into my armpit, I started an aggressive massage on her left foot again, through the scratchy wool socks.

"It's not working," she said, and I could sense her stirring panic. I stripped the sock from her foot and rolled it like a glove over her chapped, frozen fingers. I couldn't make out the details in the dark, just the outline, enough to see that all of her toes were swollen and stiff. I took her foot in my own rigid hands, trying to massage the blood back down through her calf and into her ankle, the arch, the heel, the ball. I was afraid of how cold the smallest toe felt.

"Am I going to lose my toes?"

"No," I said.

Vonn didn't resist when I drew her foot toward me, just shut her eyes as slowly I brought her toes into my mouth, warming them with my tongue, sucking gently to draw down the blood. I was moved by her groans, which were not sounds of pleasure. I couldn't save her from pain, but I hoped to save her from frostbite. We watched each other in the darkness and shared, in those strange moments, one of the greatest, strangest intimacies of my existence.

Then there was movement in the bushes to the west. Even with my senses impaired and my mouth distracted I could smell it. Vonn quickly pulled her toes out from between my teeth and put the sock back onto her foot.

"Coyote," I said, imagining he'd tracked us here, lured by Nola's blood. Or maybe our failing bodies were giving off a scent that cried out to his appetite.

Movement in the trees to the north of us meant there was more than one. Two. There were two of them, stalking us. This was happening.

I'd dragged a small branch into the alcove in case of curious wildlife—I was thinking squirrel, rat, spider. I never imagined confronting two aggressive coyotes while stranded on an outcropping over Devil's Canyon. I'd have grabbed a bigger branch.

I stood at the entrance to the cave listening to the animals stalk us from the bush, waving my stick and shouting, "Git. Git! GIT!" I tried to make myself a large menacing presence, but those canines must have been as hungry as we were because they didn't retreat very far.

Then the first dog returned, advancing from the left, the second from the right, weaving through the brush and over the rock toward our shelter. I hollered at them. So did Vonn.

Bridget woke to see the menacing coyotes and started to scream her bloody head off. The coyotes retreated into the bush and howled along with her. What a haunting sound that trio made, snatched by the canyon walls and repeated by the devil himself.

We waited. I could hear them—rustling bushes and snapping twigs—but I couldn't see them. "Git!" I shouted, but the coyotes must have thought I said, "*Come*," because they stepped out of the brush, posturing.

"Throw something at them, Wolf!" Vonn shouted.

I looked around for a rock, but when I couldn't see one within reach I grabbed the big plastic peanut butter jar and chucked it as hard as I could, beaning the closest coyote right between the eyes.

The coyote shook off the strike and came back to life snarling and snapping, able to see me better in the darkness than I could see him. The other coyote snapped up the plastic jar to crush between his incisors, then started to shake it like they do, to break the prey's neck. The jar snapped off the lid, and the beast disappeared in the cloud of ash.

The mangy animal sneezed. I stood my ground, brandishing the branch, shouting—we all were. Bridget picked up Nola's knapsack and hurled it. The dog caught it impressively in its teeth, his mate joining in the killing frenzy, tearing it to shreds. I stomped forward, swinging my

impressive stick. The beasts, confused by the bloodless sacrifice, dropped the canvas sack and bolted.

I gave chase, claiming my territory so they wouldn't come back, but I was slow in the dark, pulling myself over the rock and through the brush, following them by sound. I could tell they were headed for Devine Divide, and it occurred to me then that the wily coyotes might be tricking me—trapping me. I pressed on against my better judgment. Maybe I was afraid that if I quit they'd find out how weak I really was.

They were on the rock near the sterasote bush. I could see them moving in the shadows, then, after a brief hesitation, one after the other, the beasts made spectacular leaps over the wide gulf that separated us from the slope on the other side.

The first coyote stuck the landing gracefully in the moonlight, but the second stumbled. I was pretty sure he was limping behind his partner as they trotted up the slope and disappeared into the darkness. I worried that it was the animal I'd struck with the jar. Mostly I was relieved they were gone.

"Wolf?" Vonn called through the darkness.

Something caught my foot, and I reached down to find the remains of Nola's knapsack. The dogs had torn it up pretty bad and it didn't look salvageable for much. I looked up into the heavens, thinking, *Really?*

When I returned to the cave, I saw Vonn's shadow standing guard, holding a large spiny branch.

"They jumped the crevice," I called out. "Fifteen feet. Must be fifteen feet."

"They could come back."

"They won't come back. They won't bother. We're too much work." I wondered how much longer that would be true. "How did the Cahuilla get over?"

"Who are you talking to?" Vonn asked.

"Myself. I don't know. The Cahuilla didn't jump to get here. Not that far."

I was alarmed to turn and find that Nola hadn't been awakened by the conflict with the coyotes.

"She never woke up?"

Vonn and Bridget shook their heads.

"Fifteen feet," Bridget commented. "That's far."

I kneeled beside Nola. Her forehead was hot, her breathing labored. My body ached, and my spirit sagged. I said a silent prayer for the Devines, and rain.

IN MY dream, Vonn's toes were in my mouth. But then Vonn morphed into Bridget—you know how that happens in dreams—and she pointed out Nola's arm where the undershirt-bra-bandage was loose and sterasote leaves were falling to the ground, glowing like tiny green gems. I nearly lost it—in my dream—when I saw the wound. It was healed, entirely, miraculously. Bridget gestured for me to look into the trees ahead, and I grabbed my stick, ready to fight coyotes. Instead, I saw an angel dancing among the pines, entreating me to join her. It was my mother, in her white, batwing-sleeved dress. I followed, even when she began to run, calling out, "Glory. Glory! GLORY!"

She led me through the brush and over the rocks, back to the spot where the mangy coyotes had jumped the crevice. There she balanced impossibly at the top of a free-standing lodgepole pine. "Trust," she said.

"Trust who?" I shouted.

"Make a bridge, Wolf! Make a bridge with the mossy pine."

"Bridget what?" I shouted.

"You still here?" Byrd laughed, and plopped down beside me on the rock.

"I'm dreaming, Byrd. Did you see my mother? Where are you?"

"The matrix, dude. In between the rocks."

"Cool."

"Your eighteenth birthday blew scagg."

172

"I know."

"You're supposed to be the *guide*."

"I know. Is that the way?" I asked, pointing across to the slope.

"That's the way."

"So that will take us back up to where we fell?"

"That's the way," Byrd repeated.

"The way we get rescued?"

"It's the way you have to go," Byrd answered with a shrug. He pulled his yellow canteen out of his knapsack and took a long drink before passing it to me.

The dream drink was cool and crisp and soothed my parched throat and reconstituted my spirit.

Byrd gestured across the crevice. "There used to be a land bridge. Slender. Like the wing at Angel's Peak. It broke off. They walked across a little tightrope bridge."

"They?" I followed his finger to see evidence that there had once been a land bridge.

"Imagine what that stone sounded like when it fell . . ." Byrd mused.

"You think a person could jump that?"

Byrd shook his head. "Suicide. It's not just the leap, it's the landing. You have to be a mountain goat."

"Or coyote."

The slanted rock on the other side appeared to meet the ridge where we'd fallen. "So I make a bridge? Then I go up there? I take the Devines up there and then what?"

"You'll see a lone pine."

"A lone pine?"

"And a mesa beyond it. That's the way. Go toward the lone pine."

In this dream, Nola appeared, rising from the ridge on the other side of the slope, led by two large dogs on long leashes. Only it wasn't Nola, it was my mother wearing Nola's red poncho instead of the white dress, and they weren't dogs but coyotes.

In my dream, Nola called, "Listen to your mother, Wolf!"

That's all I remember of the dream.

I'll tell you what happened when I woke the next morning on the mountain our third day lost, but first, for the rest of this story to mean anything, you have to know what happened to Byrd.

IT WAS Lark's reappearance in my life just before I turned seventeen that set off the chain of events that led me back to the mountain, and ultimately to the Devines.

I thought about Lark Diaz every night, but I hadn't actually seen her since the day I got heatstroke the summer we'd moved from Michigan. She'd been away at boarding school, and then college in New York—Byrd had been right about his cousin never coming back to live in Santa Sophia again, not even for the summers. When she did on the rare occasion come home, she most often brought a boyfriend, some bespectacled dandy titillated by the casino culture, or some dunderheaded muscleman who wanted to hike the mountain in Jesus sandals—according to Byrd, who met the smattering of suitors at the Diaz family dinners he was obliged to attend.

I'd taken a Friday shift at the gas station for Byrd because he'd been summoned to Harley's ranch to make plans for college now that he was turning eighteen. I didn't want Byrd to leave. I hoped he wouldn't get accepted anywhere. I mocked the very notion of him going. Without Byrd, I was not just alone—without Byrd, I was just not myself.

Tinkling silver chimes—which Byrd put up when the rusty cowbell broke—announced her entrance this time. Her face was bare of makeup, her hair long and loose. She was dressed in jean shorts and desert boots, but I knew she wasn't a local. When she saw me she grinned expansively and said, "You still owe me for two sodas."

I caught the fragrance of citrus blossom. "Wow." It was all I could say, and I said it out loud. "You are . . . *Lark*."

She laughed—what a beautiful sound—and I was surprised to see that she found me charming.

"Are you moving back?" I asked, speaking from my lowest register.

"We're here for the weekend," she said. "We came all the way from New York for the big *event*." The event was the birthday party Harley was throwing for Byrd and me at the ranch on Sunday.

We? She'd brought a boyfriend?

"You know Gisele Michel? We're at school together in New York."

I was relieved when she gestured toward the parking lot to see a skinny brunette with oversized breasts climbing out of the driver's side of a silver Mercedes. Lark said solemnly as we watched her clackety-clack toward us in her too-high heels, "Her dad's a big lawyer for TV writers. Her mom's an interior designer to the stars. She has a beach house in Malibu. She's been in *People*." She shrugged as if she wasn't impressed but thought I should be.

"That's cool," I admitted.

The passenger door opened on the silver Mercedes and I was confused to see Byrd climb out. "Byrd knows your friend?"

"They met this morning."

"Okay," I said, grinning.

"I need a favor from you," Lark said but didn't say more.

When Byrd and the young woman entered the store my hair stood on end. There was some subtle hint of blood under the designer fragrance that followed her down the aisle. A predator. That's what I smelled.

Byrd strode up to us saying, "You didn't tell her, did you, Wolf?"

"No," I said. "What?"

Gisele Michel encircled Lark's slender waist from behind, licking her bottom lip as she sized me up. "He's absolutely adorable," she said in a faux-scratchy voice. "Cowboys and Indians. They're both just *yummy*."

"Don't tell them anything," Byrd said.

Tell them what? I hadn't seen Lark in the flesh in three years—now she was standing in front of me, and was she flirting? *And* she'd brought along a hot celebrity friend. *What?*

I took a closer look at Gisele, who had all the trappings of beauty but no natural grace. Her best feature (not explicitly hers) were the two expertly constructed breasts, impressive from an architectural standpoint with a hint of the surreal—almost mangaesque. Her voice put me in mind of green pepper. "Introduce me," she demanded. "I need to know the guy who knows."

"Gisele Michel, Wolf Truly," Lark said.

I was flattered that Lark knew my last name. "What do I know?"

"Don't tell them, Wolf," Byrd repeated. "I said you'd never tell."

"Tell them what?"

Gisele tugged Byrd in the direction of the pop fridge. "As I was saying before, I have a thing for Native Americans. Billy Jack. You know Billy Jack? I'm so into vintage. Film. Clothes. Everything. I long for a time when life was, like, simpler."

I could see Lark wanted to get me alone. I didn't care that I was being played. I just hoped the game was good. "We're friends, right?" Lark said.

"Yes," I said.

"When you came here that day, a long time ago, I heard you tell Byrd you found some redweed," Lark said, grinning. "I heard you, Wolf."

"Redweed?" I was shocked, a little.

"I wanted Gisele to come to the birthday party, and I was talking about the vision-quest thing and how they used to use redweed in the old ceremonies, and she said she wanted to try it, and I said I knew someone who could get it," Lark explained, her eyes huge. "It was the only way she'd come."

"Dead weed?" I deadpanned.

"You can die from a lot of things, Wolf. No one's talking about taking too much."

"You don't want redweed," I said, shaking my head.

"Please," Lark begged. "She will *hate* me if I don't come through."

At that point Gisele and Byrd crowded back into our conversation. "So," Gisele was saying, "I think Native could be hot, *super*hot: feathers, beads, buckskin, animal motifs, totem prints—if people could just sort of let it go, you know—the big injustice or whatever."

Byrd laughed, but I don't think she was trying to be funny. "When I saw your picture"—she stopped to bat her prodigious lashes at Byrd—"I said I'd only come to the party if I could do redweed with that very cute birthday boy."

Having never seen Byrd interact with a woman before, I had to admit I envied his apparent ease. You'd think he had celebrity children of celebrity lawyers and designers to celebrities throwing themselves at him every day.

"So you came all this way just to celebrate my milestone annus?" Byrd said with a grin.

Gisele mock-recoiled. "I'm not going near your anus!" Turning to Lark and me, she said, "When do we get it? The night before the party? Or would it be cool to be on it during the party?"

Byrd and I shouted, "NO!" simultaneously, and then laughed because we knew we were both thinking about Harley catching us messed up on redweed.

"What do you think, boys?" Lark asked, looking hopeful.

"You know it makes your hair fall out," Byrd said.

"It does not!" Gisele protested, clutching her mane.

"Has some chemical in it called alopeciadicide," Byrd insisted.

"He makes things up," Lark said. "He's super weird. So's Wolf. They *read. Books.*"

"You said they were straight." Gisele pouted.

"We are!" Byrd and I insisted in unison.

Lark licked her bottom lip. "So what about the redweed, Wolf?"

"I don't even know if that bush is still there," I said. That was true.

"We'll take the tiniest, littlest bit of it. Not enough to get ruined, just enough to get wrecked," Gisele promised.

"No one's gonna die," Lark said, laughing.

"You know it makes girls super horny? You know that, right, Byrd?" Gisele tipped forward on her heels and began to kiss him with an open mouth and wandering tongue. I could not look away, until Lark hopped up to sit on the counter in front of me and I caught a flash of her inner thigh.

"I've read that too," Lark said, then pulled me close so she could whisper into my ear. "I hear it makes a girl want to tear off all her clothes."

"Wouldn't it be cool to have a ceremony?" Gisele said. "A rite of passage for you birthday boys. A vision quest. Like your people used to do."

"We could do that without redweed," Byrd said.

"Eighteen is legal, you know," Gisele said, fingering Byrd's belt buckle. "For a lot of things."

Lark laced her fingers behind my neck and whispered, "I'm going to owe you so hard."

For a moment I forgot how to speak. "I don't know how to make the tea," I finally said.

"Don't look at me," Byrd said, holding up his hand. "I'm from Hamtramck."

"Seriously," Gisele sighed. "Is there nothing written down about this shit? Like a recipe or something?"

"The shamans made it," Byrd said, sounding more Native American than he ever had before in his life. "It's toxic."

"It's a hallucinogen," I said.

"It's gonna turn me into a porn star," Gisele teased.

"We won't take enough to buzz a fly," Lark promised. "So will you get it?"

I hesitated. "I don't know."

Gisele grabbed Lark by the arm then, not caring that we could hear, and hissed, "I would not have dragged my ass to Santa *Calientay* to party with, like, high school boys if you had not promised you would get us that shit, Lark!"

"I'll get the redweed," I said, to save Lark the embarrassment of disappointing her horrible friend. My intentions were good. Speaking of the road to hell . . .

Lark mouthed, *Thank you*.

To seal the deal, she pressed her bare lips to mine. My first kiss. Oranges.

The plan was that Byrd and I would locate the redweed and brew a small quantity of tea from the leaves and stems and we four would drink a thimbleful the next night to celebrate our birthdays and transition to manhood, agreeing that dusk at Secret Lake would be a momentous time and the perfect place for the ceremony. We knew the way to and from the lake well enough that we could have managed with just moonlight but we promised the girls we'd bring flashlights, and that we'd have them home by ten.

The next morning Byrd and I rode our bikes out to the path behind the high school, then hiked into the dense bush. Neither of us said anything about the rattlesnakes, but Byrd found a hefty branch for protection and watched for movement in the dense foliage. I remembered the way through the large fragrant sage bushes, past the ring of beavertail cactus. We found the redweed spread out over the fallen oak.

Byrd leaned over and took one of the small pods into his hand, then drew the Swiss Army knife from his sock. I was terrified of snakes, and I wanted to get the hell out of there.

"This is stupid," he said, fingering the pod.

"Are you kidding?"

"Seriously, Wolf. Dead weed? What are we doing?"

"We won't use much."

"Lark is playing you—you know that," Byrd said.

I knew and didn't care. Not in the slightest. I glanced at my feet, sure that any moment a rattler would come slithering up my pant leg.

"Why don't we just say we couldn't find it?" he said.

"Then they won't, you know, and I want to," I said. "Don't you want to?"

"I don't want to die." Byrd said those words and then repeated them. "I don't want to die, Wolf."

"Two pods, Byrd," I said. "We won't boil it for long. We won't drink too much. Besides, it's a vision quest! How many times have we said we should go on a trip? It's going to be cool."

"You think it might be cool?"

"So cool. So, so cool. You've never thought about a vision quest?" I asked. "You've never wondered about what it was like for your ancestors to perform their rites of passage? What kind of Indian are you? Even I've thought of that. Wondered what they saw . . . how it felt . . ."

"Might be cool, I guess," Byrd allowed.

"You read the books about it, right? The boys would have this kind of revelation where they walked through this curtain and saw themselves as animals. Felt themselves in the animal's skin."

"Cool."

"Right."

"I already know I'm a bird," Byrd said.

"Wren-tit," I said, and laughed.

"Wren-tit! How about eagle?"

"Vulture."

"Owl," Byrd said.

"Let's find out." I was saying the words, but it was my father Frankie's voice I heard, from somewhere deep within me, a genetic hot spring rising up my throat. I didn't care about my friend finding his spirit bird. I wanted Lark. It was all about Lark.

Byrd jumped in with both feet after that, seduced by the possibility of a spiritual journey in some animal realm. Back in his small apartment behind the gas station, we boiled the little red seeds from the prickly pods and used a motor oil funnel (that we cleaned) to strain the foul brew into the spout of the yellow canteen. "Too much is worse than too little," he said.

"It smells like exudate!" I cried, using a Byrd word. We laughed.

"We'll be needing protection," Byrd said, snapping his fingers. Then we collapsed with laughter all over again. We were like a couple of second graders. "We will definitely need protection."

"What if we trip on the redweed before . . . ?" Byrd asked.

"Before we need protection?" I shook my head. "That can't happen, Byrd."

"Yeah, I'll dilute it some more," Byrd said, pouring some of the brewed tea out of the canteen and replacing it with water. "A lot."

"What if they puke or something? Girls usually puke from stuff like this. Smells so bad."

"I'll bring gum," Byrd said.

"How about toilet paper?" I suggested. "In case someone gets explosive diarrhea." I was concerned about that particular side effect.

"Don't put that out there, dude," Byrd said, laughing. "Don't put shit like that out there in the universe."

"Yeah. But let's bring some," I said, then added, "It'd be cool to shape-shift. Just fly away."

"Yeah," Byrd said. He dug into the closet to get the supplies, calling out like it wasn't the biggest piece of news he'd ever told me, "Uncle Harley says I should go out of state. For the experience. Maybe back to Michigan. I think about that sometimes."

"Michigan? Back to Michigan? Why would you leave California to go to school in Michigan? What a joke! Why would you want to go there at all? Ever?!"

Byrd shrugged, then shrugged again.

"Michigan's too cold," I chided. "You won't go to Michigan." I'd looked away so he wouldn't see me swallow the lump in my throat.

IN THE late afternoon, gathered together behind a clump of trees at the Desert Station, we toasted our adventure with a bolt from a silver flask of Jamaican rum that Gisele had pilfered from her host's wet bar.

"If my dad finds out you took his Jamaican, we're dead," Lark said, and I was chilled to think of the look on Harley's face if he found out about the redweed.

We'd told the girls to dress for winter and were pleased to see they'd complied, with boots and warm coats and fuzzy hats and gloves. Gisele seemed the most eager of us all, swigging the rum and giggling. "I love being in disguise," she said. "Who would recognize me in these loser boots?"

Lark laughed mirthlessly, seeing as the boots had come from her closet. "Lucky they fit. Especially the calf. You're so much shorter than me."

Gisele straightened and said, "That was *bitchy*, Lark. Basically you just said that I'm a short cow with big feet."

"I forgot the tea!" I lied, hoping to defuse the tension between the girls. They swiveled around, turning their venom on me as I pretended to search the knapsack. I sighed with relief when I found the canteen, and we celebrated, order restored.

The girls giggled and screamed at the tram-rocking transition towers, and we used their terror as foreplay, embracing and tickling them, flinging our youth in the faces of the other riders when they frowned. But then the tram conductor warned us to dial it down or he wouldn't let us off at the Mountain Station, and Byrd and I remembered what we were risking. We were about to lose our virginity to college girls, on our shared birthday, at one of the coolest places on earth. The stakes were unusually high.

It was an unseasonably warm day, and we were sweating in our coats as we walked. When we reached *Circunsisco Gigantesco,* we paused while Byrd described, with great solemnity, the rock formation's power to produce spontaneous and multiple orgasms.

The fabled wild horses, whose ancestors were first lost on the mountain centuries before, could have been galloping in front of my stupid face, but I was so singularly focused on my pursuit of Lark I wouldn't have noticed. I couldn't wait to show her Secret Lake. Finally we stepped through the canopy of trees, past the boulders, and through the brush to reveal the smooth, framed water. I was bursting with pride.

"I thought it would be bigger," Lark said.

Gisele screamed at the sexual innuendo. "I thought it would be bigger!"

"It's a vernal lake," I said defensively. "Its size depends on the rain. This is the smallest it's been in years. Our precipitation was way below average. Way below."

Gisele laughed harder. "Smallest in years! Way below average!"

Both girls tipped back another swig of the Jamaican rum. They were not watching their step. "Watch the phlox!" I called.

We finally settled down together, sitting cross-legged on the Slab, the yellow canteen in the center of our circle. There was no wind. I'd never felt the mountain air so still and quiet. Even the birds in the tall trees were silent, a captive audience for our cautionary tale.

"Look," I said to the girls, waving my arms around like I was showing them my cool bachelor pad, crestfallen when they didn't seem the least impressed by the slim, glossy lake, or the wraiths' shadows dancing on the forest floor, or the way sunlight stroked the ragged rocks and coaxed the flecks of metal in the breccia to the fore.

"What did the Indian boys do back in old times?" Gisele asked, with surprising solemnity.

"What?"

"Did they have to pierce something? Dance? Firewalk? Or was it just drinking the redweed and going off in the forest?"

"Drinking the redweed and going off," Byrd said authoritatively.

"I think we have to make up our own ritual," I said, serious. "No going off alone. Agreed? No going off alone?"

"Agreed," we chimed.

Byrd reached for the canteen.

"Wait!" Lark cried as Byrd rose to his feet.

"Make a speech," Gisele said, grinning. "*Shirtless.*"

Lark flinched. "He's my *cousin!*"

"Don't look."

Byrd uncapped the toxic tea. "I'm starting to think this is a bad idea."

Lark frowned while Gisele sniffed the air. "It smells like *feet!*" Gisele said.

Byrd gagged and put the cap back on the canteen.

"Why don't we stick with the rum," I said.

"What about you?" Gisele asked Byrd. "You want to stick with the rum? Or are *you* ready to become a *man?*"

The dying light cast Byrd in amber as he held the canteen like a trophy and leaned into an imagined microphone. "I want to thank my agent," he said.

We all laughed.

Still holding the canteen aloft, Byrd took a solemn stance. "Today, we are men."

Lark and Gisele hooted and hollered.

"Today, we are men," Byrd repeated, and I found myself joining in. "MEN!"

I could smell the coming winter, or maybe it was a relic of winters past. Maybe the odor of pine sap was strong. Or maybe it was the rum that was so strong.

Byrd looked at me for a long time—he could have been a great actor. He spoke volumes without a word. I know it was all a big show, but I still got choked up when he asked, "Do you know, Wolf? Do you even know what it means to be a man?"

I felt like an asshole for getting emotional, because it was just Byrd and he was only goofing around, but the thing is, I didn't know the answer to that question, and I thought I should at least have some idea. I felt the weight of my father's failures and the absence of my mother, and I wondered who would teach me, or if a guy could learn on his own what it means to be a man.

Byrd reached out his hand and helped me to my feet. We bellowed, "*MEN!*" and I sucked back snot and started laughing.

Gisele rose, snatching the yellow canteen from Byrd's hand. "MEN STALLING!" she charged as she untwisted the cap.

Things seemed to happen quickly after that. Gisele dropped the cap, which bounced off the rock and fell into the brush. I laughed along with the others, but I was annoyed by her carelessness. "We should really try to find that before it gets dark," I said.

Lark was not her unflappable self. She leaped to her feet to say, "Maybe we shouldn't do this, Gisele."

A flock of preening mountain quail fluttered over our heads, flying low, sweeping the field of phlox beyond.

"We said we were gonna. Come on—we *said*." Gisele didn't sound like a grown-up college girl and neither did Lark.

Byrd reached out to take the canteen back, but Gisele held it out of his reach. "You're supposed to be brave," she said. "That's the whole point of it."

"Don't do it," Lark begged.

Gisele lifted the canteen to her mouth and took a short swig of the brew, swallowing loudly and smacking her lips. We waited, breathless, to see what would happen next. We laughed our heads off when the girl gagged theatrically before wiping her tongue. "That's seriously disgusting." She paused. "I feel nothing. Nothing."

"Déjà vu," Byrd said, looking at the yellow canteen. "I feel like I've been here before."

"Nothing?" Lark asked, staring at Gisele.

"Should we take a bigger swig?" Byrd asked.

"I definitely need more," Gisele said, belching loudly.

"You definitely need this," Byrd said, passing her some gum.

"Shouldn't I be feeling something by now?" Gisele wondered. She took another short swig as we watched and waited.

"Nothing," she said, "but pukey."

I realized, with as much relief as disappointment, that we'd diluted the brew too much.

Byrd took the canteen from Gisele, sniffing the fluid inside. "Should we just wait to see what happens?"

Just then Gisele pointed to the west, crying out, "Look at the sunset! Oh my God, you guys. That's the most beautiful thing I have ever seen. And look! That cloud looks like a woman's face. Oh my God. It's Mother Nature." Tears of joy streamed down her face. "It's so beautiful. Oh my God, you guys. She's just so beautiful."

Byrd grinned. "Mother Nature?"

No matter how reluctant we'd been, now we all wanted to tip back that yellow canteen and go to the exquisite place where even Gisele Michel sounded beautiful.

But then she started to yell. "I'm burning up, you guys! I'm so hot!" She peeled off her winter coat, even though the sun was sinking and the wind had risen, and started toward the lake. "I'm going in," she called.

Byrd and I did not swim in Secret Lake, which was buggy and coated with algae during the summer months and much too cold the remainder of the year. I'm not proud to admit that I did nothing when Gisele started peeling off her clothes. Byrd, on the other hand, gathered the girl into his arms and led her back to where Lark and I had settled on a boulder.

"You can't go into the lake, Gisele," Lark warned, trying to stop her friend from stripping completely.

"Fine," Gisele said, shivering, and put her arm around Byrd's neck. I was glad to see him return her deep kisses as she lifted his hand to the lace of her bra.

I felt Lark's hand on my shoulder and thought she meant to kiss me too, but when I turned she was gesturing at Gisele's right arm, which had begun to spasm.

"Gisele," Lark said.

Alarmed to see her jerking arm, Gisele pushed Byrd away, then fell back onto the polished granite in a fit of giggles. This bizarre behavior seemed in keeping with what I'd read about the psychotropic effects of redweed.

Before we could react, Gisele sat up. The spasms were suddenly gone, and she seemed back to her old self when she whined, "I need some water."

We'd thought to bring the tea, and the sleeping bags, three condoms each—toilet paper—and the gum . . . but no water. "We didn't bring any water," I said.

"Seriously, you guys!" Gisele shouted. "Oh my God, that stuff makes you *so* thirsty!" She belched repeatedly.

"We have gum," Byrd said.

Gisele got up and started heading toward the lake. "I need a drink. I seriously have to drink something."

Lark called out, "You can't drink the lake water, Gisele! That'll make you sick!"

"We should go back," Byrd said. "We should go back to the station and get water."

Gisele started dancing around the way people do when they're on fire, racing back to us, looking all around for something to drink, finally lunging at Byrd and yanking the yellow canteen from his hands. The sewage-scented tea splashed around our feet, but before any of us could stop her she'd downed a long gulp.

The toxin in the tea was affecting her gross motor skills so that her gait was grotesque, zombielike. "I'm thirsty," she cried as she staggered toward the edge of the Slab. It was awful to watch.

"Stop," Byrd called, running after her. "Give me the canteen!"

"Gisele!" Lark screamed.

"Stop, Gisele!" Byrd called.

She did stop, feet away from the cliff's edge, and we three breathed a sigh of relief, until she raised the canteen to her mouth again.

"NO!" Lark shouted.

Byrd stepped close. "Give it to me," he said calmly. "Give me the canteen, Gisele."

"I don't feel good," she croaked.

"Come away from the edge," Byrd said quietly. "You need to get away from the edge."

But Gisele was gone, and in her place was some altogether different creature, growling and snapping at the air. Was she on her vision quest? What the hell was she? She clung to the canteen, even as her muscles appeared to seize and her face contort. She lifted it once more.

"Put it down!" Byrd hollered, reaching out to wrestle the canteen from her hand. Gisele hung on, kicking him hard and high with her borrowed boots. He staggered backward.

"Leave her, Byrd!" I shouted.

"It's all right, Gisele, just give it to me!" Byrd started toward her again, holding out his hand. She kicked at him, losing her balance and stumbling even closer to the edge.

"Don't step back, Gisele," Byrd begged.

Gisele began to cough, and when she looked around, seemed dazed and confused. "I can't breathe."

"Don't talk," Byrd said.

"Where's my driver?"

"I don't know."

"Who are you?"

"Byrd. I'm Byrd."

"Can you fly?"

"No," Byrd said.

"Can I?" Gisele asked, then turned as if to leap. Byrd lunged for her. Byrd stumbled. And then my friend disappeared over the edge. It all happened so fast.

Gisele dropped to her hands and knees, evacuating her guts, which saved her life. Lark sobbed.

Byrd.

* * *

I SEE myself looking down at him, the wreck of his body twenty feet below on the ledge where he'd fallen. But it's a lie. The view was obscured by dense brush.

It might have taken me ten minutes to climb down to the place where he lay. I don't remember that part, only that I was there, in those last rays from the setting sun, and I thought he was dead.

He opened his eyes when he heard me crying and worked up a crooked smile.

"You're gonna be all right, buddy," I promised, but my calm was obliterated by the girls on the ridge above us, screaming their bloody heads off. Beautiful Lark. My dream girl, costarring in my nightmare.

Byrd found my eyes. He tried to say something, but blood poured forth instead of words.

"Don't talk," I said. "Your leg is broken. I know. I can see it's broken."

Please, Byrd mouthed. That's when I noticed that his arms were both broken too. There was blood in a small pool on the ground at the nape of his neck. *Please.*

"Hang on, Byrd. Hang on. We're gonna fix you."

I looked around at the sweep of forest, the ragged rock, the windworn stone, calling upon the balm of nature to heal my friend. Byrd moaned. There was a massive wound on the crown of his head.

His eyes fluttered closed. I took off my coat and covered him with it. It should have been me. That's what I thought more than anything. It should have been me. A glint of metal caught my eye—his Swiss Army knife had fallen out of his sock. I picked it up.

The girls continued their desperate concerto on the ridge as darkness fell over Secret Lake. I waited with my quiet friend as the girls continued to scream for help.

* * *

HOURS PASSED. The girls screamed. Byrd's breath grew shallow. I'd all but given up hope by the time the rescue workers, alerted by the hikers, arrived a few hours later. I looked up and recognized the man climbing down with a medical bag and ladder rope. It was Byrd's uncle Dantay. "Redweed?" he asked.

"He didn't drink it, Dantay," I said.

Dantay opened his mouth but stopped when he saw Byrd's twisted body splayed out on the rock. I don't remember what Byrd's uncle told me after that. His face said everything.

Sometime after that, I heard the sound of a helicopter. In this case it really was a helicopter, with a screamer suit dangling from a thirty-foot cable. I don't like to remember that night, that moment. Byrd didn't scream. When that helicopter took my best friend away he made no sound at all.

THE THIRD DAY

The warmth of the sun on my face confused me because the last moment I remembered was dark and cold and terror-filled. A dream. I opened my eyes to find Bridget and Vonn watching me expectantly.

"I thought you said you were from Michigan," Bridget said.

"I am."

I was surprised to see that Nola was awake and alert. "You look so much better, Mrs. Devine."

Nola nodded. "The swelling's down. So's the fever."

"The sterasote," Vonn said.

"Or the prayers," Nola said. "Don't forget about the prayers."

I didn't.

Vonn put the parka over my shoulders. "You've been weird all morning, Wolf. You okay?"

I nodded, but I was confused.

"I remember reading all about the teenagers and the redweed in the newspapers when it happened," Nola said. "My whole congregation prayed for you kids."

"Redweed?" I said. "What redweed?"

Bridget shared a look with Nola and Vonn.

"The redweed you just told us about," Vonn said. "You just told us the whole story."

"Are you okay, Wolf?" Bridget asked. "See? I told you he seemed *off*."

"I told you what happened at Secret Lake?"

"Don't you remember?"

I did not. "I thought I was dreaming it. I've had such weird dreams. I dreamed about my mother."

"I'm sorry about your friend, Byrd," Nola said.

"That Gisele Michel sounds like a piece of work," Bridget huffed. "How'd they keep her name out of the papers?"

"And that Lark person too?" Vonn said. "How does she get to walk away scot-free?"

I doubted that Lark was any more free from the memory of that night than I was.

"Why did you say you were from Michigan of all places?" Bridget asked.

"I am from Michigan. I moved to California when I was thirteen. Tin Town."

Vonn reached down, offering a hand to help me to my feet.

"It was all over the news around Thanksgiving last year," Nola said.

"Thanksgiving. Why weren't we here for Thanksgiving?" Vonn asked, trying to remember.

"There was so much going on. Remember? You were skipping school again. I had to make an appointment with the dean," Bridget said.

"You chose that weekend to move, Bridget," Nola reminded her.

"That's right. That's what it was."

"It was Thanksgiving," Nola said. "Who moves on Thanksgiving?"

"I remember now," Vonn said. "You'd just met the Realtor."

"His wife was going to Maine," Bridget recalled. "He stayed back to close my Colonial."

"Interesting euphemism," Vonn muttered.

"Stop," Bridget warned.

"You basically ate that woman's turkey," Vonn said.

"You're disgusting," Bridget hissed, then turned to Nola. "I didn't know it was going to be Pip's last Thanksgiving."

"You never know. That's the point, Bridge. Carpe diem," Nola said.

Carpe diem. My heart stopped, electrocuted by those words. *Carpe diem*. *Carpe diem. Carpe diem.*

"Wolf?"

"I'm all right," I said.

"You've got that look again," Bridget said, sharing another glance with Nola and Vonn.

We listened to the wind as we scanned the ridge for signs of life.

Vonn paused to meet my eyes before she said, "We all want to know, Wolf, what happened to your best friend? After the helicopter took him away with no sound at all?"

I WAS surprised but not necessarily relieved to see the Gremlin parked beside Kriket's trailer when the police drove me to Tin Town on the morning after Byrd's accident. Frankie hadn't been around the trailer in a few weeks.

My father must have seen the police cruiser through the kitchen window. He was out on the porch in a second. "What'd you do?" he called.

"Where were you?" I called back. "No one answered the phone all night."

Frankie turned to the cops. "What'd he do?"

"Your son here found some redweed," the officer told Frankie.

"He did?"

"That's right. He and some of his friends brewed some tea and went up to the mountain last night."

"You did?"

"I made the tea," I said.

"You drink it?"

"One girl drank it," I said.

"Redweed is not illegal," Frankie told the cops. "You can't arrest him for redweed."

"We didn't arrest him. Just had a few questions. They don't think the other boy's going to make it."

"Other boy? You said a girl drank it."

"Byrd," I said. "He fell."

"He's in a coma," one of the police officers said. "Just had word they're airlifting him to Cedars."

LESS THAN an hour later, I'd packed my knapsack and was on my way to the bus station to catch a bus to Los Angeles, where they'd transferred my best friend. I found Frankie at the table taking a belt from a greasy bottle of Scotch, a few stray children at his feet.

"I'm going," I said.

"Pull the plug," he said darkly.

"What?"

"Pull the plug."

"He's not—"

"You don't know."

"He's just in a coma."

"Pull my plug," Frankie said, "if I'm ever like that."

"I will."

"I'll do the same for you. A father should do that for his son."

"A father should do a lot of things for his son."

Frankie followed me out of the kitchen, taking another long pull from the bottle in his hand. "You want a ride?"

"Ride? With you? To Los Angeles?"

"'Course not." Frankie snorted. "Just out to the highway so you can hitch."

"I'm good. I'm taking a bus."

"I'll take you to the station. Going that way anyway." He patted his pockets, looking for his car keys. I spotted the keys on a cluttered table and moved quickly to snatch them.

"Wolf?" Frankie said, stopping me.

"Yeah." I hoped he hadn't seen me grab the keys.

"I mean it—pull my plug," he slurred.

"I'm trying, Frankie," I muttered as I tossed his car keys beside the trash bins outside the front door.

"Wolf?" Frankie called one last time.

"Yeah?" I turned back, thinking maybe he wanted a proper good-bye.

"Could you loan me fifty bucks?" Frankie asked.

I shook my head and left the trailer, heading for the bus station with Byrd's Swiss Army knife in my pocket.

THE BUS dropped me off near the hospital in LA. I entered through the lobby, got directions from a woman at the reception desk, then found the bank of elevators. I prayed as we rose that by some miracle Byrd would be sitting up, waiting for me, ready to crack a joke.

When the elevator doors parted I saw Harley standing tall over a crowd of other Diazes inside a glass-walled waiting room. Dantay was among them, Byrd's cousin Juan Carlos, a few other faces I recognized from the ranch, but not Lark. Harley turned to see me. His eyes blazed as he motioned me away.

I retreated but he came after me into the hall. He said, "You should go."

"Go? What about Byrd? How is he? What's happening?"

He shook his head. He couldn't look me in the eye. "Redweed?" Harley said. "You might as well have set a fire."

"It wasn't supposed to . . . he didn't even drink it . . . I . . ." I floundered.

"You brought the redweed," he said. "Isn't that true? You were the one who knew where it grew?"

"Yes."

He shook his head in disgust. "Your father's son after all?"

That cut deep. I glanced into the waiting room—a dizzying mass of dark hair and anxious eyes—and felt their waves of pain and fear. Dantay turned to see me standing there with Harley. I could see by his face that he blamed me too. Maybe they all did. I was sure Lark would set them straight about what happened though. She was probably just too shaken up to talk about it yet. Maybe Gisele Michel's lawyer-father had advised her to keep quiet.

I took the stairs down to the hospital lobby and found an armchair where I waited for hours, caressing the contours of Byrd's Swiss Army knife in my pocket, until I saw Dantay, and the others, and finally Harley, leave.

The floor was quiet when I stepped off the elevator—just the squeaking of my sneakers on the linoleum. When I came around the corner a nurse turned sharply, outraged to see me there. Her stern face softened when she got closer. She paused, sizing me up. "You're his *friend*?"

I nodded.

"The family has a problem with you," she said, having already decided, for reasons I didn't understand, that I wasn't a threat. "Do you have drugs or alcohol or weapons on your person?"

I shook my head, saying nothing about the knife, and dropped my gaze to her badge. NANCY HEARD—HEAD NURSE.

"What's your name?"

I looked up. "Wolf."

She motioned for me to follow, saying, "You'll want to make yourself scarce when his relatives are here."

White-haired Nurse Nancy was an angel of compassion, leading me down the hall to where I could see, through the windows of a small white room, Byrd—at least she said it was him—on a gurney, one of his legs and both of his arms encased in plaster casts. His head was huge, a big bulb wrapped in white bandages. He was intubated, machines blinking beside him.

"They don't want you to see him," the nurse said.

I nodded.

"You obviously love him very much."

It did occur to me then that Nurse Nancy misunderstood the nature of my relationship with Byrd and the reason that the Diazes didn't want to see me. Still, I wasn't lying, exactly, when I nodded. She pulled a chair up to the glass and left me there to sit at the window to his room.

I woke with my cheek against the glass, the sound of Harley Diaz's deep voice booming down the hall. A different nurse woke me and helped me out of the chair, and passed me some orange juice and stale toast on my way out the door.

Outside I walked the unfamiliar streets until my feet ached, muttering to myself like the homeless I'd seen scattered in the parks and pushing carts on the streets. I replayed the events leading up to Byrd's accident. Lark. Where was Lark in all this?

It went on like that for days. I left the hospital when the family arrived, avoiding detection with the help of the sympathetic nurses, waiting for some sign that Lark had straightened everything out so that Harley and the others would forgive me, waiting for Byrd to wake up so we could return to the desert, and the mountain, and our friendship. I wanted the nightmare to end.

Lark never appeared. The family didn't forgive me. Byrd didn't wake up. After the first couple of weeks the family only made the trip from Santa Sophia to Los Angeles on the weekends, then it was every other week, and then only Harley and Dantay. Byrd was nonresponsive. Who could blame them?

I spent all of my free time at the hospital. The nurses fed me their patients' leftovers, gave me fresh clothes from their husbands and sons, pretended they didn't know that I slept in a chair beside Byrd's bed nearly every night.

Nurse Nancy said that no one really knew if Byrd could hear me but encouraged me to talk to him anyway. I told him things—things I'd never told anyone else. I hoped to quiz him one day about my cache of secrets, certain he could hear me while he was in the coma. What an elaborate experiment, just to prove that the soul is without bounds.

Byrd had always been curious about my mother. I'd never told him or anybody about her, beyond the fact that I remembered the smell of her lemon-scented hairspray and that she was beautiful. My mother's story was the first thing I decided to tell him as I sat beside his plugged-in body draped in white sheets.

THERE WAS a picture of my mother at five years old wearing an elaborate white-lace First Communion dress in one of the boxes of photographs accidentally sold at some yard sale or lost long ago. (My mother and those white dresses.) I wonder if the image still exists somewhere of little Glory, hands clasped in prayer, eyes lifted to the ceiling in adoration. Frankie told me that when she was little my mother'd wanted to be a nun.

Glory became a saint instead of a nun, and gave her life to Frankie instead of God, at least in my father's version of their story, the one in which she forgives his every trespass and never speaks a harsh word. I've never believed his version of their marriage. What person would accept a spouse's lack of loyalty, and ambition, not to mention employment? And what workingwoman would not complain that the house is a disaster when she gets home from work each night, or flip her lid when the husband drinks Johnnie Walker while the baby plays in the cereal cupboard?

Aside from her name in Frankie's tattoo, and the repetition of her DNA in me, the only indelible thing about Glory Truly is her story. Even though everyone in Mercury already knew it, Frankie'd tell anyone who'd listen multiple times with varying facts, depending on his level of sobriety. He told strangers in bars. He told his parade of women, and the petty criminals who sat around the kitchen table, and the beautiful girl with a tulip tattoo at the carwash in Nevada when she'd asked, "Does the kid have a mother?" He told it clean. Told it sober. Told it better drunk.

My mother and I were home, sleeping on her lemon-scented pillows on the night Frankie wrecked my mother's Mustang convertible. That's usually how Frankie starts my mother's story—with the night he wrecked her car.

In the passenger seat when Frankie drove the convertible into the big oak tree on Old River Road was my mother's best friend, Pam Govay. Frankie and she had been wearing seat belts, and there wasn't a scratch on Frankie, but Pam broke her nose on the dashboard and it never did set right. The convertible (a sixteenth-birthday gift from her parents) was demolished, but the radio, as Frankie's story goes, was still blasting away when the ambulance arrived, playing some classic Detroit rock, or Motown song whose title Frankie changed with each telling, depending on his audience and his mood.

I asked him once, after moving to Santa Sophia, how it was that Aunt Kriket had a hundred kids and grandkids and Frankie had only me. He'd tilted his chin and commenced a mock national public service ad. "Condoms. Condoms work. I am here to tell you that I've made love to hundreds of women, maybe a thousand, and only one of them got pregnant. Condoms. They stop ninety-nine point ninety-nine percent of unwanted pregnancy. Use condoms—or you will have huge regrets."

On cue, my teenaged cousin's new baby started wailing in the other room and Frankie and I had a good laugh at the timing. But that night and for many nights after I'd lain awake glum with the knowledge that *I* was an unwanted child. When I asked Frankie about it, he'd shrugged. "Beats the alternative," he'd said.

"Wanted?" I'd asked, confused.

"Terminated," he'd said, thumping my head.

FROM THE day my mother brought me home from the hospital in Mercury until the day Frankie and I left for the desert, we lived in the same small bungalow on what everyone called Old Dewey Road, distinguished from New Dewey Road, where the mortgages were fatter, the sidewalks broader, and the homes had attached two-car garages instead of painted shacks out back with alley access.

The Listers, Garvin and Rayanne, who were much older than my parents and had four grown sons, lived a couple of blocks away on New Dewey. In photographs, bald, brown-eyed Garvin Lister, the principal at Saint Agnes's Catholic School, had the look of a hungry man, not that he was slender, quite the opposite. He'd hired my mother fresh from college, and he and his wife, Rayanne, a tiny woman with a strawberry birthmark on her forehead, had taken a parental interest in Glory Elizabeth Frost, whose parents had already passed by then.

When Glory met Frankie, a rudderless loser ten years her senior, Garvin and Rayanne discouraged the instantly serious relationship. Whether it was the smooth talk, or those supercharged pheromones of his, Frankie overcame the couple's objections to the point that Garvin paid for the wedding reception and walked my young mother down the aisle. Rayanne sat in the mother-of-the-groom spot, the only guest on Frankie's empty side of the church.

"They were like the parents we never had," Frankie'd say of the Listers, though I doubted Glory was similarly bereft of fond childhood memories. In the early days, the Listers would bring baked goods and casseroles to the newlyweds and send their strapping sons to help Frankie with the yard. But as the months passed, my young parents saw less and less of Rayanne, and the next year she'd developed a winter depression and stopped leaving the house altogether, or at least that's what Garvin told people.

When he turned fifty Garvin Lister bought himself a Corvette Stingray, metallic red with a custom sunroof. A car—or as Frankie put it, "That's no *car*; that's an *automobile!*"—well beyond any principal's salary, and outside of his capacity to drive comfortably. My father loved to see Garvin Lister pull up in that beautiful car. Sometimes Garvin let Frankie take the Stingray for a spin while he sat in the kitchen with my mother. I

remember that the smell of Garvin Lister would linger for days in our little house on Old Dewey—Juicy Fruit gum.

On the night Frankie crashed Glory's Mustang GT Convertible he'd
made a drunken call to Garvin afterward to ask if he'd give Glory a lift to
school the following day. Frankie was confused when Glory said she'd
rather walk. "Why would you not want a ride from Garve?"

"I'd rather walk, that's all. Besides, it's Ash Wednesday. We have to be
there early."

"So Garvin will get you there early. He's two blocks away."

My mother'd looked genuinely afraid. "The way he drives that thing!
Everyone talks about it in the teachers' lounge."

"Why would you own a Corvette if you're not gonna *drive* it? What
would be the point?" Frankie had laughed.

"It's not only that," she said.

"Give the poor guy the pleasure of your company. You're the daughter
he never had."

"I know."

"You make him smile."

"I know. Just lately he seems . . . And with the new car and everything . . ."

"So he speeds a little."

"It's not just the speeding. I'm worried about Rayanne."

"Worried about what?"

"People talk, Frankie."

"Talk about what?"

"I wouldn't want her to get the wrong idea."

"About you and Garve?" My father had laughed pretty hard at that.
"Who'd believe you'd take Garvin Lister over me?"

The following morning I noticed that gentle flakes of snow were falling outside of the bathroom window. I imagined the snow was falling in
honor of Ash Wednesday, the way children believe nature has motive and
intent.

The faculty at Saint Agnes's was expected at morning Mass to observe the first day of Lent. The priest would use his thumb to draw a cross of ashes on the foreheads of members of his congregation to remind—or was it to warn—thou are dust and to dust you shall return. My beautiful mother told me all about it as she spritzed her curls with the lemony hairspray. I felt strongly that I did not want her to leave the house.

One detail that Frankie left out when he told the story is that my mother wore a special dress that day, purchased from a secondhand shop in Mount Clemens—which I know because I was there, hidden in the rack of scratchy wool blazers, and I'd watched her find it—long and white with sheer, flowing batwing sleeves. It's the dress from my memory. The one she wore when she twirled me in the dressing room mirror.

That morning, Garvin—hungry, haunted Garvin—pulled up to the curb in his fine automobile. If I close my eyes I can smell my mother's lemon hair and feel her pink lips whisper, "Always," when she nuzzles my cheek. I cried when she let me go. Before Glory climbed inside the sports car she smiled at me and placed her pretty hand over her heart, as she did each morning. I wanted to punch Frankie in the nose when he touched his hand to his heart in kind. That farewell was meant for me.

Later that afternoon, Frankie says, he felt something shift in the air. My father claims that I started complaining about a stomachache. Soon I was feverish, vomiting, crying. Frankie couldn't comfort me, and Glory was late. Glory was never late. My father called the school office but got no answer. He called Garvin Lister's house but got no answer.

Frankie never responds when people ask where his four-year-old son was during what happened next. He seems not to remember that the feverish child with the stomachache followed him, stumbling some distance behind as he strode up the street looking for Garvin Lister's car.

I wanted to find my mother too, but I couldn't see Mr. Lister's shiny sports car in the road or in the driveway of any of the houses on New Dewey or Old. The sun was falling when Frankie turned back in the direction of home, and he must have caught the glint of red metal through the slats in a fence. I followed him through the walkway and tried to peer through the open back gate where the red Corvette was parked in the alley.

Two oily black crows tearing at a trash bag started making a racket to warn Frankie off their stash. "Go to hell," Frankie cawed back at the birds, laughing at first, then seeming confused when Garvin Lister looked up to see him and didn't crack a smile.

"What's up, Garve?" Frankie called. "You all right?"

Mr. Lister was sitting alone in the front seat of his car, ashes from the priest's sign of the cross still on his forehead. He took a long swig from a silver flask. My father had a flask exactly like it—a gift from my mother.

"Garve?" my father called, drawing closer. "That my flask?"

"Stop there, Frankie!" Garvin Lister warned.

The crows took our attention briefly, flapping away like they knew what was coming.

"You seen Glory, Garve?" my father called.

Then, rising from beneath the dashboard, was my mother's face; mascara smeared, eyes bleary, lips raw, the shadow of the ash cross on her forehead. She found me where I was hiding by the trash cans and stared at me blankly through the car window, then she turned to look at my father, and I did too.

"What the hell?" Frankie said, nearly hysterical at what he saw or thought he saw. "What the *hell*?"

My mother pulled the arms of her white dress up over her shoulders and I could see her mouthing my father's name before turning to say something to Mr. Lister in the front seat. I remember the blue and gray snapping sounds the locks made as he pressed the button to lock the doors. I remember seeing the nose of the small black gun in his hand.

My mother was struggling to get out of the car. Mr. Lister's fingers held Glory's pretty blond curls in one fist and the shiny black gun in the other.

"Frankie! Frankie!" my mother screamed.

"Okay, Glory. Okay, baby. It's okay. It's okay." Frankie made a move toward the car.

Garvin shouted, "No!"

My mother held my gaze briefly and mouthed, *Wolf.*

No time to say good-bye.

"Carpe diem!" Mr. Lister shouted, then pressed the black gun to my mother's head and pulled the trigger.

Carpe diem. I chanted those words in my head to drown out my father's howls, running down the narrow alley as fast and hard and far as my small legs had ever taken me. *Carpe diem. Carpe diem. Carpe diem.* The mantra carried me to my house, which I'd found by the green peace sign Frankie'd painted on the side of the purple garage. I busted through the back door and streaked for the safety of Glory's bed, where I'd closed my eyes, breathing her lemon scent on the pillow, imagining her whispering voice and petting hand. *Just a dream, little Wolf. Not really my face. Carpe diem. Carpe diem Carpe diem.*

The next morning I woke in my mother's bed, which usually meant I'd had a nightmare. Beneath the covers, I searched for Glory's warm skin, awash in relief when I heard my mother's footsteps in the hall.

When she pulled back the covers I blinked against the light, disturbed to find that my mother's eyes were bruised and blackened, a sloping white splint mending her broken nose. "You awake?" she said.

"Mama?" I said, hoping that my mother wouldn't have to wear the ugly white splint on her nose for long. "Mama?" I did not understand why my mother had different eyes. And darker hair.

"An awful thing happened, Wolf." The voice belonged to Pam Govay. "I'm going to tell you. Okay?"

"Okay."

"You have to be a big boy now. Okay?"

"Okay."

"Something happened to your mama."

"Mama?"

"There was an accident, okay?" Pam Govay said from behind the white splint.

I must have remembered what happened in the alley then because I stopped calling for my mother.

"She's gone," Pam Govay said. "And Frankie's gonna need someone around to help him through this and that's gonna be me. Okay?"

"Okay."

Mistaken identity—a case of mistaken identity—that was the only explanation that my child's mind could faintly grasp. In that white dress, my mother had looked too much like an angel.

THE STORY of what happened in the alley made the national news, but I never found a clipping about it in the blue house on Old Dewey Road, and I doubt that Garvin Lister's last words would have made it in anyway. In fourth grade I'd read the microfiche at the Mercury Public Library and discovered that Mr. Lister had killed himself, and his passenger, Glory Elizabeth Truly, with a small-caliber handgun registered to his wife, Rayanne. It was speculated that stress over the school board investigation into his misuse of funds and the discovery of his prescription drug abuse contributed to the murder/suicide.

The newspaper didn't say anything about Frankie being a witness. And no one seemed to know that the victim's little boy, feverish and confused, would never forget the look on his mother's face, or the words the man shouted before everything went red.

I was very young when I first told Frankie about my memory of Glory in the alley and about Garvin Lister shouting, "Carpe diem." He'd blanched, and I knew that it was a true memory because no one had ever told me that my mother was wearing a white, flowing dress on

that Ash Wednesday she was killed. One day I asked Frankie what *carpe diem* meant. "Buyer be aware," Frankie said solemnly. "Buyer be a-motherfucking-ware."

When I was a child I wondered what Garvin Lister had meant when he shouted *Buyer be aware* in the seconds before he left the planet. Who was the buyer? What was he buying? What should he be aware of? I'd accepted that what Mr. Lister did was the desperate act of a desperate man, but I wanted to find sense in his final words. Later I learned that *carpe diem* actually meant *seize the day*. I couldn't understand what Garvin Lister intended by that either, since he was not seizing the day but relinquishing it fully.

My mother has come to me over the years, a lemon-scented draft through an open window. "Wolf," she whispers.

Glory. Always.

THERE WE were, the Devines and me, on the morning of our third lost day. It was shortly after I'd unwittingly told them the whole story about what had happened to my friend.

We were quiet, watching the sun wash over the ragged terrain—the serrated green pines, the gray rock, and the brittle brush—praying for our rescue, wondering why they hadn't found us yet. *They* had grown large in all of our imaginations, to be sure. "*They'll* be coming soon," Bridget said, for the twentieth time. "*They* must have dozens out looking for us by now."

"They'll be able to track our prints," Nola said. "Won't they, Wolf?"

"Okay," I said. I was remembering something from my dream— something about a tree. And something else, something important.

"Wolf?"

I sat there, paralyzed, trying to remember what it was. Something about a pine tree. A tree trunk.

"You all right, Wolf?" Vonn asked.

"We gotta get back to the wall." I tried to stand, but my stomach was in turmoil from hunger and dehydration, and maybe a little from my story about Byrd.

"Last night you said something about making a climbing rope," Vonn said.

Nola passed the remnants of the knapsack to her granddaughter. "You're handy, Vonn. Maybe you could braid what's left of it together."

"I could try," Vonn said. "It's pretty ripped up though."

"Maybe there's something else we could use. Vines or something?" Nola turned to me. "Do you think?"

"We could look for some plant or vine. It's a good idea, Nola," I said.

"I'll go," Vonn volunteered

"Okay," I said. "You two rest, right, Nola? Bridget?"

"I'm fine," Nola said.

"You're not fine, Mim," Bridget said. "I'm having terrible stomach spasms. You must be too."

"A little."

"Am I starving? Are we starving, Wolf?"

"You can go three weeks without food. Remember?" I said. "What you're feeling now are just hunger pains."

"I used to get those between the appetizer and the entrée," Bridget said, and we all managed a laugh.

"My stomach hurts too," Vonn admitted.

"It hurt before we left," Bridget pointed out.

"You were sick last week too," Nola said. "We thought it was the rotisserie chicken."

"Maybe I caught a bug," Vonn said.

VONN AND I searched high and low for a fibrous plant that I could make a corded rope with. "We're too high up for yucca," I said to myself, then to Vonn, "Where's that mesh bag?"

"Maybe she left it up there," Vonn said, gesturing at the ridge. "Maybe she took it off to push the log and all this searching has been for nothing."

Maybe she was right. "We should go back. I can't waste time looking for something to make a rope."

"Wait, I have to . . ." Vonn said shyly.

"You do?"

"I just . . . need some privacy."

"I'll stay right here," I said. I knew she couldn't need to urinate and blushed at the thought that the girl might be menstruating.

Vonn went to a spot behind some juniper bushes, near a massive fallen log, and squatted down.

Seeing Vonn's head drop behind the fallen tree trunk, I called, "You okay?"

"Yeah," Vonn answered uncertainly.

"You want help?" I called.

"No," she called back emphatically.

After a short time she appeared again, her face blotchy from crying. I didn't wonder if her tears were for any reason beyond the obvious. When I moved to embrace her she ducked my arm. "Come on," she said. "We should look at Nola's wrist. Redress it. Kinda miraculous, isn't it? The sterasote?"

"You cleaned it. Getting rid of all that dead tissue had to have helped."

"Don't remind me," Vonn said, cringing. "That's worse than anything I've done at the Petting Zoo and they make me clean all the cages."

"The Petting Zoo?"

"That's the name of the pet clinic–animal rescue place where I work."

"I've been thinking about getting a dog," I said. "I like dogs."

"Me too," Vonn said, "but I'm such a vagabond."

I shrugged. "Maybe I'll come to the rescue place and get a dog. You know. When we get back."

"That would seem about right. Balance the universe a little," Vonn said. "I had a cat once. Sort of."

"Stray?"

"Two boyfriends before my mother brought home the idiot from Camarillo there was the Goof from Golden Hills. He had a cat. So I sort of had a cat. This fat, old black cat with a bitten-off ear. Sad cat. Lame front leg. One tooth. I don't remember the guy's name but the cat was named Midnight. I went on a junk-food binge after Bridget told me Goof was moving in. I was feeling sorry for myself, and then this fat, old black cat limps into the TV room and he nuzzles my leg, and he tries to jump into my lap but he's too old and fat, so I have to lift him up myself."

"Can't imagine Bridget as a cat person."

"Bridget didn't know the guy was bringing his cat. She didn't even know he had a cat, which is pretty shocking because it shed over everything.

"They went away for the weekend and I fed Midnight these soft cat treats made for toothless old cats that I had delivered from the grocery store, and I just let him sit there in my lap eating for two days straight. Picked him up and set him down in his litter box a few times a day. I thought I was being nice."

"Lucky cat."

"I had gas. All that crap I was eating," Vonn went on. "It was bad."

Her chin was quivering, so I didn't laugh.

"I was sitting there at Bridget's with Midnight on my lap, and Bridget and Goof walk into the room with another couple and they hit this deadly wall of stink and they start to howl and gag and all I can say is, 'Um, I think your cat's sick.'"

She paused to swallow. "The guy sees the empty packages of cat treats and grabs Midnight off my lap and kicks him out the back door. I went out to the porch to apologize, but he wouldn't come near me." Vonn sniffed, but she had no tears to spend.

"So you blamed the cat? That's all?"

"On Monday when I got home from school Midnight was gone. My mother said her boyfriend had taken him to the vet. I felt bad because I knew I'd overfed him and I hoped they could give him some pills or something. When I refilled Midnight's water bowl Bridget looked at me like I was crazy. That's when she told me that Midnight was being put down."

"Oh."

"The Goof had said any animal that smelled as bad as that cat smelled must be rotting from the inside out. He said it'd be cruel to let him live."

"Oh."

"I jumped into the car and drove straight to the vet, but it was too late."

We walked on in silence for a beat.

"I killed Midnight."

"You didn't kill Midnight. You were just part of his story at the end of his days," I said. "Besides, Midnight got to spend all that time in your lap. Paradise. I mean . . ."

"When I came up here to stay with Mim after Pip died, I saw they were hiring at the neighborhood vet. It's my job to pet the animals when they go if their owners choose not to be there."

Closer to the cave we could hear Nola humming the concerto I'd heard her hum before. It was then that Vonn realized she'd left the shredded knapsack back at the fallen log where she'd gone to cry.

Without missing a beat I spun around and began to chug back through the bushes to retrieve the thing, calling, "Go back with the others."

But I turned to find Vonn staggering after me in the wool socks and ridiculous green flip-flops. "I'll go," she said between breaths. "I'll get it!"

"I'll get it," I insisted, turning into the wind.

Breathless, I came to the place where Vonn had excused herself to be alone. I saw the shredded knapsack right away, and when I bent to scoop it up I saw something else—a sliver of silver the length and width of a toothpick sticking out from beneath a curiously set rock. I knew before I lifted it that I was about to find one of the granola bar wrappers from Bridget's lost bag.

I took it in my shaking hands—one-half of a granola bar intact inside the carefully folded foil.

Vonn had eaten the other half. I didn't need to have witnessed the crime. The night before, when I'd pressed my dry, parched lips to hers, I'd detected the merest whiff of cinnamon. That was the *something else* in her kiss. That was the something I'd noticed, and denied, and ignored, and knew I'd have to return to.

When I stood up, Vonn was there, wide-eyed. She had no words. I didn't either, only thoughts and sounds and smells—cinnamon, oats, brown sugar. The crows cawed from the pines nearby as I stared at the slim square of granola bar.

Vonn dropped to her knees, looking up at me. "I found it here, beside this log, yesterday. I called for Bridget, but she didn't hear me. I looked everywhere for the bag, the other bars, the water, but it was just this one, just sitting right there."

Together we looked up into the dense pines towering above our heads. Had the bag been hurled this far when we'd tumbled? It was possible.

"I waited for Bridget to get back, and then I couldn't . . . I was staring at the granola bar and then I opened it and I smelled it and I thought of how small it was to divide in four—such a tease . . . and no nutrition . . . being so small—but I still knew I shouldn't eat it. Couldn't eat it."

"But you did."

"I thought I'd have the tiniest nibble, and then I had another and a little more and a little more."

"And when we stopped earlier?" I asked. "A little more?"

"I'm so afraid to die," she breathed.

Even as claws sprang from my fingertips, I forgave her. Even as I growled at her, ripping at the silver foil, I forgave her.

I opened my mouth and threw the morsel of that granola bar down my throat, and then began to gag.

"Keep it down," Vonn begged. "Swallow it, for God's sake, Wolf."

I swallowed the lump of sugar and oats. Then for the first time on the mountain I began to cry, and for the first and only time since my mother died, a beautiful woman took me in her arms and rocked me like a child.

WHEN WE returned to the cave, I took a long look at Bridget, who was sallow and gaunt and exhausted. There was no question that the water bottles and other granola bars had not been found by Bridget. Or Nola—she hadn't been out of my sight. Most likely, I thought, the other granola bars had been found by the ground squirrels and dragged away. Maybe the bottles of water landed in one of the denser areas of brush or were stuck on a pine bough too high up to see.

My shame over eating that fragment of food weighed on me heavily, but it fortified me too. Redemption is a powerful motivator.

Vonn and I avoided looking at each other.

The yellow canteen, containing a cup or so of water, sat between us. I felt nauseated remembering the redweed, and worse that I'd shared the story of what happened to Byrd with the Devines.

"I'm so hungry, Wolf. Can we eat grass? Can we chew bark?" Bridget asked.

"Don't eat grass," I warned. "It'll just make you vomit and lose more fluid."

"I'm so thirsty, I feel shrunken," Bridget said.

I sniffed the air. It smelled of the rain to come. I'd been wrong before though, and didn't want to raise the Devines' hopes again. I tried to stand, mumbling, "Gotta get back to the wall."

"You're dizzy, Wolf," Vonn said.

"I'm all right." But I wasn't.

"I was thinking, maybe if I borrowed your shoes, Bridget, I could try the wall. We could let Wolf rest," Vonn said.

"Because you think I can't do it?"

"No, just to give you a rest," Vonn said.

"Vonn, you're a lot shorter than me. If I don't have the wingspan for it, you don't either."

"And my feet are half the size of yours," Bridget said.

"And how would you find your way back to the Mountain Station even if you got up there?" Nola asked.

"I'll worry about the wall, Vonn," I said. "You and Bridget need to find what's left of that blue bag."

"What do you mean, what's left of it?" Bridget asked.

"Just find the bag," I begged.

Bridget looked back and forth from me to Vonn. "Did something happen between you two?"

Vonn and I must have looked guilty.

Bridget spat on the ground at my feet, which was no mean feat considering our degree of dehydration.

"No!" I insisted.

"Bridget," Nola soothed. "You're being ridiculous. At a time like this? How could you think . . . ?"

Vonn turned toward the morning sky and said, "I found one of the granola bars."

I hung my head.

"Thank God!" Bridget cried.

"That's wonderful, Vonn!" Nola croaked.

Vonn's voice was not her own. "I ate it."

Nola sat blinking, while Bridget said, "I don't understand."

"I ate it. I found it and I ate it."

"She's not telling the truth," I said, interrupting. "I ate half of it."

The wind roared in then and spoke for all of us. Such a revelation, in different circumstances, with less fragile beings, or more fragile beings, might have elicited an entirely different response: fistfight, screaming, pushing, hair pulling. On the mountain, on that third day, the only rage came from the wind. A dubious gift to the desperate—clarity, charity, perspective.

"There's some water left in the canteen," I said after a while, grateful for their silent absolution. "Mrs. Devine, you and Bridget should finish it."

Vonn cringed. "I need the water too."

Bridget grabbed the canteen and, twisting off the cap, brought it to her lips. After a fractional sip she passed it to her daughter, who took a grateful sip before passing it to her grandmother, who drank a small amount before she passed it to me.

"Now you only have to forgive yourselves," Nola said to Vonn and me.

I took a small sip from the yellow canteen and thought of Byrd.

"Wolf?"

"I'm all right."

"You said Byrd was in the hospital in a coma. You never said . . ." Bridget ventured.

I felt my face redden.

"What happened to him?" Vonn asked.

"We have to get back to the wall," I said. "I'll tell you on the way."

Nola took my proffered arm, and we moved together, slowly, over the rock.

I didn't want to tell the rest of Byrd's story, but I did.

ALL THOSE weeks at Byrd's bedside I prayed for him to come back without actually knowing where he was. Sometimes instead of talking to Byrd's body under the white hospital sheets I spoke to the air, and sometimes I didn't even talk out loud but tried to find him in some corridor of my wandering mind. Sometimes I sang to him. Sometimes he shuddered.

Frankie's words haunted me. *Pull the plug.* I never considered pulling Byrd's plug, but the way Frankie'd said it—like he wished it were him in the coma, like he was so weary he'd rather leave the burden of his life to someone else—just have it done with. Pull the plug. I felt sorry for my father because I understood too well. While the mountain had changed me, made me stronger, brought me peace, the desert had been Frankie's final ruin. Late nights, women, alcohol, drugs, gangs, gambling and all of that without leaving Tin Town. What he'd said about clean living? He'd gone from dirty to irredeemable within weeks—selling, buying, stealing, leaving for days at a time to go on a bender, or for weeks at a time lazing around in the quiet home of some sexual conquest until she kicked him out. I saw less of Frankie at Kriket's trailer than I saw of Yago. Yago visited his stash more than Frankie visited his son.

At the hospital the nurses brought me a covered plate of turkey dinner on Christmas Day, and clean clothes from someone's tall husband, and they let me take a hot shower while the staff had their party down the hall. I was in Byrd's room, still wet from the shower and with a towel around my waist, waiting for the nurse to find the bag of clean clothes, when the door opened. It was Lark. She did not seem surprised to see me. "You're not supposed to be here," she said.

"You going to tell your dad?"

She shrugged and handed me a grocery bag, saying, "The nurse asked me to give you these. Clothes?"

It had been only weeks since that night at Secret Lake, but she was different, older somehow, wearing baggy sweats and sneakers. "How is he?" she asked, hardly taking her eyes from his body on the hospital bed.

"They're taking the tube out next week." I stepped behind a curtain in the small room to change.

"What's the point?"

"What do you mean?"

"Isn't he a . . . you know . . . ?"

I knew what she was asking. "No."

"My dad says he won't ever be the same."

"No one is."

"I'm not," she said quietly.

"I thought Harley would want you home for Christmas," I said when I joined her at Byrd's bedside.

"I'm driving to the desert this afternoon with Gisele." She turned away from me, sniffling.

"You're still friends?"

"Why wouldn't I be?" she asked.

"I don't know."

"It wasn't *her* fault," Lark said.

We were quiet, listening to the machines.

"I'm sorry," I said. "Lark, I'm so sorry."

She looked me in the eye for the first time.

"I got the redweed. I made the tea."

"For me though. You did it for me." She shifted her gaze to Byrd.

"He's going to get better," I promised.

The way she looked at me—I read so much into her expression that day. I mistook her guilt for lust, and her pity for affection, and I saw a promise for a future when there was only fervent hope she'd never have to see me again.

"I'll write to you," I said.

"Okay."

"Will you write me back?"

"I'm gonna be pretty busy."

"I'll write to you anyway. Even if you don't write me back."

Had I seen the truth in that moment, I'd never have sought Lark out at the church before her friend's wedding. Never uttered those pitiful words broadcast to the crowd—the final straw. Still, I don't like to wonder what would have become of the Devines, what would have become of all of us, if I hadn't been on the mountain that day.

* * *

ONE FRIDAY morning, early in the New Year, I rode the hospital elevator up to Byrd's floor, groggy and sore from having slept, or rather not slept, on a park bench.

His ventilator had been removed successfully, and Byrd had been breathing on his own for more than a week. Harley and the others started making more frequent, unexpected trips to the hospital, staying at Byrd's bedside long into the night. I'd have to leave to wander the streets, and sleep in the park with the other homeless. The nurses would hang a surgical mask in the window when it was all right for me to come back.

Each day Byrd breathed on his own seemed worse than the one before. He groaned almost constantly, a low growling sound that Nurse Nancy said didn't necessarily mean he was in pain, but it was awful to hear. By the end of the second week there was no improvement.

I'd watched Harley from a distance, plodding up the steps to the hospital. I knew how he felt. I was anxious that day, pacing in the parking lot, looking up at the window for my all-clear sign. When I saw Nurse Nancy hang up the surgical mask only an hour after Harley's arrival I didn't see it as a good sign and bolted for the door.

The elevator doors parted on Byrd's floor and I was shocked to see Harley there—I was sure I'd seen the surgical mask hanging in the window. Something was wrong. There were other Diaz relatives in the corridor. Dantay and Juan Carlos. Not Lark. Harley lunged forward and grasped my shoulders, embracing me warmly. Then he looked me in the eye for the first time since the accident. "Lark told me you had nothing to do with it. She told me it was all her friend's idea—that you and Byrd were against the redweed all along."

I wanted to ask what took her so long to tell the truth, but I could see there was something else going on.

"He opened his eyes," Harley said, grinning.

"Byrd's awake?"

"Last night. The nurse said he called out for you."

I shot down the hall and burst into the hospital room, where I found

Byrd being attended by several of the nurses. Something wasn't right. I knew it by the nurses' somber faces. I drew closer to the bed, where Byrd was blinking rapidly.

As I got closer to the bed he stopped blinking entirely, and focused on the ceiling with a strange expression. His upper lip twitched as his gaze shifted low, then high, like he was a lizard scoping a fly.

Leaning over the bed, crowding his eyeline, I could see that he didn't recognize me. There was no brightness whatsoever in his expression. When I said my name he didn't blink. When I said his name he didn't react. He didn't seem to know I was in the room. He didn't seem to know *he* was in the room.

Nurse Nancy appeared at my side. She put her warm hand on my shoulder, telling me with a gentle squeeze that I should have low expectations. Harley joined us in the room, repeating what the doctors had said about the unpredictable nature of brain injuries. Recovery could be slow or rapid, or there would be no recovery. Or full recovery. The only thing the doctors agreed on was that it was a miracle that Byrd survived at all.

BACK ON the mountain, I wished I'd declined the request to tell the rest of Byrd's story. The Devines were more than a little disheartened by the uncertain ending. The injustice of it was hard to bear.

Carrying sticks to protect ourselves—even Nola doing so—we made our way to the wall. From my angle at the bottom of it, the rock face appeared to have changed overnight—growing higher, steeper, more concave.

"I'm glad, at least, that you didn't pull Byrd's plug," Bridget said. "I thought that's what you were going to tell us."

Something streaked through the branches over our heads.

"Did you see that?" Nola asked, gesturing with the stick in her good hand.

"I think it was an owl," Vonn said.

"We need to crush more sterasote," I said, noting Nola's decline.

Bridget was proud to dispense a cache of the leaves from her pocket. "I got some more leaves earlier." We settled down on the metates where Nola had fallen and hit her head the day before and began to crush the sterasote. I became mesmerized by the image on the bloodstained rock in my periphery, the sharp portrait of a bird in flight. It seemed like a message. But I couldn't think of what it meant. Was Byrd saying he was here with me? Overhead, the crows cawed, attacking a Cooper's hawk that'd been swooping in to raid their nest. I thought of eggs, which made me feel hungry and sick.

A branch snapped in the brush behind us. We stopped, reaching for our sticks. Coyotes. We waited, hearts thudding, primed for the fight. I sniffed the wind but couldn't find their scent. Scenes from the previous night flashed before me: Vonn's toes in my mouth, the coyote shaking Pip's remains, the pair of animals making that magnificent leap over Devine Divide.

The memory of the leaping coyotes sparked more images from my dream, and I remembered the part where my mother told me to make a bridge. "Last night," I said, "I had this strange dream."

"A future-dream?" Bridget said, leaning in. "What did you dream?"

I had to see for myself if what I'd seen in my dream really existed, and so I rose and began to lurch over the rocks and through the brush toward the crevice. I must have looked like I'd lost my mind, mumbling, *My mother said to make a bridge.*

"Wolf?"

"WOLF!" Vonn shouted, chasing after me. "What about the sterasote?"

Bridget helped Nola to her feet, and they followed too, all of them calling my name.

"Come on," I shouted, charged with the notion that my dream had been a message. I badly wanted to believe.

And there it was, near the sterasote bush—the moss-mottled lodge-pole pine that my mother had been standing on. "Okay," I said.

The fallen pine was part-hidden in the brush, leaning against a massive boulder—not unusual in this terrain—not rooted but fallen from the ridge above. "This is it!"

The Devines could only stare.

The log was long enough to span the crevice and appeared sturdy enough too. If we could stand it up, with a good push from eight hands (well, seven with Nola's injury) it would fall across the divide and become locked in by the two large boulders that flanked the slope.

"Whatever you're thinking—no," Bridget said.

"This log was in my dream. My mother told me to make a bridge."

"I believe you, Wolf," Bridget said. "But no."

"It's our only way out," I said.

"What else did you dream?" Bridget asked.

"Byrd told me to look for a pine tree."

"So we could make a bridge?"

"No, another pine. It was standing alone near this wide bare mesa."

"You really think this is our only chance?" Vonn said to clarify.

"He said it was the way."

"The way to Secret Lake?" Nola asked. We all turned to look at her. She was shivering badly. I took off my parka and put it on her shoulders.

"The Mountain Station's that way," I said, pointing. "See up there, where the ridges connect? If we can get across here, and get back up there, I know I can find our way back now that I have my bearings."

The Devines studied the spot where the ridges joined at the top of the slope.

"It does look like it'd be easy enough to get there," Vonn said.

"I won't be crawling across any bridge," Bridget said.

"That mesa from my dream? Maybe we'll see it up there where the ridges connect."

"What if it gets foggy again?"

"Then we'll wait it out, but at least we're up there, which is better than being trapped down here."

"But won't it roll?" Nola said, pointing at the log.

"Look at the crux of those two boulders on the other side. If we can all push together, from here, the log will fall right there. See? And on this side it's stabilized by this tree and this boulder."

"How'd it get here?" Vonn asked.

"Fell from up there," Bridget said. "Like us."

"Maybe it was the Cahuilla," Nola said. "The ones who made the mortar holes. Maybe they were going to make a bridge."

"Why didn't they, then?" Vonn asked. "And how did they get here if they didn't have a bridge?"

"Would it even hold our weight?" Nola wondered.

"Lodgepole is strong," I said.

"I'll wait here. You can send back the rescue team," Bridget said.

We were silent for a while, letting the wind cool our fear. A fascinating disconnect, because while our circumstances demanded urgency, our thoughts were inclined to wander, make long detours for the right answer.

"What if no one is looking for us?" I said finally.

We stood together, staring at the moss-covered log.

"Even if we could push that log over, I will not be walking across it," Bridget said again.

"I could never do that either," Nola said.

"I'm thinking more that we straddle the log and *shimmy* across." Like me and Byrd in the storm on Angel's Peak.

A pair of crows settled near some brush higher up on the rocky steps, and when I turned to look at them I noticed the deep fault in the boulder to the right of the sterasote bush. I'd been standing on that very rock in the dusk collecting leaves only hours ago, but looking at it from this new angle, I noticed that the fissure was deep, and in fact seemed to cut through the length of the boulder.

Time. Maybe it was the rhythmically swaying pine branches that put me in mind of a clock. The sun was moving in and out of the clouds, casting shadows, then stealing them away so quickly it made me dizzy. I clapped my hands together, as much to get my own attention as that of the Devines. "We have to make decisions. I say we try the bridge."

"I say we stay," Bridget voted. "No offense to your dream, Wolf. It's too big a risk."

"But what if no one is looking?" Vonn asked. "Like Wolf said."

"They *must* be by now," Bridget said weakly.

"Look over there, Bridget!" I said, pointing to the gentle slope on the other side. "We can be home in a few hours. A few *hours*."

"Do you honestly think that I am going to *shimmy* over a hundred-foot-deep crevice?"

"If we don't do it today," I said quietly, "we might not have the strength tomorrow."

"Let's do it," Nola said. "Come on, Bridge."

"We need everyone to push it," Vonn said.

Bridget paused, then glanced at Vonn. "I guess it wouldn't hurt to try to put the log across. See if it would even work," she said.

"So we push it. And it drops down and lands right exactly there?" Vonn asked.

I nodded. And prayed.

We didn't waste another breath before gripping the big piece of timber, and on the count of three, as if we'd rehearsed it, as if we'd done it a thousand times, we heaved and hoed and pushed the log until it was vertical, then we dropped it, moss side up, across the crevice. It fell exactly at the crux, locked in by the rocks on either side, precisely where we'd intended.

We celebrated briefly before we began the next job, quickly gathering as many of the sterasote leaves and stems as we could stuff into our pockets for Nola's poultice. I cautioned the women about the large, loose boulder that could break off at any moment—or cling for another thousand years. That's how it is with rocks.

Finally there was the matter of order. "I'll go first," Vonn said, trembling. Without further ado she mounted the log, which teetered when she leaned over to grasp it, and threatened to roll when she dangled her legs on either side. Until we saw the first, then the second green flip-flop drop away and float down to the unseen bottom of the dark crevice, no one had considered that she should take them off first.

"Don't look down!" Nola called.

Vonn did look down, and my stomach turned watching her teeter and flail. I closed my eyes, expecting to hear the sound of her body splashing against the rocks below. When I opened my eyes I was shocked to see she that she was moving forward, chanting, "Please. Please. Please."

I joined in, whispering, "Please." Nola joined in, and Bridget too, until our prayer was a song. Even the crows shut the hell up to hear it.

When Vonn reached the other end she heaved herself up and flopped onto the slope like a drowning man on a beach. Chest heaving, too stunned to celebrate, she waved as I squeezed Nola's good hand on one side of me and Bridget's on the other. Vonn's bravery inspired me.

Having watched her cling to the log as she bucked forward, I realized that Nola couldn't possibly keep her balance with only one working arm. For no particular reason, I felt confident that the log would bear our joint weight.

"Come on, Nola," I called over the wind. "You and me."

She adjusted the yellow canteen on the strap around her neck as I climbed aboard the log, alarmed to find that the moss was slipperier than I'd bargained for. Once I was balanced, Nola marshaled her courage and mounted behind me, clinging to my waist with her good hand, as if we were riding a motorcycle, the yellow canteen a hard knot in my back.

"Okay," I said. "One, two, three." But when we tried to move, our dual forces were too great and we succeeded only in almost dislodging the log from where it was anchored in the rocks.

"I'll move," I told Nola. The wind had kicked up, and I needed to shout to be heard. "Then you move." And we did—in a graceless but effective fashion, until I stopped. I don't know why the hell I did it but about halfway across that log I stopped and looked down, and I saw far below, on a black river of rock, one of Vonn's green flip-flops, and attached to the green flip-flop, I was sure, the broken body of Vonn, or was that Byrd? It didn't matter that I knew I was hallucinating.

I lost my balance and swung this way and that, taking Nola with me. Gasping, I steadied our joined bodies. Paralysis came next, not literally, of course, since I controlled my muscle groups sufficiently to keep my grip, but I couldn't move forward, even when Nola nudged me. Even when she began to tremble and squeezed my torso so tightly I thought the canteen would fracture one of my ribs.

Vonn shouted from the other side. "Move, Wolf! Go!" I locked eyes with her and in a moment gained control over my muscles again and started to inch forward, dragging Nola's trembling weight on my back.

"Keep going, Wolf! Good!" It was my mother's voice now. *Glory.* I could smell her lemony hairspray. I stayed focused on Vonn's face, and when my feet met the rigid granite on the other side, I called over the wind, "Help me pull Nola up."

I turned my head to tell Nola, "Hold on for one second. Okay? Balance for one second so that Vonn and I can get you off the log!"

But Nola wobbled the second I stepped off, and I had to spin around to catch her, grabbing her by the closest limb—her broken wrist. She screamed like hell, but I didn't let go. Vonn caught her by her other arm and we pulled her to safety off the slope.

Nola tried to catch her breath as Vonn calmly tugged her wrist bones back into place, then tightened the makeshift bandage and splints.

For all the pain she must have endured, Nola didn't even look down at her wrist. She couldn't take her eyes off her daughter, standing alone and terrified on the other side.

Bridget.

We all turned to look at her alone on the other side. I've hardly pitied a person more than I pitied her in that moment. "Your turn, Bridget," I called into the wind.

"I know!" she said.

"Sit down at the edge!" Vonn shouted.

"I can't do it!" Bridget shouted, backing away.

"You can, Bridget! You're in the best shape of anyone!"

I was fully prepared to shimmy back across the crevice to bring Bridget with me the way I had Nola, but I have to admit I was relieved when she started bravely toward the log.

"Don't look down!" Nola called.

"You can do it, Bridget!" I shouted.

She was trembling. We could see it, even at fifteen feet.

Vonn shouted, "Put your legs on either side!"

Bridget crouched down, focusing on Vonn's instructions.

The wind blew hard and mean, invading the spaces between trees and rocks and us and courage.

"Swing your left leg over," Vonn called. "And now your right. Shift your weight."

"Like you're riding a horse!" I called.

"She's scared of horses," Vonn and Nola said together.

"Like you're riding a bike!" Vonn called.

Bridget swung her legs and shifted her weight and finally managed to straddle the log. The wind pushed and pulled her but she held fast.

"Slow. Start slow!" Vonn called. "The wind's picked up!"

Surprising us all, Bridget shook off the gale and began to inch forward, strong and steady, her eyes on Vonn just as mine had been.

The wind whipped us from every direction. On the slope side, Nola gripped a pine trunk with her good hand.

We held our breath watching Bridget fight the wind and maintain her balance on that moss-covered log strung out over the abyss. I had the terrible feeling that she was going to look down and see Vonn's green flip-flops like I had.

She stopped.

Vonn and I shared a look.

"What is it, Bridge?" Nola shouted.

"Ants," she called back, staring down at the log.

Then she looked up at us, and we could see a family of them scattering over her neck and cheek and into her hair.

One hand flew to her face. The other hand slipped on the velvety moss, and she teetered, only to be further undone by a stray wind that tore through the pass and almost blew her off the log altogether. She managed to regain her balance but just barely, and we watched her panic about what to do next, aware that the ants were traveling over her back and shoulders.

"This way!" we shouted, but Bridget started shimmying backward, which must have felt safer, peeling her legs off the log and throwing herself into the brush away from the cliff's edge on the other side to swat at the ants until they were dead.

The wind tore through the canyon and careened around the trees and raced toward us with alarming strength and speed. Couldn't help but take it personally.

Bridget turned toward the smoke-gray sky as we stood on the other side of Devine Divide, swerving our heads to look too—because we all heard it—the unmistakable sound of a helicopter.

I was sure I saw the outline of the blades pushing through the clouds. I remember that I pointed. Vonn and Nola scanned the sky as the wind pummeled us from the rear and nearly pushed us over the ledge. Bridget opened her mouth to the heavens and screamed, a primitive sound, like nothing I'd heard before or since, a wail that drew from the depths of her fear and grief and rage and regret. It was one of the saddest sounds I've ever heard. I held my breath waiting for the rockslide, but it didn't come.

Instead, the heavens opened up and rained down upon us. Finally. A deluge with no warning—well, of course there were many warnings, but they'd all seemed like false alarms. The rain seemed to come in answer to Bridget's scream, and it was torrential, a blessing and a curse. We held our tongues out to catch the fat, wet drops and slurped the cold fluid that collected in our cupped palms. I showed the women how to lap at the rainwater that quickly gathered in the hollows of the rocks.

On the other side of the divide Bridget quenched her thirst while the storm raged on, thunder crashing around us and jagged bolts of lightning ripping across the sky. "Keep low!" I called, sending Nola and Vonn to crouch in the brush away from the cliff's edge. All we needed was to be struck by lightning.

Everyone knows not to stand beneath a tree during a thunderstorm, but our instinct to find shelter must be superior to our fear of lightning because it's the first thing many people do. When the sky lit up with jagged bolts Bridget went directly for the shelter of a tall pine.

"NO!" I yelled.

Panting, panicked, she looked around and saw the sterasote bush, thinking to shelter herself on the rock beneath its expansive branches. The rain came fast and hard, and nothing, with the exception of earthquakes and rockslides, frees a loose rock like driving rain. It wasn't the boulder with the massive fissure that broke free though. It was the large boulder above it that bounced down the incline and hit the rock beside the rock that held the boulder that anchored the log that crossed the crevice. I counted four seconds before I heard the crash of timber down below. It made me sick to do the math.

Bridget. Oh, Bridget. She stood across the yawning distance. It was fifteen or so feet across, but it might as well have been a mile.

Vonn cried out to her mother, "We'll find another log, Bridge! Don't worry."

The look on Bridget's face—it hurts to remember it.

Nola couldn't speak. She locked eyes with her daughter.

"We'll figure it out!" I shouted.

That's when I remembered that while Nola was wearing the canteen on the strap around her neck, we'd left her oxblood poncho, our vessel for collecting the rainwater, on the bush by the cave.

"The poncho!" I called to Bridget. "It's at the cave!" I held the yellow canteen in the air. "I'm gonna throw this over so you can fill it up."

Sheet lightning captured snapshot images of Vonn and Nola, sodden, shivering, clinging to each other and to the rock. I crouched, inching closer to the edge, preparing to throw the yellow canteen across the chasm.

Maybe I should have waited until the storm was over, but we didn't know how long it would last and we needed to collect the rainwater. I held the canteen in my throwing arm, waiting for a break in the wind.

"Don't try to catch this," I called to Bridget over the rain.

Bridget nodded but still got her catching hands ready.

"Don't catch it, Bridge!" Nola called.

Bridget nodded once more and raised her hands again when I went to throw.

"Put your hands in your pockets, Bridge," Nola yelled.

Bridget stuffed her hands into her pockets.

"I'm going to throw it toward the bushes," I shouted. "Okay? Let it land nice and easy!"

Bridget took hold of a nearby tree branch so the wind wouldn't blow her away.

"Back away from the edge, Bridget!" I called over the storm.

"Back away!" Nola shouted.

"You're freaking her out!" Vonn hissed.

There was a blinding flash of lightning, followed by a butt-clenching crack of thunder. The wind was blowing sixty miles an hour, easy. I've seen wind like that bounce the screws out of sheet metal and fold it like origami. I've seen wind like that pick up an aluminum shed and throw it on its ass. I didn't want to see what that wind would do with the slightness of Bridget Devine.

I hurled the canteen. Bridget, as instructed, did not attempt to catch the vessel—not even when it was swept off course from the bushes and landed within her grasp, then was blown astray toward the ridge.

We drew a sharp collective breath as the canteen dropped into the crevice and erupted with relief when its strap caught on a fluke-shaped rock jutting out below the jagged edge.

"You have to get the canteen, Bridge!" Nola shouted.

"You're going to have to *reach*, Bridget! You're going to have to reach pretty far!" I called over the crashing thunder.

The rain lashed Bridget's face as she stood back from the ledge, shaking her head dramatically.

"On your stomach, Bridge!" Nola called. "Don't look down! Just don't look down!"

"You can do it, Bridget!" Vonn called over the freezing rain.

The wind spun the canteen this way and that, easing the strap away from the wet rock hook. "Please, Bridget! We need that canteen!" I shouted.

I didn't have to imagine the terror Bridget felt. I felt it myself watching her drop to her knees in the little patch of mud on the other side of the crevice and crawl over the rocks toward the terrifying edge. Finally she reached it, and closed her eyes, groping blindly for the strap.

"Lower!" I called above the rain.

"To the left!" Nola shouted over the thunder.

"*Your* left!" Vonn cried over the wind.

Bridget reached down, her fingers straining, and finally caught the wet leather strap of the yellow canteen between her thumb and forefinger. But as soon as she had a grip on the strap she lost it again. It went on like that for a painfully long time with Bridget almost, then not, saving the canteen. "You're going to have to open your eyes, Bridget!" I called. "You're going to have to look down!"

Bridget inched closer to the edge, so close that from our angle it looked like she might pitch forward and fall into the depths. We held our breath as Bridget's fingers inched toward the leather strap. Finally, finally, she got hold of it.

When Nola and Vonn and I saw that Bridget had saved the yellow canteen we whooped in celebration, jumping up and down in the pouring rain, and we couldn't believe our eyes when we looked across the crevice a second later and witnessed Bridget drop the thing.

The strap was slick. Bridget's hand was wet. She thought she had a grip on it, but she did not. A basic miscalculation. Life-and-death consequences. She lost her grasp on the strap and she dropped the yellow canteen, and we could only watch helplessly, hopelessly as the greedy wind rushed up from the canyon floor to fling the vessel against the rock and then out of our sight forever.

Bridget backed away from the ridge and stood up, and we all looked at one another for a slow-motion minute, shocked, and maybe a little frightened, by her calm. The rain stopped then. The deluge didn't peter out or taper off, it stopped.

The steely clouds still threatened, but we were thankful for the reprieve from the hard-driving rain. "Bridget!" I called. "You have to go and get the poncho before the wind takes it! Drink whatever's in the hood!"

We paused a moment, Bridget and me, to look at each other across the distance before she turned and disappeared into the brush. We had an understanding. I just didn't know what it was.

Vonn was sodden, teeth chattering. "I'm still so thirsty."

"Look in the rocks, here and here." I pointed out the water in the granite grooves and gullies. Nola needed help to get to her feet and support from both Vonn and me as she bent to drink. "Drink as much as you can. We don't know when we'll have water again."

We went about like that for some time, lapping water from the rocks, like animals, I remember thinking, a herd of Devines, maybe it was a *pride* of Devines. A *blessing* of Devines? My gut began to contract from too much of the gritty water, and I stopped drinking, begging God to let me keep the fluid even while I felt it rise.

Nola was shivering vigorously. Next stop—Hypothermia.

Vonn was still focused on the other side of the crevice. "Where is she?"

"Bridget!" I shouted. "BRIDGET!" No answer.

I motioned Vonn out of Nola's earshot. "We don't have a lot of time, Vonn," I said. "We need to get Nola to a doctor."

"I know," Vonn said.

"She has to come with us," I asserted, rubbing warmth into my arms.

"We can't leave Bridget here alone!" Vonn cried.

"She'll be okay. The Mountain Rescue guys'll come back for her." I believed that.

"How long will it take?"

"A few hours. Depends on where the ridges connect. From over there it looked easy enough. A couple of hours to get back to the Mountain Station, I'd guess, but I'll run into a hiker long before that."

I started up the slope.

"You're leaving?"

"I'm just going up there to look. To see where the ridges connect. I'll come right back."

"She hates being alone," Vonn said, turning back to wait for Bridget's return. "I can't leave her alone."

"I'll need you to help with Nola," I said. "What if she passes out? Vonn, I can't do it by myself."

Dark clouds raced above us as I took a quick look around, concerned that there was no shelter from the rain should it return. "I'm going up there to scout. That's all. I'll come right back." I was slurring, which put me in mind of my father. "You have to tell Nola to be ready to go. And tell Bridget to gather rocks."

"Why?"

I didn't answer.

Vonn joined Nola to wait, falling into her grandmother's embrace, careful of her broken wrist. "Bridget!" Vonn shouted across the divide.

"Bridget!" Nola called. "Bridge!"

Leaving them, I ascended the slope feeling a rush of endorphins. We were only a couple of miles from the Mountain Station, and this whole ordeal was nearly over. In minutes I'd have a clear view of our path over the ridge and back to where we'd started the rockslide. Maybe it was a gentle hike. Maybe we'd find a marked path.

I didn't climb up to the plateau—I flew. The air smelled green and citrusy from the rain. I was filled with gratitude.

Heaving, I reached the top, wishing I had a flag to plant, and that I was not alone. The view? No Palm Springs. No Tin Town. No Salton Sea. There were, instead, spiky pines as far as the eye could see, rising up from the granite, which transformed into angry gray faces the longer I stared.

That's what I did. For a very long time. I stared at the sinister forests and the shifting white rock. I stared at the gesticulating branches of the army of pines. What were they upset about? I was the one who'd been deceived. After all the work and risk to cross Devine Divide I couldn't accept what I could see with my two eyes. The ridges did not connect.

The rocky peak that contained the slope was separate from the one that contained the cave. The joint between the ridges was an optical illusion. There was no way for us to return to the place we were before the rockslide, no way back to the Mountain Station, no way back at all, only forward, into the honeycomb of Devil's Canyon, up and down and around to what?

Bridget was stranded and even if we continued on without her, Nola and Vonn and me, the only way forward appeared to lead toward our doom. We'd risked our lives to cross the crevice, and now we were worse off than before. Much worse. I had to laugh, and I heard Byrd laughing right along with me. Because it was ridiculous, and we always thought ridiculous things were hilarious.

When I was done laughing, I dropped to my haunches, gazing out on the horizon, and that's when I saw the lone pine—the tree that Byrd had shown me in my dream. And beyond it the expansive mesa he'd described. The sound of splashing confused me. I turned to find Vonn squelching up the slope in her soaking wool socks and hurried to lend her my hand, helping her up to the plateau. Déjà vu.

"My feet are killing me," she said, then stopped to take in the view.

When tears appeared in her eyes I didn't know at first if it was because of Bridget, or the pain in her feet, or if she was moved by the mountain's beauty, or if it was because she saw what I'd seen.

"It doesn't connect," she said. "The ridges don't connect."

"No. But look," I said, gesturing hopefully toward the distant lone pine. "Just like my dream. The lone pine. Byrd said it was the way."

Vonn squinted. "There must be a hundred lone pines in this wilderness."

"It's the only way for us to go, Vonn," I said, pointing out the tragic circumstances of alternate routes. "So it's the way. Do you understand?"

"What about Bridget?"

I had no answer.

"I can't leave her."

"We can't stay. We have to get Nola to a hospital. We can't expect that she'll keep on rallying. There's no time to lose," I said, choking on the cliché.

"Go on without us."

Not an option.

"You go and get help," Vonn prodded as we watched the wind stroke the treetops.

"There isn't time," I said. "It could take hours to find help and get all the way back. She needs to see a doctor. Now."

"Bridget is trapped over there. Mim is . . . with her arm . . . I can't, Wolf. How? Look at my feet. Now I don't even have the stupid flip-flops!"

I sat down on a rock then, drawing Vonn down to the spot beside me. "I hate the wind," she said.

Kneeling at her feet, I unrolled the sopping-wet wool socks. I didn't want Vonn to look at her toes, so I held her eyes with mine, humming the Bob Seger song "Against the Wind" to distract her.

"I hate that song."

Frankie used to belt that song out in the kitchen. I purposefully botched the lyrics to amuse her.

"Stop," she said, grinning. "I really hate that song."

I tried not to look at Vonn's toes, and then did, and wished I hadn't, and kept on singing to disguise my concern. Quickly I took off my own warm boots and stuffed Vonn's feet into the fleece lining, struggling to lace them with my cold, clumsy fingers.

She stared at my bare white feet as I wrung out the wool socks. "What about you?"

"I'm boiling," I said, and she laughed. "I'm used to the cold."

"Just for a little while, okay?" she said, her teeth chattering. "I'll wear the boots for a little while."

Walking barefoot in this terrain would have been challenging in the best of circumstances. The rocks were hard and sharp and cold, and my feet were already sore and bruised. I could only pray they'd stay frozen so that I wouldn't have to bear the excruciating pain of their thaw.

Clomping behind me in my hiking boots, Vonn put me in mind of a child in her father's shoes. I felt sorry, as we made our way back down the slope, for lonely children, and frozen toes, and for Nola, and Bridget, alone and afraid across the divide.

Vonn was relieved to see that Bridget had reappeared. She was wearing Nola's oxblood poncho and perched on a rock a few feet back from the edge.

"You okay?" I called.

Bridget waved.

"She lost her voice," Nola said.

"You drink lots of water?" I called.

She nodded, then pointed up at the slope behind me, looking vaguely hopeful.

"It doesn't connect," I called. "The slope doesn't connect to the ridge. It's not the way back."

Bridget shook her head, protesting.

I shouted, "It looks like it connects, but it doesn't! We're going to have to figure something else out!"

She met my gaze across the crevice.

"We're going to get you home!" I called. "I promise, Bridget!"

"I won't leave her alone," Nola said. "We'll get another log. We'll make another bridge."

"There isn't time." I caught a whiff of rotting flesh as Nola found my eyes. We were so sure the sterasote poultice would save her life, but we'd been foolish to hope for more miracles.

"You and Vonn go on," she said. "I'll stay here with Bridget."

I cupped her cold cheeks. "We're gonna be okay, Mrs. Devine. We're going to get out of this."

Soaking, shuddering, Nola said resolutely, "I won't leave my daughter."

"You have to."

"I won't go without her."

Bridget, across the divide, was waving her arms. Finally, when she had our attention, she stomped her feet angrily. *GO!* she mouthed, pointing up the slope. *GO WITH THEM!*

Nola called back hoarsely, "I'm not leaving!"

"I'm not leaving either!" Vonn called out.

Bridget, shrunken and shivering, gestured calmly toward the slope. *Go,* she mouthed again. *Please.*

I had the strongest sense of déjà vu as I watched Nola, beside me, put her hand over her heart. Vonn picked up the cue and pressed her hand to her heart. Across the crevice Bridget did the same. I didn't know that other people did that. I raised my hand to my chest and put my palm over my breast where the tattooed owl kept Byrd, and Glory, and Frankie, and now, Nola and Bridget and Vonn Devine.

Nola's face lit as she gestured to the horizon with a shaking hand. "A rainbow."

Vonn sighed with delight—*even* then, even *there*.

Bridget would not turn to look.

"It's a sign!" Nola called over the wind as the rainbow disappeared.

"I don't care about the rainbow!" Bridget squeaked hoarsely, but the mention of a *sign* did seem to intrigue her. She was about to look for the rainbow when Vonn raised her hand, trembling, to point at something else instead.

The coyote was crouched near the sterasote bush about fifteen feet from Bridget. I don't know how long the beast had been there, upwind where I couldn't smell him.

"Bridget," I called calmly. "Behind you." Then I leaped to my feet, shaking my fist at the space between the coyote and me. "GIT!" I shouted.

On the other side of the crevice Bridget stared at the coyote.

"Don't. Run. Bridget," I called evenly. "Don't. Run. Unless you're running *at* him."

Bridget could only stare at the crouched beast with the twitching haunches.

I could see she wanted to bolt. "Don't do it, Bridget!"

"Don't run!" Nola called.

"Don't run!" Vonn shouted.

But Bridget ran. She ran as fast as she could run, silently screaming, and the coyote chased her into the dense brush of the outcropping. We could hear the sound of breaking limbs and snapping twigs.

The coyote howled. Bridget couldn't scream but yowled with her broken voice. Their memorable duet.

Then the beast went silent. None of us could breathe. Even the wind paused to find out what the hell happened between the lost woman and the hungry coyote. I pictured the beast with Bridget's neck in its jaws, shaking her rag-doll body, and had to staunch the rise of vomit. I don't know what Nola and Vonn were thinking or doing. I couldn't look at either. I stood there, cursing.

Nola cleared her throat, attempting to find her voice. "Bridget?" she finally called, all business. "Bridget Devine, you answer me!" Her tone said, *I will not stand here and have you killed and eaten by a coyote, young lady!* "Bridget!"

We waited. There was a flash of lightning in the sky to the east. Another sign. I watched the outcropping, praying that Bridget would appear, but every time I closed my eyes I was assaulted by the image of the coyote burrowing into her gut and emerging with twisted lengths of steaming intestines in its teeth. I could smell the blood.

What happened next I'm slightly hazy on because I had doubled over to vomit gritty rainwater. In my periphery, I saw a massive red bird eclipse the sun. I heard the clatter of rocks behind me, and when I turned, I had to blink several times, because Bridget was, impossibly, *there*, balanced awkwardly on the slope in Nola's oxblood poncho. She tried to speak but still had no voice.

We three stood there looking at Bridget, who was flushed and confused and as shocked to find herself with us as we were to see her alive. It's hard to imagine that she did what she did without divine intervention.

Vonn reached Bridget first, almost knocking her off her feet, then Nola, then me. We embraced one another fiercely, merging our sweat and filth and flesh, but only for a moment. The coyote was still a threat.

"I have no memory. From there to here," Bridget croaked, gazing at the other side of the wide divide. We all turned to look across the crevice just in time to watch the coyote make a graceful arced leap. I stepped forward when the animal landed on the slope a few yards above us, but he disappeared before I had a chance to protest.

* * *

THAT DAY, that third day we were lost, we didn't relive Bridget's astonishing jump across the fifteen-foot crevice. We didn't even discuss the miracle of it. Once Bridget had rejoined the rest of us, we went on with the next task, which was to get us all up the slope to the plateau so that we could find a route that would take us to the distant lone pine.

We didn't talk about the loss of the yellow canteen either as we trudged up the slope, Vonn, clumsy in my boots, and me bearing Nola's almost deadweight. "Doing great, Mrs. Devine," I said.

"Nola," she said hoarsely, smiling.

"Doing great, *Nola*," I said.

"I have a good feeling about this," Bridget said.

"Me too," I lied.

When we reached the plateau, I pointed out the lone pine. "See! See the pine!" I shouted over the wind.

"And the mesa!" Bridget shouted.

"I see it! There's plenty of room to land a helicopter," Vonn said, turning to smile at her mother.

Bridget, still sailing on her crevice-leap high, smiled back at Vonn and began to search the honeycomb canyons for the best way to reach our destiny.

"Isn't this the most miraculous thing?" Nola breathed, coming alive with hope.

Something nagged at me—the truth, I suppose—which was that the lone pine was random, and the mesa likely another illusion, and the air still not stable enough for a helicopter rescue.

"What do you think, Wolf?" Nola asked.

I began to lead the Devines toward the lone pine, a place foretold by a specter in a dream.

After a short while Nola stopped, lowering herself onto a long, flat boulder. "I'm frozen. Can we rest a minute?"

We stopped.

"Frozen," she repeated as we four embraced again to share our body heat.

Cue the sun. I can't help how it sounds. That's what happened. The sun burst forth, wiping away the curtain of cloud, warming our frigid bodies, saving our souls.

Nola turned her face toward the sun. "Can we stay here for a little while?"

"We have to," I said. "There's no sun once we get down there. It'll be cold as hell. We have to dry off now, while we can."

We sat on the warm rock, leaning against one another for support.

"Feels so good." Vonn unzipped her pea coat and spread it over a rock to dry. Nola and Bridget and I did the same.

Vonn. I remember looking at Vonn Devine in that moment, with her dust-smeared face and ratty hair and crusted eyes. Our days marooned on the mountain hadn't dimmed her beauty, and her betrayal—our betrayal—with the granola bar had bound us inextricably.

The sound I was hearing wasn't humming so much as moaning but I recognized the song as the Bob Seger one I'd been singing to her before. She looked up to catch me staring. "What?"

"I thought you hated that song?"

"Pip never cared for Bob Seger," Nola said.

"He'd be proud of you," I said, surprising myself.

"He would?"

"You're tough as nails, Mrs. Devine."

"Nola," she said.

"Nola."

"It's nice to have a man call me by my first name," she said. "Pip used to call me Noli."

"I couldn't do that," I said.

"I didn't sprinkle his ashes at the lake," Nola said.

"That's okay, Mim," Bridget said.

"Pip would have thought it was cool. The coyotes and everything," Vonn said.

"He would have," Nola said.

"Even better than the lake."

"I suppose. It's just that we didn't have a moment," Nola said. "We should have had a moment."

We were quiet for a time, listening to the wind, and then Vonn started to sing the Seger song in a parched whisper. I joined in with my own scratchy, broken vocals, and finally Nola added her voice, wheezing but with perfect pitch. It must have sounded horrible, painful, but to our ears we were a gospel choir singing for Patrick Devine.

Bridget broke the spell, shushing us and pointing to the sky. But this time it wasn't a helicopter sound that she heard. It sounded like a plane. We heard it too. It sounded exactly like a prop plane.

"It sounds like a plane," I said. I knew Mountain Rescue had a couple of prop planes. *Thank you, God.*

"Maybe I got the helicopter part wrong," Bridget strained to whisper.

Planes couldn't fly as low as a helicopter, but they could see us if they were looking. We started shouting all at once. "Help! Here! Down here!" Then I had an idea. "The poncho! Stretch it out like a target!"

Bridget took off the poncho, and we stretched the plastic so that it formed a bull's-eye over the rock.

The steady, even hum of the motor grew closer, and we began to shout again. "Over here! Over here! Here!" We went on like that for longer than you might have expected, given the number of times the wind had fooled us. Eventually our necks got tired.

At last Nola stretched out on the sun-warmed rock, looking up at the sky. One by one we took our places beside her, four in a row, so we could rest while we waited to catch sight of the rescue plane that we were still convinced was about to appear from around the next peak.

Time—impudent, insufficient, incoherent time—passed. The sound of the plane died down, or shifted in tenor or tone. I couldn't say how much time passed between elation and surrender.

"The wind," I said stupidly.

"The wind," Bridget agreed.

"We have to go," I said, watching my feet attempt to plant themselves before I collapsed again on the warm rock beside the Devines. How was I going to hike without shoes or boots or even flip-flops to protect my soles? How was I going to leave the rock? It was so warm. We were so tired.

I knew it was folly to stay there. I was exhausted, dehydrated, hungry, but we had to press on or Nola would die.

"Not yet," Nola said.

"We're dry." I struggled mightily for the strength to sit up again. "The sooner we hit the trail, the quicker we'll find something edible, or maybe we'll come on a stream."

"I'm going to stay here," Nola said. "I don't see where I'll find the strength to go on."

"Don't say that."

"Maybe it's my time, Wolf."

"Not yet."

"I won't go without you, Mim," Vonn said.

Bridget nodded in agreement.

"We'll find food, Mrs. Devine," I said.

"We could have had that granola bar," Bridget said in a strained whisper.

"Bridget!" Nola snapped.

Bridget lunged at me then, swinging wildly. I caught her in my arms.

"It's your fault," she hissed.

"Bridget!" Nola shouted.

"It's all his fault!"

I backed away. Maybe she was right.

"You got us lost! You made her eat the granola bar!"

"No!" Vonn rose up from the rock. "He didn't make me do anything."

Vonn stood before us in my too-big climbing boots and, reaching into the deep pocket of her cargo pants, drew out a rectangle of silver foil. One of the other granola bars. It was one of the other granola bars. I felt punched in the gut.

It took a moment for Vonn to find her voice. "This is the only one left. I ate the other whole bar on the first day. And I drank the water. All of it."

We stared at the silver foil in Vonn's filthy palm. A shadow darkened the evidence, and we looked up to find three huge black birds soaring high overhead—three—when there had only ever been two. I don't know if the others found that strange.

Did we shout at Vonn? Did we reproach her? Did we throttle her? No. We sat there in shock. Vonn heaved a deep sigh, then mumbled something we assumed was a plea for forgiveness. *What was that she said?*

"I said I'm pregnant," Vonn repeated, and then said it once more, in case there was any lingering confusion. "I'm going to have a baby."

Dumbstruck by the first confession, dumbfounded by the second, we watched Vonn tear at the silver wrapper. I could smell it; cinnamon and oats, brown sugar. She snapped the granola bar into three equal pieces and passed one to Nola, and one to Bridget, and finally to me. "I'm sorry," she said, unable to meet our eyes. "I was throwing up so much, and I was so worried about the . . ."

We, each of us, handed our morsel of granola back to Vonn. You'd think Vonn would have demurred, but she snatched back the pieces one by one and gobbled them all.

"Does the father know?" Bridget rasped after a very long time.

Yago popped into my head again. He'd already fathered six children at this point. Wouldn't that be just my luck?

Vonn shook her head. "I don't want to talk about this right now."

"Do you know who the father is?" Bridget strained to speak.

"Are you really asking me that?"

I'd wondered the same thing.

"I know who it is. I just don't remember his name," Vonn said. "I'm not sure I ever asked his name."

Nola tsked.

"I can hardly even remember what he looked like."

"You didn't care what he looked like?" Bridget was aghast.

"I was at a low point," Vonn said. "Obviously."

"I usually turn to crossword puzzles," Nola said flatly. "Or you might try crotcheting. I can show you how to make mittens."

"Are you all right?" I asked.

Vonn just looked at me.

"I mean—does everything feel normal?"

"I guess," she said. "I'm hungry."

Nola smiled through her pain. "I hope it's a girl, Vonn. Or a boy."

"You'll be a great-grandmother, Mim," Bridget said. She seemed oblivious to the fact that she would be becoming a grandmother.

Exhausted, Vonn sat down on the rock beside me. I shifted my gaze to take in her physique. She did not look pregnant. It suddenly hit me that she might be lying. She'd already lied about the food and water.

"How pregnant?" I asked.

"First trimester," Vonn said.

I didn't know what that meant and was embarrassed to ask.

"Can we rest just a little longer?" Nola asked.

We all stretched back out on the rock again, watching the birds circling over our heads.

Vonn turned to me, speaking in a whisper. "What if we don't make it?"

"We will," I said.

"But if we don't?"

I had no response.

"*Three* crows," Nola said absently. "There used to be two. Weren't there only two crows before?"

I didn't tell Nola that these black birds were not crows.

LYING THERE in the warm sun, we must have fallen asleep, because a sound woke me—a sharp, screeching sound, metal on metal, the whirring, hacking sound of an engine turning, but not catching. My mind was filled with the image of Yago trying to start his motorcycle. When I opened my eyes I could still hear the sound of Yago's motorcycle, which obviously was not lost in the wilderness, but which I could nonetheless hear quite distinctly.

No matter which direction I looked there was nothing but trees and bush and rock. Still, the noise—I had to see what the noise was, and so I rose, searching the perimeter for coyotes. I also found a few dozen large rocks here and there, and set them near Vonn, who I reckoned could throw the hardest in my absence, and left the slumbering Devines to follow the sound.

Through the slanted forest I wandered, in and out of dappled light, then farther away, chasing that horrible screeching sound that both attracted and repelled me. I followed that pitchy gray-and-black noise beyond the bushes, near a dramatic granite sculpture—a loaf of rock fractured in equal vertical portions that looked to my hungry eyes like slices of fresh cut bread. My gut seized with wanting, and I remember having to stop myself from trying to bite the rock.

The wind must have changed direction then. I hadn't smelled the blood earlier and nearly gagged when it crawled up my nostrils and dripped down the back of my throat. I held my breath, but I'd been hallucinating and couldn't trust my own eyes. Then I dared to look, wishing that I was not alone and could ask my companion if I was currently witnessing the evisceration of my cousin Yago by two of the biggest turkey buzzards I'd ever seen.

The vultures were real, and also real were the awful, screeching, throaty, engine-revving sounds they made—the reason they're called *buzzards*—while pecking at the steaming carcass of a dead coyote.

Was it the coyote with the injured leg? The one I'd hit with the jar full of Pip? The one I'd watched leap across the canyon and stumble on the landing? Possibly. I pitied the animal. I was sorry if in some small way I was responsible for his death.

I thought, for a moment, about salvaging the meat but I wasn't sure I had the strength to shoo the birds away, let alone the guts to swallow the scraps from a vulture's lunch. I backed off from the exquisitely horrifying creatures, remembering—there had been three of them. Where was the third?

Back through the woods I ran, into the sunlight and over a ridge before I came to the Devines, still asleep on the warm granite bed. I *remember* running, but it must be a lie. I didn't have the strength to run. Still, even weak as I was, I'm sure I would have caught and strangled the vulture I saw strutting around Vonn if he hadn't flapped away on his own.

Fluid. I badly needed fluid. I tried to will myself to think of anything but water and turned to watch the sleeping Devines.

I couldn't entirely blame the bird, with the smell and all, for thinking that at least one of them was already dead. Time to move on. My sense of duty was intense. I had to protect these women. I had to get them safely home.

"Vonn," I called. "Bridget. Nola. We need to get moving."

Vonn woke first. "Bad dream," she said, her mouth so dry she could barely form words. Bridget woke next. She tried to speak, but her voice was still shredded. We all turned to look at Nola.

"Mrs. Devine," I said, leaning over her. "Nola."

She opened her eyes and smiled a little, but it was clear her condition was worsening. Her eyes were glassy from fever. "Another day," she said. I couldn't say she sounded relieved.

The sun had fallen behind some gray-bellied clouds and without it I couldn't begin to calculate the time.

After helping the Devine women back into their dry coats I lifted them, one by one, to their feet and led them onward toward our beacon—the lone pine from my dream, where the helicopter from Bridget's dream would find us.

My socks were no protection against the sharp rocks and thorny underbrush. My feet were as good as bare. "Shouldn't take more than a couple of hours," I said enthusiastically.

After a very short time I stopped thinking about our destination, focused instead on finding a path through the wilderness that would be kindest to my shoeless feet. Where we were going didn't seem as important as the fact that we were moving. As long as we were moving we might find food and water. As long as we were moving there was hope.

Far away from the vultures, we picked our way down a short slope and through a forest of young white firs. I remember I was getting dizzy looking down and had to keep finding the horizon and the gesticulating pines, and the skyscrapers of gold-veined quartz, and the patches of mugwort, and the gritty Devines.

We trudged up one short slope, then down another, only to go up again and down again, and then traverse a few improvised switchbacks until we had no sense that we were going one way or another but looping back in on ourselves.

I reminded them to look for food as we went, praying for a few paltry pine nuts forgotten by some overfed rodents. I was more optimistic that we'd come across a stream, a pond, even a puddle or two from the earlier rain.

Up and down, through a forest of black oaks, then into a mesa of manzanita and thorny chamise. After a time we came upon a collection of shaded boulders where I brushed away some dirt and acorn shells to make a place for Nola and Bridget and Vonn to rest. We huddled together as the wind rose up and the temperature fell.

My fingers were throbbing. My feet were numb, the baby toes solid as little rocks. I didn't express my pain or fear. Nola had set the tolerance bar ridiculously high in both regards. We were quiet, watching the clouds, imagining heaven—at least I was—calculating my odds.

There was no water. No blue mesh bag to hope to find. No emotional revelations. No memories to keep or share. Our mouths were dry, and I had the sense that my thoughts were becoming desiccated too.

Nola pointed to the place where the darkening sky met the ragged green mountain range. "Looks like bric-a-brac," she said, following the line with her finger. "Your aunt Louise had a dress with those colors. Louise. That's a nice name, Vonn. Louise?"

"Is it?" Vonn said.

"Sam," Bridget said with her strangled voice.

"No boys' names for girls," Nola said. "Saints' names always work. Theresa, Augusta, Sophia."

I found it disturbing that the Devine women were musing on names for a child who wouldn't live to be born.

"Season," Bridget croaked. "Isn't that one you said before, Mim?"

Nola laughed. "Season? Wasn't that you? How about Winter?"

"Winter's a boys' name," Bridget said.

It was a ghoulish exercise, and I needed them to stop. "We have to go on," I said, trying to rise.

But we couldn't. Night had fallen. Maybe it came hard and fast, or maybe it wafted in, slowly and gently, with a pink sunset in between—I don't know. I was consumed by pain and hunger and thirst and fear and already mourning the loss of Vonn's nameless baby.

"It's night," Nola said.

The Devines seemed as shocked about it as I was. We had no cave. We had no shelter. I turned to heaven, begging for mercy, unaware I was talking out loud. "You see us? You see us here? We're lost as hell. We are crying out to you from the wilderness."

"Amen." Nola squeezed my hand, and we remained like that, hand in hand, as if it were the most natural thing in the world. Bridget reached out to touch her daughter's face, but before she could, a sound startled us all—a thunderous metal sound that we felt in the rock and saw in the trembling branches and heard in the trees and the air.

We held our breath, looking around at one another, and then turning our attention to the earth. The plates had shifted. We didn't know what it meant.

Our teeth clicked in our dry mouths as we clung to one another against the cold, howling wind. Howling, yes, like a coyote, a wolf, a dying man, like a sound effect sampled from a horror show. Felt like a cheap shot, all considered. Did the wind honestly think we weren't scared enough already?

Beside me, Vonn began to gag and held her hand over her mouth as though she might vomit. After a moment she stopped.

"False alarm?"

Without anyone saying a word, we joined hands again.

WE MAY have slept, in and out of time and space. I remember hearing the owl hooting in my ear, and clawing my way back to awareness.

At some point Byrd flew into my thoughts and I studied the stars for a long while, wondering where the hell he was. The Byrd who watched the mountain from Harley's ranch was a long, dark shadow of the Byrd I knew.

I closed my eyes, conjuring my friend as I'd done a hundred times before. I saw him in my mind's eye, sitting there in one of the twin brown chairs at the big picture window, staring at the mountain, his eyes tracking the tram on the double jig-back system going up and down the steep rock face, all day and half the night. I saw myself there, saying my name, *Wolf,* wishing he understood.

Then it was as though I could feel my own presence invade that sunroom in Harley's ranch house, and even though I had no form, I sat in the twin brown leather chair across from Byrd and I said, "Dude. I am lost. I am lost with these three women, and I'm afraid we're all gonna die."

"You scare me when you talk to yourself," Vonn said.

I turned to find her wide-eyed beside me, confused to find myself surrounded by rock. "Just figuring out a plan," I said. "We have to believe we're going to get out of this."

The women, each of them, turned to stare.

I remember that scene as vividly as any memory I have from those days on the mountain.

It cut me to think of any one of them alone among corpses.

Our mouths were so dry it amazes me that we made attempts to talk at all. My toes throbbed in the damp socks. The wind crept up behind me, whispering into my ear, taunting, accusing.

I staggered to my feet, swatting at the air. In my mind I was fighting Yago. I must have looked insane.

The women knew I'd lost it, but they also knew they were in no position to judge. The wind did die down eventually, with only the barest, sweetest lullaby still playing in the black forest. I felt like I'd won.

"Shh!" Nola hissed, though no one was speaking.

I could not stomach another discussion about a rescue helicopter.

"Listen," she said.

We were quiet, listening for whatever it was Nola heard. Vultures, I thought. Maybe the surviving coyote? He had our scent. Or others? There were mountain lions here too. Bobcats were plentiful and could certainly kill a person with those jagged teeth and sharp claws.

Nola sat up, her face lit by the moon. "There's something out there."

And I heard it then, cracking branches, rustling leaves. It sounded like an animal, a large animal, crashing through the brush like Frankie on a bender. Mountain lion? Maybe we were threatening her cubs.

Could be a male bighorn. They could gore you to death if you were in their territory during rutting season. But how did you know where their territory was?

The crashing sound stopped on the other side of the darkness. The animal—mountain lion, I'd decided—having been lured away by some other, smaller prey.

"It's gone," I said.

We fell silent. The women gave in to exhaustion. I stayed awake, comforted by Bridget's fluty snores.

The branches broke around me. Leaves rustled in the breeze. We were being stalked again, or it was just the wind, or a rat. I reached for my stick and gathered several more rocks at my feet. The icy air stung my lungs.

To keep myself awake I thought about Frankie.

MY FATHER was one of those guys people loved until they hated. The greatest guy, the funniest guy, the most generous guy, until he cheated on you, or stole from you, or moved you away from your home in Michigan and abandoned you in a trailer in the desert. I don't know if his presence in my life would have been less or more painful than his absence. Everything with Frankie was a toss-up.

From time to time Frankie would burst into Kriket's trailer in the night. I could hear him laughing, beer cans smacking against the kitchen table, the ashtray falling to the floor. Sometimes he left without saying hello. Twice he woke me in my sleeping bag on the floor. Once he wanted to borrow sixty dollars. Once he wanted to give me ten. I could never decide if I was glad or sorry he'd come.

I didn't attend classes at SSHS much past the middle of my freshman year. Like Byrd, I had trouble fitting in. Instead, I signed up for correspondence classes, forging my father's signature on the necessary documents, not because he wouldn't have signed them but because he was never around when they needed to be signed. I finished the four-year course in less than three and was mailed my diploma the fall before I turned seventeen. Frankie didn't know any of that. He never asked about school.

He appeared out of the blue one night, a few weeks after my fifteenth birthday, which he'd missed. "Where you been, Frankie?"

"Around."

"You're never here."

"I met a woman." He grinned. "She lives way the hell out in Indio. Divorced. Swimming pool."

"Still . . ."

"You wouldn't expect me to bring her here?"

I saw his point.

"Heard you're working out at the gas station."

"Early-morning shift. Have been for a long time."

Frankie wasn't a morning person. "Try to get a later one."

"Byrd's got the later one."

"They careful about inventory?"

Frankie was always looking for an angle. Maybe it was in his genes. I didn't see him again until Christmas Day. He showed up at the trailer like Santa Claus with gifts for everybody. For me—a high-end car audio system wrapped up in a kid's jacket and stuffed into a plastic pail. I still have it.

I saw Frankie much more regularly after our return to the desert following Byrd's hospital stay because I moved into Byrd's apartment behind the gas station and started working the night shift as well as the day shift. Frankie dropped by at least once a week. He was there to snare free cigarettes and gas, but we both pretended he cared.

Harley brought Byrd to his ranch to recover, and day by day, with the help of a private nurse and the best physical therapists, he continued to improve in the basic functions of walking and eating and going to the toilet. But he still had no language. No one knew what he was thinking or feeling or how much he understood of what was said to him.

He was Byrd but not Byrd, brought back from the dead like Lazarus from the Bible, or the gruesome pets in Stephen King.

At first I visited him every day in the sunroom Harley'd built for him with its stunning view of the mountain. He'd sit there for hours on end in that brown leather chair—remembering? Trying to forget? I was so sure if I could get him to say my name, *Wolf* or even *Wilfred*, something would reboot in his brain.

One day, out of the blue, Byrd's hand shot out to grab my hand. He looked me dead in the eye as he raised my hand and tapped *my* finger against *his* forehead. I swear he was telling me something. But it never happened again, and day after day, he flew farther away.

I'd say I saw more of Frankie in the three months after we returned to the desert than I had in the few years I'd lived at Kriket's. Our conversations were brief—awkward. Frankie stopped by on Halloween night, just a few hours, in fact, before he killed the young couple on the desert road.

No one knows that part of the story either—except Frankie—and the woman he was with.

Frankie limped into the store wearing a too-small pirate hat, his left eye covered by a cheap felt eye patch, the elastic of which looked ready to burst. "Aye, aye, matey!" he shouted.

That set me off. It didn't seem right that a guy like Byrd was lost in space and a guy like Frankie was walking around in a kid-size pirate hat and eye patch. "What do you need, Frankie?"

He'd driven to the gas station straight from the casino, where he'd just lost all the money he'd won the night before. To top it off, he'd fallen off a barstool and hurt his leg. He stunk of booze and cigars. "I need a little luck," he said.

I plucked his brand of cigarettes from the rack above the register and flipped the package to him. He thought they were freebies. I'd pay for them later.

"You good?" he asked, his eyes darting to the high shelf behind me.

"Top-notch," I said dryly, noting he was looking at the premium tequila.

"Good." He glanced out at the parking lot. I wondered if he was
being followed. Or thought he was. "Don't sleep."

"Right."

"Can't eat."

"Me too." He kept looking out into the parking lot. "I have night-
mares about Byrd," I said. It was the truth.

Frankie didn't hear a word I said. He was distracted by honking in
the parking lot, and we looked out to see the woman in the Gremlin.

"She's not the most patient." He started to limp down the aisle,
groaning in pain.

"What do you want? I'll get it."

"A six-pack, some tissues, some lip balm. She wants some of that
spicy jerky you got on the display rack at the back."

I walked to the back of the store only to find that we were out of the
spicy jerky. I turned back to ask Frankie what I should bring instead, and
that's when I saw my father in the security mirror over the register,
straining for the tequila on the high shelf behind the counter. When he
couldn't reach the tequila he grabbed a bottle of wine and hid it under
his jacket. Then he opened the register to peel away half the stack of
twenty-dollar bills.

"Thanks, Wolf." Frankie said when I approached the counter with
his other things.

I put the items in a bag while he pretended to search his pockets. He
was a terrible actor. "So you're good out here?" he asked.

"You back at the trailer?"

Frankie shook his head. "I owe Yago a little money."

I passed him the bag. "It's on me, Frankie."

"Thanks, Wolf."

"Good luck with Yago."

"What's that supposed to mean?"

"Nothing."

Frankie grabbed the bag and headed for the door, but then he came back. I wish he hadn't.

"I know what you think."

"I don't think anything, Frankie."

"I see the way you look at me. You think I'm a loser."

I couldn't disagree.

He paused. "I'm sorry about what happened to Byrd."

"Yeah."

"That was bad luck, Wolf. Don't think I don't understand."

"Yeah, Frankie."

"But you don't get to look down on me." He looked ridiculous in the hat and eye patch. "I didn't push Byrd off the cliff, Wolf. All that shit's your fault, right? You brought the redweed."

I surprised both of us with what I did next. I turned and climbed the stepladder to reach the top shelf and selected the premium tequila Frankie'd had his eye on before.

"The good stuff," I said, setting the bottle on the counter.

"Just when I think you're an asshole," he said, touched.

"We should stop underestimating each other," I said, hiding my contempt.

"This means a lot to me, Wolf," Frankie said. "I've been going through a rough time. The thing with Yago. You know what he's like. We gotta have each other's back."

I wondered if he noticed my hands were shaking when I reached for the second bottle of tequila and passed it to him.

Did I mean for Frankie to get drunk and get behind the wheel to get burgers that Halloween night? No. But I did hope he would choke on it.

THE FOURTH DAY

I woke shivering, swallowing the harvest of dread in my throat, to find the black night still around us. I felt like it should be morning, and for a second believed I'd gone blind. The rocks trembled beneath me, but it wasn't the plates shifting this time. I remember being afraid that if I closed my eyes and allowed myself to return to whatever dream I'd been having, I'd never see the Devines, or the mountain, again.

Hypothermia was a coward's way out, and I was afraid I'd take it if I got the chance. *Stay awake, scut,* I told myself.

I checked to make sure the women were all still asleep and panicked when Nola felt stiff beside me. I stared at her face in the dim light. "Nola," I said. My mouth was frozen. She didn't move. I disengaged myself from Vonn on my other side, searching Nola's neck for a pulse. Finding none, I held my finger beneath her nose. I was prepared to face her death.

I was not prepared to be bitten. I suppose a person is never *prepared* to be bitten. My scream must have carried all the way to Palm Springs. Nola woke screaming too, creating a chain reaction as Vonn woke and began to scream. Bridget, could she have screamed, would have screamed, but her face spoke volumes. When the screaming was over, I was confident that no animal within three miles would dare to challenge the demon we'd just unleashed. And that if there was a rescue team within two miles, they'd heard us.

"What the heck, Nola?" I croaked, holding out my damaged finger.

"I'm so sorry."

We gathered one another into our arms, rooting for warmth. "It's all right. Go back to sleep. Go back to sleep."

"My heart's racing," Vonn said.

"Mine too," Bridget said.

My eyes had adjusted surprisingly quickly to the dark, and when I looked around I could make out the triad of boulders cleaving to the high ridge, defying gravity. I could distinguish the cottonwood from the ironwood, and I could pick the limber pine from the Coulter, and as Mother Nature's long-winded sorrow came tearing through the trees, I had to admit that I could see, in this light, in any light, that we were losing Nola.

"I'm so hungry," Bridget said.

"Don't talk about it," Nola said.

I thought Bridget might start up about the granola bars but she didn't.

"They must be looking for us," Vonn said.

"Tomorrow," Bridget said. "I have a feeling."

"Will you ever come back if . . . ?" Vonn asked after a time. I knew she was talking to me and I knew she meant the mountain, and I understood what remained unspoken. *If we survive this.*

"No," I said definitively. I stroked the rock to soften the blow and instantly changed my mind. "Yes." I didn't know then if I'd ever see the mountain again.

Vonn's hands reached reflexively for her stomach.

"Vonn?"

"It hurts," she said.

"You're hungry," I said.

"Mine hurts too," Bridget said.

My hunger had grown black wings and a sharp, hooked beak, consuming me gut-first. We tried to let the sound of the wilderness lull us back to sleep. At least we would have, had Bridget not shifted and touched something wet.

"Is that blood?" she asked, pointing.

Blood. I could smell it, even in the dark. To be sure I dipped my finger into the apple-size wetness and brought it to my nose. The wound on Nola's forehead was crusted over and dry. My finger wasn't bleeding from where she'd bitten me—at least not much. The blood hadn't come from Nola's swollen purple wrist either.

"Who's bleeding?" Bridget asked.

When Vonn clutched her cramping gut, I did not want to believe that the blood was hers. "Okay," I said, which wasn't a question. "You're all right, Vonn."

Vicious nature teaches us dark lessons, and experience taught me to be ready for anything, especially the worst.

Vonn grasped my arm. "It hurts."

I shuddered.

"I had some cramping when I was pregnant with you too," Bridget said.

"You did?"

"Spotting too."

"You did?"

"She did and look at you. You're perfect, Vonn," Nola said.

"Hardly," Vonn said.

"I've miscarried," Bridget said.

"You never told me."

"It's not something you want to talk about," Bridget said.

"Before I was born or after?"

"Four times. All after."

"Four times?"

"Anyway, I had five pregnancies and only had the spotting with you."

I feared Bridget was giving her daughter false hope.

"What did the doctor say?" Vonn asked.

"He said I needed to take it easy."

"Did you?"

"I had a job. I was alone," Bridget said, straining her voice. "I didn't have a car."

"Why didn't you move back here so Mim could help?"

"I didn't want to run into him."

"My father?"

"Mim and Pip came to Golden Hills a lot," Bridget said. "And then I met Carl."

"His house was a palace," Vonn said, nodding.

"It was."

"And you always wanted to be queen," Vonn added.

Bridget shook her head. "I wanted you to be a princess."

Vonn stroked her womb through her coat.

There came the whoosh of wide black wings. My stomach roiled at the recollection of the black buzzards bobbing at those steaming coyote remains. I thought I was alone with my thoughts and shuddered when Vonn said, "Vultures."

"It was the owl."

"Not the owl," she said.

"I think it was the owl."

"The vultures, Wolf."

We reached for the comfort of each other's hands. I held Vonn's frozen fingers to my lips but failed to warm them.

"Wolf?"

"Vonn."

"The vultures . . . ?" She paused.

"The vultures."

"If anything happens . . ."

I didn't want her to see my face.

"You know what I'm saying, Wolf?"

I did.

"They're just hungry too."

THERE WAS a dreamlike quality to that fourth day. I woke again to the metallic scent of the rock, and the rustle of the pines, and the weight of our bodies entwined, and then, surprisingly, pinpricks of cold landing on my cheek.

My first thought was that the dampness was saliva, and I was grateful when I opened my eyes to find no carnivorous beast looming over my face, just the chaotic weave of branch and needle from the towering trees overhead.

A flake of white hit my cheek. Snow. Another flake found my forehead, another, my eyelid. When I realized the flakes were not melting on my skin, I wondered if I were dead.

Only a few flakes had made it through the dense pines above our heads, but when I sat up I discovered that the surrounding rocks were blanketed in a thin layer of white. We had to head to a lower elevation, I knew, or I would lose more than my baby toes to frostbite.

"Snow." Vonn sat upright, opening her mouth to accept the flakes. She shook her mother, saying, "Bridget. Snow."

Bridget woke, confused. When she saw my eyes she must have realized how grave our risk if we stayed here in the snow. She turned to wake her mother, stroking her cold cheek, "Mim? Mim?"

I was relieved when Nola blinked herself awake, and encouraged when she managed to sit up.

Vonn reached down with her white fingers, scooping the snowflakes from where they'd gathered in the folds of her coat and bringing the mound to Nola's mouth. We all followed suit, scooping handfuls of snow to melt between our tongues and our dry, frozen palates.

"We have to go. We have to get out of the snow," I said, helping Vonn, then Bridget to their feet.

Stepping down from the rock, I winced at the slicing pain in my heel. I remember telling myself that pain was my friend. I remember telling myself that whatever parts of my feet hurt would be the parts I'd be keeping if we got out of this alive.

In the distance we heard the screeching of a hawk.

We hiked down a long rocky slope for nearly half an hour until we'd walked out of the snowfall. Each step was excruciating. We were chilled to our marrow.

We came to a fork in the brush, and I was grateful to rest as we paused to consider the granite shrapnel and spiny brush in the direction of the lone pine. The other way presented a gentle slope and what appeared to be a long stretch of meadow grass that would be much kinder to my tortured feet. The whole *lone pine* thing now struck me as fool-hardy, arbitrary, an ill-conceived goal. I chose the simpler path, announcing, "This way."

"But that's not the way to the pine tree," Bridget said.

"This is the best way to get there."

"Away from the tree?"

"It's a shortcut."

Nola was overcome by dizziness. I almost didn't catch her when she started to fall.

"Will they pick up our scent all this way?" Vonn wondered.

"The coyotes?"

"No. The rescue dogs."

"Would they know we got over the crevice?" Bridget wondered. "How could they know?"

I didn't tell them that even if Search and Rescue had the dogs and were looking for us, and even if the dogs had tracked us all the way to the ridge from where we'd fallen, and down onto the outcropping and past the cave and to the crevice, they would never believe that we'd made it safely to the other side. They would have abandoned the search—reclassified it as *recovery*.

Wouldn't *they* be surprised to find Vonn's lime-green flip-flops at the bottom of the crevice but no bodies?

We stumbled onward, anywhere the path was less stony and the hawkweed less dense, inching through forests and over tumbled boulders, luxuriating in patches of meadow grass, traipsing through knee-high fields of chilled skunk cabbage, Nola supported by Bridget and Vonn.

We'd been walking for a while—there was no sun to tell us the hour—when Vonn spied something unusual ahead. "What's that?" she asked, pointing. "That turquoise thing."

"A flower?" Nola guessed.

"It's a bird," I said, squinting.

"It's not moving," Vonn said.

We inched through the forest toward the turquoise beacon, and only when we were all standing over it did we realize what we were looking at.

Vonn picked the square of plaid fabric from the branch and held it in her hand. "It's a pocket," she said. "Ripped from a shirt."

A shirt pocket? Here?

Vonn handed the square to me. No telling how long it had been there.

"Hello!" we shouted, scanning the trees. "Hello! Hello!"

There came the sound of cracking branches and we spun—each toward a different direction—to find nothing but rock and tree and root-mangled soil. The wind roared through the canyon.

"Hello," I called tentatively. "Hello?"

"One of the rescue fellows?" Nola said hopefully.

We hastened our pace, calculating all it meant to imagine that we were not alone. We didn't know if we needed to be hurrying to something or away from something.

"Hello?" Vonn called again.

We paused to listen to her echoing voice.

"Please let him have food and water," Bridget murmured.

"Please," Nola said.

"What if he has some but he doesn't want to share?" Vonn asked.

"This bit of fabric could have been here for years," I said.

"Think he came from the same direction we did?" Vonn asked, stumbling over a boulder.

Then the scent of cat stopped me in my tracks. Bobcats mark territory with their acrid urine just like domestic cats do. I did not wonder at that point if the plaid shirt was in any way connected to the pungent odor.

"Smells like cat," Vonn said.

"Hello?" we called, surveying the rock and trees for the plaid shirt's owner.

There was rustling in the brush to the left of us, up a short escarpment of rusty manganese-covered granite. "Hello!" I shouted.

"The wind," Vonn said.

I choked the square of blue fabric, calling, "Hello! Is anyone there?"

We kept on through the forest, dizzy from the onslaught of trees. The heels and toes and balls of my feet begged me to stop. We did when, once again, there was movement in the brush.

Bridget heard it first this time and crouched, calling, "Hey! Hello!?"

There was a crashing on the other side of some thick manzanita. We stopped, holding our breath, waiting, but no animal came rushing at us and in a moment it was quiet once again.

"What was that?" Vonn asked.

"The wind," I said reflexively, which was inane, unless the wind had legs and weighed enough to crack a branch.

"What's that?" Vonn asked, pointing up ahead.

"Just Byrd," I said as I watched the figure of my friend move on through the trees.

"It's not a bird," she said.

"Are you all right, Wolf?" Bridget asked.

I could hear Byrd's laughter, and because it sounded so real, I started laughing too, until I saw myself in Nola's glassy eyes.

"Look," Vonn said, pointing out another blue fragment half buried in the dirt between two boulders.

It was denim. I leaned down and pinched it with my fingers and pulled it from the earth. It was like a magic trick, almost comical, as I kept tugging and tugging and finally freed a sizable pair of jeans from their earthen tomb.

"Hello! Hello! Hel-lo!" we all called out to the wilderness, shivering, not in the least because the jeans belonged to a very big man.

"His coat," Vonn said, pointing to a large camouflage-style raincoat hanging weathered from the branch of a nearby tree.

"Stay here," I told the women. I didn't want to alarm them, but I'd spied through the brush a dirty red hunter's cap on what appeared to be the slumbering head of a shirtless man. It was freezing cold, and the man was without his coat, so he was either dead or crazy.

"Oh my God," Vonn said, gripping her mother and grandmother as I limped toward him.

My mental state was such that I knew I should fear *his*. I wondered if he had a gun. "Hello," I called.

As I walked toward him, with each painful step, I was praying that he was dead so I could have his boots.

He was dead. He had no boots. No legs for that matter. Missing too was an arm. Scavengers had gutted him, made bowls of his hip bones and licked him clean. Poor bastard. Poor bastard.

A ground squirrel startled the hell out me, darting from beneath a granite ledge nearby where I noticed the remnants of the man's missing leg, the right, judging by the shape of the brown-socked foot. I looked around for the twin, but the left leg was nowhere to be seen. Neither was the boot that the man must have at some point had on his foot.

Struck by a thought, I went to the leg, looking around for the bush knife I hoped the stranger kept there, grasping the dried muscle and desiccated skin through the rotting brown sock. No knife.

After a second's hesitation I picked up the blackened leg bone and headed back to the spot where the man's torso lay, though I had no strength in *my* bones to dig a grave for *his*.

"Why did he take off his clothes?" Vonn called to me, watching from the distance as I returned the man's leg to his carcass.

"Happens sometimes when people are freezing to death. Their brain short-circuits. Maybe they think they're burning up with heat. They take off all their clothes."

Vonn turned, darting into the brush nearby. I was afraid she needed to vomit. But Vonn didn't vomit. After a moment she returned triumphantly, carrying a large pink knapsack she'd spotted in some meadow grass. I can't recall if she raced back to us or if we ran to her, but I remember we four on our knees gathered around the knapsack.

"Is it his wife's?" Vonn wondered. "What if she's alive? What if she's still here?" She dumped the contents of the knapsack into the dirt: a damp and moldy Florida State T-shirt and a yellow canteen, an exact match to Nola's and the one I gave to Byrd. The canteen was dry, I knew, the second I picked the thing up.

"This can't be all," Vonn cried, clutching the empty knapsack. "It can't be!" She shook it again. I almost laughed when a penny fell out, clattering onto the rock. Her face changed then, as she felt, in the seam of the knapsack, a long, zippered compartment. She opened it and drew out a leather-sheathed hunting knife.

I took the knife from Vonn's trembling hand, pulling out the blade to examine it, before I returned it to its sheath and the sheath to my pocket. Tenacious Vonn continued to search, and found two more treasures in the same compartment as the knife—a small jar of Tabasco sauce along with some waterlogged pouches of salt and pepper and a tiny tin of peppermints. I naturally saw the tin of peppermints as a sign from my mother—it was the same brand she always carried in her purse.

Watching Vonn open the tin, I drooled in anticipation. Inside were a full complement of twenty miniscule mints—five each, two of which we quickly agreed we would have immediately, saving the next for sunset, and the next for sunrise, and the last we'd decide later. We watched one another place the tiny treasures on our tongues, the most sublime thing any of us had ever tasted.

"What about this?" Vonn asked, opening the Tabasco sauce. "Can we drink it? A drop? Please?"

"No!" I said, taking it from her, jamming it into my coat pocket. "That would make the thirst worse."

"It couldn't be worse," Bridget said.

"Couldn't we have a little?" Vonn begged.

I shook my head and started forward, disgusted to find myself salivating over the thought of shaking the hot sauce over some steaming ground squirrel flesh.

Vonn slipped into the harness of the flaccid pink knapsack.

"That would be the worst," Vonn said. "Being alone. Up here."

"Shouldn't someone say a prayer over the poor man's body?" Nola asked, and all of us stopped to look back.

"I did," I said, which was a lie. I'd said a prayer for Nola.

(Later I found out the man's name was Pedro Rodriquez. While living his dream to hike the Pacific Crest Trail alone, he'd gotten lost and became trapped in Devil's Canyon. The man left his wife, four daughters, and seven grandchildren. The pink knapsack belonged to his eldest granddaughter, and he was carrying it for luck. When we found him he'd been missing for three months.)

The trees gave way to a long stretch of corrugated granite. I felt my life-force draining into the veins of the rock as I charted the white bands of feldspar, drawn like chalk arrows we were meant to follow.

Vonn called from behind me, pointing at something in the woods to the west, "Wolf, look over there."

We four changed course to investigate a nearby rock and what appeared to be a large lizard but was instead the corpse's left leg, and a few feet away from it, astonishingly, a single weathered leather hiking boot.

The pine boughs above me shivered as I sat down to pull the hiking boot over my stiff left foot. It was several sizes too large, which meant that I could switch feet easily to give each of my soles a break from the rocky ground. I looked around for its mate but couldn't find the right boot anywhere.

"This is bad," Bridget murmured.

"We need to move to higher ground again," I said. "Looks like the snow's stopped, but there's not much daylight left."

Behind me, Vonn opened the bandage on Nola's wound, releasing a potpourri of infection from the blood-blackened sterasote. Bridget gagged. I moved upwind.

"That does not smell good," Nola said, holding her breath.

"I need to clean Mim's wound. And I'm going to need fresh bandages," Vonn said, taking off her coat.

"No," Bridget strained. "My shirt."

"Not now," I said. "We need to keep moving."

"Why are we going back up?" Vonn asked. "It's cold up there."

"I know, but we need to get visible. In case there's a plane looking for us."

"Or a helicopter," Bridget added. "They have to be looking for us by now."

The committee of vultures was circling again, and I worried they'd get the wrong idea if we stopped for too long. "Come on."

One of the circling vultures broke ranks to swoop down. He settled on a tree growing out from a fault in a rock nearby, the eager reaper with his pickled red head and massive talons getting an estimate on Nola to report to his friends. I hate spies.

"Git!" I shouted, and he did, but I knew he'd be back.

"Come on," I told the Devines. "We need to keep moving."

Vonn hastily rewrapped Nola's wound, and we carried on toward higher ground, maneuvering over boulders and branches and roots, our path presenting itself as a multiple choice of barely possible and impossible routes.

I limped along in the lead with my one excellent boot and my aching socked foot and my only remaining stick. Turning to check on the Devines, I'd had to blink away visions of the coyotes and mountain lions and Yago attacking from behind. "Okay?"

Bridget behind me in the red poncho supported Nola from one side, while Vonn took the other, clomping in my hiking boots. No one an-swered.

The most successful people in the most impossible situations are the ones who are sure they're gonna get out of it, and they go on thinking that, even if they die trying.

"Okay," I shouted again.

Vonn looked up, grateful. "Okay," she said.

We carried on through the cold, bleak forest, intending to move to higher ground but finding ourselves at the mercy of the canyon.

WE WERE alternately chilled in the long stretches between the rocks and baked on the bare ridges. We stopped to rest every quarter hour or so, but only for a moment, all of us knowing instinctively that our next stop could also be our tomb. Our pace was torpid. Our stomachs were empty. Our thirst was wretched. Our spirits were weak.

"I was dreaming last night," Nola said.

"You bit me," I said.

"Yes, I did. I remember why. I was eating anniversary cake. In my dream. Pip was feeding it to me. We always did buttercream frosting."

"We have to keep moving," I said.

"The vultures are back." Vonn pointed at the black bird hunkered down on a nearby branch.

Bridget shivered.

"I dreamed about Pip being so happy to see me," Nola said.

"We'll rest a little. Okay?" I offered, hurling a rock to scare the black bird away.

The vulture fled the branch but found another.

"Stay with us, Nola," I said.

"Come on, Mim,"

"I'm ready," Nola said, struggling to keep her eyes open. "It's okay."

Bridget held up her hand then, shushing us. "Listen."

I wanted to strangle her—I did. Especially because the air was still, and the mountain was quiet, eerily so. Nothing sounded like a helicopter or waterfall or rescue plane or barking dog.

The only sound, and it was crazy-making, was the rhythmic kiss of water hitting rock.

That's what Bridget was hearing too, and now I could smell the water. I moved through the trees trying to sniff out its source, and at last spotted a timid dripping stream moistening the fractures in the granite over our heads, then falling one drop at a time into a loose, glistening cairn of pebbles below.

We didn't whoop. We didn't celebrate. We helped Nola to the ground, where she struggled into position with her head resting on the rock, and waited openmouthed, like a baby bird, for the sandy, dripping water to accumulate on her tongue. After swallowing a few mouthfuls, she murmured a prayer and gave her spot to Bridget. Bridget took no more or less time than Nola to drink a mouthful, then made way for Vonn, who drank a few drops and made way for Nola again, who insisted Vonn drink some more.

After the women had several drinks, I took my turn. The water tasted sour, but the wetness on my lips and tongue and throat was inspirational. We took turns resting our heads on the rock to accept the dripping water—the process was interminably slow.

What prompted my urge I can't say, but I was seized by the impulse to write my name on our new canteen's yellow enamel. I couldn't find a stone sharp enough to scratch the surface, so I asked to borrow Nola's diamond wedding ring, which Bridget had been wearing on her index finger. When I finished, Nola asked me to write hers too, then Vonn scratched her name, and finally Bridget. We were here. Damn it.

"We have to fill it," I said.

"It'll take all day," Vonn said.

We set the canteen on the ground, propped up by a few rocks, to take the dripping water. Every drop was a second, a heartbeat, another grain of sand.

Looking around at my motley crew, I waited for a sign about what to do next. Drip, drip, drip. We were quiet and still for a long time.

Vonn was the first to double over, vomiting, and then we all began to purge in tragically embarrassing bouts. The water we'd thought would save us might instead dehydrate us further.

"Oh, Wolf," Nola said. I took her in my arms.

We needed cleaner water. I tore a piece of nylon from the pocket of my parka and used it as a filter over the mouth of the canteen. We watched the water. Drip, drip, drip.

We did fall asleep then, or maybe we fell unconscious. We were all in and out that fourth day. Mostly out of it.

When I opened my eyes, I was startled by our reality. Was I really on the mountain? Lost with three Devines? Were we really only hours away from dehydration, hypothermia? I took a moment to look around, reacquaint myself with the rock, moved by the sky. I hoped, in taking that moment, the hallucination I was having—of three hungry vultures waiting out our lives—would fade.

But it didn't. One of the birds was bobbing in a Coulter pine. Another, strutting on a rock. The third was flapping within two feet of Nola. It was no illusion.

"Nola," I said, shaking her awake.

She saw the vultures and shrieked in terror. Bridget and Vonn woke, screaming when they saw the birds too. Amid the mayhem, I knocked over the yellow canteen, spilling a tragic amount of the carefully collected water. I looked at the spilled water, homicidal.

Vonn set the canteen back under the drip.

Stomping toward the biggest buzzard in my single boot, I hollered, "Get out of here!"

The vulture raised his crooked wings, flapping aggressively.

"Shoo!" Nola cried.

I charged at it, the pain of each step a shot to my skull. "GO!"

Finally the bird took flight, hovering, smug.

Bridget hurled a rock at the pine branch where another was perched. She missed, and when the rock hit the ground, all three of the vultures converged upon it for a taste of our scent.

"They're like seagulls," Bridget said. "Do they think we're feeding them?"

Nola chastised them. "We're not a food court."

The birds were too close for comfort. I charged again, shouting, "Go! Git! GIT!"

The vultures cocked their heads. Do vultures laugh?

I picked up a large rock and threw it into their midst, but that didn't scare them away. They pecked at the rock like they hoped it was human sacrifice.

Vonn threw handfuls of dirt at the birds and, after that, just insults.

Bridget folded herself, sharp angles like origami. "Make them go away, Wolf," she cried, covering her filthy face with her filthy fingers.

"GIT!" I shouted, charging toward the vultures again. I fell against a rock and some hard object slammed my hip bone. The Tabasco sauce from the dead hiker's knapsack.

My first thought was that maybe I could drink the whole thing in a single gulp and kill myself—not suicide but sacrifice to the buzzards. My second thought was that the Devines might try to save me and I imagined it would all end quite badly. Not that, at this point, it looked like it would end especially well.

"Vonn," I said. "I need Nola's bandages."

"They're disgusting."

"Not to vultures," I said.

She saw that I was holding the bottle of Tabasco sauce in my hand and realized my intention. "Okay, but aren't birds immune to hot peppers? Didn't I read that somewhere?"

"They won't taste it," I said as she peeled the puss-welded bandages from Nola's arm and handed the repulsive mess to me. "But if we're lucky, it'll irritate the hell out of their eyes."

It was both disgusting and gratifying to watch the sinister birds swarm the pepper-soaked cloth. They shook and shredded the bandages—oh, and the horrible sound they made—and I guess I was right about the pepper sauce because they seemed agitated and then they flapped away.

"It worked," Vonn breathed.

Nola and Bridget grinned with the victory. Even the trees praised our gross ingenuity, creaking and clapping in the wind, blowing away the clouds and bringing back the sun to torch us. The temperature must have been twenty degrees hotter in the sun than the shade. I was afraid to sweat and lose more fluid. The odor.

Bridget turned away from the sight of Nola's festering wound. There was no choice but to redress her broken wrist properly at that point.

"Nola," I said. "We have to take care of your injury."

"Please don't waste time with that. We have to keep moving."

"Vonn's going to clean it, Mim. She knows what she's doing."

"It's not like I'm a doctor." I could see that Vonn was pleased by her mother's confidence.

"We obviously can't leave it exposed like that," Bridget said sternly, turning to work herself out of her T-shirt. "Use this to bandage it back up."

"That's the only other layer you have under there, Bridget," Vonn said, tending to Nola's putrid arm. "You'll freeze."

"I'm numb," Bridget said, more as a statement than a complaint.

Vonn found some fresh branches to use as splints, and with no time and no place to crush them, took a fistful of the sterasote leaves and wrapped Bridget's T-shirt around Nola's injured wrist.

"You must have a high tolerance for pain, Nola," I said.

"Perk of aging," Nola said, trying to smile. She gestured toward the dripping water.

"We have to be patient," I said, checking in with Bridget and Vonn. "Right? We'll feel better when we've had some more water. And we'll have some energy to get back at it. Right?"

Drip. Drip. Drip.

"Hot," Vonn said when she saw me watching her. She was unaware that her cracked lip was bleeding.

"Hot," I agreed, noticing a branch beside Vonn moving in the wind.

"It's going to take forever," Nola said.

Drip, drip, drip. Nola was right. It would take all our daylight hours to fill the canteen, and then what? The temperature in this part of Devil's Canyon would drop to near freezing when the sun shifted. Not to mention that in the unlikely event there was a plane looking for us, we would not be spotted here.

I studied the slender septum in the varnished rock where the water dripped but I couldn't see a way to climb up to find its source.

"We can't stay here," I said finally.

"Three days without water, Wolf," Vonn returned.

"We need the water," Bridget said. "I think we should stay."

"I'm staying with my daughter," Nola said.

I turned to Vonn for a tie vote. "Vonn?"

"I'm with Bridget and Mim," Vonn declared. The clouds were reflected in her pretty eyes. Her mouth was set defiantly. "What?"

I blinked when the branch moved beside her, and I went on blinking until I understood that I was not looking at a branch but a snake, slithering along the fracture in the marbled rock where Vonn was leaning. A Pacific rattler, olive and brown, and judging by the yellowish tail, young.

Rising slowly, I said, "It's time to move on."

"You just said to be patient," Bridget pointed out.

I wanted to pull Vonn away from the snake without any of the women being the wiser. I offered my hand, along with a corny bow.

"Why are you being weird?" Vonn asked.

"Let's go," I said.

"I'm staying here," she said, staring at my outstretched hand.

The young snake slithered in and out of the cracks in the rock beside Vonn's head.

"We need to go now, Vonn," I said, my hand waiting in midair.

"I'm not going."

"Trust me, Vonn."

"What's with you?"

"Trust me," I repeated, telling myself not to look at the snake.

"I do trust you, Wolf." She held my gaze. "But I'm staying here."

"Please."

Bridget turned to Vonn then, promptly spotting the snake a hair's width from her daughter's neck. She shouted in her broken voice, "Snake!"

Nola shrieked.

Vonn turned, startling the snake.

"Don't move," I whispered as the snake reared up, caught between a rock and a soft place, and rattled his tail.

Bridget took a step forward. "Get away from her!" she growled, finding her voice in the moment.

"Bridget!" I shouted.

I saw it happen before it happened, and I had no way to stop it from happening.

Bridget swiped at the snake with her bare hands.

"No!"

The slithering snake, striking at its tormentor, found Vonn's upper arm instead.

People say snakebites are incredibly painful, but Vonn didn't shriek or scream. "He got me," she said, holding her breath.

"Okay," I said. "Stay still. The most important thing is to be calm. And still."

"I'm sorry. I'm so sorry," Bridget cried.

Vonn smiled reassuringly, reaching out for her mother. "Mama," she said, and then fainted before any of us could catch her. She slumped and fell back and hit her head on the edge of a rock, before she fell to the ground unconscious. Just like that.

"Vonn!" I dropped to her side, my hands on her face.

Bridget murmured, "Oh my God."

"Where's the snake?" I whipped my head around but couldn't see it.

"Vonn! Vonn!" Nola cried, squeezing Vonn's leg.

Shot with adrenaline, I bent to lift Vonn to my shoulder. I wasn't afraid of snakes anymore. I wasn't afraid of anything, except maybe time. It felt like twenty miles but it was more likely twenty feet before I found a patch of soft earth where I could lay her down.

"Maybe she wasn't bitten," Nola offered desperately. "Maybe she only thought she was. Like Bridge with the bee."

Opening Vonn's jacket, we saw right away where the young rattler's razor fangs had sliced through the layers of clothing and punctured her arm. I remember Byrd saying that bites from baby rattlers were the worst. My mind raced through the don'ts of a snakebite.

"Shouldn't we suck out the venom?" Bridget asked.

"No."

"Should we tie it off?"

"No."

"Should we try to wake her up?"

"No. Not yet."

"We can't do *nothing*," Nola said.

There was something about urine. Wrong. That was Frankie. *Be still. Remove jewelry. Don't use pressure. Don't use a tourniquet. Don't apply ice. Keep the bite lower than the heart.*

"We have to keep her still," I said, "so her heart doesn't pump too fast and make the venom spread faster. And keep the bite area lower than her heart. You can't suck out the venom because you'd get sick too. That won't help anyone."

"He was trying to bite me," Bridget said.

"Some bites are dry. Maybe it was a dry bite," I said unconvincingly.

"No venom? Does that happen?"

"How will we know?" Nola asked.

I thought of what Byrd had said. *She doesn't expire.*

"What now?" Bridget asked.

"We have to go on," I said.

Nola had had the presence of mind, even in the chaos with the snake, to bring along the hiker's yellow canteen with its meager quantity of water. She even remembered the pink knapsack. Bridget made sure the canteen lid fit tightly while I bent down to attend to Vonn. I didn't have the strength to lift her again. So I prayed for it.

Byrd whispered into my ear, "Take back your boots. She'll be easier to lift."

I did. She was, and my feet were grateful. I left the dead hiker's single boot behind.

It seemed as though the air changed after that. Time sped up again, and I was out of my body, hovering above, observing the man-child carry the pretty, dying girl through the sloping forests and over the tumbled boulders and up the hill so steep that at some points he practically had to crawl on his knees with the girl draped over his back. I watched his shins banging against the rock, his fingers bleeding, cheeks snagged by thorns. I bet that hurt, I thought, before returning to my body to discover I was right.

I might have congratulated myself for my strength had I not turned around to find that Bridget, whose shoulders were significantly smaller, and whose legs were stick thin, had hoisted her failing mother and was following in my footsteps.

That was a hell of a thing to witness. Speaking of heroes.

After a time, we reached a small, forested plateau where we thought we could gain a sense of direction. I found a worn boulder and eased Vonn down. She was still unconscious, and the bump on the back of her head worried me as much as the swelling at the site of the snakebite. Her breathing was shallow, her heartbeat faint.

Glancing around, I was sorry to find that this vantage point brought us no clear perspective, no sense of direction, just more trees and rock. Bridget staggered up, and I helped her settle Nola down beside her granddaughter. Nola, critically injured. Vonn, bitten by a snake. Bridget, on the verge of a breakdown.

I'd counted Nola out every hour for the past three days and she kept coming back. Now she wasn't the worst off. Resilience, thy name is Devine. Stay with us, Vonn.

"How is she?" Nola asked, reaching out to take Vonn's limp hand.

"Still breathing," I said.

"It's my fault," Bridget said quietly. "All of this."

"It's the snake's fault," Nola said.

The bees. The snakes. Damnable nature.

We passed around the yellow canteen, from which we each took a single small sip, then Bridget and I stepped a few feet away to survey the undulation of rocks and trees. "Not ideal," she said quietly, looking around, unaware that she sounded just like her mother.

"No," I said.

"We have to get them to a hospital."

"We will."

"We've lost sight of the pine tree."

"What?"

"The pine tree."

"Right." I'd forgotten about the beacon altogether.

There was a sound then. Distant at first. Bridget and I shared a look. The hooting owl again.

"Where?" I asked.

Bridget spied him in a tree on a rocky hillside.

The bird woke Nola. "Maybe it's a sign," she croaked.

"Would the sterasote help Vonn's bite?" Nola asked.

"We could try," I said.

With the dead man's hunting knife I cut a length of fabric from the hood of my sweatshirt and tore it in two. Then we took the leaves from our pockets and divided what remained of our cache, cramming half into the putrid casserole that was Nola's wound, and spreading the rest on the area around Vonn's snakebite.

Nola watched me return the knife to the sheath. "Sharper than you'd think," she said.

We drank a little more of the cloudy water from the canteen and felt stronger, ready to push on. Nola managed to find the strength to walk on her own, which impressed the hell out of me. Vonn remained unconscious.

The owl hooted again, and Bridget pointed to where the bird was flapping away up the hill.

"We should follow him," I said. I don't know why.

I hoisted Vonn back onto my shoulders. Nola leaned on Bridget, and we traversed the rock and climbed the boulders and dragged our heels through a short grassy meadow and on again over another ridge, following the hooting owl.

The choice to follow the bird made as much sense as any choice I've ever made, any direction I've ever taken. We followed the bird for what must have been hours, hiking up, and down again, lost in our own finales, letting the mountain, and the owl, lead the way.

"We're going nowhere," Bridget said at one point.

"We're gonna get out of this," I said. But I wasn't sure anymore and thought I must have sounded like a fool.

We carried on, shuffling over the rocky ground, Vonn growing heavier on my strained shoulders. No point in cursing God. Besides, you had to hand it to him for his gamesmanship.

The beauty of the setting sun on that night, the last night, was not lost on me, even with Vonn unconscious and Bridget huffing behind me, Nola leaning on her shoulder. I wished I had my camera. "Haven't heard the owl in a while," Bridget said.

She was right.

Another night on the mountain. Our last, but I didn't know it then. Owl or no owl, we had to stop soon, and we'd need shelter for the night. It was cold.

"Why are we climbing?" Bridget asked. "It's just getting colder. There's nothing to see from up here but more rocks and more trees."

Just then the owl hooted again, and when we turned to look for him we spied a rock formation farther up the hill, slabs of white granite that had fallen to create a house shape, complete with a tilted chalet roof.

We headed for the shelter feeling optimistic, but each awful step brought us deeper into a deafening wind tunnel. If the owl was still hooting, I'll be damned if I could hear it.

When we reached the place, Bridget helped me lay Vonn down on a bed of granite within. Nola sat down beside her. "Four days is a long time to be lost," she said.

I scanned the area for loose rocks, which I tossed within reach of Nola and Bridget. I wanted to be well-armed in case of an attack.

"Please, Wolf," Nola said. "Come here."

"Okay," I said slowly.

She gestured for me to lean down, and I did. Then she whispered something into my ear that I didn't understand. I asked her to repeat it.

"You know the Andes survivors?"

"Yes," I said.

"*Eat me*," Nola mouthed.

Let's say that there followed a long pause.

"You know what they did, Wolf?"

"I know what they did."

"In the book, they dried it like *jerky*."

I could only thank God for the roaring wind so that Bridget did not hear what her mother had asked me to do.

"What are you saying, Mim?" Bridget asked.

"I was telling Wolf thanks," Nola said, then turned back to me in earnest. "We wouldn't be here without you."

I looked around at the three Devines. Vonn's complexion was ash. Nola was drained. Bridget still had a flicker of hope. She smiled when she saw my concern. "She's breathing," she said, spreading her palm over her daughter's chest. "She's gonna be fine."

The wind was deafening. Louder than it had been at any other moment on any other day in any other place on the mountain. It was hard to think over the roar.

"Why does it have to be so loud?" Bridget said, holding her ears.

That wind raged all night long, from time to time storming into our shelter to remind everyone who was the boss. I suppose I must have slept. I do recall that after a long stretch of being awake I was startled to see Nola struggling to rise from where she'd been sleeping beside Vonn, as if she was being lifted by the wind and coaxed out of the shelter, under a spell. That's what it seemed like.

"Nola," I said.

The wind appeared to guide her with its hand on the small of her back as she moved to find her place under the shimmering stars. "Nola," I called after her, but she didn't respond.

I watched her there, with the wind whipping her hair, as her posture changed, and she was young again, lovely in the moonlight, sparkling against the night.

I crept toward her. "Nola," I said, but she didn't turn around.

I found a rock to sit down on.

Nola murmured something to the heavens, turned, then—looking straight through me—arranged herself on the rock, and raised her arm in the air. Her head began to swivel strangely, and she dropped her chin to her chest.

Her arms began to flail about in what appeared to be a seizure. I was paralyzed over what to do, watching her saw the dark with speed and vigor, even with her injured wrist, while her face was joyful and serene. If it was a seizure, I finally decided, I would let her seize.

After watching her for a time, I began to see that her gestures were not random or epileptic but precise, her motions rhythmic. She was holding aloft a ghost instrument, stroking a set of strings with her infection-ravaged broken wrist. Spiccato. Legato. Pizzicato. Détaché. She wasn't playing air violin. Nola was playing the wind.

I listened, enrapt by the music, every poignant note.

When she was done her arms fell limp at her sides. The forest begged for an encore, but she'd left it all on the stage. Without acknowledging my presence, she made her way back to her place beside Bridget and Vonn, eased herself back down on the rock, and closed her eyes.

THE FIFTH DAY

The wind on the morning of the fifth day blew so cold and hard I had to pry open my frozen eyelids with my frozen fingers. I couldn't have spoken, even if I'd wanted to. My teeth felt loose. My mouth was a grave.

Vonn? I couldn't summon the strength to turn toward her. Of course I was afraid. As the sun rose over the ridge, all I could do was lie still with my eyes closed, imagining the assemblage of spirits waking in Tin Town. Kriket and Yago and the legions of Trulys in that trailer. And the Diazes too. Lark. Harley. Dantay. My friend Byrd. My father in jail.

Regrets. Sure, you think about regrets, but it's not regret for the things you've done that occupy you as much as it is a longing for the things you'll never have the chance to do.

I had the strangest sense of being watched, and I glanced over to find Nola, pale and still, eyes wide and fixed on me. I shuddered. "Nola?"

I was startled when she blinked.

"The knife," Nola said.

"What?"

"Please," Nola said.

I could not connect the dots.

"Please," Nola said.

Knife. Was she suggesting I kill her? Slit her throat like the sacrificial lamb?

"We're going to make it out of this."

She shook her head.

"Faith," I said. "Three seconds, remember?"

I worked up the guts to turn then, to find Vonn still and stiff beside me. I touched her face. "Vonn?" I said. "Wake up." But she wouldn't. I checked her wrist, surprised to find a pulse, and whispered into her ear, "You're not leaving me."

She whimpered faintly, which I took as confirmation.

Bridget woke then and stretched to stroke Vonn's forehead. "The swelling around the bite mark looks about the same," Bridget said. "Mim?"

"I'm here," Nola said weakly.

I located the dead man's canteen.

"The peppermints!" Bridget blurted.

She found the flaccid pink knapsack on the rock, and the container of mints inside, but could not pry open the tiny tin.

"Careful," I said, watching her frustration build.

Bridget banged the tin against the rock.

"That won't work."

"I think I got it." She slammed the tin against the rock once more and did succeed in opening the lid but upset the contents, and all we could do was watch the tiny peppermints bounce down the rock and roll into the dense vegetation on either side.

I managed to salvage only three of the remaining mints.

Nola tried to comfort Bridget. "A couple of mints won't make a difference."

"Here," I said, passing one of the tiny mints to Bridget.

"Save mine for Vonn," Bridget said.

"Mine too," Nola said.

I put the mints in my pocket, and we spoke no more of peppermints or hunger.

The canteen contained barely enough water to moisten our lips. I passed it to Nola, who only pretended to take a sip, before passing it to

Bridget, who gave it right back to me. I remember thinking of the dead man to whom the canteen belonged, wishing I knew his name so that I could carve it there along with ours.

"We have to," I said, pressing the canteen back into Nola's good hand. "Just a little."

We were careful to save a few drops for Vonn.

"We should go out there and look around," I said, rising and offering a hand to Bridget.

"The air's different," Nola said.

"Lower elevation," I said.

"Maybe we'll find berries," Bridget said.

"Listen to that wind!" I shouted as we stepped out of the stone chalet. Like it heard me, the wind shoved me from behind. Bridget covered her ears against the howling.

Something moved on the ridge to my left—a flash of tawny fur. I turned slowly, about to come face-to-face with the mountain lion I'd feared had been stalking us. But it wasn't a mountain lion, it was a massive bighorn ram. Six feet tall, I'd guess, and just as long, with white-spotted flanks and huge, curled horns.

I didn't dare alert Bridget, whose back was to me. She had a poor track record in situations requiring calm.

When the ram snorted in my direction I sensed no threat. In fact, I can tell you that I saw his appearance as a good omen. I felt forgiven for killing the lamb. Mercy killing or not, the deed had haunted me.

When the ram tired of looking at me—I'd never have tired of looking at him—he leaped, clattering from boulder to rock, then disappeared beyond a crag.

"So loud," Bridget strained to shout, turning in time to miss the bighorn.

I nodded and looked toward the shelter to find Nola sitting up and staring in wonder at the place on the rock where the bighorn had been. It was rare to see a bighorn, and when our eyes met we acknowledged the privilege and the opportunity to share it. Bridget turned around, pulling at my frozen hands. "Let's go see."

Assaulted by the raging wind, we started up the slope, but Bridget barely had the strength to put one foot in front of the other, and so I hauled her most of the way, gripping her waist, bearing her weight on my hip. We looked back to check in with Nola every few steps. Neither of us remarked that the wind sounded like a helicopter or a waterfall. We were sick of the wind making us look stupid.

I sniffed the air to find that it smelled like water again. An olfactory mirage.

"Smells like water," Bridget said.

The wind changed direction and the sweet scent disappeared.

"I keep thinking about that little baby. Vonn's baby," Bridget said.

"Me too." It was true. I was already grieving her child.

"The father'll never know," she said.

"Who?"

"Vonn's baby—the father."

"Maybe he wouldn't care. Maybe he already has a bunch of kids out there who he doesn't take care of." I squirmed, thinking of Yago.

"Maybe," Bridget said.

"Anyway, she said she didn't know him."

"I heard her talking about him on the phone." Bridget's eyes flickered with hope. "Maybe it was more than a one-night thing."

"Maybe."

"Maybe he's looking for her right now." She struggled to form each word.

"Maybe." We both knew she was grasping at straws, but I admired her spirit. "We're not giving up yet."

Just then we crested the ridge. And I fell to my knees. That's what I did. I fell to my knees when I saw what I saw. When I turned to look I could see by Bridget's face that she was seeing it too, in all its majesty—

roaring, thundering, cascading. It was not some cruel mirage. It was Corazon Falls.

Few eyes have looked on Corazon Falls. The waters are remote, and the canyons are a deathtrap for even the most experienced of hikers. On top of that the winds are usually high and unpredictable. I felt honored, humbled to see it.

Back at the shelter, Nola could see that something had stopped Bridget and me in our tracks. I shouted down to her. "It's the falls, Nola! We've found Corazon Falls!"

She couldn't hear me, of course. I turned to Bridget, who was standing away from the edge of the cliff, entranced.

The scent of the water was intoxicating. So close but so far. We inhaled the clouds of moisture as we studied the landscape. The rocks were ragged, big as cars, descending toward the shallow rapids at the crashing falls. The river's banks were slight and rocky too.

I couldn't see a way down. "We just need to get down. Water leads to people. Right?"

"What about over there? By those trees?"

I shook my head. The route was impossibly steep.

"What about there?"

"Maybe," I said, drawing closer to the edge.

Bridget closed her eyes. "I can feel the spray."

I searched the rocks for a route to the bottom. "Maybe there," I said, gesturing at a collection of tumbled boulders to the right of the falls. But just as I said it, one of the smaller boulders came loose. We watched it bounce down to the water and shatter when it hit the riverbank. I was overcome by vertigo and had to close my eyes and lie flat on my back to let it pass.

"You all right?"

"Vertigo," I said darkly.

"There's got to be a way."

285

"Look for yourself."

Bridget fought her own vertigo, getting down on her knees and crawling over the rocks like a lizard, the plastic poncho squeaking as she found a place beside me near the bushes at the cliff's edge. "What about there?" she said, inching closer, pointing with a shaky finger.

"Careful," I said, feeling a tremble in the granite upthrust beneath us. "Maybe."

Bridget pushed back the branches of some fragrant sage for a better view. "What about there?"

"Even if I got all the way down," I said, "how would I get from that rock to that one?"

Impossible. She saw it too. We were quiet, watching the water fall, breathing our last breaths, thinking our final thoughts, drawing inevitable conclusions.

Moved by the beauty of the falls and the scattering clouds and the pale blue sky against the amber rock, Bridget sighed.

I agreed. The rushing water. The clearing sky. Good place to die.

We looked around, nodding—we might have been considering a vacation property, that's how content we must have appeared.

Looking back at Nola in the shelter, I waved and felt reassured when she waved back. I was worried that she was going to lose consciousness, or worse. I didn't want to be robbed of the chance to say good-bye.

"Nola has to see this," I said. "And Vonn. When she wakes up."

IT TOOK some time for me to hike down to the shelter and carry Nola back up to reunite her with Bridget. My knees were burning, and my shoulders were aching, but I went once more to collect Vonn. She was deadweight. I'd had to pick her up like a child and cradle her, each step torture. Finally I reached the ridge. We four were together again, in view of the roaring falls. I laid Vonn down beside Nola a few steps away from the edge.

The sun shone down on us and warmed us. In the water's white noise we heard helicopters, and airplanes, and the whispers of our dead. I began to fixate on the likelihood that the scavengers would become ill from feasting on Vonn's snake-poisoned cadaver. We hadn't been successful at finding our way back, but I felt no small amount of pride in the blessing of Devines. We were quiet there in the sunshine for a very long time.

Bridget's words broke through my reverie. "I can't seem to make peace with it."

I struggled for composure, but by that point I was too weak and confused.

"In my dream we were saved, Wolf. I remember the *feeling*. The greatest feeling," she said.

"I believe you, Bridget," I said.

"You do?"

"I do." It was the truth. I believed she believed.

On my hands and knees I went to Nola, who was beside Vonn in the shade of a bush. "Come on. Come over here with us. It's a hell of a view."

We crawled, Nola on her elbows, back to the edge of the cliff beside Bridget. She was too spent for awe and wonder. Tears rolled down her cheeks.

We watched the water, mesmerized, preparing for our last breaths— at least that's what I was doing. I suppose I'd accepted it. I prayed that Vonn would wake long enough to see this rare sight.

I don't remember feeling agitated but rather calm. That is, until Bridget grabbed my arm, shouting, "What's that?"

I squinted, trying to find what she was looking at.

She pointed with a trembling hand. "There! Down there! On the riverbank!"

"Where?"

"THERE!"

Then I saw it. An orange vest. It was an orange vest attached to a man, leading two other men, also wearing orange vests, and carrying knapsacks through the bush and over the rocky riverbank heading toward the falls.

"Hikers," Nola croaked, pointing. She did not have the strength to call out.

They weren't hikers. They were Mountain Rescue.

"Hello! HELLO!" I shouted, but couldn't be heard over the raging water.

We watched, breathless, as the lead hiker took his binoculars in hand to scour the area. Even from this distance we could see they had walkie-talkies and ropes. Mountain Rescue. They were *they*. They were the *they* we'd prayed for.

"Help!" I screamed thinly.

Nola watched, paralyzed, as Bridget pulled herself to her feet.

The ridge was so dense with brush there were few places we could be seen. Bridget started jumping up and down, waving her arms above the bushes.

I jumped up and down too, and when that didn't work I threw rocks and branches, but the men in the orange vests were much too far away and appeared to be concentrating their search efforts on the ground.

Finally one of the men trained his binoculars on the ridge where we stood.

"Wave your arms!" I screamed to Bridget, and we did, insanely, re-peatedly. Nola waved with her good arm, until the man put down his bin-oculars and turned to scan another area. He hadn't seen us. It was a long way and a ragged ridge, and he'd passed us over.

"There are big rocks back at the shelter!" I shouted.

"I'll get them," Nola said, then tried to stand but couldn't.

Down below, the man in the orange vest trained his binoculars on our ridge once more. I jumped and waved and shouted. The man looked like Dantay, even from that great distance. I was terrified that I was hal-lucinating.

Bridget turned to look at her mother, and noticed Vonn trembling.

"She's seizing," Nola said.

Vonn went still, then limp. We dropped down beside her. It was only a moment. I didn't know at that point if she was still breathing.

When I leaped to my feet again, I saw that the man in the orange vest had put his binoculars down. He'd missed us. Again.

"They're leaving!" I jumped up and down, hollering. Bridget joined, waving her arms.

Turning to look at Vonn, slumped and pale on the ground behind us, I was shaking with fear. We were losing her. And the baby too. With a final surge I shouted at the top of my lungs, "HELP!"

Just then the last man stopped—as if he'd heard me—and turned back to scan the rocky river and its shallow banks.

I shouted, "UP! LOOK UP!" We waved our arms madly.

The man in the orange vest looked everywhere but up.

"PLEASE!" I shouted.

The orange vest was about to walk away again but appeared to change his mind.

"Here!" I shouted.

He moved closer to the river and settled there on one knee to wash his face. Then he took a canteen from a pocket inside his coat and dipped it into the cold churning water.

"The pink knapsack!" Bridget said suddenly. "Put rocks in it! Make it heavy enough to splash!"

Down by the water, the other two rescue men joined the first to wash their faces and fill their canteens.

I raced down the hill to get the bag.

"Hurry," Nola called.

The short journey was an eternity, my toes screaming each step of the way. Finally I reached the bag and stooped to fill it with large heavy rocks.

As I staggered back up the hill with the bag, Bridget called out in her strangled voice, "They're leaving! Hurry!"

"Take this!" I hollered, holding out the knapsack as I struggled to climb the final steps to where Bridget stood near the edge.

She grabbed the pink bag from my hand, and then in a panic she swung it around her shoulder and let it fly. I knew before the thing left her hands that she didn't have the weight or muscle to throw the bag as far as it needed to go to clear the ridge and hit the water with enough force to get the rescuers' attention.

"No," Bridget breathed, watching the bag as it snagged on some manzanita on a slight projection under the ledge.

Below us, the rescuers rose, preparing to leave. Nola sank down on a nearby rock. All hope was lost.

Bridget turned to look at Vonn, unconscious on the ground. Then she looked at Nola. Then at me.

"It's okay, Bridget," I said. "It wasn't heavy enough anyway."

Bridget turned and started to run.

Nola shouted, "Not now, Bridge! Please!"

I was annoyed with her too, thinking of the precious energy we would have to spend finding her when she got lost in the woods. "Bridget!" I hollered, but I guess I didn't blame her for wanting to die alone.

"Bridget Devine!" Nola shouted sternly.

Bridget stopped.

"We need to stay together!" Nola called.

"Stay with us, Bridget!" I shouted.

Bridget turned back to us, holding her hand over her heart.

"Bridge?!" Nola called. "Come back here!"

Then Bridget started to run again. Only this time she wasn't running away from us but toward us. There were no bees chasing her. No snarling coyotes. And there was nowhere to run but the cliff's edge.

"Bridget!" I shouted when I realized what she meant to do.

The look on Bridget's face wasn't fear. It wasn't horror. Bridget knew before she leaped, when she raised her arms in that big red plastic poncho, before she cast off from that ridge and dropped to the rocks below, Bridget Devine knew that it was the single greatest moment of her life.

Clairvoyant after all.

NOLA STARED at the empty place where her child had been.

It all happened so fast.

Bridget must have looked like a giant red bird—that's how I imagined her—gliding down to land on the jagged wet rock. She surprised the hell out of us all.

I crept toward the edge and peered down into the river to see Bridget's body limp on a rock near the bank several yards from where the men in the orange vests had stopped to fill their canteens. That was a hell of a good jump if you can say such a thing about such a thing.

Even at a distance I could see where her blood splashed across the white rocks on the riverbank. It looked like a fresh petroglyph. I imagined it said, in some uninvented tongue, *Bridget Devine was here.*

The three rescue workers in orange vests were staring, dumbfounded, at the oxblood lump that had shot down from the ridge and landed with a thud.

Finally they looked up.

I waved.

I knew the men returned my wave, but I could not take my eyes off Bridget and the red ribbons of blood.

THE WIND died down and the air was silk, more stable than anyone had ever seen it near Corazon Falls. I remember lying there quietly on the rocks, watching the helicopter hover and land. The sun was high.

I think it gave Nola and me a little comfort to know how much Bridget would have enjoyed being right.

I could barely muster a whisper of thanks when men appeared with water and chocolate. I kept lifting my head to check on Vonn and Nola.

The rescue is a blur. Odd-angled images as they loaded us into the gurneys. Nola first, then Vonn, then me. Nola was beside me in the helicopter. I heard her rasp apologetically to the pilot, even near death as she was, "We must smell *awful!*"

Nola Devine being sorry. I turned to look for Bridget. Then remembered.

Looking down from inside the helicopter, I spotted the red dot on the riverbank and watched it grow smaller and smaller until we were at such a distance that it looked like a pushpin in a topographical map. That was the last time I saw the mountain.

AFTER

I woke in the hospital four days later missing three toes, thirteen pounds, and what had been left of my boyhood.

My first word upon gaining full consciousness after our rescue? *Vonn*.

A nurse appeared at my side, raising my bed, checking my vitals. The water in the glass she lifted to my lips tasted of bleach. I thought of Nola. I sniffed the air for something familiar—rock, earth, pine, snow—but could detect only the dueling qualities of ammonia and blood.

I fell back to sleep and woke sometime later, smiling when Nola Devine appeared at my door, folded into a wheelchair pushed by an orderly. Her arm was set in a sling, the swelling down significantly.

"Vonn?" I said.

Nola wheeled closer to my bed. "She's okay. She's confused. She's been in and out of it since we got here."

"The baby?"

"A fighter. Everyone says so."

Bridget, I remembered. Nola seemed to read my thoughts.

"She hasn't asked about her mother yet. She's sleeping a lot. She really doesn't remember much."

"Has she asked about me?" I had no voice.

Nola shook her head.

"She doesn't remember the rockslide, or crossing over the crevice, or being bitten by the snake. None of it. I haven't known how to tell her."

"Can I see her?"

"The nurse said we could go up and see her in a few hours. They're doing some tests. In the meantime, the guys from Mountain Rescue are here," Nola said.

I tried to sit up.

"They've stopped by every day since they brought us in. It was Harley Diaz, Wolf. He started the whole thing in motion. No one was looking for us."

"Harley," I said when he entered the room. Harley wasn't on the Mountain Rescue team and I was a little confused.

"You forgot your knapsack," he said.

"Yeah."

Harley leaned over, embracing me warmly.

"You saved us, Harley," I managed to say. "Thanks."

"Thank this guy," Harley said as the next man entered the room. I knew it would be Dantay.

Dantay embraced me too. "Don't try to talk."

The third man was Native American also. I recognized him but couldn't remember his name. He held a motorcycle helmet in his hand. "I'm Byrd's cousin," he said. "Juan Carlos. We've seen each other out at Harley's ranch."

"Thank you," I said.

"There's one more from our team," Dantay said.

My eye stopped on the person who entered the room next. His posture was stooped, his expression solemn. He was familiar, but I didn't know him. When I realized who it was I couldn't speak for a long time. "Byrd," I said at last.

He approached my hospital bed with his crooked smile and drooping left lid.

"Yo," I said, grinning.

"*Arra fah ken ut,*" Byrd said, without missing a beat.

Harley told us then that he'd been startled awake by noises in the early-morning hours. He'd gone to check on Byrd and found him sitting in the leather chair by the window, watching dawn break over the mountain. He was about to take him back to his bed when Byrd said, "Wolf." It was the first word Byrd had spoken in the year and four days since his accident. Harley couldn't ignore it.

Byrd followed Harley out to the car and they drove straight to the gas station, where Byrd pointed out the accumulation of newspapers outside the apartment door. Harley's concern grew when they entered the small apartment and saw my knapsack on the hook by the door. Within the hour a team from Mountain Rescue had been dispatched to the mountain.

"Bridget," I said, flashing back to the mountain—that moment. "Vonn doesn't know."

"I understand," Harley said.

Nola gestured for Harley, Dantay, and Juan Carlos to leave Byrd and me alone, and so they did.

"Wilfred," he said, grinning. There was a glimmer of the old Byrd.

Something in his face changed then, and I had the sense my friend was gone, bodysurfing some parallel universe.

"Byrd?"

He blinked hard. "Wolf," he said, taking a seat by the window. And that was the last word Byrd said for nearly a month.

Byrd's been like a brother to me, but sometimes like my son, and sometimes, in the most irritating way, like a father too. That's the beauty of Byrd—you don't know, one moment to the next, where or who he'll be.

I suspect, when he tilts his head a certain way, he's on the mountain, taking in the view from the peak. When he talks to himself, when he's incoherent, like he is sometimes, I imagine he's standing on the spot where those fractures intersect, getting answers to questions he didn't know he had.

THAT DAY I woke up in the hospital, and after Byrd had gone, one of the nurses finally came in to say that Vonn was ready to see us. But when I attempted to roll into her room behind Nola, another nurse said, "Family only."

Nola had me covered, telling the woman, "He's the baby's father."

It was as if we'd been separated for ten years, instead of a few days, and known each other forever, instead of less than a week—at least for me. The fetal monitor at Vonn's bedside beeped steadily. I played the role of dutiful father, but it was more than an act, even then.

"Vonn," I said, when I saw that her eyes were open. She tracked me with a blank stare as I wheeled closer to her bed. Finally a smile began to pull at the corner of her dry mouth.

Intimate strangers that we were, I wasn't sure if I should embrace her and was relieved when she reached for my hand, and then for Nola's beside me. Finally she turned toward the door.

"Where's my mother?" she asked.

Nola and I shared a look. Neither of us could find our voice.

"Is she coming?"

"You remember a little about the mountain, Vonn?" I asked.

"Not much."

"The rockslide? You remember how Nola hurt her wrist?"

"I remember we were lost and it was cold and my toes hurt so much."

"Do you remember the crevice?"

Vonn shook her head. "The doctor said I had a rattlesnake bite but no venom. Dry bite. I don't remember the rattlesnake. Did I see it?"

I shared another look with Nola. "Maybe we should talk about all of this later."

"You let me put my feet under your shirt," Vonn remembered.

"Yes."

"You let me wear your boots."

"Yes."

"Where's my mother?" she asked.

I paused. "Bridget died on the mountain."

Vonn turned to look at her grandmother, who could only nod.

"We made it all the way to Corazon Falls," I said.

Vonn stopped me. "No."

"Bridget saved us, Vonn," Nola said.

"No," Vonn said again.

"She was amazing," I said.

"Don't tell me," Vonn said.

"I was so proud," Nola said.

"Please."

"It was just like her dream," Nola said.

A nurse swept into the room, responding to a change in both of her patients' vital signs. "We need to keep her quiet and calm," she said.

"Should we go?"

"No," Vonn said.

We were quiet for some time. Nola reached out with her good hand, squeezing Vonn's leg. "The doctor said you'll recover most of your memories eventually."

"What if I don't want to?" Vonn laid a hand on the gentle swell of her womb.

"We can fill in the blanks for you," I said.

"No more talk about the mountain, okay? I don't want to remember. I don't want to know."

"Sure," I said.

"Whatever you need, Vonn," Nola said.

We were quiet again, listening to a man whistling somewhere out in the hall.

"We'll make rose sachets," Vonn said.

* * *

I WAS doing well on my crutches, and Nola's arm had improved significantly. We left the hospital within days of each other a week or so later. Vonn developed complications from our ordeal. The baby was at risk. Each day brought some new worry for Vonn, another threat to the baby. Thanks to Harley's generosity, she received the finest of medical care, and spent the remaining weeks of her pregnancy at the hospital.

I took the morning shift at her bedside. She was restless and irritable, but I could usually distract her with a story, something I'd read, or remembered, or lived. Vonn told as many stories as I did, but most of hers were memories—not of the mountain—never of the mountain. She talked about happy family times—and referred to Bridget as "my mom" or "Mama." She'd completely rewritten the story of their difficult past.

I wish I could do the same with Frankie.

I'VE SEEN him only once since he went to prison, and it was nearly twenty years ago. It was just before Easter. He knew about what happened with me and the Devines on the mountain in November, but he didn't reach out to me until late March, when he tried to contact me at the gas station. He couldn't have known I was staying in the guest room at Nola Devine's condo, conveniently located near the hospital, where Vonn and the baby were being monitored around the clock.

Eventually Frankie left word with the receptionist at the physical therapy desk, asking that I visit him in prison as soon as possible. He went from nothing—no contact for four months—to insisting that I visit him immediately.

I bought a new shirt.

On that long bus ride to the prison gates I thought only of Vonn. All my life I'd wanted Frankie's full attention and I was about to get it and I just wanted to be at Vonn's side. I was worried she would need me. It'd been only a few short months since I last saw my father, but it felt like a lifetime. My heart was thudding when I entered the musty prison visitors' room. I found Frankie waiting behind the warped glass at the end of a long row of seats. He flinched when I came into view, at his mortality, mine. I'd become a man during those five endless days I was lost. He could see it.

When I sat down I dropped my crutches. Neither one of us smiled. It wasn't the time for insincerity.

Frankie'd aged in those few months too. His hair was still thick but threaded with silver. His eyes appeared a paler shade of blue. He picked up the handset and gestured for me to do the same.

I noticed his thickened neck and pectorals, the ridge of trapezoid when he scratched his head. "You're hitting the weights," I said, pantomiming a bicep curl.

"Thanks," he replied. "Had to see for myself."

"In the flesh." I grinned. "Your hair went gray."

"'Bout fifteen years ago," he chortled.

He'd been dyeing it? I had no idea.

"Yours will too," he said.

I watched him swallow something else he was about to say then and could not imagine what it might have been. *I love you, son? I'm sorry?*

I leaped for the opening. "I'd come every week if you wanted."

"Through this?" He knocked on the thick glass between us, then went silent a moment. "What the hell, Wolf?" he said. "What happened?"

"Between *us*?" I asked stupidly.

"On the mountain." He laughed in a way that should have thrown up a red flag or two.

"I got lost," I said.

"But what all *happened*? People have so many questions."

I had questions too. I wanted to know what the hell happened the night we left Mercury. I wanted to know if Frankie was there, in the shadows, watching his dying self in Warren's filthy bedroom. I wanted to know if Frankie had seen me kick him. If he was sorry I'd brought him back from the light. If he ever saw visions of my mother as an angel. I wondered if he was sorry he all but abandoned me when we moved to the desert. If he believed in heaven. Instead, I said, "Okay."

His eyes rested on my hands. "Your picture was in the paper every day there for a while."

"I know."

"What's it like being famous?"

"What's going on, Frankie?"

"Nothing. I just had to see for myself that you're okay."

I was touched, sorry I misjudged him. "I'm good."

"My son the hero."

"It's not like that."

"I kept all the articles. Got 'em up on my wall."

"Most of what they wrote isn't true," I said.

"Why not talk about it, then?"

I'd refused interviews. I'd made no comments whatsoever to the media. It seemed an affront to the universe to speak of our ordeal.

"I heard all the talk shows want you to go on and tell your story," Frankie said.

"Yeah."

"Why would you not go on the talk shows?"

"Why would I?"

"Because opportunity is knocking, Wolf!"

"Why am I here, Frankie? Why did you want me to come?"

Frankie leaned in. "I'm in touch with this agent who thinks he can sell your story. More than anything, I'm thinking about your reputation."

"You're worried about my reputation?"

"I'm just saying that you're leaving people with a lot of questions."

"I have to go," I said.

"Think about it," Frankie said, stroking the *Glory Always* tattoo on his arm.

"I don't need to think about it, Frankie."

"A tidbit?" he asked. "How about one tidbit to keep him on the line, until you decide?"

I paused. I don't know what I was waiting for. "I got nothing, Frankie."

"I'm sorry to hear that," he said. He looked into my eyes for a long moment before he motioned to the guard that he was done.

When he rose to leave I noticed that he struggled with balance, his back hadn't recovered from his car accident, his knees still hadn't healed. He limped when he walked away and raised his arm—the one with the rainbow *Glory Always* tattoo—but he didn't turn to look at me.

IN THE months after our rescue Nola and I found ourselves in the hospital parking lot, which had an unobstructed view of the mountain, several times a day. Nola always turned to look at the magnificent batholith. I never did. We didn't talk about our ordeal. We were too busy dealing with the aftermath, and too preoccupied by our concerns for Vonn and the unborn baby. Vonn devoured parenting books while Nola crocheted mittens. I paced on my crutches, restless.

I guessed that Nola, like me, missed aspects of the mountain. Nature's mirror is sharply reflective and I missed the clarity the mountain brought, even the way our dilemma defined our purpose. I missed the hypnotic beauty of the wet rock, and the crisp, fragrant air, and Bridget. I missed Bridget.

I was at the hospital for a physical therapy appointment, three floors down from Vonn, when an orderly came to tell me that I was needed immediately. The baby. I'd switched to canes at that point, and I was slow as hell getting around. The phantom pain in my toes made me irritable, then there was a long wait at the elevator and a long, clumsy walk to Vonn's room.

I found her alone, slumped in a wheelchair, unplugged from the monitor.

"Daniel," I said, falling to my knees, spreading my hands over the lump under her hospital gown.

"They're moving me to the next floor for the surgery," Vonn was heaving with emotion.

I was confused. I thought the unplugged monitor meant . . .

"Cesarean section." Vonn took my chin in her hands. "What did you call him? The baby?"

"Daniel?" I said.

"How did you know it's a boy? I just found out today."

I didn't know. The name had come to me like a memory when I placed my hands on Vonn's womb. *Daniel*.

"Bridget's middle name was Danielle," Vonn said.

I kissed Vonn then. And she kissed me back. And when we parted, we looked up to find Nola and two nurses leaning against the door in the thrall of our romance.

ON THE day you were born, tiny as you were, they let me hold you while your mother slept. I'd looked at your angel face, the face I already loved so deeply, and said, because I couldn't help it, "He looks like Yago."

The resemblance was uncanny—the black hair, the square jaw, the wide eyes.

Nola, sitting beside me, said, "You have to stop this."

"I know."

"Can't we just enjoy today? Our healthy, beautiful boy?"

We paused to smile at your sleeping face. "Have you ever thought about moving to Michigan, Nola?"

"Michigan? Who moves from California to Michigan?"

"There's an opportunity. Harley presented it to me. To Vonn and me."

"To move to Michigan?"

"Byrd's grandparents had this restaurant. It's been shuttered for years, but the area's coming back up. We could all go up there—Byrd, you, Vonn, Danny, me. Open a family business."

"Michigan?" Nola said. "We'd all move to Michigan?"

"Might be good for Byrd's recovery. It might be good for all of us."

"What's this really about, Wolf?"

I glanced down to make sure Vonn was still asleep. "It's about an opportunity."

"In Michigan."

"Yes."

"It's about the baby's father, isn't it?" Nola said.

"Yes."

"Just ask her, Wolf."

"She doesn't remember. She doesn't want to remember."

"It's crazy to think it's your cousin!"

"Okay, what if it's not Yago? What if it's someone *like* Yago?"

"What do you mean?"

"You don't know these guys from Tin Town, Nola."

"We don't even know for sure that he lived in Tin Town."

"What if the guy finds out about Danny? What if he finds out about him and kidnaps him?"

"I hadn't thought of that."

"What if he takes him out of the country?"

"Where would he take him?"

"I don't know. Europe. Mexico. South America."

Nola shook her head. "The father wasn't European though," she said.

"What are you talking about?"

"I don't know. Did I dream that?"

"Did you?"

"When Bridget told me she overheard Vonn on the phone I didn't pay all that much attention, but I'm thinking now—it wasn't European, she said. Or Mexican. He's something else."

"Something else?"

"He's something else. What did she say?"

My mind raced.

Nola snapped her fingers. "French Canadian!"

I froze.

"That was it! French Canadian!" Nola said. "You see? *Not* your cousin."

"French Canadian?"

"French Canadian." She grinned. "Don't you feel better?"

I couldn't breathe.

"He was French Canadian. He'd been wearing a rainbow T-shirt or something like that. Those are the two things I remember. All that worrying for nothing."

"A rainbow?" I said.

"Actually, there was also something about him being religious. That doesn't sound right, but I think there was also something he said or did. Glory be. Glory something . . ." Nola said.

Glory *Always*.

"Never mind." Nola shook some wool loose from the skein. "Michigan, huh?"

I felt the flutter of your tiny heart against mine. "Hold on tight, Daniel Truly," I said. "There will be sway."

I CAN imagine how you're feeling, and I'm sorry that I'm the cause of it, or the messenger of it, or whatever label, however foul, you'd like to apply right now. I felt the same confusion when I first put it all together on the day you were born.

You understand now why it's been so hard to tell you, and why I've kept this story from you, and your mother, all these years. It's a father's instinct to protect his child, and you are—every cell of you—my son. Besides, Frankie taught me that mysterious people survive better in harsh climates.

We left the desert when you were three months old, you with Nola and Byrd in the backseat of the Dodge van Harley loaned us for the trip. Vonn sat beside me and took over at the wheel when I got tired. When I wasn't driving I sat beside you in your car seat. I could watch you for hours—never got bored.

We headed northeast to Michigan and took over the old boarded-up Victorian house where Byrd had lived as a boy, and we reopened Brodski's Polish Deli, and bought you ice skates, and raised you to love winter. Kriket and Yago and Tin Town and the desert and the mountain and, most important, Frankie were worlds away.

No one ever questioned your paternity, including you, I know. From time to time your mother and I discussed the right moment to make the disclosure, but each time the subject came up I was sure you weren't ready. Your mother wasn't eager to explain the circumstances of your conception either, and she even wondered if it was too cruel a blow to discover you have a biological father whose name she never knew. Still, I promised myself, and you, that someday I'd tell you. You have a right to know.

I guess I waited this long because I didn't want Frankie to ruin our paradise in Hamtramck. I did try to tell you, I wanted to tell you, and I almost told you, but then I'd picture the prison visits, imagine the look on your face as you're running to the mailbox looking for a letter from jail. I thought about you crying at night because Frankie'd disappointed you again, and worse, I knew that one day he'd get out of prison. What if he somehow found out the truth? What if he wanted to take you from me? I always thought it was easier to say nothing. Now I'm wondering if my silence was the real burden all along.

I'm relieved you finally know about Bridget. It's time your mother knew the truth too—all of it. Her mother was a hero. You should feel proud that you carry her blood. There should be a plaque honoring her at the Mountain Station, a monument to her in Wide Valley. People should hear about what Bridget Devine did for love.

I REMEMBER one day, Danny, when you were six, about to start first grade. You came down to the basement to help me sort through some of your baby stuff for our yard sale, and while I was digging out the high chair, you found some old boxes.

"Look here," you said.

I nearly lost my knees when I turned to see you holding the yellow canteen. I hadn't seen that canteen since I was eighteen years old. I'd packed it up in the aftermath of our mountain ordeal and stored it away, I guess.

"I haven't seen that in a while," I said quietly. I didn't want your mother to hear.

"It's a canteen," you said. Then you turned the thing around in your wondering hands, brushing bits of dried mud from the dented yellow face, exposing the letters etched into the tin.

You sounded out the words, "No-la. Brid-get. Vonn. *Wolf.*"

"Good," I said.

"You didn't wash it."

"I just wanted to put it away."

"You wanted to keep it, you just didn't want to clean it?"

"Yeah."

"It's from when you were lost on the mountain."

"It is."

"It's not neat writing."

"We were tired."

"And hungry." You pretended to eat your own arm and I laughed.

"Yes, Danny. Hungry and thirsty and all of those things."

"How did you *get* lost on the mountain?"

"I got lost the way everybody gets lost," I said.

"You went the wrong way?"

"I did."

"Were you scared?"

"Sometimes. I was scared sometimes."

"Of what?"

"There were a lot of things to be scared of."

"You said you'd tell me."

"Not today."

"Tonight?"

"Not tonight."

"Tomorrow?"

"When you're older. When you've lived a little."

"How old?"

"When you're ready for it."

"Ten?"

"Twelve."

"Will you take me there someday?"

"To the mountain? No." I was emphatic.

"Do you wish you never got lost?"

If I hadn't crossed paths with the Devines on that November day, I wouldn't *be* at all. If we hadn't lost our way in the wilderness, I wouldn't have been your father. I wouldn't have met Nola, who I'm still in the habit of thinking is alive. I wouldn't have fallen in love with your beautiful mother, or witnessed Bridget's brave act.

I said I'd never return, but over the past few weeks I've decided I *have* to go back, ride the tram again, smell the butterscotch pines in Wide Valley, stroke the cool speckled granite, listen to the warblers, feel the tectonic shifts.

Maybe you'll come with me, Danny. We could hike all the way to the peak and look out over the dry, white desert, see the orchards of wind turbines and Tin Town shimmering in the distance.

Frankie was right when he said that a father should see it with his son. It's a hell of a view.

Always,
Dad

ACKNOWLEDGMENTS

I understand how people fall in love over the Internet. I fell for my Knopf editor, Anne Collins, over the "scribbles" on the numerous manuscripts we passed back and forth. I loved every query, savored each remark, concurred with all of the slashed paragraphs, adored the arrows. Anne never tired of making the climb—never even seemed out of breath—bringing insight and clarity to each page, every step of the way. She has been a gift to me and to this novel.

I'm enormously grateful to my editor at Simon & Schuster, Millicent Bennett, for her support and energy, and thank you also to Carolyn Reidy, Jonathan Karp, Marysue Rucci, Amanda Lang, and Dana Trocker. Thanks to Jackie Seow for the beautiful cover.

And thank you, as ever, to Knopf Canada, who launched my first novel, and its successors. Your collective faith and your efforts are deeply appreciated: Louise Dennys, Brad Martin, Marion Garner, Sharon Klein, Deirdre Molina, Michelle Roper, and all of the other dedicated and talented people under that very tall roof. Thank you, Diane Martin, for guiding my first three novels, and for being a bright and generous light.

I'm also most grateful to Arve Juritzen, my Norwegian publisher, for his extraordinary efforts on behalf of my books. I will never forget my trip to Oslo, all the wonderful people that my husband and I met at Juritzen Forlag, as well as the Norwegian booksellers, journalists, and readers. It's one of the highlights of my career and in many ways emboldened me to write this novel.

ACKNOWLEDGMENTS

Thank you to Jo Dickinson and Suzanne Baboneau at Simon & Schuster UK. I'm honored to be part of your tribe and look forward to a long relationship.

Denise Bukowski has been my book agent and friend since I became an author. She's a warrior and I admire the hell out of her. I'm indebted to Denise for her faith in my first novel, *Rush Home Road*, and for always being on the first line in a large assemblage of dynamic women and men who make my books better. Denise was the earliest reader of *The Mountain Story* and gave me notes that helped shape the narrative, just as she's done with all of my novels. I appreciate our long phone conversations, her wise counsel, her candor, and her sense of humor.

Bill Hamilton, my UK agent, has worked doggedly on my behalf for years and I'm so thankful for all he does. Bill was an early reader, too and I very much appreciated his perspective.

Claire Cameron, author of the beautifully tense novel *The Bear*, took the time to read that long first draft and emailed me with a lovely note— just the sort that one author would appreciate from another. Her comments, coming from a skilled outdoorsperson, not to mention talented writer, were valuable and enormously appreciated.

The copy editors on both sides of the border brought their clear eyes and narrative skills, without which the novel would suffer. Thank you to Doris Cowan in Canada and, in particular, thanks to Erica Ferguson in the U.S., who made a number of great saves and didn't miss a single detail.

With fondness and respect, thank you, Michael and Judy and Lennie. Thanks also to Alison Callahan and Jennifer Bergstrom.

Before I wrote the first sentence of this novel, I spent time on Mount San Jacinto with my husband, my family, and then alone while I worked out the story. Wolf Truly and the others had been waiting in the character queue for some time, but the narrative came in chapters, more vivid with each trip up in the tram. When I had the story in broad strokes I needed to consult someone familiar with the mountain and surrounding area of Palm Springs and the Coachella Valley. I found Matt Jordon.

ACKNOWLEDGMENTS

months at a time and don't answer the phone. Thank you to my dear friends—the ones I walk the hills and laugh with, the ones who dance with me at birthday parties, the ones who keep inviting me even though I can never come, and the ones who call and email from far away. I'm blessed to have such generous women in my life, and so grateful to know they'll be there when I emerge from underground.

It took me three years to write *The Mountain Story*. Our son, Max, was entering middle school when I began. Our daughter, Tashi, was eight. I wrote. They grew. Max just graduated and Tashi will soon be twelve. In between? There was sway. My family is folded into the pages of this book. Their love sustains me and their tenacity inspires.

Milan. My partner in life. You.

ACKNOWLEDGMENTS

Matt Jordon is a member of the Riverside Mountain Rescue Unit. He was my guide on a number of mountain hikes, patient with my questions of "Would it be possible to . . . ?" "Would it be accurate to say . . . ?" "Is it believable that . . . ?" I thank Matt for sharing his knowledge and for keeping me safe on the mountain—even in darkness and deep snow. I'm also thankful to Matt and his wife and fellow outdoors enthusiast, Kim, for reading and making important comments about the final draft. Their thumbs-up meant a lot to me.

Search and rescue teams all over the world—these extraordinary people, many of whom are volunteers, risk their lives to save lost, imperiled, and stranded strangers and are heroes in every sense. Go to rmru. org to read about true mountain rescues on Mount San Jacinto, and learn more about safe wilderness practices.

Mount San Jacinto. The unnamed mountain in the novel is a fictional projection of the real mountain that overlooks Palm Springs. I changed the mountain's geography slightly, and created Santa Sophia and Tin Town within view of it.

I have a great affection for nature, the mountain, Palm Springs, and the surrounding desert. While doing research for this book I became interested in the Cahuilla Indians, who inhabited the desert and foothills, and enjoyed reading *Mukat's People* by Lowell John Bean, and *Not for Innocent Ears* by Ruby Modesto and Guy Mount, and learning from *Temalpakh* by Katherine Siva Saubel and Lowell John Bean, among many books about Cahuilla culture and history. I'm grateful to the Cahuilla for what I learned about their people. In mysterious ways they influenced my voice in the telling of *The Mountain Story*.

Thanks to my mother and father, two of my favorite humans on the planet, whose sense of humor and compassion continue to inspire me, and to my brothers, Todd and Curt, and my sisters-in-law, Kelly and Erin, and my extended family of Loyers and Rowlands, and Stielers and Gecelovskys, for their love and support.

It can't be easy to be friends with an author. We disappear for